Y0-BDI-639

ROMANCE OF THE THREE KINGDOMS VOL.IV

LUO GUANZHONG

ISBN: 1495285944
ISBN-13 :978-1495285943

Contents

Acknowledgements

Cover: Looking three times at the Thatched Hut, Dai Jin (1388-1462)

Translation by: C. H. Brewitt-Taylor and www.threekingdoms.com

Edition: www.tresreinos.es

Contact: contactar@tresreinos.es

English text used with permission of www.threekingdoms.com.

South Xiongnu
Qiang Tribes
Liangzhou
Xizhou
Yongzhou
Didao
Tianshui
Jieting
Nanan
Yellow River
Changan
Jicheng
Yinping
Jiangyou
Nanzheng
River Han
Wancheng
Hanzhong
Yizhou
Luocheng
Shangyong
Xiangyang
Xincheng
Langzhong
The Great River
Dangyang
Jingzhou
Chengdu
Baidicheng
Zigui
Yidu
Lingling
Gongan
Wuling
Guiyang

n Tribes

Youzhou
Liadong
Jizhou
Bohai
Yejun
Handan
Maocheng
Pingyuan
Qingzhou
Liyang
Yanzhou
Wuchao
Xuzhou
Puyang
Guandu
Juancheng
Yuzhou
Xuchang
Yingchuan
Runan
Shouchun
Xiangcheng
The Great River
Hefei
Wuhu
Wuchang
Wujun
Lukou
Fankou
Chaisang
Yangzhou
Changsha

Chapter 91

Sacrificing At River Lu, The Prime Minister Marches Homeward;
Attacking Wei, The Lord Of Wuxiang Presents A Memorial.

Meng Huo at the head of the Mang Chieftains and Notables attended to do honor to the army of Shu on its departure. They reached the River Lu in autumn, the ninth month. But on trying to cross the river, a tremendous storm came and hindered them. Wei Yan having reported his difficulty to Zhuge Liang, Meng Huo was asked if he knew of any reason for such a storm.

Meng Huo replied, "Wild spirits have always troubled those who would cross this river. It is necessary to propitiate them with sacrifices."

"What is the sacrifice?" asked Zhuge Liang.

"In the old days when malicious spirits brought misfortune, they sacrificed humans to the number of seven sevens and offered their forty-nine heads. They also slew a black ox and a white goat. Sacrifice thus, the wind will subside and the waters come to rest. The same used to be done to secure a plenteous harvest."

"How can I slay a single person now that fighting is done and peace has returned?" said Zhuge Liang.

Zhuge Liang went down to the river to see for himself. The north wind was blowing hard, and the waves were high. Both humans and horses seemed frightened. He himself was perplexed. Then he sought out some of the natives and questioned them.

They said, "We have heard the demons moaning every night since your army crossed the river. The cries begin at dusk and continued till dawn. There are many dark demons in the malarial vapors, and no one dared cross."

"The sin is mine," sighed Zhuge Liang, "for more than a thousand soldiers of Ma Dai perished in these waters beside many southern people. Their poor distressed souls are not yet freed. Therefore I will come this night and sacrifice to them."

"According to the ancient rule the number of victims ought to be forty-nine. Then the spirits will disperse," said the natives.

"As the resentful demons are here because of the deaths of people, where is the sense in slaying more humans? But I know what to do."

Zhuge Liang bade them make balls of flour paste after the manner of human heads and stuff them with the flesh of oxen and goats. These would be used instead of human heads, and they called these 'mantou' or 'human heads'.

By nightfall, an altar had been set up on the bank of the river with the sacrificial objects all arranged. There were also forty-nine lamps. Flags were flying to summon the souls. The forty-nine mantous were piled up on the ground. In the middle of the third watch, at midnight, Zhuge Liang, dressed in Taoist garb, went to offer the sacrifice in person, and he bade Dong Jue read this prayer:

"On the first day of the ninth month of the third year of the era Beginning Prosperity of the Han Dynasty, I, Zhuge Liang, Prime Minister of Han, Lord of Wuxiang, Imperial Protector of Yizhou, reverently order this sacrifice to appease the shades of those soldiers of Shu who have died in their country's service and those of the southern people who have perished.

"I now declare to you, O ye shades, the majesty of my master, the Emperor of the mighty Han Dynasty, excelling that of the Five Feudatories[i] and brilliantly continuing the glory of the Three Dynastic Kings[ii]. Recently, when the distant south rebelliously invaded his territory, contumeliously sent an army, loosed the venom of their sorcery, and gave free rein to their savagery in rebellion, I was commanded to punish their crimes. Wherefore my brave armies marched and utterly destroyed the contemptible rebels. My brave soldiers gathered like the clouds, and the insensate rebels melted away. Hearing of the easy successes I won, they were entirely demoralized.

"My army consists of heroes from the Nine Regions[iii], and officers and people are famous in the empire; all are expert in war and skilled in the use of arms. They go whither light leads them and serve the Emperor. All have exerted themselves to obey orders and carried out the plans for the seven captures of Meng Huo. They were whole-hearted in their service and vied in loyalty. Who could foresee that you, O Spirits, would be sacrificed in the strategy and be involved in the enemies' wicked wiles? Some of you went down to the deep springs wounded by flying arrows. Others went out into the long night hurt by lethal weapons. Living you were valorous, dead you left behind a name.

"Now we are returning home. The victors' song is in our mouths and our prisoners accompany us. Your spirits are with us still and certainly hear our prayers. Follow the banners, come with the host, return to your country, each to his own village, where you may enjoy the savor of the meat offerings and receive the sacrifices of your own families. Do not become wandering ghosts in unfamiliar hamlets of restless shades in strange cities. I will memorialize our Emperor that your wives and little ones may enjoy his gracious bounty, every year gifts of food and clothing, every month donations for sustenance. Comfort yourselves with this provision.

"As for you, Spirits of this place, shades of the departed people of the south, here is the usual sacrifice. You are near home. Year-round sacrifice is not lacking. Living you stood in awe of the celestial majesty, dead you come within the sphere of refining influence. It is right that you should hold your peace and refrain from uttering unseemly cries. With bowed head I pray you partake of the sweet savor of this sacrifice.

"Alas, ye dead! To you this offering!"

Zhuge Liang broke into loud lamentations at the end of this prayer and manifested extreme emotion, and the whole army shed tears. Meng Huo and his followers also moaned and wept, and amid the sad clouds and angry mists they saw the vague forms of many demons floating away on the wind till they disappeared.

The material portion of the sacrifice was then thrown into the river. Next day the army stood on the south bank with a clear sky over their heads and calm waters at their feet, the clouds gone and the winds hushed, and the crossing was made without misadventure. They continued their way, whips cracking, gongs clanging, spurs jingling, and ever and anon the song of victory rising over all.

Passing through Yongchang, Wang Kang and Lu Kai were left there in command of the four territories---Yizhou, Yongchang, Zangge, and Yuesui. And then Meng Huo was permitted to leave. He was ordered to be diligent in his administration, maintain good control, and soothe and care for the people left to him to govern and to see to it that agriculture was promoted. He took leave with tears rolling down his cheeks.

When the army neared Capital Chengdu, the Latter Ruler came out ten miles in state to welcome his victorious minister. The Emperor stood by the roadside as Zhuge Liang came up, and waited.

Zhuge Liang quickly descended from his chariot, prostrated himself and said, "Thy servant has offended in causing his master anxiety. But the conquest of the south was long."

The Emperor took Zhuge Liang kindly by the hand and raised him. Then the chariots of the Son of God and his minister returned to Chengdu side by side. In the capital were great rejoicings with banquets and rewards for the army. Henceforward distant nations sent tribute to the Imperial Court to the number of two hundred.

As proposed in a memorial, the Emperor provided for the families of the soldiers who had lost their lives in the expedition, and they were made happy. And the whole land enjoyed tranquillity.

Meanwhile in the Middle Land, the Ruler of Wei, Cao Pi, had now ruled seven years, and it was the fourth year of Beginning Prosperity in Shu-Han calendar. Cao Pi had taken to wife a lady of the Zhen family, formerly the wife of the second son of Yuan Shao. He had discovered Lady Zhen[iv] at the sack of Yejun and had married her. She bore him a son, Cao Rui, who was very clever and a great favorite with his father.

Later Cao Pi took as Beloved Consort a daughter of Guo Yong in Guangzong. Lady Guo was a woman of exceeding beauty, whom her father said, "She is the king among women!" And the name "Lady King" stuck to her.

But with Lady Guo's arrival at court, Lady Zhen fell from her lord's favor, and the Beloved Consort's ambition led her to intrigue to replace the Empress. She took Zhang Tao, a minister at the court, into her confidence.

At that time the Emperor was indisposed, and Zhang Tao alleged, saying, "In the palace of the Empress has been dug up a wooden image with Your Majesty's date of birth written thereon. It is meant to exercise a maleficent influence."

Cao Pi in his anger forced his Empress to commit suicide; and he set up the Beloved Consort in her place.

But Lady Guo had no issue. Wherefore she nourished Cao Rui as her own. However, loved as Cao Rui was, he was not then named heir by the Empress.

When he was about fifteen, Cao Rui, who was an expert archer and a daring rider, accompanied his father to the hunt. In a gully they started a doe and its fawn. Cao Pi shot the doe, while the fawn fled. Seeing that the fawn's course led past his son's horse, Cao Pi called out to him to shoot it. Instead the youth bursts into tears.

"Your Majesty has slain the mother. How can one kill the child as well?"

The words struck the Emperor with remorse. He threw aside his bow, saying, "My son, you would make a benevolent and virtuous ruler."

From this circumstance Cao Pi decided that Cao Rui should succeed, and conferred upon him the princedom of Pingyuan.

In the fifth month the Emperor fell ill, and medical treatment was of no avail. So the chief officers were summoned to the bedside of the Emperor. They were Commander of the Center Army Cao Zhen, General Who Guards the West Chen Qun, and Grand Commander Sima Yi.

When they had come, the Emperor's son was called, and the dying Emperor spoke thus: "I am grievously ill, and my end is near. I confide to your care and guidance this son of mine. You must support him out of good feeling for me."

"Why does Your Majesty talk thus?" said they. "We will do our utmost to serve you for a thousand autumns and a myriad years."

"No; I know that I am about to die," said the Emperor. "The sudden fall of the gates of Xuchang this year was the omen, as I well knew."

Just then the attendants said that General Who Conquers the East Cao Xiu had come to ask after the Emperor's health. They were told to call Cao Xiu into the chamber.

When he had entered, Cao Pi said to him, "You and these three are the pillars and cornerstones of the state. If you will only uphold my son, I can close my eyes in peace."

These were his last words. A flood of tears gushed forth, and Cao Pi sank back on the couch dead. He was forty years of age and had reigned seven years (AD 229).

The four ministers raised the wailing for the dead and forthwith busied themselves with setting up Cao Rui as the Emperor of Great Wei. The late Emperor received the posthumous style of "Emperor Pi". The late Empress, the consort who had suffered death, was styled "Empress Zhen".

Honors were distributed freely in celebration of the new reign. Zhong Yao was made Imperial Guardian; Cao Zhen, Regent Marshal; Cao Xiu, Minister of War; Hua Xin, Grand Commander; Wang Lang, Minister of the Interior; Chen Qun, Minister of Works; Sima Yi, Imperial Commander of the Flying Cavalry; and many others, conspicuous and obscure, were promoted. A general amnesty was declared throughout all the land.

About this time a vacancy existed in the commandership of Yongzhou and Liangzhou. Sima Yi asked for the post and got it. He left for his new office as soon as he had received the appointment. All military affairs of the west were now under his command.

In due time the news of all these doings reached Zhuge Liang and perturbed him not a little.

He was anxious, saying, "Cao Pi is dead, and his son Cao Rui has succeeded him. But that is not my concern. Only I am worried about Sima Yi, who is very crafty and skillful in the art of war, and who, in command of all western forces of Yongzhou and Liangzhou, may prove a serious danger to Shu. This Sima Yi ought to be attacked at once."

Counselor Ma Su spoke of this matter. "You, O Prime Minister, have just returned from an arduous and exhausting expedition, and you should take time to recuperate before you undertake such another. However, I have a scheme by which Cao Rui may be brought to work the destruction of Sima Yi. May I lay it before you?"

"What plan have you?" said he.

"The young emperor has no confidence in Sima Yi although Sima Yi is a high minister of state. Now send someone secretly to Luoyang and Yejun to disseminate reports that Sima Yi is about to rebel. Further, prepare a proclamation in his name and post it up so as to cause Cao Rui to mistrust him and put him to death."

Zhuge Liang adopted the suggestion.

Whence it came about that many notices suddenly appeared, and one found its way to the city gate of Yejun. The wardens of the gate took it down and sent it to Cao Rui. This is what it said:

"I, Sima Yi, Imperial Commander of the Flying Cavalry, Commander of the Forces of Yongzhou and Liangzhou, confident in the universal principles of right, now inform the empire, saying:

"The Founder of this Dynasty, Emperor Cao, established himself with the design of recurring the empire to the Lord of Linzi, Cao Zhi. Unfortunately, calumny spread abroad, and the Dragon Ruler could not manifest himself for many years. Emperor Cao's grandson, Cao Rui, does not follow a virtuous course, though sitting in the high place, and has not fulfilled the great intention of his ancestor. Now I, in accordance with the will of Heaven and favoring the desires of the people, have decided upon a day to set my army in motion in order to secure the wish of the people. When that day arrives, I call upon each one to gather to his lord, and I will destroy utterly the family of any who shall disobey. You are hereby informed that you may all know."

This document frightened the young Emperor, and he turned pale. At once he called a council of his officials to consider it.

Hua Xin said, "That was the reason for his having requested the commandership of Yongzhou and Liangzhou. Now Emperor Cao, the Founder of Great Wei, frequently said to me that Sima Yi was ambitious and hungry, and should not be entrusted with military authority lest he harm the state. This is the first beginning of rebellion, and the author should be put to death."

Wang Lang said, "Sima Yi is a master of strategy and skilled in tactics. Moreover, he is ambitious and will cause mischief if he be allowed to live."

Wherefore Cao Rui wrote a command to raise an army, which he would lead to punish the minister.

Suddenly Cao Zhen stood forth from the rank of military officers and said, "What you advise is impossible. His Late Majesty, Emperor Pi, confided his son to the care of certain officers of state, of whom Sima Yi is one, wherefore it is certain that he felt sure of Sima Yi's probity. So far nothing is known certainly. If you hastily send an army to repress him, you may force him into rebellion. This may be but one of the base tricks of Shu or Wu to cause dissension in our midst so that occasion be found to further their own aims. As no one knows, I pray Your Majesty reflect before you do anything."

"Supposing Sima Yi really contemplates a revolt. What then?" said Cao Rui.

Cao Zhen replied, "If Your Majesty suspects him, then do as did Liu Bang the Supreme Ancestor of Han when, under pretense of taking a trip on the Lake Yunmeng, he summoned his vassals---and seized Han Xin, who had been denounced. Go to Anyi; Sima Yi will assuredly come out to meet you, and his actions and demeanor may be watched closely. He can be arrested if needed."

Cao Rui changed his mind. Leaving Cao Zhen to

regulate the affairs of state, the young Emperor went out with the Imperial Guards, to the number of one hundred thousand, and traveled to Anyi.

Ignorant of the reason of the Emperor's coming, and anxious to show off his dignity, Sima Yi went to welcome his ruler in all the pomp of a commander of a great army of one hundred thousand.

As Sima Yi approached, the courtiers told the Emperor, saying, "Sima Yi's defection is certain since such a large army can only mean that he is prepared to resist."

Whereupon Cao Xiu, with a large force, was sent in front to meet him. Sima Yi thought the Imperial Chariot was coming, and he advanced alone and stood humbly by the roadside till Cao Xiu came up.

Cao Xiu advanced and said, "Friend, His Late Majesty entrusted you with the heavy responsibility of caring for his son. Why are you in revolt?"

Sima Yi turned pale, and a cold sweat broke out all over him as he asked the reason for such a charge. Cao Xiu told him what had occurred.

"This is a vile plot on the part of our rivals, Shu and Wu, to cause dissension," said Sima Yi. "It is a design to make the Emperor work evil upon his ministers that thereby another may profit. I must see the Son of Heaven and explain."

Ordering his army to retire, Sima Yi went forward alone to the Emperor's chariot.

Sima Yi bowed low and said, weeping, "His Late Majesty gave me charge of his son. Could I betray him? This is a wile of the enemy. I crave permission to lead an army, first to destroy Shu and then to attack Wu, whereby to show my gratitude to the late Emperor and Your Majesty and manifest my own true heart."

However, Cao Rui did not feel quite convinced, and Hua Xin said, "In any case withdraw his military powers and let him go into retirement."

And thus it was decided. Sima Yi was forced to retire to his native village. Cao Xiu succeeded to his command, and Cao Rui returned to Luoyang.

The news was soon reported to Shu. Zhuge Liang rejoiced when they told him of the success that had attended the ruse.

"Sima Yi and the forces he commanded in Yongzhou and Liangzhou have been the obstacles in my long-wished-for attack on Wei. Now he has fallen, I have no more anxiety."

At the first great assembly of officers at court, Zhuge Liang stepped forth and presented to the Ruler of Shu a memorial on the expedition he contemplated.

"The First Ruler had accomplished but half his great task at his death. At this moment the empire is in three parts, and our country is weak; it is a most critical moment for us. Still, ministers are not remiss in the capital, and loyal and devoted soldiers sacrifice their lives abroad, for they still remember the special kindness of the First Ruler and wish to show their gratitude to him by service to Your Majesty. Therefore it would be indeed fitting that you should extend your holy virtue to glorify his virtuous memory in the stimulation of the will of your purposeful officers. Your Majesty should not lose yourself in the pursuit of mean things, quoting phrases to confound the eternal principles of rectitude, and so preventing remonstrance from honest people. One rule applies to the palace of the Emperor and the residence of a courtier; there must be one law rewarding the good and punishing the evil. Evil-doers and law-breakers, as also true and good people, should be dealt with according to their deserts by the officers concerned in order to manifest Your Majesty's impartial and enlightened administration. Partiality is wrong, as is one law for the court and another for the regions.

"The High Ministers Fei Yi, Guo Youzhi, and Dong Yun are honest men, devotedly anxious to be loyal to the last degree; wherefore His Late Majesty chose them in his testament. My advice is to consult them in all Palace matters, great or small, before taking action. Your Majesty will reap the enormous advantage of having any failings corrected.

"General Xiang Chong is a man of well-balanced temperament, versed in military matters, to whom, after testing him, the late Emperor applied the epithet 'capable'. The consensus of opinion is that Xiang Chong should be Grand Commander. My advice is to consult him in all military matters, great or small, whereby your military forces will yield their maximum, each one being employed to the best advantage.

"Attract worthy people; repel mean ones. This policy achieved the glory of the Former Hans, while its reversal ruined the Latter Hans. When the late Emperor was with us, he often discussed this with your servant, and he took much to heart the story of Emperors Huan and Ling.

"The Chair of the Secretariat Chen Zhen, Commander Zhang Si, and Minister Jiang Wan are both incorruptible and enlightened people, honest to the death. I wish that Your Majesty should have them near and hold them in confidence. If this be done, then the glory of the House of Han will be quickly consummated.

"I was originally a private person, a farmer in Nanyang, concerned only to secure personal safety in a troubled age and not seeking conversation with the contending nobles. His Late Majesty, the First Ruler, overlooking the commonness of my origin, condescended to seek me thrice in my humble cot and consult me on the trend of events. His magnanimity affected me deeply, and I consented to do my utmost for him. Then came defeat, and I took office at a moment of darkest outlook and at a most difficult crisis. This is twenty-one years ago. The First Ruler recognized my diligent care, and when dying he confided the great task to me. From that day I have lived a life of anxiety lest I should fail in my trust and so dim his glory.

"That is why I undertook the expedition to the lands beyond the River Lu. Now the Southern Mangs has been quelled, and our army is in good condition. I ought to lead it against the north, where I may meet with a measure of success in the removal of the wicked ones, the restoration of Han, and a return to the old capital. This is my duty out of gratitude to the late Emperor and loyalty to Your Majesty. As to a discussion of the pros and cons and giving a true version of the whole matter, that belongs to Guo Youzhi and Fei Yi and Dong Yun. I desire Your Majesty to confide to me the task of slaying the rebels and restoring the Hans. If I fail, then punish me by telling the spirit of the late Emperor. If you know not what restoration implies, that is the fault of your advisers.

"Your Majesty should take pains to be guided into the right path and examine carefully what is laid before you, carefully remembering the late Emperor's testament.

"I cannot express what would be my delight if you had the goodness to accept and act on my advice.

"Now I am about to depart on a distant expedition, I write this with tears and clearly know what I have said."

The Emperor read it through and said, "My Father Minister, you have only just returned from a distant and fatiguing expedition against the Southern Mangs. You are not yet refreshed, and I fear this march to the north will be almost too much even for you."

Zhuge Liang replied, "The heaviest responsibility lies upon me, the well-being of Your Majesty confided to me by the First Ruler. My efforts may not be relaxed night or day. The south is at rest, at home is no anxiety. What better time could be hoped for to destroy the rebels and recover the Middle Land?"

Forth from the ranks of courtiers stood Minister Qiao Zhou and said, "I have studied the aspect of the stars. The northern quarter is brilliant and strong. The scheme will not speed."

Then turning toward the Prime Minister, he continued, "You, O Prime Minister, understand the mysteries of the skies. Why do you oppose the stars?"

"Because the stars are in infinite changes," replied Zhuge Liang. "One may rely on the stars too much. Moreover, I have already sent the army into Hanzhong, where I shall act as soon as I have studied what is afoot."

Qiao Zhou pleaded in vain. Zhuge Liang was too strongly set upon his purpose to yield. So Guo Youzhi, Dong Yun, and Fei Yi were ordered to attend to matters in the Palace; Xiang Chong was to control all military affairs and became Grand Commander; Jiang Wan was made Military Adviser; Chen Zhen became Chair of the Secretariat; Zhang Si, Controller of the Prime Minister's palace; Du Qiong, Imperial Censor; Du Wei and Yang Hong, Ministers; Meng Guang and Lai Min, Libationers; Yin Mo and Li Zhuan, Academicians; Xi Zheng and Fei Shi, General Secretaries; Qiao Zhou, Chief Secretary; and others to the number of over a hundred, all to manage the administration of Shu in the absence of Zhuge Liang.

Having received his Emperor's command to lead an expedition against the north, Zhuge Liang returned to his palace and summoned the officers of the army to listen to the orders. And they came, and to each was appointed a duty in the great army:

Front Army Commander---Wei Yan
Front Army Marching Generals---Zhang Yi, Wang Ping
Rear Army Commander---Li Hui
Rear Army Marching General---Lu Yin
Left Army Commander and Chief of the Commissariat---Ma Dai
Left Army Marching General---Zhang Ni
Right Army Commander---Ma Zheng
Right Army Marching General---Deng Zhi
Center Army Director---Liu Yang
Center Army Marching Generals---Liao Hua, Hu Ji
Center Army Front Generals---Yuan Lin, Liu Ba, Xu Yun
Center Army Rear General---Hu Ban
Center Army Left Generals---Wu Yi, Ding Xian
Center Army Right Generals---Gao Xiang, Guan Yong, Liu Min
Center Army Center Generals---Du Qi, Sheng Bo, Fan Qi
Advisers---Ma Su, Yang Yi, Cuan Xi, Du Yi
Secretaries---Fan Jian, Dong Jue
Left Guard---Guan Xing
Right Guard---Zhang Bao
Inspector---Yan Yan

Li Yan was given the task of guarding the passes

against Wu from the southeast.

Zhuge Liang was the Commander-in-Chief of the Northern Expedition.

All being ready, a day was chosen for the start: The fifth year, the third month, on the day of "tiger".

After the appointments had all been made, there came forward a veteran who had listened in vain for the duty assigned him.

"Old I may be," said he, "yet have I still the valor of Lian Po[v] and the heroism of Ma Yuan[vi]. Why am I thought useless any more than these two who refused to acknowledge old age?"

It was Zhao Yun.

Zhuge Liang said, "I have lost my friend Ma Chao by illness since I returned from the Southern Expedition, and I feel as I had lost an arm. Now, General, you must own that the years are mounting up. Any slight lapse would not only shake the life-long reputation of yourself, but might have a bad effect on the whole army."

Zhao Yun replied bitterly, "I have never quailed in the presence of the enemy from the day I first joined the First Ruler. I have ever pressed to the front. It is a happy ending for a person of valor to die on the frontier. Think you that I should resent it? Let me lead the van, I pray."

Zhuge Liang used all his skill to dissuade the veteran, but in vain.

Zhao Yun was set on it, saying, "If you, O Prime Minister, do not let me lead the van, I will smash my head on the floor and die at your feet."

At last Zhuge Liang yielded, saying, "General, you can have the post of Van Leader, but you must choose a colleague to support you."

"I will go to help the Veteran Leader!" cried Deng Zhi, without a moment's hesitation. "I am not worth much, but I will help lead the attack on the enemy."

Accordingly five thousand of veterans were chosen for the advanced guard, and with them, to assist Zhao Yun, went Deng Zhi and ten other generals.

After the vanguard had set out, the main body marched by the north gate, the Latter Ruler himself going to see his minister start. The farewell was taken three miles from the gate, in the face of the grand army with its banners and pennons flaunting in the wind, and spears and swords gleaming in the sun.

Then they took the road leading to Hanzhong.

Naturally, this movement was duly reported in Luoyang at a court held by Cao Rui, when a minister said, "A report from the border stations says that Zhuge Liang has marched three hundred thousand troops into Hanzhong. Zhao Yun and Deng Zhi are leading the advanced guard."

The report alarmed Cao Rui, and he asked, "Who can lead an army to repel the advance?"

At once out spoke one, saying, "My father died in

Hanzhong, and to my bitter resentment his death is unavenged. Now I desire to lead the army against Shu, and I pray that the armies west of the Pass may be given me for this purpose. I shall render a service to the state, as well as taking vengeance for my father. I care not what fate may befall me."

The speaker was Xiahou Yuan's son, Xiahou Mao. He was by nature very impulsive and also very miserly. When young he had been adopted by Xiahou Dun. When Xiahou Yuan was killed by Huang Zhong, Cao Cao was moved and married Xiahou Mao to one of his daughters, Princess Qinghe, so that he was an Imperial Son-in-Law. As such he enjoyed great deference at court. But although he held a military commission, he had never been with the army. However, as he requested the command, he was made Commander-in-Chief of the western armies and was ready to march.

But Minister of the Interior Wang Lang spoke against the appointment, saying, "The appointment is wrong. Xiahou Mao, the Son-in-Law, has never seen a battle and is unsuitable for this post, especially when his opponent is the clever and crafty Zhuge Liang, a man thoroughly versed in strategy."

"I suppose you have arranged with Zhuge Liang to be his ally," sneered Xiahou Mao. "Ever since I was a boy, I have studied strategy, and I am well acquainted with army matters. Why do you despise my youth? Unless I capture this Zhuge Liang, I pledge myself never again to see the Emperor's face."

Wang Lang and his supporters were silenced. Xiahou Mao took leave of the Ruler of Wei and hastened to Changan to get his army in order. He had two hundred thousand troops from the western areas.

He would go to battle, take the signal flags in grip,
But could he play the leader, he a lad with callow lip?

The next chapter will deal with this campaign.

Chapter 92

Zhao Yun Slays Five Generals;
Zhuge Liang Takes Three Cities.

Zhuge Liang's army marched northward, passing through Mianyang, where stood Ma Chao's tomb. In honor of the dead Tiger General, Zhuge Liang sacrificed there in person, Ma Chao's cousin---Ma Dai---being chief mourner for the occasion.

After this ceremony, when the Commander-in-Chief was discussing his plans, the spies came in to report: "The Ruler of Wei, Cao Rui, has put in motion all western forces under Xiahou Mao."

Then Wei Yan went in to offer a plan, saying, "Xiahou Mao is a child of a wealthy family, soft and stupid. Give me five thousand troops, and I will go out by Baozhong, follow the line of the Qinling Mountains east to the Ziwu Valley and then turn north. In ten days I can be at Changan. Hearing of my rush, Xiahou Mao will hasten to vacate the city. Then he must flee by way of Royal Gate. I will come in by the east, and you, Sir, can advance by the Xie Valley with the main army. In this way all west of Changan will be ours in just one move."

Zhuge Liang smiled at the suggestion.

"I do not think the plan quite perfect," said he. "You are gambling by thinking there is no northerner worth considering guarding Changan. If anyone suggests sending a force across to block the exit of the mountains, I am afraid we should lose five thousand troops, to say nothing of the check to our elan. The plan will not work."

"If you, O Prime Minister, march by the high road, they will bring against you the whole host Within the Passes and will thus hold you indefinitely. You will never get to the Middle Land."

"But I shall go along the level road on the right of Longyou. I cannot fail if I keep to the fixed rules of war."

Wei Yan withdrew, gloomy and dissatisfied.

Then Zhuge Liang sent Zhao Yun orders for the advanced guard to move.

Xiahou Mao was at Changan preparing his force. There came to him a general from Xiliang, named Han De, a man of great valor, whose weapon was a mighty battle-ax called "Mountain Splitter". He brought with him eighty thousand of the Qiang tribesmen and offered his services. They were gladly accepted, and his army was made the van of the attack.

This Han De had four sons, all very expert in archery and horsemanship. They were named Han Ying, Han Yao, Han Qiong, and Han Qi, and they came to serve under their father. Han De led his sons and the eighty thousand troops by the road to Phoenix Song Mountain, where they were near the army of Shu, and here they drew up the array.

When the battle line was in order, the father, with his four sons, rode to the front and began to revile their enemy, shouting, "Rebels and raiders! How dare you invade our territory?"

Zhao Yun quickly lost his temper, rode forward and challenged. The eldest son, Han Ying, accepted and galloped out; but he was slain in the third bout. Immediately his brother Han Yao went out, whirling his sword. But now Zhao Yun's blood was up, and the old dash and vigor came upon him so that the young man had no chance to win the battle. Then the third son, Han Qiong, took his great halberd and dashed out to his brother's aid. Zhao Yun had now two opponents; nevertheless he held his own, nor blenched nor failed a stroke. Seeing that his two brothers were nearing defeat, the fourth son Han Qi went to join in the fray with his pair of swords that he had named "Sun and Moon". And there was the veteran warrior with three against him, and he still kept them at bay.

Presently a spear thrust got home on Han Qi, who fell. Another general then coming out to take his place. Zhao Yun lowered his spear and fled. Han Qiong then took his bow and shot three arrows at the fugitive, who turned them aside so that they fell harmless. Angry at this, Han Qiong again seized his halberd and went in pursuit. But Zhao Yun took his bow and shot an arrow that wounded his pursuer in the face. So Han Qiong fell and died. Han Yao then galloped up and raised his sword to strike, but Zhao Yun slipped past, got within his guard and made Han Yao a prisoner. Zhao Yun quickly galloped into his own array with his captive, dropped him and then, dashing out, recovered his spear, which had fallen when he seized his man.

Han De was overwhelmed with the loss of all his sons and went behind the battle array. His Qiang tribesmen were too frightened at the prowess of Zhao Yun to be of any use in battle, and no one dared to meet the old warrior. So they retired, while Zhao Yun rode to and fro among them slaying at his will.

I thought of brave old people, of Zhao Yun,
Who, in spite of numbered years three scores and ten,
Was marvelous strong in battle; who one day
Slew four opposing generals, as great as
When at Dangyang he had saved his lord.

Seeing the successful battle that Zhao Yun was waging, Deng Zhi led on his troops to join in the fight. This completed the discomfiture of the Xiliang army, and they ran away. Han De, seeing the danger of being captured, threw off his armor and went on foot. The soldiers of Shu drew off and returned to their camp.

In camp Deng Zhi felicitated his veteran colleague.

"For a man of seventy years, you are unique and wonderful," said he. "You are as much the hero as you ever were. It is almost an incomparable feat to have slain four generals in one day."

"Yet the Prime Minister thought me too old and did not wish to employ me. I had to give him a proof."

The captive Han Yao was sent to the main body with the messenger who bore an account of the victory.

In the meantime, Han De led his defeated army back to his chief, to whom he related his sad story with many tears. Then Xiahou Mao got angry and decided to lead his own army out against Zhao Yun.

When the scouts reported his coming, Zhao Yun took his spear and mounted his steed. He led one thousand troops out to Phoenix Song Mountain, at the foot of which he made his array. Xiahou Mao was wearing a golden casque, riding a white horse, and carrying a huge sword. From his place beneath the great standard, he saw Zhao Yun galloping to and fro. He was going out to give battle, when Han De checked him.

"Is it not mine to avenge my four sons?" said Han De.

Han De seized his mountain-splitter ax, and rode directly at the warrior, who advanced with fury. The contest was but short, for in the third encounter Zhao Yun's spear thrust brought Han De to the earth. Without waiting a moment he made for Xiahou Mao, who hastily dashed in behind his ranks and so escaped. Then Deng Zhi led on the main body and completed the victory. The force of Wei retired three miles and made a camp.

This first battle having gone against him, Xiahou Mao called his officers to consult.

He said, "I have heard Zhao Yun long ago, but have never met face-to-face. Now though that warrior is old, he still has incredible prowess. The story of Dangyang where he alone fought against a whole host and came out victor is really not fabricated. But what to be done against such a champion?"

Then Cheng Wu, son of Cheng Yu, said, "My opinion is that this Zhao Yun, though brave in the field, is lacking in the council chamber. Really he is not greatly to be feared. Give battle again soon, but first prepare a two-pronged ambush. You can retreat and so draw him into it. Then go up on the hill top and direct the attack from that point of vantage so that he may be hemmed in on all sides and be captured."

The necessary plans for this were made, and two parties of thirty thousand each, led by Dong Xin and Xue Ze, went into ambush right and left. The ambush laid, Xiahou Mao advanced once more to attack, drums rolling and flags flying. As soon as he appeared, Zhao Yun and Deng Zhi went to meet him.

Deng Zhi said, "The army of Wei were beaten only yesterday. This renewed attempt must mean that they are trying some trick. You should be cautious, General."

"I do not think this youth, with the smell of mother's milk still on his lips, worth talking about. We shall surely capture him today."

Zhao Yun pranced out, and Pan Sui came to meet him from the side of Wei. But Pan Sui made no stand and quickly ran away. Zhao Yun plunged in to try to capture Xiahou Mao. Then there came out to stop him no less than eight generals of Wei, all of whom passed in front of Xiahou Mao. But one by one they too fled. Zhao Yun pressed forward at full speed, Deng Zhi coming up behind.

When Zhao Yun had got deeply involved, with the battle raging all around him, Deng Zhi decided to retire. This was the signal for the ambush to come out, Dong Xin from the right and Xue Ze from the left. Deng Zhi was so hampered that he could not attempt to rescue his colleague. Zhao Yun was thus entirely surrounded. However, he struggled on, losing men at every dash, till he had but one thousand troops left. He was then at the foot of the hill whence Xiahou Mao was directing operations, and observing his enemy from this point of vantage, Xiahou Mao sent troops to check Zhao Yun whithersoever he went. Zhao Yun decided to charge up the hill, but was stopped by rolling bulks of timber and tumbling rocks.

The battle had lasted long, and Zhao Yun was fatigued. So he halted to rest a time, intending to renew the struggle when the moon should be up. But just as he had taken off his armor the moon rose and, with it, his enemies began to attack with fire as well, and the thunder of the drums was accompanied by showers of stones and arrows.

The oncoming host shouted, "Zhao Yun! Why don't dismount and be bound?"

However, Zhao Yun did not think of that, but got upon his steed to strive once more to extricate himself. And his enemies pressed closer and closer, pouring in flights and flights of arrows. No advance was possible, and the end seemed very near.

"I refused the repose of age," sighed he, "and now my end will come to me here!"

Just then he heard new shouting from the northeast, and the array of Wei became disordered. To his joy, Zhao Yun saw Zhang Bao coming toward him, the serpent halberd in his hand, and a man's head hanging at his bridle.

Soon Zhang Bao reached the veteran general's side and cried, "The Prime Minister feared some misfortune had befallen you, so he sent me to your help! I have five thousand troops here. We heard that you were surrounded. On the way I met Xue Ze and slew him."

Zhao Yun's courage revived, and he and the young general went on toward the southwest, driving the soldiers of Wei before them in disorder. Soon another cohort came in from the side, the leader wielding the green-dragon saber.

This was Guan Xing, and he cried, "The Prime Minister sent me with five thousand troops to your aid. On the way I encountered Dong Xin and slain him. Here is his head. The Prime Minister is coming up too!"

"But why not press on to capture Xiahou Mao since you have had such wonderful success?" cried Zhao Yun.

Zhang Bao took the hint and went forward. Guan Xing followed.

"They are as my own children," said Zhao Yun to those who stood near. "And they press on wherever there is merit to be won. I am an old leader and high in rank, but I am not worth so much as these two youths. Yet will I risk my life once more for the sake of my old lord the First Ruler."

So he led the remnant of his troops to try to capture Xiahou Mao.

During that night the army of Wei was smitten till corpses covered the earth and gore ran in rivers. Xiahou Mao was unskillful, and young, and inexperienced in battle. His army was in utter rout, and he could not think but only flee. At the head of a hundred cavalries, he made for Nanan. His army, leaderless, scattered like rats.

Zhang Bao and Guan Xing set out for Nanan. At the news of their coming, Xiahou Mao closed the city gates and urged his soldiers to defend. Zhao Yun soon joined the generals, and they attacked on three sides. Deng Zhi arrived also, and the city was quite surrounded.

After vain efforts for ten days, they heard the news: "The Prime Minister has stationed the rear army in Mianyang, the left army in Yangping Pass, the right army in Shicheng. He himself is leading the center army toward Nanan."

The four generals went to visit Zhuge Liang and told him their failure at the city. He got into his light chariot and rode out to view the city, after which he returned and summoned the officers to his tent.

Zhuge Liang said, "The moat is deep, the walls are

steep. Wherefore the city is well defended and difficult to take. My present plan omits this place. If you persist in the attack and the Wei armies march to try for Hanzhong, our army will be in danger."

"Consider what the capture of Xiahou Mao would mean," said Deng Zhi. "He is an Imperial Son-in-Law, and worth more than slaying a hundred ordinary leaders. We have begun the siege, and we should not raise it."

Zhuge Liang said, "I have other plans. West of this lies Tianshui and north Anding. Does anyone know the governors of these two places?"

"Ma Zun is the Governor of Tianshui, Cui Liang that of Anding," replied a scout.

Zhuge Liang then called to him one by one---Wei Yan, Zhang Bao, Guan Xing, and two trusted subordinates---and gave each certain instructions. They left to carry out their orders.

Next Zhuge Liang ordered the soldiers to pile up beneath the walls heaps of firewood and straw, saying he was going to burn the city. The defenders on the wall derided him.

Cui Liang, the Governor of Anding, was much frightened when he heard that Xiahou Mao was besieged, and began to see to his own defenses. He mustered his four thousand soldiers, resolved to defend his city as long as possible. Then there came a man from the south direction, who said he had secret letters.

Cui Liang had him brought into the city, and, when

questioned, the man said, "I am one of Xiahou Mao's trusted soldiers and named Pei Xu. I was sent to beg for help from Tianshui and Anding. The city of Nanan is hard pressed. Every day we have raised fires to call the attention of your cities to our plight, but our signals have all failed. No one has come. I was ordered to fight my way through the besiegers and come to tell you. You are to give assistance immediately, and our General will open the gates to help you."

"Have you a letter from the General?" asked Cui Liang.

A letter was produced from inside the man's dress, all moist with perspiration. After the Governor had read it, the soldier took it back and went on to the direction of Tianshui.

Two days later a mounted messenger came to Anding and said to Cui Liang: "Governor Ma Zun of Tianshui with his troops have already started for Nanan. The troops of Anding should march at once to their aid."

Cui Liang took the advice of his officers. Most of them said, "If you do not go, and Nanan is taken, we shall he blamed for giving up the Imperial Son-in-Law. He must be rescued."

Thereupon Cui Liang marched. The civil officers were left in charge of the city. The army took the high road to Nanan. They saw flames shooting up to the sky all the time, and the Governor urged the army to march faster. When fifteen miles from the city, there was heard the drums of an attacking force, and the scouts came to say that the road ahead was held by Guan Xing, while Zhang Bao was coming up quickly in their rear.

At this news the soldiers scattered in all directions. Cui Liang had a hundred men left with whom he tried to cut his way out that he might return to his own city. He got through.

But when he came to his own city, a flight of arrows greeted him from the wall, and Wei Yan shouted to him, saying, "I have taken the city. You had better yield!"

This was what had happened. Wei Yan and his soldiers, disguised as an Anding soldiers, in the darkness of the night had beguiled the wardens of the gate into opening it, and the men of Shu had got in.

Cui Liang set off for Tianshui. But one march away a cohort came out, and beneath the great flag he saw a light chariot. In the chariot sat a man in Taoist robe with a feather fan in his hand. Cui Liang at once recognized Zhuge Liang, but as he turned, up came Guan Xing and Zhang Bao, who summoned him to surrender. As he was entirely surrounded, no other course was open to him, so he gave in. He went to the great camp with Zhuge Liang, who treated him with courtesy.

After a time Zhuge Liang said, "Is the Govenor of Nanan a friend of yours?"

"He is one Yang Ling, a cousin of Yang Fu. Being neighboring counties, we are very good friends."

"I wish to trouble you to persuade him to capture Xiahou Mao. Can you?"

"If you, O Prime Minister, order me to do this, I would ask you to withdraw your troops and let me go into the city to speak with him."

Zhuge Liang consented and ordered the besiegers to draw off seven miles and camp. Cui Liang himself went to the city and hailed the gate. He entered and went forthwith to his friend's residence. As soon as he had finished the salutations, he related what had happened.

"After the kindness we have received from Wei, we cannot be traitors," said Yang Ling. "But we will meet ruse with ruse."

He led Cui Liang to the Commander-in-Chief and told the whole story.

"What ruse do you propose?" asked Xiahou Mao.

"Let us pretend to offer the city, and let the army of Shu in. Once they are in, we can massacre them."

Xiahou Mao agreed to plot the scheme.

Cui Liang went back to Zhuge Liang's camp, where he said, "Yang Ling wants to offer the Prime Minister the city. He also wants to capture Xiahou Mao, but he is so afraid of having few soldiers that he has made no hasty move."

"That is simple enough," replied Zhuge Liang. "Your hundred troops are here. We can mix with them some of my generals dressed as your officers and so let them get into the city. They can hide in Xiahou Mao's dwelling and arrange with Yang Ling to open the gates in the night. And my grand army will come in to make the capture for you."

Cui Liang thought within himself, "If I do not take the Shu generals, they will arouse suspicion. I would rather take them and will kill them as soon as they get within the walls. Then, I will give the signal and beguile Zhuge Liang to enter, and so dispose of him."

So Cui Liang consented to Zhuge Liang's proposal.

Zhuge Liang gave him instructions, saying, "I will send my trusty Guan Xing and Zhang Bao with you. You will pass them off as the rescuers just to set Xiahou Mao's mind at rest. But when you raise a fire, I shall take that as my signal and come in."

At dusk the two trusty generals, having received their secret orders, put on their armor, mounted, took their weapons, and got in among the Anding troops. Cui Liang led the small force to the gate. Yang Ling was on the wall. The drawbridge was hoisted. He leaned over the guard rail and scanned those below.

"Who are you?" asked he.

"We are rescuers from Anding."

Now Cui Liang shot an arrow over the wall, to which a secret letter was bound, saying:

"Zhuge Liang is sending two generals into the city that they may help him to get in, but do nothing till we get inside lest the ruse gets known and the game be spoiled."

Yang Ling went to show this letter to Xiahou Mao,

who said, "Then Zhuge Liang is going to be our victim. Put a company of ax and bill men in the palace, and as soon as these two generals get inside, shut the gates and fall on. Then give the signal. As soon as Zhuge Liang gets inside the gate, seize him."

All arrangements being made, Yang Ling went back to the wall and said, "Since you are Anding troops, you may be allowed in."

The gate was thrown open and, while Guan Xing followed close after Cui Liang, Zhang Bao was a little way behind. Yang Ling came down to the gate to welcome them. As soon as Guan Xing got near, he lifted his sword and smote Yang Ling, who fell headless. Cui Liang was startled and lashed his steed to flee.

But Zhang Bao rushed forth and cried, "Scoundrel! Did you think your vile plot would be hidden from the eyes of our Prime Minister?"

With that Cui Liang fell from a spear thrust of Zhang Bao. Then Guan Xing went up on the wall and lit the fire. Soon the army of Shu filled the city. Xiahou Mao could make no defense, so he tried to fight his way through the south gate. There he met Wang Ping and was captured. Those with him were slain.

Zhuge Liang entered the city of Nanan and at once forbade all plunder. The various generals reported the deeds of valor. The captive Commander-in-Chief was placed in a prisoner's cart.

Then Deng Zhi asked, "O Prime Minister, how did you know the treachery of Cui Liang?"

Zhuge Liang said, "I knew the man was unwilling in his heart to yield, so I sent him into the city that he might have a chance to weave a counter plot with Xiahou Mao. I saw by his manner he was treacherous, and so I sent my two trusty generals with him to give him a feeling of security. Had he been true to me, he would have opposed this. But he accepted it gaily and went with them lest I should suspect him. He thought they could slay the two leaders and entice me in. But Guan Xing and Zhang Bao already had orders of what to do. Everything turned out as I thought, and as they did not expect."

The officers bowed their appreciation of his wonderful insight.

Then Zhuge Liang said, "I sent one of my trusty people to pretend he was a certain Pei Xu of Wei and so deceive this Cui Liang. Then I sent another messenger to reinforce the ruse. I also sent them to Tianshui to repeat the plan, but nothing has happened yet. I do not know the reason. We will take this opportunity to capture that place."

It was decided to take Tianshui next, and thither they moved. Wu Yi and Liu Yang were to guard Nanan and Anding. Wei Yan was ordered to move toward Tianshui.

When Ma Zun, Governor of Tianshui, heard of Xiahou Mao's being besieged in Nanan, he called a council at which one party---headed by Yin Shang and Liang Xu---were strongly of opinion that a rescue should be attempted.

"If anything sinister happens to the Imperial Son-in-Law, 'golden branch and jade leaf' as he is, we shall be held guilty of having made no attempt to save him. Wherefore, O Governor, you must march all the forces you have to his rescue," said Yin Shang and Liang Xu.

Ma Zun found decision difficult, and while thinking over what was best to do, the arrival of Pei Xu, a messenger from Xiahou Mao, was announced. Pei Xu was taken to the Governor's residence and there produced his dispatch and asked for aid. Soon came another man saying that the Anding troops had set out and calling upon Ma Zun to hasten. This decided him, and he prepared his army.

Then an outsider came in and said, "O Governor, you are the sport of one of Zhuge Liang's wiles."

All looked at him with surprise. He was one Jiang Wei. His father was Jiang Jiong, a former local official who had died in the court's service while quelling one of the Qiang rebellions. Jiang Wei was well up in books, seeming to have read everything, and was also skilled in all warlike exercises. He had studied books on war. He was a very filial son and much esteemed. He held military rank of General.

Jiang Wei said to the Governor, "I hear Zhuge Liang is attacking Xiahou Mao, who is now in Nanan most closely besieged. How then can this messenger have got out? Pei Xu is an unknown officer whom no one has heard of, and the other messenger from Anding bears no dispatch. The fact is the men are imposters sent to beguile you into leaving your city undefended so that it may be the more easily captured."

The Governor began to understand. He said, "Were it not for you, I would fall into a ruse."

Then Jiang Wei said, "But do not be anxious. I have a scheme by which we can capture Zhuge Liang and relieve Nanan."

The fates all changing bring the man that's needed,
And warlike skill comes from a source unheeded.

The next chapter will unfold the ruse proposed by Jiang Wei.

Chapter 93

Jiang Wei Goes Over To Zhuge Liang; Zhuge Liang's Reviles Kill Wang Lang.

Jiang Wei propounded his scheme of defense, saying, "Zhuge Liang will lay an ambush behind the city, induce our soldiers to go out and then take advantage of its undefended state to capture it. Now give me three thousand good soldiers, and I will place them in ambush at a certain critical place. Lead your troops out, but go slowly and not further than ten miles, and then turn to retire. However, look out for a signal, and if you see one, attack, for the attack will be double. If Zhuge Liang is there himself, we shall capture him."

The Governor adopted this plan, gave the needed troops to Jiang Wei, who marched at once, and then Ma Zun went forth himself with Liang Qian. Only two civil officials---Liang Xu and Yin Shang---were left to guard the city.

Zhao Yun had been sent to lie in ambush in a secret place among the hills till the Tianshui army left the city, when he was to rush in and capture it. His spies reported the departure of the Governor, and only civil officials remained within the city. Zhao Yun sent on the news to those who were acting with him, Zhang Yi and Gao Xiang, that they might attack Ma Zun.

Zhao Yun and his five thousand troops then quickly marched to the city wall and called out, "I am Zhao Yun of Changshan. You have fallen into our trap, but if you will surrender quickly, you will save many lives."

But instead of being alarmed, Liang Xu looked down from the wall and said, "On the contrary, you have fallen into our trap. Only you do not know it yet!"

Zhao Yun began his attack on the walls. Soon there was heard a roar, and fire broke out all round, and forth came a youthful leader armed with a spear, riding a curvetting steed.

"Look at me, Jiang Wei of Tianshui!" cried he.

Zhao Yun made at him, but after a few bouts he found Jiang Wei was getting very eager.

Zhao Yun was surprised, and wondered, "No one knows there is such an able man in Tianshui."

As the fight went on, along came the two other forces under Ma Zun and Liang Qian, now returning. As Zhao Yun found he could not prevail, he set to cut an alley through and lead off his defeated troops. He was pursued, but Zhang Yi and Gao Xiang poured forth to save him, and he got away safely.

Zhuge Liang was surprised when he heard what had happened.

"Who is this?" said he. "Who has thus seen into the dark depths of my secret plan?"

A man of Nanan, who happened to be there, told him, "He is Jiang Wei from Jicheng of Tianshui County. He is very filial to his mother. Civil skill and military prowess, wisdom and courage, he has all. Truly, he is a hero of the age."

Zhao Yun also praised his skill with the spear, which was superior to any other's.

Zhuge Liang said, "I want to take Tianshui now. I did not expect to find such a man as this."

The Shu army then advanced in force.

Jiang Wei went back to Ma Zun and said, "Zhao Yun's defeat will bring up Zhuge Liang with the main body. He will conclude that we shall be in the city, wherefore you had better divide your force into four. I, with one party, will go into hiding on the east so that I may cut off our enemies if they come that way. You, O Governor, and Liang Qian and Yin Shang will lie in ambush on the other sides of the city. Let Liang Xu and the common people go up on the wall to make the defense."

Ma Zun agreed to the plan and prepared everything.

Due to Jiang Wei, Zhuge Liang himself led the main army to Tianshui.

When they reached the city, Zhuge Liang gave a general orders: "Attacking a city must be proceeded as soon as the army reaches it. At the rolling of drums, incite and urge the soldiers to advance with a rush. The keenness of the soldiers will be spoiled by any delay."

So this time also the army came straight up to the rampart. But they hesitated and dared not attack when they saw the flags flying in such good order and apparently such thorough preparation.

About the middle of the night, fires started up all around and a great shouting was beard. No one could see whence the Wei soldiers were coming, but there were answering shouts from the wall. The soldiers of Shu grew frightened and ran. Zhuge Liang mounted a horse and, with Guan Xing and Zhang Bao as escort, got out of danger. Looking back, they saw many mounted troops with torches winding along like a huge serpent.

Zhuge Liang bade Guan Xing find out what this meant, and Guan Xing report: "These are Jiang Wei's troops."

Zhuge Liang remarked, "An army owes more to its leading than to its numbers. This Jiang Wei is a true genius."

Zhuge Liang led the army back to camp, and then he thought for a long time. Suddenly he called up one of the Anding men and said, "Where is the mother of this Jiang Wei?"

"She lives in Jicheng," replied he.

Zhuge Liang called Wei Yan and said to him, "March off with a body of troops, giving out that you are going to take Jicheng. If Jiang Wei comes up, let him enter the city."

Then Zhuge Liang asked, "What is the most important place in connection with this place?"

The man from Anding replied, "The storehouse of Tianshui is at Shanggui. If that is taken, the supplies are cut off."

This was good news, so Zhao Yun was sent to attack Shanggui, while Zhuge Liang made a camp ten miles south of the city.

The spies took the news of the movements of these three forces into Tianshui.

When Jiang Wei heard that one army was to attack his own place, he pleaded with Ma Zun, saying, "My mother is in Jicheng, and I am worried about the attacking force. Let me go to its defense, that I may keep the city and do my duty by my mother at the same time."

So Jiang Wei received command of three thousand troops and marched toward his home.

When Jiang Wei came near the walls, he saw a cohort under Wei Yan. He attacked. After a show of defense Wei Yan retreated, and Jiang Wei entered the city. He closed the gates and prepared to defend the wall. Then he went home to see his mother.

In the same way Liang Qian was allowed to enter Shanggui.

Then Zhuge Liang sent for his prisoner, Xiahou Mao, and, when he was brought to his tent, Zhuge Liang said suddenly, "Are you afraid of death?"

Xiahou Mao prostrated himself and begged for his life.

"Well, Jiang Wei of Tianshui, who, is now gone to guard Jicheng, has sent a letter to say that he would surrender if only that would secure your safety. Now I am going to let you go if you will promise to induce Jiang Wei to come over to me. Do you accept the condition?"

"I am willing to induce him to yield to you," said Xiahou Mao.

Zhuge Liang then gave his prisoner clothing and a horse and let him ride away. Nor did he send anyone to follow him, but let him choose his own road.

Having got outside, Xiahou Mao wanted to get away, but he was perfectly ignorant of the roads and knew not which to take. Presently he came across some people, apparently in flight, and he questioned them.

"We are Jicheng people," said they. "Jiang Wei has surrendered the city and deserted to Zhuge Liang. The troops of Shu are looting and burning, and we have escaped. We are going to Shanggui."

"Do you know who is holding Tianshui?"

"Governor Ma Zun is in there," said they.

Hearing this, Xiahou Mao rode quickly toward Tianshui. Presently he met more people, evidently fugitives, leading sons and carrying daughters, who told the same story. By and by he came to the gate of the city, and, as he was recognized, the wardens of the gate admitted him, and the Governor came to greet him and asked of his adventures. He told all that had happened, that Jiang Wei had surrendered and related what the fugitives had said.

"I did not think Jiang Wei would have gone over to Shu," said the Governor sadly.

"It seems he thought by this to save you, Sir Commander-in-Chief," said Liang Xu. "I am sure he has made only a pretense of surrendering."

"Where is the pretense when it is a fact that he has surrendered?" said Xiahou Mao.

They were all perplexed. Then at the third watch the troops of Shu came to begin an attack. The fires round the wall were very bright, and there in the glare was seen Jiang Wei, armed and riding up and down under the ramparts calling out for Xiahou Mao. Xiahou Mao and Ma Zun ascended the wall, whence they saw Jiang Wei swaggering to and fro.

Seeing the chiefs on the wall, Jiang Wei called out, "I surrendered for the sake of you, O General. Why have you gone back on your word?"

"Why did you surrender to Shu after enjoying so much of Wei's bounty?" said Xiahou Mao. "And why do you talk thus?"

"What do you mean talking thus after writing me a letter telling me to surrender? You want to secure your own safety by involving me. But I have surrendered, and as I am a superior general in their service now, I see no sense in returning to Wei."

So saying, he urged the soldiers on to the attack. The assault continued till dawn, when the besiegers drew off.

Now the appearance of Jiang Wei in this fashion

was but a ruse. Zhuge Liang had found among his men one who resembled Jiang Wei and had disguised him so that Jiang Wei appeared to be leading the attack on the ramparts. In the smoke and fire during the night no one could penetrate the disguise.

Zhuge Liang then led the army to attack Jicheng. The grain in the city was insufficient to feed the people. From the wall Jiang Wei saw wagons of grain and forage being driven into the Shu camp, and he determined to try to secure some. So he led three thousand troops out of the city to attack the train of wagons. As soon as he appeared, the convoy abandoned the carts and fled. Jiang Wei seized them, and was taking them into the city, when he was met by a cohort under the command of Zhang Yi. They plunged into battle. After a short time Wang Ping came to reinforce Zhang Yi, so that Jiang Wei was attacked on two sides. All Jiang Wei's efforts were vain, and he had to abandon the spoil and try to reenter the city.

But as he drew near, he saw the walls were decorated with Shu ensigns, for Wei Yan had captured the place and was in possession. By desperate fighting Jiang Wei got clear and set off for Tianshui. But he only had a few score horsemen left. Presently the small force fell in with Zhang Bao, and at the end of this engagement Jiang Wei found himself alone, a single horseman. He reached Tianshui and hailed the gate. The watchers above the gate knew him and went to tell the Governor.

"This fellow has came to beguile me into opening the gate," said Ma Zun.

So Ma Zun ordered the defenders to shoot at the fugitive. Jiang Wei turned back, but there were the army of Shu close at hand. He set off as fast as he could for Shanggui. But when he got there Liang Qian hurled a volley of abuse at him.

"You traitor!" cried Liang Qian. "Dare you come to try to cajole me out of my city? I know you have surrendered to Shu."

Liang Qian's soldiers also began to shoot at the hapless fugitive.

Jiang Wei was helpless. He could not explain the real truth to those who doubted him. Lifting his eyes to heaven, while tears rolled down his cheeks, he whipped up his steed and rode off toward Changan.

Before he had got very far, he came to a spot where were many heavy foliaged trees. From among these appeared a company of soldiers, led by Guan Xing. Weary as were both horse and rider, there was no chance of successful resistance, and Jiang Wei turned back. But soon appeared a small chariot in which sat Zhuge Liang, dressed simply as usual in a white robe and carrying his feather fan.

"Friend Jiang Wei," said Zhuge Liang, "is it not time to yield?"

Jiang Wei stopped and pondered. There was Zhuge Liang, and Guan Xing's troops were behind him. There was no way out. So he dismounted and bowed his head in submission.

Zhuge Liang at once got out of the chariot and

bade him welcome, taking him by the hand and saying, "Ever since I left my humble cottage, I have been seeking some worthy person to whom I might impart the knowledge that my life has been spent in acquiring. I have found no one till this moment, and now my desire is attained. You are the one."

Jiang Wei bowed and thanked him, and they two returned to camp.

Soon after their arrival, the new recruit and Zhuge Liang consulted how to capture Tianshui and Shanggui. Jiang Wei had a scheme.

"The two civil officers in charge of the city, Yin Shang and Liang Xu, are excellent friends of mine," said he, "and I will write a letter to each, shoot it over the wall tied to an arrow, and ask them to help by raising a revolt within the city."

They decided upon this, and two secret letters were duly written and sent flying over the ramparts, where they were found and taken to the Governor. Ma Zun was doubtful what action to take and consulted with Xiahou Mao, asking him to decide.

Said Ma Zun, "Yin Shang and Liang Xu are in league with Jiang Wei, and they plot to aid the enemy from within. What should be done?"

"Put both the men to death," Xiahou Mao replied.

But Yin Shang heard what was toward and said to Liang Xu, "The best course for us is to yield the city to Shu and trust to them to treat us well as our recompense."

That evening Xiahou Mao sent many times to summon the two officers to him, but they thought it too great a risk to answer the call. Instead, they armed themselves and rode at the head of their own soldiers to the gates, opened them and let in the troops of Shu. Ma Zun and Xiahou Mao fled by the west gate with a hundred faithful followers and sought refuge with the Qiang tribespeople.

Liang Xu and Yin Shang welcomed Zhuge Liang, who entered the city, restored order, and calmed the people.

This done, Zhuge Liang asked how he might capture Shanggui.

Liang Xu said, "My brother, Liang Qian, holds that city, and I will call upon him to yield it."

Thereupon Liang Xu rode over to Shanggui and called out his brother to submit. Zhuge Liang rewarded the two brothers and then made Liang Xu Governor of Tianshui; Yin Shang, Magistrate of Jicheng; and Liang Qian, Magistrate of Shanggui. Next the army prepared to advance.

His officers asked, "O Prime Minister, why do you not pursue and capture Xiahou Mao?"

Zhuge Liang replied, "I let him go as I would release a duck. In my friend Jiang Wei I recognized a phoenix."

Such awe and fear seized upon the country around when these exploits of Zhuge Liang were heard of that many other cities simply opened their gates without making any resistance. Zhuge Liang brought all soldiers from Hanzhong, horse and foot, and marched on to Qishan.

When the Shu army reached the west bank of River Wei, the scouts reported their movements in Luoyang, and, at a court held in the first year of the era of Calm Peace (AD 227), the ministers told the Ruler of Wei of the threatened invasion.

They said, "Xiahou Mao, the Imperial Son-in-Law, has lost the three counties and fled to the Qiangs. The enemy has reached Qishan, and their advanced columns are on the west bank of River Wei. I pray that an army be sent to repulse them."

The Emperor, Cao Rui, was alarmed and asked, "Who shall go out and drive off the enemy for me?"

Minister Wang Lang stepped forward and said, "I observed that whenever General Cao Zhen was sent by the late Emperor on any expedition he succeeded. Why not send him to drive off these soldiers of Shu?"

Cao Rui approved of the suggestion.

Whereupon he called up Cao Zhen and said to him, "The late Emperor confided me to your guardianship. You cannot sit by while the enemy ravages the country."

Cao Zhen replied, "Your Majesty, my talents are but poor and unequal to the task you propose."

"You are a trusted minister of state, and you may not really refuse this task. Old and worn as I am, I will use the little strength left me to accompany you," said Wang Lang.

"After the bounties I have received, I cannot refuse," replied Cao Zhen. "But I must ask for an assistant."

"You have only to name him, O Noble One," said the Emperor.

So Cao Zhen named Guo Huai, a man of Yangqu, whose official rank was Lord of Sheting; he was also Imperial Protector of Yongzhou.

Thereupon Cao Zhen was appointed Commander-in-Chief, and the ensigns of rank were conferred upon him. Guo Huai was appointed his second, and Wang Lang was created Instructor of the Army. Wang Lang was then already old, seventy-six.

The army of Cao Zhen consisted of two hundred thousand troops, the best from both capitals. His brother, Cao Zun, was made Leader of the Van with an assistant, Zhu Zan, General Who Opposes Brigands. The army moved out in the eleventh month of that year, and the Ruler of Wei went with it to the outside of the west gate.

Cao Zhen marched by way of Changan and camped on the west bank of the River Wei. At a council, which the Commander-in-Chief called to consider the best mode of attack, Wang Lang asked that he might be allowed to parley with the enemy.

Said Wang Lang, "Let the army be drawn up in complete battle order and unfurl all the banners. I will go out and call a parley with Zhuge Liang, at which I will make him yield to us without a blow, and the army of Shu shall march home again."

Cao Zhen agreed to the plan. So orders were given to take the early meal at the fourth watch and have the men fall in with their companies and files at daylight, all in review order. Everything was to be grand and imposing, the flags fluttering and the drums rolling, every soldier in his place. Just before this display, a messenger was to deliver a declaration of war.

Next day, when the armies were drawn up facing each other in front of the Qishan Mountains, the soldiers of Shu saw that their enemies were fine, bold warriors, very different from those that Xiahou Mao had brought against them. Then after three rolls of the drums, Minister of the Interior Wang Lang mounted his horse and rode out, next to him rode Commander-in-Chief Cao Zhen, and followed behind was Deputy Commander Guo Huai. The two Leaders of the Van remained in charge of the army.

Then a messenger rode to the front and called out in a loud voice, "We request the leader of the opposing army to come out to a parley."

At this, within the Shu army, an opening was made at the main standard, through which came out Guan Xing and Zhang Bao, who took up their stations right and left. Then followed two lines of generals, and beneath the standard, in the center of the array, was seen a four-wheeled carriage wherein sat Zhuge Liang, with turban, white robe and black sash. A leather fan was in his hand. He advanced with the utmost dignity. Looking up, he saw three commander umbrellas and flags bearing large white characters. In the middle was an aged, white-haired figure, Minister Wang Lang.

"He intends to deliver an oration," thought Zhuge Liang. "I must answer as best I may."

His carriage was then pushed to the front beyond the line of battle, and he directed one of his officers to reply, saying, "The Prime Minister of the Hans is willing to speak with Minister Wang Lang."

Wang Lang advanced. Zhuge Liang saluted him from the carriage with raised hands, and Wang Lang replied from horseback with an inclination. Then Wang Lang began his oration.

"I am happy to meet you, Noble Sir. Your reputation has been long known to me. Since you recognize the decrees of Heaven and are acquainted with the conditions of the world, why do you, without any excuse, lead out such an army?"

Zhuge Liang replied, "How mean you no excuse? I hold an edict to destroy rebels."

Wang Lang replied, "Heaven has its mutations, and change its instruments from time to time. The supreme dignity comes at last to the person of virtue. This is the inevitable and immutable law. In the days of Emperors Huan and Ling arose the Yellow Scarves rebellion, and the whole earth was involved in wrangling and warfare. Later, in the eras of Inauguration of Tranquillity and Rebuilt Tranquillity, Dong Zhuo arose in revolt, a revolt which Li Jue and Guo Si continued after Dong Zhuo had been destroyed. Next Yuan Shu usurped the imperial style, and his brother Yuan Shao played the man of might and valor in the land of Yejun. Liu Biao occupied Jingzhou, and Lu Bu seized and held Xuzhou. Thus rebels have arisen in the land like swarm of wasps and bold spirits have followed their own will, to the danger of the supreme dignity and the peril of the people.

"Then the Founder of Wei, Emperor Cao, swept away rebellion in eight directions, purged the land, and restored order. All hearts turned to him in gratitude, and the people of the four quarters admired his virtue. He gained his position by no manifestation of force: It was simply the will of Heaven. His son and successor, Emperor Pi, was wise and warlike, adequate to the great heritage and fitted to wield supreme power. Wherefore, in accordance with the will of Heaven and the desires of humans, and following the example of the earliest emperors, he took his place as arbiter of the Central Government, whereby the myriad countries are ordered and governed. Can any maintain that it was not the desire of Heaven and the wish of the people?

"Noble Sir, you are a man of natural talent and acquired attainments, worthy, you say yourself, to be compared with Guan Zhong[vii] and Yue Yi[viii]. Why then place yourself in opposition to the decree of Heaven and turn away from the desire of humankind to do this thing? You cannot be ignorant of the wise old saying: 'He who accords with the Heaven shall flourish, while he who opposes shall be destroyed.'

"Now the armies of Wei are countless legions, and their able leaders are beyond number. Can the glowworm in the parched stubble rival the glorious moon in the sky? If you will turn down your weapons and throw aside your armors and dutifully yield, you shall not lose your rank. The state will have tranquillity and the people rejoice. Is not that a desirable consummation?"

Zhuge Liang laughed.

Said he, "I regarded you as an old and tried servant of the Han Dynasty and thought you would hold some noble discourse. Could I imagine you would talk so foully? I have a word to say that all the armies may hear. In the days of Emperors Huan and Ling the rule of Han declined, the officers of state were the authors of evil, the government fell into confusion, and misfortune settled on the country. Trouble was rife in every quarter. The Yellow Scaves, Dong Zhuo, Li Jue and Guo Si, and other rebels arose one after another, deposing the emperor and afflicting the people. Because the household officers were corrupt and foolish, and the court officials were as brute beasts, living only that they might feed; because high people, wolfishly cruel in their hearts, savagely mean in their conduct, were in office one after another, and slavish flatterers bending slavish knees confounded the administration, therefore the Throne became as a waste heap, and the people were trodden into the mire.

"I know all about you. You came from the eastern seashore. You got into office with a recommendation of filial piety and integrity; you properly aided your sovereign and supported the state, cared for the tranquillity of Han and magnified the Lius. But could one have imagined that you would turn and assist rebels and enter into a plot to usurp the Throne? Indeed your crime is great and your guilt heavy. Heaven and earth will not suffer you. The inhabitants of this land would devour you.

"But happily the design of Heaven is to retain the glorious dynasty. The late Emperor Bei continued the line in the River Lands, and I have been entrusted by the present Emperor with the task of destroying you rebels.

"Since you are such a false and specious minister, you have but to hide your body and cover your head, concern yourself about your belly and your back. Do not come out before the armies to rave about the decrees of Heaven. You fool and rebel! Mark you, today is your last day. This day even you descend to the Nine Golden Springs. How will you stand before the twenty-four emperors of Latter Han that you will meet there? Retire, you rebel! Go tell your rebellious companions to come and fight one battle with me that shall decide the victory."

Fierce wrath filled the old man's breast. With one despairing cry Wang Lang fell to the earth dead.

This exploit of Zhuge Liang's has been lauded in verse:

In west Qin, when the armies met in the field,
He, the bold one, singly faced a myriad warriors,
And with a simple weapon, just his tongue,
He did to death a wicked minister.

After Wang Lang had fallen, Zhuge Liang waved the fan toward Cao Zhen and said, "As for you, I leave you alone for this occasion. Go and get your army in order for tomorrow's battle."

The chariot turned and left the ground. Both armies retired for that day. To Cao Zhen fell the melancholy duty of rendering the last services to the aged Minister and setting his coffin on its journey to Changan.

Then said General Guo Huai, "Zhuge Liang will certainly think the army occupied with mourning and make a night attack. Let us anticipate him and set out an ambush about our camp. Let two bodies of our troops be hidden outside and two others take the occasion to raid the camp of the enemy."

"I thought of such a scheme myself," said Cao Zhen. "It exactly suits my plans."

So Cao Zhen gave order to Cao Zun and Zhu Zan: "You are to take ten thousand troops each, get away by the rear of the mountain, and look out for the passing of the soldiers of Shu. When they have gone by, you are to make for their camp. But you are only to attempt a raid if they have left."

Cao Zun and Zhu Zan took the order and left. Then the Commander-in-Chief arranged with Guo Huai each to lead a force and hide outside the camp to wait for the raid of Shu. Only a few soldiers were to be left within to make a fire if the enemy were seen to be coming. And all generals set about the necessary preparations.

When Zhuge Liang reached his tent, he called to him Zhao Yun and Wei Yan, and said to them, "You two are to make a night attack."

"Cao Zhen is a man of experience and will be on the lookout," ventured Wei Yan.

"But that is just what I want: I want him to know we shall attack tonight. He will then put some troops in hiding in rear of the Qishan Mountains, who will make for our camp as soon as they see us pass toward theirs. I am sending you to let yourselves be seen passing the hill. but you are to camp behind it and at a distance. When the soldiers of Wei attack this camp, you will see a signal. Then Wei Yan will hold the approach to the hill, and Zhao Yun will make his way back in fighting order. He will meet the army of Wei returning and will let them pass. The enemy will assuredly fall to fighting among themselves, and we shall finish the battle."

These two having gone away to carry out their portions of the plan, Zhuge Liang next called up Guan Xing and Zhang Bao: "You are to take each ten thousand troops and hide in the high road to the mountain. When the troops of Wei come, let them pass and then march along the road they came by to their camp that they have just left."

These two having left, Zhuge Liang placed Ma Dai, Wang Ping, Zhang Ni, and Zhang Yi in ambush about the camp.

Within the camp the tents and shelters were left standing as if the camp was occupied, while wood and straw were heaped up ready to give the signal. This done, Zhuge Liang and his officers retired to the rear of the camp to watch the proceedings.

On the side of Wei the two Van Leaders, Cao Zun and Zhu Zan, left at dusk and hastened toward the camp of Shu. About the second watch they saw troops busily moving about in front of the hill.

Cao Zun thought to himself, "General Guo Huai is an excellent strategist and of wonderful prevision."

Then he hastened the march, and in the third watch reached the camp of Shu. He at once dashed into the enclosure, but only to find it totally deserted. Not a man was visible. At once he knew he had stumbled into a trap, and began to withdraw. Then the flames sprang up. Zhu Zan arrived already to fight, and the two bodies of troops, thrown into confusion, fought with each other till the two leaders met, when they found out they were fighting their own men.

As they were restoring order, on came the four bodies of troops of Shu under Ma Dai, Wang Ping, Zhang Ni, and Zhang Yi who had lain in ambush ready for them. Cao Zun and Zhu Zan, with more than a hundred of those nearest to them, ran away to get to the high road. But before long the rolling drums announced another body of their enemy, and their flight was stopped by Zhao Yun.

"Whither go ye, O rebel leaders?" cried Zhao Yun. "Stop, for here is death!"

But Cao Zun and Zhu Zan still fled. Then came up

a force led by Wei Yan and completed the defeat. The soldiers of Wei were wholly beaten and ran away to their own camp. But the guard left in the camp thought they were the enemy who come to raid, so they lit the fires, and at this signal Cao Zhen rushed up from one side and Guo Huai from the other, and a fierce fight with their own troops began.

While this was going on, three cohorts under Wei Yan, Guan Xing, and Zhang Bao arrived from three points, and a great and confused battle began. The soldiers of Wei were driven off and chased for three miles.

In the fight Wei lost many leaders, and Zhuge Liang gained a great success. Cao Zhen and Guo Huai got together their beaten troops and went back to their own camp.

When they discussed the fight, Cao Zhen said, "The enemy are too strong for us. Have you any plan to drive them away?"

Replied Guo Huai, "Our defeat is one of the ordinary events of war. Let us not be cast down. I have a plan to suggest that will disorder them so that one body cannot help the other, and they will all be compelled to flee."

Wei leaders fail and sadly send
To pray tribespeople help to lend.

The plan will be unfolded in the next chapter.

Chapter 94

Zhuge Liang Defeats The Qiangs In A Snowstorm;
Sima Yi Quickly Captures Meng Da.

Guo Huai laid before his colleague the scheme to overcome the army of Shu, saying, "The Qiang tribes have paid tribute regularly since the days of the Founder of Wei. Emperor Pi regarded them with favor. Now let us hold such points of vantage as we may, while we send secret emissaries to engage their help in exchange for kindly treatment. We may get the Qiangs to attack Shu and engage their attention, while we gather a large army to smite them at another place. Thus attacking, how can we help gaining a great victory?"

A messenger was sent forthwith bearing letters to the Qiang tribespeople.

The King of the western Qiangs was named Cheli Ji. He had rendered yearly tribute since the days of Cao Cao. He had two ministers, one for civil and the other for military affairs, named, respectively, Prime Minister Ya Dan and Chief Leader Yue Ji.

The letter was accompanied by presents of gold and pearls, and when the messenger arrived, he first sought Prime Minister Ya Dan, to whom he gave gifts and whose help he begged. Thus he gained an interview with the King, to whom he presented the letter and the gifts. The King accepted both and called his counselors to consider the letter.

Ya Dan said, "We have had regular intercourse with the Wei kingdom. Now that Cao Zhen asks our aid and promises an alliance, we ought to accede to his request."

Cheli Ji agreed that it was so, and he ordered his two chief ministers to raise an army of two hundred fifty thousand of trained soldiers, archers and crossbowmen, spearmen and swordsmen, warriors who flung maces and hurled hammers. Beside these various weapons, the tribesmen used chariots covered with iron plates nailed on. They prepared much grain and fodder and many spare weapons, all of which they loaded upon these iron-clad chariots. The chariots were drawn by camels or teams of horses. The carts or chariots were known as "iron chariots".

The two leaders took leave of their King and went straightway to Xiping Pass.

The commander in charge of the Pass, Han Zhen, at once sent intelligence to Zhuge Liang, who asked, "Who will go to attack the Qiangs?"

Guan Xing and Zhang Bao said they would go.

Then Zhuge Liang said, "You shall be sent. But as you are ignorant of the road and the people, Ma Dai shall accompany you."

To Ma Dai he said, "You know the disposition of the Qiangs from your long residence there. You shall go as guide."

They chose out fifty thousand of veterans for the

expedition. When they had marched a few days and drew near their enemy, Guan Xing went in advance with a hundred horsemen and got first sight of them from a hill. The Qiangs were marching, the long line of iron chariots one behind another in close order. Then they halted and camped, their weapons piled all along the line of chariots like the ramparts of a moated city. Guan Xing studied them for a long time quite at a loss to think how to overcome them. He came back to camp and consulted with his two colleagues.

Ma Dai said, "We will see tomorrow what they will do when we make our array, and discuss our plans when we know more."

So the next day they drew up their army in three divisions, Guan Xing's division being in the center, Zhang Bao's in the left, and Ma Dai's in the right. Thus they advanced.

The enemy also drew up in battle order. Their Chief Leader, Yue Ji, had an iron mace in his hand and a graven bow hung at his waist. He rode forward on a curvetting steed boldly enough. Guan Xing gave the order for all three divisions to go forward. Then the enemy's ranks opened in the center and out rolled the iron chariots like a great wave. At the same time the Qiangs shot arrows and bolts, and the men of Shu could not stand against them.

The wing divisions under Ma Dai and Zhang Bao retired, and the Qiangs were thus enabled to surround the center. In spite of every effort, Guan Xing could not get free, for the iron chariots were like a city wall and no opening could be found.

The troops of Shu were absolutely helpless, and Guan Xing made for the mountains in hope of finding a road through.

As it grew dark a Qiang leader with a black flag approached, his warriors like a swarm of wasps about him.

Presently the leader cried out to him, "Youthful general, flee not. I am Yue Ji!"

But Guan Xing only hastened forward, plying his whip to urge his steed. Then he suddenly came on a deep gully, and there seemed nothing but to turn and fight. Yue Ji come close and struck at him with the mace. Guan Xing evaded the blow, but it fell upon his steed and knocked it over into water. Guan Xing went into the water too.

Presently he heard a great noise again behind him. Yue Ji and his troops had found a way down into the gully and were coming at him down the stream. Guan Xing braced himself for a struggle in the water.

Then he saw Zhang Bao and Ma Dai coming up on the bank fighting with, and driving off, the Qiangs. Yue Ji was struck by Zhang Bao, and he too fell into the gully. Guan Xing gripped his sword and was about to launch a stroke at Yue Ji as he came up, when Yue Ji jumped out of the water and ran away.

At once Guan Xing caught the steed Yue Ji had left, led it up the bank and soon had it ready to mount. Then he girded on his sword, got on the horse, and joined the battle with his colleagues.

After driving off the Qiangs, Guan Xing, Zhang Bao, and Ma Dai gathered together and rode back. They quickly gained the camp.

"I do not know how to overcome these men," said Ma Dai. "Let me protect the camp while you go back and ask the Prime Minister what we should do."

Guan Xing and Zhang Bao started at once and made the best of their way back. They told Zhuge Liang what had happened. He at once sent off Zhao Yun and Wei Yan to go into ambush. After this he went himself with thirty thousand troops and Jiang Wei, Zhang Yi, Guan Xing, and Zhang Bao and soon came to Ma Dai's camp. The day after, from the summit of a hill, Zhuge Liang surveyed the country and the enemy, who were coming on in a ceaseless stream.

"It is not difficult," said Zhuge Liang.

He called up Ma Dai and Zhang Yi and gave them certain orders.

They having gone, he turned to Jiang Wei, saying, "My friend, do you know how to overcome them?"

"The enemy only depend upon force and courage. They shall not expect this fine strategy," was the reply.

"You know," said Zhuge Liang, smiling. "Those dark clouds and the strong north wind mean snow. Then I can do what I wish."

The two leaders, Guan Xing and Zhang Bao, were sent into ambush, and Jiang Wei went out to offer battle. But he was to retire before the iron chariots. At the entrance to the camp were displayed many flags, but the soldiers that should serve under them were not there.

It was now full winter, the twelfth month, and the snow had come. The army of Shu went out to offer battle. When the iron chariots came forward, they retired and thus led the Qiangs to the gate of the camp, Jiang Wei going to its rear. The Qiangs came to the gate and stopped to look. They heard the strumming of a lute, but there were no soldiers there; the flags meant nothing. They told Yue Ji, and he suspected some ruse. Instead of entering, he went back to Prime Minister Ya Dan and told him.

"It is a ruse," said Ya Dan. "Zhuge Liang's base trick is the pretense of a pretense, and you had better attack."

So Yue Ji led his troops again to the camp gate, and there he saw Zhuge Liang with a lute just getting into his chariot. With a small escort, he went toward the back of the camp. The tribesmen rushed into the camp and caught sight of the light chariot again just as it disappeared into a wood.

Then said Ya Dan, "There may be an ambush, but I think we need not be afraid of these soldiers."

Hence they decided to pursue. Ahead of them they saw the division under Jiang Wei hastening off through the snow. Yue Ji's rage boiled up at this sight, and he urged his men to go faster. The snow had filled in the roads among the hills, making every part look like a level plain.

As they marched, one reported that some of the

enemy were appearing from the rear of the hills. Some thought this meant an ambush, but Ya Dan said it did not matter, and they need not fear. He urged them to hasten.

Shortly after this they heard a roaring as if the hills were rending asunder and the earth falling in, and the pursuers on foot fell one atop of the other into great pits that were invisible in the snow. The iron chariots, being close behind and hurrying along, could not stop, and they went into the pits also. Those still farther in the rear halted, but just as they were facing about, Guan Xing and Zhang Bao came up, one on either side, and attacked. Myriads of bolts flew through the air. Then three other divisions under Jiang Wei, Ma Dai, and Zhang Yi arrived and confusion was worse than ever.

The Qiang leader, Yue Ji, fled to the rear and was making for the mountains when he met Guan Xing, who slew him in the first encounter. Prime Minister Ya Dan was captured by Ma Dai and taken to the main camp. The soldiers scattered.

Hearing of the capture of one leader, Zhuge Liang took his seat in his tent and bade them bring the prisoner. He told the guards to loose his bonds, and he had wine brought to refresh him and soothed him with kindly words.

Ya Dan was grateful for this kindness, and felt more so when Zhuge Liang said, "My master, the Emperor of the Great Han, sent me to destroy those who are in revolt. Why are you helping them? But I will release you, and you will return to your master and say that we are neighbors and we will swear an oath of everlasting friendship, and tell him to listen no more to the words of those rebels."

Ya Dan was released and so were all the soldiers that had been captured, and all their stuff was given back to them. They left for their own country.

The Qiangs being thus disposed of, Zhuge Liang quickly marched again to Qishan. He sent letters to Capital Chengdu announcing his success.

Meanwhile Cao Zhen anxiously waited for news of his expected allies. Then a scout came in with the news that the army of Shu had broken camp and were marching away.

"That is because the Qiangs have attacked," said Guo Huai gleefully, and the two made ready to pursue.

They saw ahead of them the army of Shu seemed to be in confusion. The Van Leader Cao Zun led the pursuit.

Suddenly, as he pressed on, there came a roll of drums, followed by the appearance of a cohort led by Wei Yan, who cried, "Stop! You rebels!"

But Cao Zun did not obey the summons. He dashed forward to meet the attack. He was killed in the third encounter. His colleague Zhu Zan in similar fashion fell in with a cohort under Zhao Yun, to whose long spear he soon fell victim. The loss of these two made Cao Zhen and Guo Huai hesitate, and they made to retire.

But before they could face about, they heard the

drums of an army in their rear, and Guan Xing and Zhang Bao came out and surrounded them. Cao Zhen and Guo Huai made a stand for a time, but were soon worsted and fled. The army of Shu pursued the beaten enemy to the bank of River Wei, where they took possession of the Wei camp.

Cao Zhen was greatly chagrined at his defeat and sad at the loss of his generals. He send a report of his misfortune to his master and asked for reinforcements.

At the court of Wei one of the ministers told the story, saying, "Cao Zhen has been defeated repeatedly, and his two Van Leaders were slain. Further, his Qiang allies have suffered great loss. Cao Zhen is sending for help, and the case is very urgent."

Cao Rui was alarmed and asked for someone to say how to drive off the victorious foe.

Thereupon Hua Xin said, "It will be necessary for Your Majesty to go in person. You should call together all the nobles, and each will have to exert himself. Unless this is done, Capital Changan will be lost and the whole Land Within the Passes be in danger."

But Imperial Guardian Zhong Yao opposed him.

Said he, "The knowledge of every leader must exceed that of those led; then only will he be able to control them. Sun Zi the Strategist sums it up very briefly: 'Know the enemy, know thyself, and every battle is a victory.' I know Cao Zhen has had great experience in the field, but he is no match for Zhuge Liang. Still there is such a match, and I will pledge my whole family that he will succeed. But Your Majesty may be unwilling to listen to me."

The Ruler of Wei replied, "You are a minister of high rank and old. If you know any wise person able to repel these soldiers of Shu, call him without delay and ease my mind."

Then said Zhong Yao, "When Zhuge Liang decided to invade us, he was afraid of the one man I will name. Wherefore he spread calumnies concerning him, raising suspicion in Your Majesty's mind that you might dismiss him. That done, Zhuge Liang invaded. Now employ this man again, and the enemy will retire."

"Who is it?" asked the Ruler of Wei.

"I mean the Imperial Commander of the Flying Cavalry, Sima Yi."

"I have long regretted my action," said Cao Rui. "Where now is friend Sima Yi?"

"He is at the city of Wancheng, idle."

An edict was prepared recalling Sima Yi and restoring him to his rank and titles, and conferring upon him the new title Commander-in-Chief of the Western Forces and General Who Pacifies the West. All troops of Nanyang were set in motion, and Cao Rui led them to Changan. At the same time Cao Rui ordered Sima Yi to be there to meet him on a certain day. And the orders were sent by a swift messenger to the city of Wancheng.

At this time Zhuge Liang greatly rejoiced at the success he had had. He was at Qishan, busy with plans for other victories, when Li Yan, who was in command at the Palace of Eternal Peace, sent his son Li Teng to the camp. Zhuge Liang concluded that such a visit could only mean that Wu had invaded them, and he was in consequence cast down. However, he summoned Li Teng to his tent, and when asked the object of his mission, Li Teng replied that he had joyful news to impart.

"What is your joyful news?" said Zhuge Liang.

"Formerly Meng Da deserted to Wei, but only because he could do nothing else. Cao Pi thought much of his capabilities, treated him most generously, kept him at his side, gave him titles of General Who Establishes Strong Arms and Lord of Pingyang, and appointed him to the posts of Governor of Xincheng and Commander of Shangyong and Jincheng, and so on. But when Cao Pi died, all was changed. In Cao Rui's court were many who were jealous of Meng Da's influence and power, so that he enjoyed no peace.

"He used to talk about being originally one of the Shu leaders, and he was forced to do so-and-so. Lately he has sent several confidants with letters to my father asking that he would state his case to you as to the happenings. When the five armies came upon Shu, he wanted to rejoin the River Lands. Now he is at Xincheng, and, hearing you are attacking Wei, he proposes to lead the army of the three counties about Xincheng, Jincheng, and Shangyong to attack Luoyang while you attack Changan, whereby both capitals will be taken. I have brought with me his messenger and his letters."

This was good news, and the bearer was fittingly rewarded. But at that moment came the news that Cao Rui was leading an army to Changan and had recalled the banished Sima Yi to office. This piece of bad news saddened Zhuge Liang not a little.

He told Ma Su, who said, "Cao Rui should not be your worry. If he goes to Changan, we will march there and capture him on the road, and there will be an end of him."

"Do you think I fear him?" said Zhuge Liang bitterly. "But the recall of Sima Yi is another matter; that troubles me. And Meng Da's proposal will avail nothing if he comes across this man. Meng Da is no match for him. He will he captured, and, if he should be, the Middle Land will be hard to conquer."

"Why not put Meng Da on his guard then?" said Ma Su.

Zhuge Liang decided to write, and the letter was dispatched immediately.

Meng Da was then at Xincheng, anxiously expecting the return of his last confidential messenger, when, one day, the man returned and gave him this letter from Zhuge Liang himself:

"Your last letter has convinced me of your loyal rectitude, and I still remember with joy our old friendship. If your plan succeeds, you will certainly stand in the first rank of most worthy ministers. But I scarcely need impress upon you the extreme necessity for most perfect secrecy. Be very careful whom you trust. Fear everyone, guard against everyone. This news of the recall of Sima

Yi and the proposed junction of armies at Changan is very serious. If a word reaches Sima Yi, he will come to you first. Therefore take every precaution and do not regard this as a matter of unimportance."

"They say Zhuge Liang leaves nothing to chance," said Meng Da, smiling as he read. "This proves it."

He lost no time in preparing a reply, which he sent also by a trusty messenger. This letter was like this:

"I acknowledge your most valuable advice, but is it possible that I should be remiss? For my part I do not think the Sima Yi's affair need cause anxiety, for Wancheng is three hundred miles from Luoyang and four hundred miles from Xincheng. Should he hear anything, it would take a month to send a memorial to the capital and get a reply. My ramparts here are strong and my forces posted in the best positions. Let him come! I am not afraid of the result, so you, O Prime Minister, need feel no anxiety. You have only to wait for the good news of success."

Zhuge Liang read the letter and threw it on the ground, stamping his foot with rage.

"Meng Da is a dead man!" said he, "A victim of Sima Yi."

"Why do you say that?" said Ma Su.

"What does the Art of War say? 'Attack before the enemy is prepared; do what he does not expect.' What is the use of reckoning upon a month's delay for sending up a memorial? Cao Rui's commission has already gone, and Sima Yi may strike whom he will. He will not have to wait to memorialize the Throne. Ten days after he hears of Meng Da's defection, he will be upon Meng Da with an army, and Meng Da will be helpless."

The others agreed. However, Zhuge Liang sent the messenger back again with a message:

"If the matter has not yet actually started, no other person is to be told of it; for if anyone knows, it shall certainly come to nothing."

And the messenger left for Xincheng.

In his idle retreat in Wancheng, Sima Yi had heard of his master's ill-success against the armies of Shu, and the news made him very sad. He lifted up his eyes and sighed.

He had two sons, Sima Shi the elder and Sima Zhao, both clever and ambitious, and both earnest students of military books. One day they were present when their father seemed very cast down, and Sima Shi asked his father the reason.

"You would not understand," said the father.

"I think you are grieving because the Ruler of Wei does not use you," replied Sima Shi.

"But they will send for you presently," said Sima Zhao.

The prophecy was not long in fulfillment, for even then the bearer of the command stood at the gate, and the servant announced a messenger from the court bearing a commission.

As soon as he heard its terms, Sima Yi set about ordering the armies of Wancheng. Soon came a messenger from Governor Shen Yi of Jincheng with a secret message for Sima Yi. The messenger was taken into a private chamber, and his message was that Meng Da was on the point of rebellion. The leakage of this news was due to Li Gu, a confidential subordinate of Meng Da, and Deng Xian, Meng Da's nephew. Li Gu and Deng Xian went to confess the plot in exchange for a promise of amnesty.

Sima Yi smote his forehead.

"This is the Emperor's great good fortune, high as heaven itself. Zhuge Liang's army is at Qishan already, and all people's courage is at the brink of breakdown. The Emperor must go to Changan, and if he does not use me soon, Meng Da will carry out his plan; his plot will succeed, and both capitals will be lost. Meng Da is surely in league with Zhuge Liang, and if I can seize this Meng Da before he makes any move, that will damp Zhuge Liang's spirits and he will retreat."

His elder son Sima Shi remarked, "It is necessary to memorialize the Throne."

"No," replied his father, "that would take a month, and delay would mean failure."

Sima Yi gave orders to prepare to advance by double-rapid marches and threatened death to all loiterers. In order to avert suspicion, he sent letters to Meng Da by the hand of Military Adviser Liang Ji to tell Meng Da to prepare to join the western expedition.

Sima Yi quickly followed Liang Ji. After two days' march Sima Yi fell in with an army of General Xu Huang over the hills.

Xu Huang got an interview with Sima Yi, and he said, "The Emperor has arrived at Changan to lead an expedition against Shu. Whither is the Commander-in-Chief going?"

Sima Yi, in a low voice, said to him, "Meng Da is on the verge of rebellion, and I am going to seize him."

"Let me go as your Van Leader," said Xu Huang.

So Xu Huang's troops were joined to the expedition and marched in the van. Sima Yi commanded the center, and his sons brought up the rear.

Two days farther on, some of the scouts captured Meng Da's confidential messenger, and with him Zhuge Liang's reply.

Sima Yi said to the man, "I will let you live if you tell all you know."

So the messenger told all about the letters and messages he had taken from one to the other.

When Sima Yi read, he remarked, "All able people think the same way. Our plan would have been foiled by Zhuge Liang's cleverness unless, by the good luck of the Emperor, this messenger had been captured. Now Meng Da will be helpless."

The army pressed on still more rapidly.

Meng Da had arranged for his stroke with Governor Shen Yi of Jincheng and Governor Shen Dan of Shangyong and was awaiting the day he had fixed. But Shen Yi and Shen Dan were only pretending to abet him, although they went on training and drilling their troops to keep up appearances till the soldiers of Wei could arrive. To Meng Da they pretended delay in their transport as the reason for being unable to start. And he believed them.

Just then Liang Ji came, and when he had been ceremoniously received, he produced the order from Sima Yi and said, "The Commander-in-Chief has received the edict of the Emperor to call in all the forces in this area, and he has sent me to direct you to hold your troops in readiness to march."

"On what day does the Commander-in-Chief start?" asked Meng Da.

"He is just about starting now, and is on the way to Changan" replied Liang Ji.

Meng Da smiled inwardly, for, this being so, he saw success before him. He gave a banquet to Liang Ji. After Liang Ji took his leave, Meng Da sent to his fellow conspirators---Shen Yi and Shen Dan---to say the first step must be taken next day by exchanging the banners of Wei for those of Han and marching to attack Luoyang.

Then the watchmen reported a great cloud of dust in the distance as though an army was coming. Meng Da was surprised and went up on the ramparts to see for himself. Soon he made out the banner of Xu Huang leading. He ran down from the wall and in a state of trepidation ordered the raising of the drawbridge. Xu Huang still came on and in due time stood on the bank of the moat.

Then Xu Huang called out, "Let the traitor Meng Da yield quickly!"

Meng Da, in a rage, opened upon him with arrows, and Xu Huang was wounded in the forehead. He was helped to a place of safety while the arrows flew down in great numbers. When the soldiers of Wei retired, Meng Da opened the gates and went in pursuit. But the whole of Sima Yi's army soon came up, and the banners stood so thick that they hid the sun.

"This is what Zhuge Liang foresaw!" said Meng Da despairingly. The gates were closed and barred.

Meanwhile the wounded general, Xu Huang, had been borne to his tent, where the arrow head was extracted and the physician attended to him. But that night he died. He was fifty-nine. His body was sent to Luoyang for burial.

Next day, when Meng Da went up on the wall, he saw the city was entirely surrounded as with a girdle of iron. He was greatly perturbed and could not decide what to do. Presently he saw two bodies of troops coming up, their banners bearing the names of his fellow conspirators---Shen Yi and Shen Dan. He could only conclude that they had come to his help, so he opened the gates to them and went out to join them in the fight.

"Rebel, stay!" cried they both as they came up.

Realizing that they had been false, he turned and galloped toward the city, but a flight of arrows met him, and the two who had betrayed him, Li Gu and Deng Xian, began to revile him.

"We have already yielded the city!" they cried.

Then Meng Da fled. But he was pursued, and as he and his horse were both exhausted, he was speedily overtaken and slain. They exposed his head, and his soldiers submitted. Sima Yi was welcomed at the open gates. The people were pacified, the soldiers were rewarded and, this done, a report of their success was sent to Cao Rui.

Cao Rui ordered the body of Meng Da to be exposed in the market place of Luoyang, and he promoted Shen Yi and Shen Dan and gave them posts in the army of Sima Yi. He gave Li Gu and Deng Xian command of the cities of Xincheng and Shangyong.

Then Sima Yi marched to Changan and camped. The leader entered the city to have audience with his master, by whom he was most graciously received.

"Once I doubted you," said Cao Rui, "but then I did not understand, and I listened to mischief-makers. I regret it. Had you not suppressed Meng Da, both capitals would have gone wrong."

Sima Yi replied, "Shen Yi gave the information of the intended revolt and thought to memorialize Your Majesty. But there would have been a long delay, and so I did not await orders, but set forth at once. Delay would have played into Zhuge Liang's hands."

Then Sima Yi handed in Zhuge Liang's letter to

Meng Da.

When the Emperor had read that, he said, "You are wiser than both the great strategists of old---Wu Qi[ix] and Sun Zi[x]."

The Ruler of Wei conferred upon the successful leader a pair of golden axes and the privilege of taking action in important matters without first obtaining his master's sanction. Then Sima Yi was ordered to lead the army to the pass against the enemy.

Sima Yi said, "May I name the Leader of the Van?"

"Whom do you nominate?"

"Zhang He, General of the Right Army, can shoulder this task."

"Just the man I wished to send," said Cao Rui, smiling. And Zhang He was appointed.

Sima Yi took his army off Changan and marched it to the camp of the Shu army.

By strategy the leader shows his skill;
He needs bold fighting men to work his will.

The result of the campaign will appear in the next chapter.

Chapter 95

Ma Su's Disobedience Causes The Loss Of Jieting;
Zhuge Liang's Lute Repulses Sima Yi.

Beside sending Zhang He as Van Leader of Sima Yi, Cao Rui appointed two other generals, Xin Pi and Sun Li, to assist Cao Zhen. Xin Pi and Sun Li led fifty thousand troops.

Sima Yi's army was two hundred thousand strong. They marched out through the pass and made a camp.

When encamped, Sima Yi summoned Zhang He to his tent and admonished him, saying, "A characteristic of Zhuge Liang is his most diligent carefulness; he is never hasty. If I were in his place, I should advance through the Ziwu Valley to capture Changan and so save much time. It is not that he is unskillful, but he fears lest that plan might miscarry, and he will not sport with risk. Therefore he will certainly come through the Xie Valley, taking Meicheng on the way. That place captured, he will divide his force into two, one part to take Gu Valley. I have sent Cao Zhen orders to guard Meicheng strictly and on no account to let its garrison go out to battle. The generals Sun Li and Xin Pi are to command the Gu Valley entrance, and should the enemy come, they are to make a sudden attack."

"By what road will you advance?" asked Zhang He.

"I know a road west of Qinling Mountains called Jieting, on which stands the city Liliu. These two places are the throat of Hanzhong. Zhuge Liang will take advantage of the unpreparedness of Cao Zhen and will certainly come in by this way. You and I will go to Jieting, whence it is a short distance to Yangping Pass. When Zhuge Liang hears that the road through Jieting is blocked and his supplies cut off, he will know that all the lands of West Valley Land is impossible to keep, and will retire without losing a moment into Hanzhong. I shall smite him on the march, and I ought to gain a complete victory. If he should not retire, then I shall block all the smaller roads and so stop his supplies. A month's starvation will kill off the soldiers of Shu, and Zhuge Liang will be my prisoner."

Zhang He took in the scheme and expressed his admiration, saying, "O Commander, your calculation exceeds human!"

Sima Yi continued, "However, it is not to be forgotten that Zhuge Liang is quite different from Meng Da. You, as Leader of the Van, will have to advance with the utmost care. You must impress upon your generals the importance of reconnoitering a long way ahead and only advancing when they are sure there is no ambush. The least remissness will make you the victim of some ruse of the enemy."

Zhang He, having received his instructions, marched away.

Meanwhile spies had come to Zhuge Liang in Qishan with news of the destruction of Meng Da and the failure of his conspiracy.

They said, "Sima Yi marched rapidly in eight days to Xincheng. He had Shen Yi, Shen Dan, Li Gu, and Deng Xian plot against Meng Da from within. Meng Da had not been able to do anything and was killed. Now Sima Yi has gone to Changan, when he has marched through the pass with Zhang He."

Zhuge Liang was distressed.

"Meng Da's destruction was certain," said he. "Such a scheme could not remain secret. Now Sima Yi will try for Jieting and block the one road essential to us."

So Jieting had to be defended, and Zhuge Liang asked who would go. Ma Su offered himself instantly.

Zhuge Liang urged upon him the importance of his task.

"The place is small, but of very great importance, for its loss would involve the loss of the whole army. You are deeply read in all the rules of strategy, but the defense of this place is difficult, since it has no wall and no natural defenses."

"I have studied the books of war since I was a boy, and I may say I know a little of the art of war," Ma Su replied. "Why alone is Jieting so difficult to hold?"

"Because Sima Yi is an exceptional man, and also he has a famous second in Zhang He as Leader of the Van. I fear you may not be a match for him."

Ma Su replied, "To say nothing of these two, I would not mind if Cao Rui himself came against me. If I fail, then I beg you to behead my whole family."

"There is no jesting in war," said Zhuge Liang.

"I will give a written pledge."

Zhuge Liang agreed, and a written pledge was given and placed on record.

Zhuge Liang continued, "I shall give you twenty-five thousand veterans and also send an officer of rank to assist you."

Next he summoned Wang Ping and said to him, "As you are a careful and cautious man, I am giving you a very responsible position. You are to hold Jieting with the utmost tenacity. Camp there in the most commanding position so that the enemy cannot steal by. When your arrangements are complete, draw a plan of them and a map of the local topography, and let me see it. All my dispositions have been carefully thought out and are not to be changed. If you can hold this successfully, it will be of the first service in the capture of Changan. So be very, very careful."

After Ma Su and Wang Ping had gone and Zhuge Liang had reflected for a long time, it occurred to him that there might be some slip between his two leaders.

So he called Gao Xiang to him and said, "Northeast of Jieting is a city named Liliu, and near it an unfrequented hill path. There you are to camp and make a stockade. I will give you ten thousand troops for this task. If Jieting should be threatened, you may go to the rescue."

After Gao Xiang had left, and as Zhuge Liang thought Gao Xiang was not a match for his opponent Zhang He, he decided there ought to be additional strength on the west in order to make Jieting safe. So he summoned Wei Yan and bade him lead his army to the rear of Jieting and camp there.

But Wei Yan thought this rather a slight, and said, "As Leader of the Van, I should go first against the enemy. Why am I sent to a place where there is nothing to do?"

"The leadership of the van is really a second-rate task. Now I am sending you to support Jieting and take post on the most dangerous road to Yangping Pass. You are the chief keeper of the throat of Hanzhong. It is a very responsible post and not at all an idle one. Do not so regard it and spoil my whole plan. Be particularly careful."

Wei Yan, satisfied now that he was not being slighted, went his way.

Zhuge Liang's mind was at rest, and he called up Zhao Yun and Deng Zhi, to whom he said, "Now that Sima Yi is in command of the army, the whole outlook is different. Each of you will lead a force out to Gu Valley and move about so as to mislead the enemy. Whether you meet and engage them or not, you will certainly cause them uneasiness. I am going to lead the main army through the Xie Valley to Meicheng. If I can capture that, Changan will fall."

Zhao Yun and Deng Zhi took the orders and went off.

Zhuge Liang appointed Jiang Wei as Leader of the Van, and they marched to the Xie Valley.

When Ma Su and Wang Ping had reached Jieting and saw what manner of place it was, Ma Su smiled, saying, "Why was the Prime Minister so extremely anxious? How would the Wei armies dare to come to such a hilly place as this?"

Wang Ping replied, "Though they might not dare to come, we should set our camp at this meeting of many roads."

So Wang Ping ordered his soldiers to fell trees and build a strong stockade as for a permanent stay.

But Ma Su had a different idea.

"What sort of a place is a road to make a camp in? Here is a hill standing solitary and well wooded. It is a heaven-created point of vantage, and we will camp on it."

"You are wrong, Counselor," replied Wang Ping. "If we camp on the road and build a strong wall, the enemy cannot possibly get past. If we abandon this for the hill, and the troops of Wei come in force, we shall be surrounded, and how then be safe?"

"You look at the thing like a child," said Ma Su, laughing. "The rules of war say that when one looks down from a superior position, one can overcome the enemy as easily as cleaving bamboo. If they come, I will see to it that not a breastplate ever goes back again."

"I have followed our Commander-in-Chief in many campaigns, and always has he explained in details about the topography and given out well-thought orders. Now I have studied this hill carefully, and it is a critical spot. If we camp thereon and the enemy cut off our water supply, we shall have a mutiny."

"No such thing!" said Ma Su. "Sun Zi says that victory lies in desperate positions. If they cut off our water, will not our soldiers be desperate and fight to the death? Then everyone of them will be worth a hundred. I have studied the books, and the Prime Minister has always asked my advice. Why do you presume to oppose me?"

"If you are determined to camp on the hill, then give me part of the force to camp there on the west so that I can support you in case the enemy come."

But Ma Su refused. Just then a lot of the inhabitants of the hills came running along saying that the Wei soldiers had come.

Wang Ping was still bent on going his own way, and so Ma Su said to him, "Since you will not obey me, I will give you five thousand troops and you can go and make your own camp. But when I report my success to the Prime Minister, you shall have no share of the merit."

Wang Ping marched about three miles from the hill and made his camp. He drew a plan of the place and sent it quickly to Zhuge Liang with a report that Ma Su had camped on the hill.

While Sima Yi was marching toward Jieting, he sent his younger son to reconnoiter the road and to find out whether it had a garrison.

Said Sima Yi, "If there is a garrison, do not advance further."

Sima Zhao returned to report: "Jieting has already been occupied by Shu."

"Zhuge Liang is rather more than human," said his father regretfully when Sima Zhao gave in his report. "He is too much for me."

"Why are you despondent, Father? I think Jieting is not so difficult to take."

"How dare you utter such bold words?"

"Because I have seen. There is no camp on the road, but the enemy are camped on the hill."

This was glad news.

"If they are on the hill, then Heaven means a victory for me," said his father.

At night Sima Yi changed into another dress, took a small escort, and rode out to see for himself. The moon shone brilliantly, and he rode to the hill whereon was the camp and looked all round it, thoroughly reconnoitering the neighborhood. Ma Su saw him, but only laughed.

"If Sima Yi has any luck, he will not try to surround this hill," said he.

Ma Su issued an order to his generals: "In case the enemy come, you are to look to the summit for a signal with a red flag, when you shall rush down on all sides."

Sima Yi returned to his camp and sent out to inquire who commanded in Jieting.

They told him, "He is Ma Su, brother of Ma Liang."

"A man of false reputation and very ordinary ability," said Sima Yi. "If Zhuge Liang uses such as Ma Su, he will fail."

Then he asked, "Are there any other camps near the place?"

And they reported, "Wang Ping's camp is about three miles off."

Wherefore Zhang He was ordered to go and check Wang Ping from coming to rescue. Zhang He marched out and placed himself between Wang Ping and the hill.

This done, Sima Yi ordered Shen Yi and Shen Dan to surround the hill and to block the road to the water supply. Lack of water would cause a mutiny; and when that occurred, it would be time to attack.

Then Sima Yi led the main body to attack the hill on all sides.

From the summit of his hill, Ma Su could see the banners of his enemy all round, and the country about was full of soldiers. Presently the hemming in was complete, and the soldiers of Shu became dejected. They dared not descend to attack although Ma Su hoisted the red flag signaling for them to move. The generals stood huddled together, no one daring to go first. Ma Su was furious. He cut down two generals, which frightened the others to the point of descending and making one desperate rush. But the troops of Wei would stand firm against their attack, and they reascended the hill.

Ma Su saw that matters were going ill, so he issued orders to bar the gates and defend till help should come from outside.

When Wang Ping saw the hill surrounded, he started to go to the rescue, but Zhang He checked him, and after exchanging some ten encounters Wang Ping was compelled to retire whence he had come.

The Wei troops kept a close siege. The Shu soldiers in the hill camp, having no water, were unable to prepare food, and disorder broke out. The shouting was audible at the foot of the hill and went on far into the night. The soldiers on the south side got out of hand, opened the gates and surrendered. The men of Wei went round the hill setting fire to the wood, which led to still greater confusion in the beleaguered garrison. At last Ma Su decided to make a dash for safety toward the west.

Sima Yi allowed him to pass, but Zhang He was sent to pursue and chased him for ten miles. But then there came an unexpected roll of drums. Zhang He was stopped by Wei Yan while Ma Su got past. Whirling up his sword, Wei Yan dashed toward Zhang He, who retired within his ranks and fled. Wei Yan followed and drove Zhang He backward toward Jieting.

The pursuit continued for fifteen miles, and then Wei Yan found himself in an ambush, Sima Yi on one side and Sima Zhao on the other. They went around the hill and closed in behind Wei Yan, and he was surrounded. Zhang He then turned back, and the attack was now on three sides. Wei Yan lost many troops, and all his efforts failed to get him clear of the press. Then help appeared in the person of Wang Ping.

"This is life for me," said Wei Yan as he saw Wang Ping coming up, and the two forces joined in a new attack on the force of Wei. So the troops of Wei drew off, while Wei Yan and Wang Ping made all haste back to their own camp in Jieting---only to find them in the hands of the enemy.

Shen Yi and Shen Dan then rushed out and drove Wei Yan and Wang Ping to Liliu.

About that time Gao Xiang got news of the attack on Jieting, and he marched out his army from Liliu to the rescue. But halfway he fell in with Wei Yan and Wang Ping.

When Gao Xiang heard their story, he at once proposed a night attack on the Wei camp and the recovery of Jieting. They talked this over on the hillside and arranged their plans, after which they set themselves to wait till it was dark enough to start.

They set out along three roads. Wei Yan was the first to reach Jieting. Not a soldier was visible, which looked suspicious. He decided to await the arrival of Gao Xiang, and they both speculated as to the whereabouts of their enemy. They could find no trace, and the third army under Wang Ping had not yet come up.

Suddenly a bomb exploded, and a brilliant flash lit up the sky; drums rolled as though the earth was rending, and the enemy appeared. In a trice the armies of Shu found themselves hemmed in. Both Wei Yan and Gao Xiang pushed here and shoved there, but could find no way out. Then most opportunely from behind a hill rolled out a thunder of drums, and there was Wang Ping coming to their rescue. Then the three forced their way to Liliu. But just as they drew near to the city, another body of soldiers came up, which, from the writing on their flags, they read Wei Commander Guo Huai.

Now Guo Huai had talked over Sima Yi's recall with his colleague Cao Zhen, and, fearing lest the recalled general should acquire too great glory, Guo Huai had set out to anticipate him in the capture of Jieting. Disappointed when he heard of Sima Yi's success there, he had decided to try a similar exploit at Liliu. So he had diverted his march thither.

He engaged the three Shu armies at once and slew many of them. Wei Yan feared the Wei army might pour into Hanzhong; so Wang Ping, Gao Xiang, and Wei Yan rushed to Yangping Pass and mustered its defense.

Guo Huai, pleased with his success, gathered in his army after the victory and said to his officers, "I was disappointed at Jieting, but we have taken this place, and that is merit of high order."

Thereupon he proceeded to the city gates. Just as he arrived, a bomb exploded on the wall, and, looking up, he saw the rampart bedecked with flags. On the largest banner he read the characters Sima Yi, General Who Pacifies the West. At that moment Sima Yi himself lifted a board that hung in front of him and looked over the breast-high rail.

He looked down and smiled, saying, "How late you are, friend Guo Huai!"

Guo Huai was amazed. "He is too much for me," said he.

So Guo Huai resignedly entered the city and went to pay his respects to his successful rival.

Sima Yi was gracious, and said, "Zhuge Liang must retire now that Jieting is lost. You join forces with Cao Zhen and follow up quickly."

Guo Huai agreed and took his leave.

Sima Yi called to him Zhang He, and said, "Cao Zhen and Guo Huai thought we should win too great merit, so they tried to get ahead of us here. We are not the only ones who desire to achieve good service and acquire merit, but we had the good fortune to succeed. I thought Wei Yan, Ma Su, Wang Ping, and Gao Xiang would first try to occupy Yangping Pass. If I went to take it, then Zhuge Liang would fall on our rear. It says in the books on war that one should crush a retreating enemy, not pursue broken rebels. So you may go along the by-roads and smite those withdrawing down the Gu Valley, while I oppose the Xie Valley army. If they flee, do not press them too much, but just hold them up on the road and capture the baggage train."

Zhang He marched away with half the force to carry out his part of this plan.

Then Sima Yi gave orders: "We are going to the Xie Valley by way of Xicheng. Though Xicheng is a small place, it is important as a depot of stores for the Shu army, beside commanding the road to the three counties of Nanan, Tianshui, and Anding. If this place can be captured, the other three can be recaptured."

Sima Yi left Shen Yi and Shen Dan to guard Liliu and marched his army toward the Xie Valley.

After Zhuge Liang had sent Ma Su to guard Jieting, his mind was constantly disturbed. Then arrived the messenger with the topography and plan prepared by Wang Ping. Zhuge Liang went over to his table and opened the letter. As he read it he smote the table in wrath.

"Ma Su's foolishness has destroyed the army!" he cried.

"Why are you so disturbed, O Prime Minister?" asked those near.

"By this plan I see that we have lost command of an important road. The camp has been made on the hill. If the Wei army come in force, our army will be surrounded and their water supply interrupted. In two days the soldiers will be in a state of mutiny. If Jieting shall be lost, how shall we be able to retire?"

Here High Counselor Yang Yi said, "I am none too clever I know, but let me go to replace Ma Su."

Zhuge Liang explained to Yang Yi how and where to camp; but before he could start, a horseman brought the news of the loss of Jieting and Liliu.

This made Zhuge Liang very sad, and he sighed, saying, "The whole scheme has come to nought, and it is my fault."

Zhuge Liang sent for Guan Xing and Zhang Bao, and said, "Each of you takes three thousand of good soldiers and go along the road to Wugong Hills. If you fall in with the enemy, do not fight, but beat drums and raise a hubbub and make them hesitate and be doubtful, so that they may retire. Do not pursue, but when they retire, make for Yangping Pass."

He also sent Zhang Yi to put Saber Pass in order for retreat and issued instructions for making ready to march. Ma Dai and Jiang Wei were told to guard the rear, but they were to go into ambush in the valleys till the whole army would have retreated. Trusty messengers were sent with the news to Tianshui, Nanan, and Anding that the officers, army, and people might go away into Hanzhong. He also sent to remove to a place of safety in Hanzhong the aged mother of Jiang Wei.

All these arrangements made, Zhuge Liang took five thousand troops and set out for Xicheng to remove the stores.

But messenger after messenger, more than ten of them, came to report: "Sima Yi is advancing rapidly on Xicheng with an army of one hundred fifty thousand troops."

No leader of rank was left to Zhuge Liang. He had only the civil officials and the five thousand soldiers, and as half this force had started to remove the stores, he had only two thousand five hundred left.

His officers were all frightened at the news of near approach of the enemy. Zhuge Liang himself went up on the rampart to look around. He saw clouds of dust rising into the sky. The Wei armies were nearing Xicheng along two roads.

Then he gave orders: "All the banners are to be removed and concealed. If any officer in command of soldiers in the city moves or makes any noise, he will be instantly put to death."

Next he threw open all the gates and set twenty soldiers dressed as ordinary people cleaning the streets at each gate. He told them not to react at the coming of the Wei army, as he had a plan ready for the city defense.

When all these preparations were complete, he donned the simple Taoist dress and, attended by a couple of lads, sat down on the wall by one of the towers with his lute before him and a stick of incense burning.

Sima Yi's scouts came near the city gate and saw all this. They did not enter the city, but went back and reported what they had seen. Sima Yi smiled incredulously. But he halted his army and rode ahead himself. Lo! It was exactly as the scouts had reported: Zhuge Liang sat there, his face with all smiles as he played the lute. A lad stood on one side of him bearing a treasured sword and on the other a boy with the ordinary symbol of authority, a yak's tail. Just inside the gates a score of persons with their heads down were sweeping as if no one was about.

Sima Yi hardly believed his eyes and thought this meant some peculiarly subtle ruse. So he went back to his armies, faced them about and moved toward the hills on the north.

"I am certain there are no soldiers behind this foolery," said Sima Zhao. "What do you retire for, Father?"

Sima Yi replied, "Zhuge Liang is always most careful and runs no risks. Those open gates undoubtedly mean an ambush. If our force enter the city, they will fall victims to his guile. How can you know? No; our course is to retire."

Thus were the two armies turned back from the city, much to the joy of Zhuge Liang, who laughed and clapped his hands as he saw them hastening away.

The officials gasped with astonishment, and they asked, "Sima Yi is a famous general of Wei, and he was leading one hundred fifty troops. By what reason did he march off at the sight of you, O Prime Minister?"

Zhuge Liang said, "He knows my reputation for

carefulness and that I play not with danger. Seeing things as they were made him suspect an ambush, and so he turned away. I do not run risks, but this time there was no help for it. Now he will meet with Guan Xing and Zhang Bao, whom I sent away into the hills to wait for him."

They were still in the grip of fear, but they praised the depth of insight of their chief and his mysterious schemes and unfathomable plans.

"We should simply have run away," said they.

"What could we have done with two thousand five hundred soldiers even if we had run? We should not have gone far before being caught," said Zhuge Liang.

Quite open lay the city to the foe,
But Zhuge Liang's lute of jasper wonders wrought;
It turned aside the legions' onward march
For both the leaders guessed the other's thought.

"But if I had been in Sima Yi's place, I should not have turned away," said Zhuge Liang, smiling and clapping his hands.

He gave orders that the people of the place should follow the army into Hanzhong, for Sima Yi would assuredly return.

They abandoned Xicheng and returned into Hanzhong. In due course the officials and soldiers and people out of the three counties also came in.

It has been said that Sima Yi turned aside from the city. He went to Wugong Hills. Presently there came the sounds of a Shu army from behind the hills.

Sima Yi turned to his sons, saying, "If we do not retire, we shall yet somehow fall victims to this Zhuge Liang."

Then appeared a force advancing rapidly, the main banner displaying Tiger General of the Right Guard, Zhang Bao. The soldiers of Wei were seized with sudden panic and ran, flinging off their armors and throwing away their weapons. But before they had fled very far, they heard other terrible sounds in the valley and soon saw another force, with the main banner Dragon General of the Left Guard, Guan Xing. The roar of armed troops echoing up and down the valley was terrifying. As no one could tell how many men there were bearing down on them, the panic increased. The Wei army abandoned all the baggage and took to flight. But having orders not to pursue, Zhang Bao and Guan Xing let their enemies run in peace, while they gathered up the spoils. Then they returned.

Seeing the valley apparently full of Shu soldiers, Sima Yi dared not marched by the main road. He hurried back to Jieting.

At this time Cao Zhen, hearing that the army of Shu was retreating, went in pursuit. But at a certain point he encountered a strong force under Ma Dai and Jiang Wei. Valleys and hills seemed to swarm with enemies, and Cao Zhen became alarmed. Then Chen Zao, his Van Leader, was slain by Ma

Dai, and the soldiers were panic-stricken and fled in disorder. And the soldiers of Shu were hastening night and day along the road into Hanzhong.

Zhao Yun and Deng Zhi, who had been lying in ambush in Gu Valley, heard that their comrades were retreating.

Then said Zhao Yun, "The army of Wei will surely come to smite us while we are retreating. Wherefore let me first take up a position in their rear, and then you lead off your troops and part of mine, showing my ensigns. I will follow, keeping at the same distance behind you, and thus I shall be able to protect the retreat."

Now Guo Huai was leading his army through the Gu Valley.

He called up his Van Leader, Su Yong, and said to him, "Zhao Yun is a warrior whom no one can withstand. You must keep a most careful guard lest you fall into some trap while they are retreating."

Su Yong replied, smiling, "If you will help me, O Commander, we shall be able to capture this Zhao Yun."

So Su Yong, with three thousand troops, hastened on ahead and entered the valley in the wake of the Shu army. He saw upon a slope in the distance a large red banner bearing the name Zhao Yun of Changshan. This frightened him, and he retired.

But before he had gone far a great uproar arose about him, and a mighty warrior came bounding forth on a swift steed, crying, "Do you recognize Zhao Yun?"

Su Yong was terrified.

"Whence came you?" he cried. "Is there another Zhao Yun here?"

But Su Yong could make no stand, and soon fell victim to the spear of the veteran. His troops scattered, and Zhao Yun marched on after the main body.

But soon another company came in pursuit, this time led by a general of Guo Huai, named Wan Zheng. As they came along Zhao Yun halted in the middle of the road to wait for the enemy. By the time Wan Zheng had come close, the other Shu soldiers had gone about ten miles along the road. However, when Wan Zheng drew nearer still and saw who it was standing in his path, he hesitated and finally halted. Zhao Yun guarded the road until the sunset, when he he turned back and retired slowly.

Guo Huai and his army came up and met Wan Zheng, who said, "Zhao Yun is as terrible as ever. He guards the rear carefully, and I dare not be reckless."

However, Guo Huai was not content and ordered Wan Zheng to return to the pursuit of the retreating army. This time Wan Zheng led a company of several hundred horsemen.

Presently they came to a wood, and, as they entered, a loud shout arose in the rear, "Zhao Yun is here!"

Terror seized upon the pursuers, and many fell from their horses. The others scattered among the hills. Wan Zheng braced himself for the encounter and went on. Zhao Yun shot an arrow which struck the plume on his helmet. Startled, Wan Zheng tumbled into a water stream.

Then Zhao Yun pointed his spear at him and said, "Be off! I will not kill you. Go and tell Guo Huai to come quickly, if he is coming."

Wan Zheng fled for his life, while Zhao Yun continued his march as rear guard, and the retreat into Hanzhong steadily continued. There were no other episodes by the way.

Cao Zhen and Guo Huai took to themselves all the credit of having recovered the three counties---Nanan, Tianshui, and Anding.

Before the cautious Sima Yi was ready to pursue the army of Shu, it had already reached Hanzhong. He took a troop of horse and rode to Xicheng and there heard from the few people who had formerly sought refuge in the hills, and now returned, that Zhuge Liang really had had no men in the city, with the exception of the two thousand five hundred soldiers, that he had not a single military commander, but only a few civil officers. Sima Yi also heard that Guan Xing and Zhang Bao had had only a few troops whom they led about among the hills making as much noise as they could.

Sima Yi felt sad at having been tricked.

"Zhuge Liang is a cleverer man than I am," said he with a sigh of resignation.

He set about restoring order, and presently marched back to Changan.

He saw the Ruler of Wei, who was pleased with his success and said, "It is by your good service that all counties of West Valley Land is again mine."

Sima Yi replied, "But the army of Shu is in Hanzhong undestroyed. Therefore, I pray for authority to go against them that you may recover the West River Land also."

Cao Rui rejoiced and approved, and authorized the raising of an army.

But then one of the courtiers suddenly said, "Your servant can propose a plan by which Shu will be overcome and Wu submits."

The generals lead their beaten soldiers home,
The victors plan new deeds for days to come.

Who offered this plan? Succeeding chapters will tell.

Chapter 96

Shedding Tears, Zhuge Liang Puts Ma Su To Death;
Cutting Hair, Zhou Fang Beguiles Cao Xiu.

The proposer of the great plan that was to conquer the empire was the Chair of the Secretariat, named Sun Zu.

"Noble Sir, expound your excellent scheme," said the Ruler of Wei.

And Sun Zu said, "When your great progenitor, Emperor Cao, first got Zhang Lu, he was at a critical stage in his career, but thenceforward all went well. He used to say the land of Nanzheng is really a natural hell. In the Xie Valley there are one hundred fifty miles of rocks and caves, so that it is an impossible country for an army. If Wei be denuded of soldiers in order to conquer Shu, then for sure we shall be invaded by Wu on the east. My advice is to divide the army among the various generals and appoint each a place of strategic value to hold, and let them train their forces. In a few years the Middle Land will be prosperous and wealthy, while the other two Shu and Wu, will have been reduced by mutual quarrels and will fall an easy prey. I hope Your Majesty will consider whether this is not a superior plan."

"What does the General think?" said Cao Rui to Sima Yi.

He replied, "Chairman Sun Zu says well."

So Cao Rui bade Sima Yi draw up a scheme of defense and station the soldiers, leaving Guo Huai and Zhang He to guard Changan. And having rewarded the army, the Ruler of Wei returned to Luoyang.

When Zhuge Liang got back to Hanzhong and missed Zhao Yun and Deng Zhi, the only two generals who had not arrived, he was sad at heart and bade Guan Xing and Zhang Bao go back to afford them assistance. However, before the reinforcing parties could leave, the missing men arrived. Furthermore, they came with their army in excellent condition and not a man short, nor a horse nor any of their equipment.

As they drew near, Zhuge Liang went out of the city to welcome them.

Thereupon Zhao Yun hastily dismounted and bowed to the earth, saying, "The Prime Minister should not have come forth to welcome a defeated general."

But Zhuge Liang lifted him up and took his hand and said, "Mine was the fault. Mine were the ignorance and unwisdom that caused all this. But how is it that amid all the defeat and loss you have come through unscathed?"

And Deng Zhi replied, "It was because friend Zhao Yun sent me ahead, while he guarded the rear and warded off every attack. One leader he slew, and this frightened the others. Thus nothing was lost or left by the way."

"A really great general!" said Zhuge Liang.

He sent Zhao Yun a gift of fifty ounces of gold, and to his army ten thousand rolls of silk.

But these were returned as Zhao Yun said, "All armies have accomplished nothing, and that is also our fault. The rules for reward and punishment must be strictly kept. I pray that these things be kept in store till the winter, when they can be distributed among the army."

"When the First Ruler lived, he never tired of extolling Zhao Yun's virtues. The First Ruler was perfectly right," said Zhuge Liang.

And his respect for the veteran was doubled.

Then came the turn of the four unfortunate leaders Ma Su, Wang Ping, Wei Yan, and Gao Xiang to render account. Wang Ping was called to the Commander-in-Chief's tent and rebuked.

"I ordered you and Ma Su to guard Jieting. Why did you not remonstrate with him and prevent this great loss?"

"I did remonstrate many times. I wished to build a rampart down in the road and construct a solid camp, but the Counselor would not agree and showed ill temper. So I led five thousand troops and camped some three miles off. When the army of Wei came in crowds and surrounded my colleague, I led my army to attack them a score of times. But I could not penetrate, and the catastrophe came quickly. Many of our troops surrendered, and mine were too few to stand. Wherefore I went to friend Wei Yan for help. Then we were intercepted and imprisoned in a valley and only got out by fighting most desperately. We got back to my camp to find the enemy in possession, and so we set out for Liliu. On the road I met Gao Xiang, and we three tried to raid the enemy's camp, hoping to recover Jieting. But as there was no one soldier there, I grew suspicious. From a hill I saw Wei Yan and Gao Xiang had been hemmed in by the soldiers of Wei, so I went to rescue them. Thence we hastened to Yangping Pass to try to prevent that from falling. It was not that I failed to remonstrate. And you, O Prime Minister, can get confirmation of my words from any of the officers."

Zhuge Liang bade him retire, and sent for Ma Su. He came, bound himself, and threw himself on the earth at the tent door.

Zhuge Liang got angry, saying, "You have filled yourself with the study of the books on war ever since you were a boy. You know them thoroughly. I enjoined upon you that Jieting was most important, and you pledged yourself and all your family to do your best in the enterprise. Yet you would not listen to Wang Ping, and thus you caused this misfortune. The army is defeated, generals have been slain and cities and territory lost, all through you. If I do not make you an example and vindicate the law, how shall I maintain a proper state of discipline? You have offended, and you must pay the penalty. After your death the little ones of your family shall be my care, and I will see that they get a monthly allowance. Do not let their fate cause you anxiety."

Zhuge Liang told the executioners to take Ma Su away.

Ma Su wept bitterly, saying, "Pity me, O Prime Minister! You have looked upon me as a son; I have looked up to you as a father. I know my fault is worthy of death, but I pray you remember how King Shun employed Yu, after executing Yu's father[xi]. Though I die, I will harbor no resentment down in the depths of the Nine Golden Springs."

Zhuge Liang brushed aside his tears and said, "We have been as brothers, and your children shall be as my own. I know what to do."

They led the doomed man away. Without the main gate, just as they were going to deal the fatal blow, High Counselor Jiang Wan, who had just arrived from Capital Chengdu, was passing in. He bade the executioners wait a while, and he went in and interceded for Ma Su.

"Formerly the King of Chu put Minister Cheng Dechen[xii] to death due to a defeat, and his rival Duke Wen of Jin[xiii] rejoiced. There is great confusion in the land, and yet you would slay a man of admitted ability. Can you not spare him?"

Zhuge Liang's tears fell, but he said, "Sun Zi maintains that the one way to obtain success is to make the law supreme. Now confusion and actual war are in every quarter. If the law be not observed, how may rebels be made away with? He must die."

Soon after they bore in the head of Ma Su as proof, and Zhuge Liang wailed bitterly.

"Why do you weep for him now that he has met

the just penalty for his fault?" said Jiang Wan.

"I was not weeping then because of Ma Su, but because I remembered the words of the First Ruler. At his last moment in Baidicheng, he said: 'Ma Su's words exceed his deeds. Do not make much use of him.' It has come true, and I greatly regret my want of insight. That is why I weep."

Every officer wept. Ma Su was but thirty-nine, and he met his end in the fifth month of the sixth year of Beginning Prosperity (AS 228).

A poet wrote about him thus:

That was pitiful that he who talked so glib
Of war, should lose a city, fault most grave,
With death as expiation. At the gate
He paid stern law's extremest penalty.
Deep grieved, his chief recalled the late Prince's words.

The head of Ma Su was paraded round the camps. Then it was sewn again to the body and buried with it. Zhuge Liang conducted the sacrifices for the dead and read the oration. A monthly allowance was made for the family, and they were consoled as much as possible.

Next Zhuge Liang made his memorial to the Throne and bade Jiang Wan bear it to the Latter Ruler. Therein Zhuge Liang proposed his own degradation from his high office.

"Naturally a man of mediocre abilities, I have enjoyed your confidence undeservedly. Having led out an expedition, I have proved my inability to perform the high office of leader. Over solicitude was my undoing. Hence happened disobedience at Jieting and the failure to guard the Gu Valley. The fault is mine in that I erred in the use of officers. In my anxiety I was too secretive. The 'Spring and Autumn' philosophy has pronounced the commander such as I am is blameworthy, and whither may I flee from my fault? I pray that I may be degraded three degrees as punishment. I cannot express my mortification. I humbly await your command."

"Why does the Prime Minister speak thus?" said the Latter Ruler after reading the memorial. "It is but the ordinary fortune of war."

Court Counselor Fei Yi said, "The ruler must enhance the majesty of the law, for without law how can people support him? It is right that the Prime Minister should be degraded in rank."

Thereupon an edict was issued reducing Zhuge Liang to the rank of General of the Right Army, but retaining him in the same position in the direction of state affairs and command of the military forces. Fei Yi was directed to communicate the decision.

Fei Yi bore the edict into Hanzhong and gave it to Zhuge Liang, who bowed to the decree. The envoy thought Zhuge Liang might be mortified, so he ventured to felicitate him in other matters.

"It was a great joy to the people of Shu when you, O Prime Minister, captured the four northwest counties," said he.

"What sort of language is this?" said Zhuge Liang, annoyed. "Success followed by failure is no success. It shames me indeed to hear such a compliment."

"His Majesty will be very pleased to hear of the acquisition of Jiang Wei."

This remark also angered Zhuge Liang, who replied, "It is my fault that a defeated army has returned without any gain of territory. What injury to Wei was the loss of Jiang Wei?"

Fei Yi tried again, saying, "But with an army of one hundred thousand bold veterans, you can attack Wei again."

Said Zhuge Liang, "When we were at Qishan and Gu Valley, we outnumbered the enemy, but we could not conquer them. On the contrary, they beat us. The defect was not in the number of soldiers, but in the leadership. Now we must reduce the army, discover our faults, reflect on our errors, and mend our ways against the future. Unless this is so, what is the use of a numerous army? Hereafter everyone will have to look to the future of his country. But most diligently each of you must fight against my shortcomings and blame my inefficiencies. Then we may succeed, rebellion can be exterminated, and merit can be set up."

Fei Yi and the officers acknowledged the aptness of these remarks. Fei Yi went back to the capital, leaving Zhuge Liang in Hanzhong resting his soldiers and doing what he could for the people, training and heartening his troops and turning special attention to the construction of apparatus for assaults on cities and crossing rivers. He also collected grain and fodder and built battle rafts, all for future use.

The spies of Wei got to know of these doings in the River Lands and reported to Luoyang. The Ruler of Wei called Sima Yi to council and asked how Shu might be annexed.

"Shu cannot be attacked," was the reply. "In this present hot weather they will not come out, but, if we invade, they will only garrison and defend their strategic points, which we should find it hard to overcome."

"What shall we do if they invade us again?"

"I have prepared for that. Just now Zhuge Liang shall imitate Han Xin who secretly crossed the river into Chencang. I can recommend a man to guard the place by building a rampart there and rendering it absolutely secure. He is a nine-span man, round shouldered and powerful, a good archer and prudent strategist. He would be quite equal to dealing with an invasion."

The Ruler of Wei was very pleased and asked for his name.

"His name is Hao Zhao, and he is in command at Hexi."

The Ruler of Wei accepted the recommendation, and an edict went forth promoting Hao Zhao to General Who Guards the West, and sending him to command in the county of Chencang.

Soon after this edict was issued, a memorial was received from Cao Xiu, Minister of War and Commander of Yangzhou, saying that Zhou Fang, the Wu Governor of Poyang, wished to tender his submission and transfer his allegiance, and had sent a man to present a memorandum under seven headings showing how the power of the South Land could be broken and to ask that an army be dispatched soon.

Cao Rui spread the document out on the couch that he and Sima Yi might read it.

"It seems very reasonable," said Sima Yi. "Wu could be quite destroyed. Let me go with an army to help Cao Xiu."

But from among the courtiers stepped out Jia Kui, who said, "What this man of Wu says may be understood in two ways. Do not trust it. Zhou Fang is a wise and crafty man and very unlikely to desert. In this is some ruse to decoy our soldiers into danger."

"Such words must also be listened to," said Sima Yi. "Yet such a chance must not be missed."

"You and Jia Kui might both go to the help of Cao Xiu," said the Ruler of Wei.

Sima Yi and Jia Kui went.

A large army, led by Cao Xiu, moved to Huancheng. Jia Kui, assisted by General Man Chong and Governor Hu Zhi of Dongwan, marched to capture Yangcheng, and facing the East Pass. Sima Yi led the third army to Jiangling.

Now the Prince of Wu, Sun Quan, was at the East Pass in Wuchang, and there he assembled his officers and said, "The Governor of Poyang, Zhou Fang, has sent up a secret memorial saying that Cao Xiu intends to invade. Zhou Fang has therefore set out a trap for Cao Xiu and has drawn up a document giving seven plausible circumstances, hoping thereby to cajole the Wei army into his power. The armies of Wei are on the move in three divisions, and I need your advice."

Gu Yong stood forth, saying, "There is only one man fit to cope with the present need: He is Lu Xun."

So Lu Xun was summoned and made Grand Commander, General Who Pacifies the North, Commander-in-Chief of all the State Armies, including the Imperial Guards, and Assistant in the Royal Duties. He was given the White Banners and the Golden Axes, which denoted imperial rank. All officers, civil and military, were placed under his orders. Moreover, Sun Quan personally stood beside him and held his whip while he mounted his steed.

Having received all these marks of confidence and favor, Lu Xun wanted two persons to be his assistants.

Sun Quan asked their names, and Lu Xun said, "They are Zhu Huan, General Who Fortifies Prowess, and Quan Zong, General Who Calms the South. These two should be in command."

Sun Quan approved and appointed Zhu Huan and Quan Zong as Left Commander and Right Commander respectively.

Then the grand army, comprising all the forces of the eighty-one counties of the South Land and the levies of Jingzhou, seven hundred thousand troops in total, was assembled and marched out in three divisions, Lu Xun in the center, with Zhu Huan and Quan Zong supporting him left and right with the other two columns.

Then said Zhu Huan, "Cao Xiu is neither able nor bold. He holds office because he is of the blood. He has fallen into the trap laid by Zhou Fang and marched too far to be able to withdraw. If the Commander-in-Chief will smite, Cao Xiu must be defeated. Defeated, he must flee along two roads, one Jiashi on the left, the other Guichi on the right, both of which are precipitous and narrow. Let me and my colleague go to prepare an ambush in these roads. We will block them and so cut off their escape. If this Cao Xiu could be captured, and a hasty advance made, success would be easy and sure. We should get Shouchun, whence Xuchang and Luoyang can be seen. This is the one chance in the thousand."

"I do not think the plan good," said Lu Xun. "I have a better one."

Zhu Huan resented the rejection of his scheme and went away. Lu Xun ordered Zhuge Jin and certain others to garrison Jiangling and oppose Sima Yi and made all other dispositions of forces.

Cao Xiu neared Huancheng, and Zhou Fang came out of the city to welcome him and went to the general's tent.

Cao Xiu said, "I received your letter and the memorandum, which was most logical, and sent it to His Majesty. He has set in motion accordingly three armies. It will be a great merit for you, Sir, if the South Land can be added to His Majesty's dominions. People say you are abundant in craft, but I do not believe what they say, for I think you will be true to me and not fail."

Zhou Fang wept. He seized a sword from one of his escort and was about to kill himself, but Cao Xiu stopped him.

Still leaning on the sword, Zhou Fang said, "As to the seven things I mentioned, my regret is that I cannot show you all. You doubt me because some persons from Wu and Wei have been poisoning your mind against me. If you heed them, the only course for me is to die. Heaven only can make manifest my loyal heart."

Again he made to slay himself.

But Cao Xiu in trepidation threw his arms about him, saying, "I did not mean it. The words were uttered in jest. Why do you act thus?"

Upon this, Zhou Fang, with his sword, cut off his hair and threw it on the ground, saying, "I have dealt with you with sincerity, Sir, and you joke about it. Now I have cut off the hair, which I inherited from my parents, in order to prove my sincerity."

Then Cao Xiu doubted no more, but trusted him fully and prepared a banquet for him, and when the feast was over Zhou Fang returned to his own.

General Jia Kui came to Cao Xiu, and when asked whether there was any special reason for the visit, he said, "I have come to warn you, Commander, to be cautious and wait till you and I can attack the enemy together. The whole army of Wu is encamped at Huancheng."

"You mean you want to share in my victory," sneered Cao Xiu.

"It is said Zhou Fang cut off his hair as a pledge of sincerity. That is only another bit of deceit. According to the Spring and Autumn Annals, Yao Li cut off his arm as a pledge of loyalty before he assassinated King Qing Ji. Mutilation is no guarantee. Do not trust Zhou Fang."

"Why do you come to utter ill-omened words just as I am opening the campaign? You destroy the spirit of the army," said Cao Xiu.

In his wrath he told the lictors to put Jia Kui to death.

However, the officers interceded, saying, "Before the march, killing our general is not favorable to the army. O Commander, spare him until after the expedition."

And Jia Kui was reprieved. But he was not assigned any part in the campaign, and his troops were left in reserve. Cao Xiu himself went away to the East Pass.

When Zhou Fang heard that Jia Kui had been broken, he rejoiced in his heart, saying, "If Cao Xiu had attended to his words, then Wu would have lost. Heaven is good to me and is giving me the means of achieving great things."

Then he sent a secret messenger to Huancheng, and Lu Xun knew that the time had come. He assembled the officers for orders.

Lu Xun said, "Shiding, lying over against us, is a hilly country fit for preparing an ambush. It will be occupied as suitable to array our army and await the coming of Wei. Xu Sheng is to be Leader of the Van, and the army will move there."

Now Cao Xiu told Zhou Fang to lead the way for his attack. While on march, Cao Xiu asked, "What is the place lying ahead?"

Zhou Fang replied, "Shiding, a suitable place to camp in."

So a great camp was made there.

But soon after the scouts reported, "Wu soldiers, unknown in number, have camped among the hills."

Cao Xiu began to feel alarmed, saying, "Zhou Fang said there were no soldiers. Why these preparations?"

Cao Xiu hastily sought Zhou Fang to ask him, but was told, "Zhou Fan has gone away with a few dozen riders. No one knows whither."

"I have been deceived and am in a trap," said Cao Xiu, now very repentant of his easy confidence. "However, there is nothing to fear."

Then he made his arrangements to march against the enemy, and when they were complete and the array drawn up, Zhang Pu, the Leader of the Van, rode out and began to rail at the men of Wu.

"Rebel leader, come and surrender!" cried Zhang Pu.

Then rode out Xu Sheng and fought with him. But Zhang Pu was no match for Xu Sheng, as was soon evident, wherefore he led his troops to retire.

"Xu Sheng is too strong," said Zhang Pu when he saw Cao Xiu.

"Then will we defeat him by a surprise," said Cao Xiu.

He sent Zhang Pu with twenty thousand troops to hide in the south of Shiding, while another equal party under Xue Qiao was sent north.

And Cao Xiu arranged, saying, "Tomorrow I will lead a thousand soldiers to provoke the troops of Wu into battle, then I will feign defeat and lead them to the hills in the north, when a bomb will explode and a three-pronged ambush will bring us victory."

On the other side Lu Xun called his two generals, Zhu Huan and Quan Zong, and said, "Each of you is to lead thirty thousand troops and take a cross cut from Shiding to the enemy's camp. Give a fire signal behind the camp on arrival, and then the main army will advance to the camp's front for a double attack."

As evening fell these two moved out their troops, and by the middle of the second watch both had got behind the camp of Wei. Due to darkness, Zhang Pu, Cao Xiu's general, who was there in ambush, did not recognize that the troops who approached him were enemies, but went as to meet friends and was at once slain by the blade of Zhu Huan. The soldiers of Wei then fled, and Zhu Huan lit his signal fires.

Quan Zong, marching up, came across the northern ambush under Xue Qiao. Quan Zong began a battle at once, and the troops of Wei were soon put to flight. Both the armies of Wu pursued, and confusion reigned in Cao Xiu's camp, troops fighting with others of their own side and slaying each other.

Cao Xiu despaired and fled toward Jiashi. Xu Sheng, with a strong force, came along the high road and attacked. And the soldiers of Wei killed were very many. Those who escaped did so by abandoning all their armors.

Cao Xiu was in straits, but he struggled along the Jiashi Road. Here came a cohort into the road from the side. It was led by Jia Kui. Cao Xiu's alarm gave place to shame on meeting Jia Kui.

"I took no notice of what you said, and so this evil came upon me," said he.

Jia Kui replied, "Commander, you should quickly get out of this road. For if the troops of Wu block it, we shall be in grave danger."

So Cao Xiu hastened, while Jia Kui protected his retreat. And Jia Kui ordered his soldiers to set flags and banners up among trees and in thickets and along by-paths, so as to give an impression of having many men posted all round. Wherefore when Xu Sheng came in pursuit, he thought the country was full of ambushing men and dared not proceed far. So he gave up the pursuit and retired.

By these means Cao Xiu was rescued, and finally Sima Yi withdrew his army upon the news of Cao Xiu's defeat.

In the meantime, Lu Xun was awaiting news of victory. Soon Xu Sheng, Zhu Huan, and Quan Zong came and reported their successes, and they brought great spoil of carts and bullocks, horses and mules, and military material and weapons. And they had also ten thousand prisoners. There was great rejoicing, and Lu Xun with Zhou Fang led the army home into Wu.

On their return Sun Quan, the Prince of Wu, came out with a numerous cortege of officers to welcome the victors, and an imperial umbrella was borne over the head of Lu Xun as they wended their way homeward.

When the officers presented their felicitations, Sun Quan noticed that Zhou Fang had no hair.

Sun Quan was very gracious to him, saying, "This deed of yours, and the sacrifice you made to attain it, will surely be written in the histories."

He made Zhou Fang the Lord of the Gate Within. Then there were great feastings and greetings and much revelry.

Lu Xun said, "Cao Xiu has been thoroughly beaten, and the soldiers of Wei are cowed. I think now is an occasion to send letters into Shu to advise Zhuge Liang to attack Wei."

Sun Quan agreed, and letters were sent to the River Lands.

The east, successful in one fight,
Would unto war the west incite.

The next chapter will say if Zhuge Liang once more tried to overcome Wei.

Chapter 97

Sending A Second Memorial, Zhuge Liang Renews The Attack On Wei; Forging A Letter, Jiang Wei Defeats The Northern Army.

It was in the autumn of the sixth year of Beginning Prosperity (AD 229) that the Wei army was defeated, with very great loss, by Lu Xun of Wu. Cao Xiu's mortification brought on an illness from which he died in Luoyang. By command of Cao Rui, the Ruler of Wei, Cao Xiu received most honorable burial.

Then Sima Yi brought the army home again.

The other officers went to welcome him and asked, "The defeat of Commander Cao Xiu is also partly yours. Why, O General, did you hurry home?"

Sima Yi replied, "I came for reasons of strategy, because of Zhuge Liang's probable intentions. If he knows I have suffered a defeat, he may try to attack Changan. The whole West Valley Land would be helpless if I did not return."

They listened and smiled, for they thought he was afraid.

Letters from Wu came to Shu proposing a joint attack on Wei and detailing their recent victory. In these letters two feelings were gratified---that of telling the story of their own grandeur and prowess, and that of furthering the design of a treaty of peace. The Latter Ruler was pleased and sent the letters to Zhuge Liang in Hanzhong.

At that time the army was in excellent state, the soldiers hardy, the horses strong. There were plentiful supplies of all kinds. Zhuge Liang was just going to propose a new war.

On receipt of the letter he made a great banquet to discuss an expedition. A severe gale came on from the northeast and brought down a fir tree in front of the general's shelter. It was an inauspicious omen to all the officers, and they were troubled.

Zhuge Liang cast lots to know what portent was intended, and announced, "That gale signals the loss of a great leader."

They hardly believed him. But before the banquet ended, two sons of Zhao Yun, Zhao Tong and Zhao Guang, came and wished to see the Prime Minister.

Zhuge Liang, deeply affected, threw aside his wine cup and cried, "That is it. Zhao Yun is gone!"

When the two young men came in, they prostrated themselves and wept, saying, "Our father died the night before at the third watch."

Zhuge Liang staggered and burst into lamentation.

"My friend is gone. The country has lost it great beam, and I my right arm!"

Those about him joined in, wiping away their tears. Zhuge Liang bade the two young men go in person to Chengdu to bear the sad tidings to the Emperor.

And the Latter Ruler wept bitterly.

"Zhao Yun was my savior and friend. He saved my life when I was a child in the time of great confusion!" cried the Latter Ruler.

An edict was issued creating Zhao Yun Regent Marshal and Lord of Shunping and giving burial on the east of Silky Hills near Capital Chengdu. A temple was ordered to his memory and sacrifices were offered in four seasons.[xiv]

From Changshan came a general, tiger bold,
In wit and valor he was fitting mate
For Guan Yu and Zhang Fei, his exploits rivaling
Even theirs. River Han and Dangyang recall
His name. Twice in his stalwart arms he bore
The prince, his well-loved leader's son and heir.
In storied page his name stands out, writ large.
Fair record of most brave and loyal deeds.

The Latter Ruler showed his affectionate gratitude to the late leader, not only in according him most honorable burial, but in kindness to his sons. The elder, Zhao Tong, was made General in the Tiger Army and the younger, Zhao Guang, Station General. He also set guards over the tomb.

When the two sons had left, the ministers reported to the Latter Ruler: "The dispositions of the army are complete, and the Prime Minister proposes to march against Wei without delay."

Talking this over with one and another, the Latter

Ruler found the courtiers much inclined to a cautious policy and somewhat fearful. And the doubts entered into the Latter Ruler's mind so that he could not decide. Then came a memorial from Zhuge Liang, and the messenger, Yang Yi, was called into the presence and gave it to the Latter Ruler. The Emperor spread it on the table and read:

"The First Ruler always said: 'Han and rebels cannot coexist; a ruler's domain cannot be confined.' Wherefore he laid upon me, thy minister, to destroy the rebels. Measuring my powers by his perspicacity, he knew that I should attack and oppose my talents, inadequate as they might be, to their strength, for, if I did not, the royal domain would be destroyed. It was a question whether to await destruction without effort, or to attack? Wherefore he assigned me the task confidently. Thenceforward this task occupied all my thoughts.

"Considering that the south should be made secure before the north could be attacked, I braved the heat of summer and plunged deep into the wilds of the Mang nations. Not that I was careless of myself or the soldiers, but urged by the one consideration, that the royal domain should not be restricted to the capital of Shu, I faced dangers in obedience to the First Ruler's behest. But there were critics who said that I should not do it.

"Now the rebels have been weakened in the west and have become defeated in the east. The rule of war is to take advantage of the enemy's weakness, and so now is the time to attack. I shall discuss the various circumstances in order.

"The enlightenment of the Founder of the Hans, Liu Bang, rivaled the glory of the sun and moon; his counselors were profound as the ocean abyss. Nevertheless, he trod a hazardous path and suffered losses, only attaining repose after passing through great dangers. Your Majesty does not reach his level, nor do your counselors equal Zhang Liang and Chen Ping. Yet while we desired victory, we would sit idle, waiting till the empire should become settled. This attitude is beyond my comprehension.

"Imperial Protector Liu Yao and Governor Wang Lang each occupied a territory. They passed their time in talking of tranquillity and discussing plans, quoting the sayings of the sages till they were filled with doubts and obsessed with difficulties. So this year was not the time to fight, nor next year the season to punish, and, thus talking, it came about that Sun Ce grew powerful and possessed himself of all the South Land. This sort of behavior I cannot understand.

"In craft Cao Cao surpassed all humans. He could wield armies like the great strategists of old, Sun Zi and Wu Qi. Yet he was surrounded in Nanyang, was in danger at Wuchao, was in difficulties at Qilian, was hard pressed in Liyang, was nearly defeated at Beishan, and nearly killed at Tong Pass. Yet, after all these experiences, there was a temporary and artificial state of equilibrium. How much less can I, a man of feeble powers, bring about a decision without running risks? I fail to understand.

"Cao Cao failed in five attacks on Changba, and four times crossed Lake Chaohu without success.

He employed Li Zu, who betrayed him, and put his trust in Xiahou Yuan, who was defeated and died. The First Ruler always regarded Cao Cao as an able man, and yet Cao Cao made such mistakes. How then can I, in my worn-out condition, avoid any error? I do not understand why.

"Only one year has elapsed since I went into Hanzhong, yet we have lost Zhao Yun, Yang Qun, Ma Yun, Yan Zhi, Ding Li, Bo Shou, Liu He, Deng Tong, and others, and leaders of rank and generals of stations, to the number of near eighty, all people unsurpassed in dash and valor, and more than a thousand of the specialized forces of horse and trained cavalry of the Sou and the Tangut tribespeople in the Gobi Desert, whose martial spirit we have fostered these ten years all about us, and not only in one region. If we delay much longer, two-thirds of this will have dissipated, and how then shall we meet the situation? I do not understand delay.

"The people are stretched and the army exhausted indeed, but confusion does not cease. If confusion does not cease, then, whether we go on or stand still the drain is the same. Does it seems that attack should not be made yet? Is it that the rebels are to be allowed to obtain a permanent hold on some territory? I do not understand the arguments.

"A stable condition of affairs is indeed difficult to obtain. Once, when the First Ruler was defeated in Jingzhou, Cao Cao patted himself on the back and said that the empire was settled. Yet, after that, the First Ruler obtained the support of Wu and Yue on the east, took Ba and Shu on the west, and undertook an expedition to the north, wherein

Xiahou Yuan lost his life. So Cao Cao calculations proved erroneous, and the affairs of Han seemed about to prosper. But, still later, Wu proved false to pledges, our Guan Yu was defeated, we sustained a check at Zigui---and Cao Pi assumed the imperial style. Such events prove the difficulty of forecast. I shall strive on to the end, but the final result, whether success or failure, whether gain or loss, is beyond my powers to foresee."

The Latter Ruler was convinced, and by edict directed Zhuge Liang to start on the expedition.

Zhuge Liang marched out with three hundred thousand well-trained soldiers, Wei Yan leading the first division, and made all haste to Chencang.

The news soon reached Luoyang, and Sima Yi informed the Ruler of Wei, who called his council.

Then Cao Zhen stepped forth and said, "In the previous campaign I failed to hold West Valley Land, and my disgrace is terrible to bear. But now I beg to be given another command that I may capture Zhuge Liang. Lately I have found a stalwart soldier for a leader, a man who wields a ninety-pound sword, rides a swift and savage steed, bends the three-hundred-pound bow, and carries hidden about him when he goes into battle three meteor maces with which his aim is certain. So valorous is he that none dare stand against him. He comes from Didao in West Valley Land and is named Wang Shuang. I would recommend him for my leader of the van."

Cao Rui approved at once and summoned this marvel to the hall. There came a nine-span man with a dusky complexion, yellowish eyes, strong as a bear in the hips and with a back supple as a tiger's.

"No need to fear anything with such a man!" said Cao Rui, laughing.

He gave the new hero rich presents, a silken robe and golden breastplate, and gave him the title General Who Possesses the Tiger Majesty. And Wang Shuang became Leader of the Van of the new army. Cao Zhen was appointed Commander-in-Chief.

Cao Zhen took leave of his master and left the court. He collected his one hundred fifty thousand veterans and, in consultation with Guo Huai and Zhang He, decided upon the strategic points to be guarded.

The first companies of the army of Shu sent out their scouts as far as Chencang. They came back and reported: "A rampart has been built and behind it is a general named Hao Zhao in command. The rampart is very strong and is further defended by thorny barriers. Instead of taking Chencang, which seems difficult, it would be easier to go out to Qishan by the Taibo Mountains, where is a practicable, though winding, road."

But Zhuge Liang said, "Due north of Chencang is Jieting, so that I must get this city in order to advance."

Wei Yan was sent to surround Chencang and take it. He went, but days passed without success. Therefore he returned and told his chief the place was impregnable. In his anger, Zhuge Liang was going to put Wei Yan to death, but an officer stepped forth.

Said he, "I have followed the Prime Minister for a long time, but have not achieved worthy service. Now I want to go to Chencang and persuade Hao Zhao to yield. Thus, our army does not need to use a single bow or arrow."

Others turned their attention to Counselor Jin Xiang.

"How do you think you will persuade him?" said Zhuge Liang. "What will you say?"

"Hao Zhao and I are both from West Valley Land and pledged friends from boyhood. If I can get to see him, I will so lay matters before him that he must surrender."

Jin Xiang got permission to try, and rode quickly to the wall of Chencang.

Then he called out, "Friend Hao Zhao, your old chum Jin Xiang has come to see you!"

A sentry on the wall told Hao Zhao, who bade them let the visitor enter and bring him up on the wall.

"Friend, why have you come?" asked Hao Zhao.

"I am in the service of Shu, serving under Zhuge Liang as an assistant in the Tactical Department. I am created exceedingly well, and my chief has sent me to say something to you."

Hao Zhao was rather annoyed, and said, "Zhuge Liang is my enemy. I serve Wei while you serve

Shu. Each serves his own lord. We were brothers once, but now we are enemies. So do not say any more."

And the visitor was requested to take his leave. Jin Xiang tried to reopen the conversation, but Hao Zhao left him and went up on the tower. The Wei soldiers hurried Jin Xiang on to his horse and led him to the gate. As he passed out, he looked up and saw his friend leaning on the guard rail.

He pulled up his horse, pointed with his whip at Hao Zhao, and said, "My friend and worthy brother, why has your friendship become so thin?"

"Brother, you know the laws of Wei," replied Hao Zhao. "I have accepted their bounty, and if that leads to death, so be it. Say no more, but return quickly to your master and tell him to come and attack. I am not afraid."

So Jin Xiang had to return and report failure.

"He would not let me begin to explain," said he.

"Try again," said Zhuge Liang. "Go and really talk to him."

So the go-between soon found himself once more at the foot of the wall.

Hao Zhao presently appeared on the tower, and Jin Xiang shouted to him, "My worthy brother, please listen to my words while I explain clearly. Here you are holding one single city. How can you think of opposing one hundred thousand troops? If you do not yield, you will be sorry when it is too late. Instead of serving the Great Han, you are serving a depraved country called Wei. Why do you not recognize the decree of Heaven? Why do you not distinguish between the pure and the foul? Think over it."

Then Hao Zhao began to get really angry. He fitted an arrow to his bow and he called out, "Go! Or I will shoot. I meant what I said at first, and I will say no more."

Again Jin Xiang returned and reported failure to Zhuge Liang.

"The fool is very ill-mannered," said Zhuge Liang. "Does he think he can beguile me into sparing the city?"

He called up some of the local people and asked about the forces in the city. They told him about three thousand.

"I do not think such a small place can beat me," said Zhuge Liang. "Attack quickly before any reinforcements can arrive."

Thereupon the assailants brought up scaling ladders, upon the platforms of which ten or more men could stand. These were surrounded by planks as protection. The other soldiers had short ladders and ropes, and, at the beat of the drum, they attempted to scale the walls.

But when Hao Zhao saw the ladders being brought up, he made his soldiers shoot fire-arrows at them. Zhuge Liang did not expect this. He knew the city was not well prepared for defense, and he had had the great ladders brought up and bade the soldiers take the wall with a rush. He was greatly chagrined when the fire arrows set his ladders on fire and so many of his soldiers were burned. And as the arrows and stones rained down from the wall, the soldiers of Shu were forced to retire.

Zhuge Liang angrily said, "So you burn my ladders! Then I will use battering rams."

So the rams were brought and placed against the walls and again the signal given for assault. But the defenders brought up great stones suspended by ropes, which they swung down at the battering rams and so broke them to pieces.

Next the besiegers set to work to bring up earth and fill the moat, and Liao Hua led three thousand soldiers to excavate a tunnel under the ramparts. But Hao Zhao cut a counter-trench within the city and turned that device.

So the struggle went on for near a month, and still the city was not taken. Zhuge Liang was very depressed.

That was not all. The scouts reported: "From the east there is coming a relief force of Wei, the flags of which bears the name Wei Van Leader, General Wang Shuang."

Zhuge Liang asked, "Who wants to go out and oppose this force?"

Wei Yan offered himself.

"No;" said Zhuge Liang, "you are too valuable as Leader of the Van."

General Xie Xiong offered his services. They were

accepted, and Xie Xiong was given three thousand troops. After he had gone, Zhuge Liang decided to send a second force, and for command of this General Gong Qi volunteered and was accepted. Gong Qi also had three thousand troops.

Then Zhuge Liang feared lest there would be a sortie from the city to aid the relief force just arriving, so he led off the army seven miles and made a camp.

The first body sent against Wang Shuang had no success: Xie Xiong fell almost immediately under Wang Shuang's great sword. The men fled and Wang Shuang pursued, and so came upon Gong Qi, who had come to support his colleague. Gong Qi met a similar fate, being slain in the third bout.

When the defeated parties returned, Zhuge Liang was anxious and called up Liao Hua, Wang Ping, and Zhang Ni to go out to check this Wang Shuang, They went and drew up in formal array, and then Zhang Ni rode to the front. Wang Shuang rode to meet him, and they two fought several bouts. Then Wang Shuang ran away and Zhang Ni followed.

His colleague, Wang Ping, suspected this flight was but a ruse, so he called to Zhang Ni, "Do not follow the fleeing general!"

Zhang Ni then turned, but Wang Shuang turned also and hurled one of his meteor hammers, which hit Zhang Ni in the back, so that he fell forward and lay over the saddle. Wang Shuang rode on to follow up this advantage, but Liao Hua and Wang Ping poured out and checked him. Wang Shuang's whole force then came on and slew many of the troops of Shu.

Zhang Ni was hurt internally and vomited blood at times. He came back and told Zhuge Liang, saying, "Wang Shuang is very terrible and no one can stand up to him. He camps outside Chencang, building a strong stockade, and so making the city with double walls and a deep moat."

Having lost two generals, and a third being wounded, Zhuge Liang called up Jiang Wei and said, "We are stopped this way. Can you suggest another road?"

"Yes," said Jiang Wei. "Chencang is too well protected and, with Hao Zhao as defender and Wang Shuang as supporter, cannot be taken. I would propose to check Chencang by leaving a general here, who shall make a strong camp with the support of the hills. Then try to hold the roads so that the attack from Jieting may be prevented. Then if you will send a strong force against Qishan, I can do something which will capture Cao Zhen."

Zhuge Liang agreed. He sent Wang Ping and Li Hui to hold the narrow road to Jieting, and Wei Yan was sent to guard the way from Chencang. And then the army marched out of the Xie Valley by a small road and made for Qishan.

Now Cao Zhen still remembered bitterly that in the last campaign Sima Yi had filched from him the credit he hoped to obtain. So when he received the commission of defending the capitals against the invading forces, he detached Guo Huai and Sun Li and sent them to hold positions east and west. Then he had heard that Chencang was threatened, so had sent Wang Shuang to its relief, and now to his joy he heard of his henchman's success. He placed Grand Commander Fei Yao in command of the van and stationed other generals at strategic and commanding points.

Then they caught a spy. He was taken into the presence of the Commander-in-Chief to be questioned.

The man knelt down and said, "I am not really a spy in the bad sense. I was bringing a secret communication for you, Sir, but I was captured by one of the parties in ambush. Pray send away your attendants."

The man's bonds were loosed and the tent cleared.

The captive said, "I am a confidant of Jiang Wei, who has entrusted me with a secret letter."

"Where is the letter?"

The man took it from among his garments and presented it to Cao Zhen, who read:

"I, Jiang Wei, your guilty general, make a hundred prostrations to the great leader Cao Zhen, now in the field. I have never forgotten that I was in the employment of Wei and disgraced myself; having enjoyed favors, I never repaid them. Lately I have been an unhappy victim of Zhuge Liang's wiles and so fell into the depths. But I never forgot my old allegiance. How could I forget?

"Now happily the army of Shu has gone west, and Zhuge Liang trusts me. I rely upon your leading an army this way. If resistance be met, then you may simulate defeat and retire, but I shall be behind and will make a blaze as signal. Then I shall set fire to their stores, whereupon you will face about and attack. Zhuge Liang ought to fall into your hands. If it be that I cannot render service and repay my debt to the state, then punish me for my former crime.

"If this should be deemed worthy of your attention, then without delay communicate your commands."

The letter pleased Cao Zhen, and he said, "This is heaven-sent help to aid me in an achievement."

Cao Zhen rewarded the messenger and bade him return to say that it was accepted.

Then he called Fei Yao to his councils and said, "I have just had a secret letter from Jiang Wei telling me to act in a certain fashion."

But Fei Yao replied, "Zhuge Liang is very crafty, and Jiang Wei is very knowing. If by chance Zhuge Liang has planned all this and sent this man, we may fall into a snare."

"But Jiang Wei is really a man of Wei. He was forced into surrender. Why are you suspicious?"

"My advice is not to go, but to remain here on guard. Let me go to meet this man, and any service I can accomplish will redound to your credit. And if there be any craft, I can meet it for you."

Cao Zhen approved this and bade Fei Yao take fifty thousand troops by way of the Xie Valley.

Fei Yao marched away and halted after the second

or third stage and send out scouts. This was done, and the scouts reported that the Shu army was coming through the valley. Fei Yao at once advanced, but before the troops of Shu got into contact with him, they retired. Fei Yao pursued. Then the troops of Shu came on again. Just as Fei Yao was forming up for battle, the Shu army retreated again. And these maneuvers were repeated thrice, and a day and a night passed without any repose for the Wei army.

At length rest was imperative, and they were on the point of entrenching themselves to prepare food when a great hubbub arose all around, and with beating of drums and blaring of trumpets, the whole country was filled with the soldiers of Shu. Suddenly there was a stir near by the great standard, and out came a small four-wheeled chariot in which sat Zhuge Liang. He bade a herald call the leader of the Wei army to a parley.

Fei Yao rode out and, seeing Zhuge Liang, he secretly rejoiced.

Turning to those about him, Fei Yao said, "If the soldiers of Shu come on, you are to retire and look out for a signal. If you see a blaze, you are to turn and attack, for you will be reinforced by Jiang Wei."

Then Fei Yao rode to the front and shouted, "You rebel leader in front there. How dare you come here again after the last defeat?"

Zhuge Liang replied, "Go and call Cao Zhen to a parley."

"My chief, Cao Zhen, is of the royal stock. Think

you that he will come to parley with rebels?"

Zhuge Liang angrily waved his fan, and there came forth Ma Dai and Zhang Ni and their troops with a rush. The Wei army retired. But ere they had gone far, they saw a blaze in the rear of the advancing host of Shu and heard a great shouting. Fei Yao could only conclude that this was the signal of Jiang Wei he was looking for, and so he faced about to attack.

But the enemy also turned about and retired. Fei Yao led the pursuit, sword in hand, hastening to the point whence the shouting came. Nearing the signal fire, the drums beat louder than ever, and then out came two armies, one under Guan Xing and the other under Zhang Bao, while arrows and stones rained from the hill-tops. The Wei troops could not stand it and knew not only they were beaten, but beaten by a ruse. Fei Yao tried to withdraw his force into the shelter of the valley to rest, but the enemy pressed on him, and the army of Wei fell into confusion. Pressing upon each other, many fell into the streams and were drowned.

Fei Yao could do nothing but flee for his life. Just as he was passing by a steep hill there appeared a cohort, and the leader was Jiang Wei.

Fei Yao began to upbraid him, crying, "Faithless ingrate! I have haplessly fallen in your treachery and craftiness!"

Jiang Wei replied, "You are the wrong victim. We meant to capture Cao Zhen not you. You would do well to yield!"

But Fei Yao only galloped away toward a ravine. Suddenly the ravine filled with flame. Then he lost all hope. The pursuers were close behind, so Fei Yao with a sword put an end to his own life.

Of the army of Wei many surrendered. The Shu army pressed home their advantage and, hastening forward, reached Qishan and made a camp. There the army was mustered and put in order.

Jiang Wei received a reward, but he was chagrined that Cao Zhen had not been taken.

"My regret is that I did not slay Cao Zhen," said he.

"Indeed, yes," replied Zhuge Liang. "It is a pity that a great scheme should have had so small a result."

Cao Zhen was very sad when he heard of the loss of Fei Yao. He consulted Guo Huai as to a new plan to drive back the enemy.

Meanwhile, flying messengers had gone to the capital with news of Zhuge Liang's arrival at Qishan and the defeat. Cao Rui called Sima Yi to ask for a plan to meet these new conditions.

"I have a scheme all ready, not only to turn back Zhuge Liang, but to do so without any exertion on our part. They will retire of their own will."

Cao Zhen's wits are dull; so he
Fights on Sima Yi's strategy.

The strategy will appear in the next chapter.

Chapter 98

Pursuing The Shu Army, Wang Shuang Meets His Death;
Raiding Chencang, Zhuge Liang Scores A Victory.

Now Sima Yi spoke to the Ruler of Wei, saying, "I have said repeatedly that Zhuge Liang would come against us by way of Chencang; wherefore I set Hao Zhao to guard it. If an Zhuge Liang did invade, he could easily obtain his supplies by that road. But with Hao Zhao and Wang Shuang on guard there, he will not dare to come that way. It is very difficult to get supplies any other way. Therefore I can give the invaders a month to exhaust their food. Hence their advantage lies in forcing a battle; ours is postponing it as long as possible. Wherefore I pray Your Majesty order Cao Zhen to hold passes and positions tenaciously and on no account to seek battle. In a month the enemy will have to retreat, and that will be our opportunity."

Cao Rui was pleased to hear so succinct a statement, but he said, "Since, Noble Sir, you foresaw all this so plainly, why did you not lead an army to prevent it?"

"It is not because I grudged the effort, but I had to keep the army here to guard against Lu Xun of Wu. Sun Quan will declare himself 'Emperor' before long. If he does, he will be afraid of Your Majesty's attack, and so he will try to invade us first. I shall be ready to defend our frontier. The army is prepared."

Just then one of the courtiers announced dispatches from Cao Zhen on military affairs, and Sima Yi closed his speech, saying, "Your Majesty should send someone especially to caution the Commander to be careful not to be tricked by Zhuge Liang, not to pursue rashly, and never to penetrate deeply into the enemy country."

The Ruler of Wei gave the order, and he sent the command by the hand of Minister Han Ji and gave him authority to warn Cao Zhen against giving battle.

Sima Yi escorted the royal messenger out of the city and, at parting, said, "I am giving this magnificent opportunity to obtain glory to Cao Zhen, but do not tell him the suggestion was mine; only quote the royal command. Tell him that defense is the best, pursuit is to be most cautious, and he is not to send any impetuous leader to follow up the enemy."

Han Ji agreed and took leave.

Cao Zhen was deep in affairs connected with his army when they brought news of a royal messenger, but he went forth to bid Han Ji welcome. When the ceremonial receipt of the edict had come to an end, he retired to discuss matters with Guo Huai and Sun Li.

"That is Sima Yi's idea," said Guo Huai with a laugh.

"But what of the idea?" asked Cao Zhen.

"It means that he perfectly understands Zhuge Liang's plans, and he will eventually have to be called in to defeat Shu."

"But if the Shu army holds its ground?"

"We will send Wang Shuang to reconnoiter and keep on the move along the by-roads so that they dare not attempt to bring up supplies. They must retreat when they have no more to eat, and we shall be able to beat them."

Then said Sun Li, "Let me go out to Qishan as if to escort a convoy from the West Valley Land, only the carts shall be laden with combustibles instead of grain. We will sprinkle sulfur and saltpeter over wood and reeds. The troops of Shu, who lack supplies, will surely seize the convoy and take it to their own camp, when we will set fire to the carts. When they are blazing, our hidden men can attack."

"It seems an excellent plan," said Cao Zhen.

And he issued the requisite orders: Sun Li to pretend to escort a convoy; Wang Shuang to prowl about the by-roads; Guo Huai and various generals to command in the Gu Valley, Jieting, and other strategic points. Also Zhang Hu, son of Zhang Liao, was made Leader of the Van, and Yue Chen, son of Yue Jing, was his second. These two were to remain on guard in the outermost camp.

Now at Qishan, Zhuge Liang sought to bring on a battle, and daily sent champions to provoke a combat. But the men of Wei would not come out.

Then Zhuge Liang called Jiang Wei and certain

others to him and said, "I do not know what to do. The enemy refuse battle, because they know we are short of food. We can get none by way of Chencang, and all other roads are very difficult. I reckon the grain we brought with us will not last a month."

While thus perplexed, they heard that many carts of provisions for Wei were passing by from the West Valley Land, and the convoy was commanded by Sun Li.

"What is known of this Sun Li?" asked Zhuge Liang.

A certain man of Wei replied, "He is a bold man. Once he was out hunting with the Ruler of Wei on Great Rock Hill, and a tiger suddenly appeared in front of his master's chariot. He jumped off his horse and dispatched the beast with his sword. He was rewarded with a Commandership. He is an intimate friend of Cao Zhen."

"This is a ruse," said Zhuge Liang. "They know we are short of food, and those carts are only a temptation. They are laden with combustibles. How can they imagine that I shall be deceived by this sort of thing, when I have fought them with fire so many times? If we go to seize the convoy, they will come and raid our camp. But I will meet ruse with ruse."

Then Zhuge Liang sent Ma Dai with order: "You and three thousand troops are to make your way to the enemy's store camp and, when the wind serves, to start a fire. When the stores are burning, the soldiers of Wei will come to surround our camp. That is how we will provoke a battle."

He also sent Ma Zheng and Zhang Ni with five thousand troops each to halt near the camp so that they might attack from without.

These having gone, he called Guan Xing and Zhang Bao, and said, "The outermost camp of Wei is on the main road. This night, when the enemy see a blaze, our camp will be attacked, so you two are to lie in wait on the two sides of the Wei camp and seize it when they have left."

Calling Hu Ban and Wu Yi, he said, "You are to lie in wait outside the camp to cut off the retreat of the force of Wei."

All these arrangements made, Zhuge Liang betook himself to a summit of the Qishan Mountains to watch the results.

The soldiers of Wei heard that their enemies were coming to seize the grain convoy and ran to tell Sun Li, who sent on a message to Cao Zhen.

Cao Zhen sent to the chief camp for Zhang Hu and Yue Chen and told them, "Look out for a signal blaze; that would mean the coming of the army of Shu, and then you are to raid the Shu camp immediately."

Zhang Hu and Yue Chen sent watchers on the tower to look out for the promised blaze.

Meanwhile Sun Li marched over and hid in the west hills to await the coming of the men of Shu. That night, at the second watch, Ma Dai came with his three thousand troops all silent, the soldiers with gags, the horses with a lashing round their muzzles. They saw tier after tier of carts on the hills, making an enclosure like a walled camp, and on the carts were planted many flags.

They waited. Presently the southwest wind came up, and then they launched the fire. Soon all the carts were in a blaze that lit up the sky. Sun Li saw the blaze and could only conclude that the troops of Shu had arrived and his own side were giving the signal, so he dashed out to attack. But soon two parties of soldiers were heard behind him closing in. These were Ma Zheng and Zhang Ni, who soon had Sun Li as in a net. Then he heard a third ominous roll of drums, which heralded the approach of Ma Dai from the direction of the blaze.

Under these several attacks, the troops of Wei quailed and gave way. The fire grew more and more fierce. Soldiers ran and horses stampeded, and the dead were too many to count. Sun Li made a dash through the smoke and fire of the battle and got away.

When Zhang Hu and Yue Chen saw the fire, they threw open the gates of their camp and sallied forth to help defeat the army of Shu by seizing their camp. But when they reached the Shu camp, they found it empty. So they hurried to set out to return. That was the moment for Hu Ban and Wu Yi to appear and cut off their retreat. However, they fought bravely and got through. But when at length they reached their own camp, they were met by arrows flying thick as locusts. For Guan Xing and Zhang Bao had taken possession in their absence.

They could only set out for headquarters to report

their mishap. As they neared Cao Zhen's camp, they met another remnant marching up. They were Sun Li's soldiers, and the two parties went into camp together and told the tale of their victimization. Cao Zhen thereafter looked to his defenses and attacked no more.

Thus victorious, the soldiers of Shu went to Zhuge Liang, who at once dispatched secret directions to Wei Yan. Then Zhuge Liang gave orders to break camp and retreat.

This move was not understood, and Yang Yi asked the leader, "O Prime Minister, you have just scored a victory, and the enemy have lost their bravery; why retreat?"

"Because we are short of food," said Zhuge Liang. "Our success lay in swift victory, but the enemy will not fight, and thus they weaken us day by day. Though we have worsted them now, they will soon be reinforced, and their light horse can cut off our provisions. Then we could not retreat at all. For a time they will not dare look at us, and we must take the occasion to do what they do not expect, and retreat. But I am solicitous about Wei Yan, who is on the Chencang road to keep off Wang Shuang. I fear he cannot get away. So I have sent him certain orders to slay Wang Shuang, and then the force of Wei will not dare to pursue."

Therefore the retreat began, but to deceive the enemy the watchmen were left in the empty camp to beat the watches through the night.

Cao Zhen was depressed at his recent misfortune. Then they told him Zhang He, General of the Left Army, had come. Zhang He came up to the gate, dismounted, and entered.

When he saw Cao Zhen, he said, "I have received a royal command to come and to be into your arrangements."

"Did you take leave of friend Sima Yi?" asked Cao Zhen.

Zhang He said, "His said to me that if you won the field the Shu army would stay, but if you did not, the Shu army would retreat. It seems that our side has missed success. Have you since found out what the troops of Shu are doing?"

"Not yet."

So Cao Zhen sent out some scouts, and they found empty camps. There were flags flying, but the army had been gone two days. Cao Zhen was disgusted.

When Wei Yan received his secret orders, he broke up camp that night and hastened toward Hanzhong. Wang Shuang's scouts heard this and told their chief, who hurried in pursuit. After about seven miles, he came in sight of Wei Yan's ensigns.

As soon as Wang Shuang got within hailing distance, he shouted, "Do not flee, Wei Yan!"

But no one looked back, so he again pressed forward.

Then he heard one of his guards behind him shouting, "There is a blaze in the camp outside the city wall. I think it is some wile of the enemy!"

Wang Shuang pulled up and, turning, saw the fire. He therefore tried to draw off his troops. Just as he passed a hill, a horseman suddenly came out of a wood.

"Here is Wei Yan!" shouted the horseman.

Wang Shuang was too startled to defend himself and fell at the first stroke of Wei Yan's blade. Wang Shuang's troops thought this was only the beginning of an ambush and serious attack, so they scattered. But really Wei Yan only had thirty men with him, and they moved off leisurely toward Hanzhong.

No man could better Zhuge Liang's foresight keen;
Brilliant as a comet where it flashed:
Back and forth at will his soldiers dashed,
And Wang Shuang's dead body marked where they had been.

The secret orders sent to Wei Yan was that he was to keep back thirty men and hide beside Wang Shuang's camp till that warrior left. Then the camp was to be set on fire. After that the thirty were to wait till Wang Shuang's return to fall upon him. The plan being successfully carried out, Wei Yan followed the retreating army into Hanzhong and handed over his command.

The Shu army having retreated safely to Hanzhong, feastings were held in celebration of the event.

Zhang He, who, failing to come up with the retiring enemy, presently returned to camp. Hao Zhao sent a letter to say that Wang Shuang had met his end. This loss caused Cao Zhen deep grief, so that he became ill and had to return to Luoyang. He left Zhang He, Sun Li, and Guo Huai to guard the approaches to Changan.

Meanwhile in the South Land, at a court held by Sun Quan, the Prince of Wu, a certain spy reported: "Prime Minister Zhuge Liang has invaded Wei twice, and Commander-in-Chief Cao Zhen has suffered great losses."

Thereupon his ministers urged on Sun Quan that he should attack Wei and try to gain the Middle Land.

However, Sun Quan could not make up his mind, and Zhang Zhao endeavored to prove to him that his hour was come by this memorial:

have heard that a phoenix has lately appeared in the hills east of Wuchang and bowed; that a yellow dragon has been seen in the Great River. My lord, your virtue matches that of Kings Yu and Tang, and your understanding is on a level with that of Kings Wen and Wu[xv]. Wherefore you should now proceed to the imperial style and then raise an army to maintain your authority."

And many other officers supported Zhang Zhao's proposal. They finally persuaded Sun Quan to decide upon the 'tiger' day in the forth month, in summer. They prepared an altar on the south of Wuchang, and on that day his courtiers formally requested him to ascend to the high place and assume the style of "Emperor".

"Yellow Dragon" was chosen as the style of the reign (AD 229). Sun Jian, the deceased father of the new Emperor, was given the title of the Martially Glorious Emperor, his mother Empress Wu, and his elder brother, Sun Ce, was made posthumously Prince of Changsha, and his son, Sun Deng, was styled Heir Apparent. The rank of Left Companion of the Heir Apparent was conferred upon the eldest son of Zhuge Jin, Zhuge Ke. The rank of Right Companion of the Heir Apparent was bestowed upon the second son of Zhang Zhao, Zhang Xi.

This son of Zhuge Jin was a person seven-span height, very clever, and especially apt at capping verses. Sun Quan liked him much. When Zhuge Ke was six, he went with his father to a banquet. Sun Quan noticed that Zhuge Jin had a long face, so he bade a man lead in a donkey, and he wrote on it with chalk, "My friend Zhuge Jin". Everyone roared with laughter. But the youngster ran up and added a few strokes making it read, "My friend Zhuge Jin's donkey". The guests were astonished at his ready wit, and praised him. Sun Quan was also pleased and made him a present of the donkey.

Another day, at a large official banquet, Sun Quan sent the boy with a goblet of wine to each courtier.

When he came to Zhang Zhao, the old man declined it, saying, "This is not the proper treatment for old age."

"Can you not make him drink?" said Sun Quan.

Then said Zhuge Ke to the old gentleman, "You remember Lu Wang[xvi]; he was ninety and yet gripped the signaling flags and wielded the axes of an army commander in the field. He never spoke of age. Nowadays in battle we put seniors behind, but at the banquet board we give them a front place. How can you say we do not treat old age properly?"

Zhang Zhao had no reply ready, and so had to drink. This sort of precocity endeared the boy to Sun Quan, and now Sun Quan made him the Left Companion to the Heir Apparent.

Zhang Zhao's son, Zhang Xi, was chosen for honor on account of the eminent services of his father, whose rank was only below that of Prince. Then Gu Yong became Prime Minister and Lu Xun, Regent Marshal. And Lu Xun assisted the Heir Apparent in the custody of Wuchang. Sun Quan himself returned to Jianye.

As Sun Quan seemed powerful and well established, the whole of his court turned their thoughts toward the suppression of Wei. Only Zhang Zhao opposed it and tendered counsels of internal reform.

"It is not well to begin Your Majesty's new reign with fighting. Rather improve learning and hide the sword; establish schools and so give the people the blessings of peace. Make a treaty with Shu to share the empire, and lay your plans slowly and carefully."

Sun Quan saw the wisdom of the advice. He sent

an envoy into the River Lands to lay the scheme of an alliance before the Latter Ruler. The Latter Ruler called his courtiers to discuss it. Many were opposed to Sun Quan as an upstart usurper and advised rejection of any friendly proposals from him.

Then Jiang Wan said, "We should get the opinion of Zhuge Liang."

So they sent and put the matter before the Prime Minister.

Zhuge Liang said, "Send an envoy with presents and felicitations and ask Sun Quan to send Lu Xun against Wei. Then Sima Yi will be engaged with Wu, and I may once more march to Qishan and attempt Capital Changan."

Wherefore the Chair of the Secretariat, Chen Zhen, was sent with presents of horses, a jeweled belt, gold and pearls, and precious things into the South Land to congratulate the Ruler of Wu on his newly assumed dignity. And the presents were accepted, and the bearer thereof honored and allowed to return.

When this was all over, Sun Quan called in Lu Xun and asked his opinion about the concerted attack on Wei. Lu Xun saw through the scheme at once.

"We owe this to Zhuge Liang's fear of Sima Yi," said he. "However, we must consent since Shu asks it. We will make a show of raising an army and in a measure support them. When Zhuge Liang has actually attacked Wei, we will make for the Middle Land ourselves."

Orders went forth for enlisting and training Jingzhou soldiers ready for an expedition to start presently.

When Chen Zhen returned to Hanzhong and reported to the Prime Minister, Zhuge Liang was still worried that he could not advanced hastily by the road through Chencang. So he sent scouts out first.

Soon the scouts brought the news back: "The defender of the city, Hao Zhao, is being very ill."

"That means success for me," cried he, cheering.

He called in Wei Yan and Jiang Wei, and said, "Take five thousand troops and hasten to Chencang. If you see a blaze, then attack."

They could hardly believe what the order was meant, and came again to see their chief and asked the exact date of departure.

Replied Zhuge Liang, "In three days you should be ready to march. Do not come to take leave of me, but set out as soon as possible."

After they had left his tent, he summoned Guan Xing and Zhang Bao and gave them secret instructions.

Now when Guo Huai heard that Commander Hao Zhao of Chencang was ill, he and Zhang He talked over the matter.

Guo Huai said, "Hao Zhao is very ill. You had better go and relieve him. I will report to the capital what we have done that they may arrange."

So Zhang He started with his three thousand troops to relieve the sick man.

Hao Zhao was indeed at the point of death, and suddenly they told him that the army of Shu had reached the walls. Hao Zhao roused himself and bade them go on the ramparts. But then fire broke out at each gate, a panic spread in the city, and the noise of the confusion startled the dying man so that he passed away just as the troops of Shu were bursting in.

When Wei Yan and Jiang Wei reached the walls, they were perplexed to find no sign of life. No flags were flying and no watchmen struck the hours. They delayed their attack for a time. Then they heard a bomb, and suddenly the wall was thick with flags, and there appeared the well-known figure of the minister.

"You have come too late," cried Zhuge Liang.

Both dropped out of the saddle and prostrated themselves.

"Really, you are supernatural, O Prime Minister!" they cried.

They entered the city, and then he explained to them, saying, "I heard the news that Hao Zhao was seriously sick, so I sent you with the deadline of three days as a decoy to calm the people of this city. Then I hid myself in the ranks of another force under Guan Xing and Zhang Bao, which came to Chencang by double marches. Also, I had sent spies into the city to start the fires and throw the defenders into confusion. An army without a leader could never fight, and I could take the city easily. This is an instance of the rule of war: 'Do the unexpected; attack the unprepared.'"

They bowed. In commiseration Zhuge Liang sent all the family of Hao Zhao, and his coffin, over to Wei, thus showing his sense of the dead man's loyalty.

Turning once more to Wei Yan and Jiang Wei, he said, "But do not divest yourself of your armor. Go and attack San Pass and drive away the guards while they are in a state of surprise. If you delay, Wei will have sent reinforcements."

They went. Surely enough the capture of San Pass was easy as the Wei soldiers scattered. But when they went up to look around, they saw a great cloud of dust moving toward them. The Wei reinforcements were already near.

They remarked to each other, "The Prime Minister's foresight was superhuman."

When they had looked a little longer, they saw the leader of the Wei army then approaching was Zhang He.

They then divided their soldiers to hold the approaches. When Zhang He saw that all was prepared, he retired. Wei Yan followed and fought a battle, defeating Zhang He heavily.

Wei Yan sent to report his success, but Zhuge Liang had already left Chencang and had gone into the Xie Valley to capture the county of Jianwei. Other armies from Shu followed. Moreover, the

Latter Ruler sent Chen Shi to assist in the campaign. Zhuge Liang then marched his main force to Qishan and there made a camp. Then he called an assembly of officers.

"Twice have I gone out by Qishan without success, but at last I am here. I think Wei will resume the former battle ground and oppose us. If so, they will assume that I shall attack Yongcheng and Meicheng and send armies to defend them. But I see Yinping and Wudu are connected with Hanzhong. If I can win these, I can drive a wedge into the Wei force. Who will go to take these places?"

Jiang Wei and Wang Ping offered themselves. The former was sent with ten thousand troops to capture Wudu; the latter, with an equal force, went to Yinping.

Zhang He went back to Changan and saw Guo Huai and Sun Li, to whom he said, "Chencang is lost, Hao Zhao is dead, and San Pass is taken. Zhuge Liang is again at Qishan, and thence has sent out two armies."

Guo Huai was frightened, saying, "In that case, Yongcheng and Meicheng are in danger."

Leaving Zhang He to guard Changan, Guo Huai sent Sun Li to Yongcheng, and he himself set out at once for Meicheng. He sent an urgent report to Luoyang.

At Wei's next court the Emperor was informed of all the misfortunes in the west: "Chencange has fallen, and Hao Zhao has died. Zhuge Liang has captured San Pass. He is camping at Qishan and is planning to invade Wei."

Cao Rui was alarmed.

Just then Man Chong reported, "Sun Quan has declared himself Emperor, and Lu Xun is drilling his army in Wuchang. An invasion from the east can be expected soon."

Cao Rui was embarrassed and frightened. Cao Zhen, being ill, could not be consulted, and Sima Yi was called. He was ready with a proposal.

"In my humble opinion, Wu will not attack us," said Sima Yi.

"What makes you think so?" asked the Ruler of Wei.

"Because Zhuge Liang still resents, and wishes to avenge, the event at Xiaoting. He never ceases to desire to absorb Wu. His only fear is that we may swoop down upon Shu. That is why there is an alliance with Wu. Lu Xun knows it also quite well, and he is only making a show of raising an army as they arranged. The truth is he is sitting on the fence. Hence Your Majesty may disregard the menace on the east, and only protect yourself against Shu."

"Your insight is very profound," said the Ruler of Wei.

Sima Yi was created Commander-in-Chief of all the forces in the west, and the Ruler of Wei directed a courtier to go to Cao Zhen for the seal.

"I would rather go myself," said Sima Yi.

So Sima Yi left the audience and went to the palace of Cao Zhen, where presently he saw the invalid. First he asked after his health and then gradually opened his errand.

"Shu and Wu have made an alliance to invade Wei and share its domains, and Zhuge Liang is at Qishan the third time. Have you heard, Illustrious Sir?"

"My people have kept back all news as I am ill," said he, startled. "But if this is true, the country is in danger. Why have they not made you Commander-in-Chief to stop this invasion?"

"I am unequal to the post," said Sima Yi.

"Bring the seal and give it to him," said Cao Zhen to his attendants.

"You are anxious on my account. Really I am only come to lend you an arm. I dare not accept the seal."

Cao Zhen started up, saying, "If you do not take it, I shall have to go to see the Emperor, ill as I am. The Middle Land is in danger."

"Really the Emperor has already shown his kindness, but I dare not accept his offer."

"If you have been appointed, then Shu will be driven off."

Thrice Sima Yi declined the seal, but eventually he received it into his hands as he knew Cao Zhen was sincere. Then he took leave of the Ruler of Wei and marched to Changan.

The seal of office changes hands,
Two armies now one force become.

Sima Yi's success or failure will be told in the next chapter.

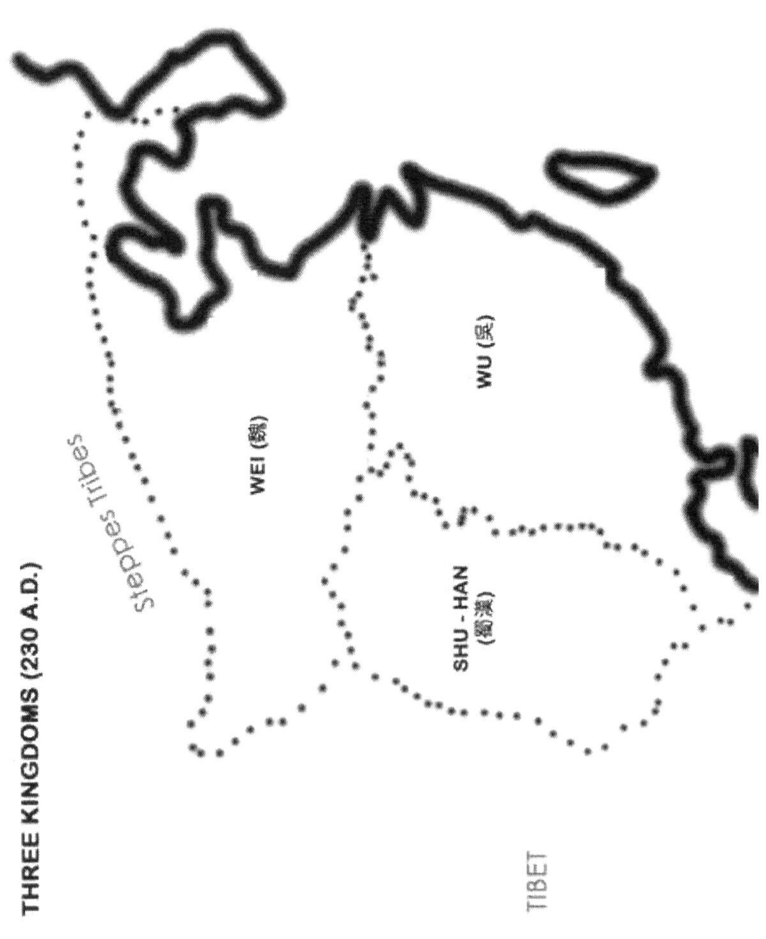
THREE KINGDOMS (230 A.D.)
Steppes Tribes
WEI (魏)
WU (吳)
SHU - HAN
(蜀漢)
TIBET

Chapter 99

**Zhuge Liang Defeats The Wei Army;
Sima Yi Invades The West River Land.**

The fourth month of Beginning Prosperity, seventh year (AD 229), found Zhuge Liang camped at Qishan in three camps, waiting to attack Wei.

When Sima Yi reached Changan, the officer in command, Zhang He, told him all that had happened. He gave Zhang He the post of Leader of the Van, with Dai Ling as his Assistant General and a hundred thousand troops, and then marched out toward the enemy, camping on River Wei's south bank.

When the local commanders Guo Huai and Sun Li went to see the new Commander-in-Chief, he asked, "Have you fought any battle with Shu?"

"Not yet," said they.

Sima Yi said, "The enemy had a long march; their chance lay in attacking quickly. As they have not attacked, they have some deep laid scheme to work out. What news have you from the counties of West Valley Land?"

Guo Huai replied, "The scouts say that the greatest care is being taken in every county. But there is no news from Wudu and Yinping."

"I must send someone to fight a decisive battle with them there. You get away as quickly and privily as you can to the rescue of those two cities, and then attack the rear of the Shu army so as to throw them into disorder."

They set out to obey these orders, and on the way they fell to discussing Sima Yi.

"How does Sima Yi compare with Zhuge Liang?" said Guo Huai.

"Zhuge Liang is by far the better," replied Sun Li.

"Though Zhuge Liang may be the cleverer, yet this scheme of our leader's shows him to be superior to most people. The enemy may have got those two cities. Yet when we unexpectedly fall upon their rear, they will certainly be disordered."

Soon after this a scout came in to report: "Wang Ping has captured Yinping, and Wudu is in possession of Jiang Wei. Furthermore, the Shu army is not far in front."

Said Sun Li, "There is some crafty scheme afoot. Why are they prepared for battle in the open when they hold two cities? We had better retire."

Guo Huai agreed, and they issued orders to face about and retreat. Just then a bomb exploded, and, at the same time, there suddenly appeared from the cover of some hills a small body of troops. On the flag that came forward they read Han Prime Minister Zhuge Liang, and in the midst of the company they saw him, seated in a small chariot. On his left was Guan Xing, and on his right Zhang Bao.

They were quite taken aback.

Zhuge Liang laughed and said, "Do not run away! Did you think that your leader's ruse would take me in? Sima Yi sent a challenge to fight every day, indeed, while you were to slip round behind my army and attack! I have the two cities---Wudu and Yinping. If you have not come to surrender, then hurry up and fight a battle with me."

By now Guo Huai and Sun Li were really frightened. Then behind them there rose a shout as of battle, and Wang Ping and Jiang Wei began to smite them in the rear, while Guan Xing and Zhang Bao bore down upon them in front. They were soon utterly broken, and the two leaders escaped by scrambling up the hillside.

Zhang Bao saw them, and was urging his steed forward to catch them, when unhappily he and his horse went over together into a gully. When they picked him up, they found that he had been kicked in the head and was badly hurt.

Zhuge Liang sent him back to Chengdu.

It has been said that Guo Huai and Sun Li escaped. They got back to Sima Yi's camp and said, "Wudu and Yinping were both in the enemy's possession, and Zhuge Liang had prepared an ambush, so that we were attacked front and rear. We lost the day and only escaped on foot."

"It is no fault of yours," said Sima Yi. "The fact is he is sharper than I. Now go to defend Yongcheng and Meicheng and remain on the defensive. Do not go out to give battle. I have a plan to defeat them."

These two having left, Sima Yi called in Zhang He and Dai Ling and said, "Zhuge Liang has captured

Wudu and Yinping. He must restore order and confidence among the people of these places and so will be absent from his camp. You two will take ten thousand troops each, start tonight and make your way quietly to the rear of the Shu army. Then you will attack vigorously. When you have done that, I shall lead out the army in front of them and array ready for battle. While they are in disorder, I shall make my attack. Their camp ought to be captured. If I can win the advantage of these hills, their defeat will be easy."

These two left, Dai Ling marching on the left and Zhang He on the right. They took by-roads and got well to the rear of the Shu army. In the third watch they struck the high road and joined forces. Then they marched toward the enemy. After about ten miles there was a halt in front. The two leaders galloped up to see what had caused it, and found many straw-carts drawn across the road.

"The enemy has been prepared," said Zhang He. "We should return."

Just as they ordered the troops to turn about, torches broke into flame all over the hills, the drums rolled, trumpets blared, and soldiers sprang out on every side.

At the same time Zhuge Liang shouted from the hill-top, "Dai Ling and Zhang He, listen to my words! Your master reckoned that I should be busy restoring order in the two cities and so should not be in my camp. Wherefore he sent you to take the camp, and you have just fallen into my snare. As you are leaders of no great importance, I shall not harm you. Dismount and yield."

Zhang He's wrath blazed forth at this, and he pointed at Zhuge Liang, crying, "You peasant out of the woods, invader of our great country! How dare you use such words to me? Wait till I catch you: I will tear you to shreds!"

He galloped forward to ascend the hill, his spear ready for the thrust. But the arrows and stones pelted too quickly. Then he turned and dashed in among the Shu soldiers, scattering them right and left. He got clear, but he saw Dai Ling was not with him. At once he turned back, fought his way to his comrade and brought Dai Ling out safely.

Zhuge Liang on the hill-top watched this warrior and saw he was a right doughty fighting man.

"I have heard that soldiers stood aghast when Zhang Fei fought his great fight with Zhang He. Now I can judge Zhang He's valor for myself. He will do harm to Shu one day if I spare him. He will have to be removed."

Then Zhuge Liang returned to his camp.

By this time Sima Yi had completed his battle line and was waiting the moment of disorder in the Shu army to attack. Then he saw Zhang He and Dai Ling come limping back dejected and crestfallen.

They said, "Zhuge Liang forestalled us. He was well prepared, and so we were quite defeated."

"He is more than human!" exclaimed Sima Yi. "We must retreat."

So the whole army retired into the fortified camps and would not come out.

Thus a great victory fell to Shu, and their booty was immense: Weapons and horses innumerable. Zhuge Liang led his army back to camp. Thereafter he sent parties to offer a challenge at the gate of the Wei camp every day, but the soldiers remained obstinately behind their shelters and would not appear. When this had continued half a month Zhuge Liang grew sad.

Then came Fei Yi from Capital Chengdu with an edict of the Emperor. Fei Yi was received with all respect, and incense was burnt as propriety demanded. This done, the command was unsealed, and Zhuge Liang read:

"The failure at Jieting was really due to the fault of Ma Su. However, you held yourself responsible and blamed yourself very severely. It would have been a serious matter for me to have withstood your intentions, and so I did what you insisted on.

"However, that was a glorious exploit last year when Wang Shuang was slain. This year, Guo Huai has been driven back and the Qiangs have been reduced; the two counties of Wudu and Yinping have been captured; you have driven fear into the hearts of all evil doers and thus rendered magnificent services.

"But the world is in confusion, and the original evil has not been destroyed. You fill a great office, for you direct the affairs of the state. It is not well for you to remain under a cloud for any length of time and cloak your grand virtue, wherefore I restore you to the rank of Prime Minister and pray you not to decline the honor."

Zhuge Liang heard the edict to the end and then

said, "My task is not yet accomplished. How can I return to my duties as Prime Minister? I must really decline to accept this."

Fei Yi said, "If you decline this, you flout the desires of the Emperor and also show contempt for the feelings of the army. At any rate accept for the moment."

Then Zhuge Liang humbly bowed acquiescence.

Fei Yi took leave and returned.

Seeing that Sima Yi remained obstinately on the defensive, Zhuge Liang thought of a plan by which to draw him. He gave orders to break camp and retire.

When the scouts told Sima Yi, he said, "We may not move. Certainly there is some deep craftiness in this move."

Zhang He said, "It must mean that their food is exhausted. Why not pursue?"

"I reckon that Zhuge Liang laid up ample supplies last year. Now the wheat is ripe, and he has plenty of every sort. Transport might be difficult, but yet he could hold out half a year. Why should he run away? He sees that we resolutely refuse battle, and he is trying some ruse to inveigle us into fighting. Send out spies to a distance to see what is going on."

They reconnoitered a long way round, and the scouts returned to say that a camp had been formed ten miles away.

"Ah, then he is not running away," said Sima Yi. "Remain on the defensive still more strictly and do not advance."

Ten days passed without further news; nor did the soldiers of Shu offer the usual challenge. Again spies were sent far afield, and they reported a further retreat of ten miles and a new encampment.

"Zhuge Liang is certainly working some scheme," said Sima Yi. "Do not pursue."

Another ten days passed and spies went out. The enemy had gone ten miles farther and encamped.

Zhang He said, "What makes you so over-suspicious? I can see that Zhuge Liang is retreating into Hanzhong, only he is doing it gradually and arousing our suspicion. Why not pursue before it is too late. Let me go and fight one battle."

"No," said Sima Yi. "A defeat would destroy the morale of our soldiers, and I will not risk it. Zhuge Liang's vile tricks are innumerable."

"If I go and get beaten, I will stand the full rigor of military punishment," said Zhang He.

"Well, if you are set on going, we will divide the army. You take your wing and go, but you will have to fight your best. I will follow to help in case of need. Tomorrow you should march only halfway and rest your troops for the battle."

So Zhang He got independent command of thirty thousand troops and took Dai Ling as his second in command, and he had a few score of generals as assistants. Halfway they camped. Then Sima Yi, leaving a substantial guard for his camp, set out along the same road with fifty thousand troops.

Zhuge Liang knew the movements of the army of Wei and when Zhang He's army camped to rest. In the night he summoned his generals and told them.

"The enemy are coming in pursuit and will fight desperately. You will have to fight everyone of you like ten, but I will set an ambush to attack their rear. Only a wise and bold leader is fit for this task."

Wang Ping stepped forth and said he was willing to go on this expedition.

"But if you fail, what then?" said Zhuge Liang.

"Then there is the military rule."

Zhuge Liang sighed. "Wang Ping is most loyal. He is willing to risk wounds and death in his country's service. However, the enemy are in two divisions, one coming in front, the other trying to get round to the rear. Wang Ping is crafty and bold, but he cannot be in two places at once, so I must have yet another general. Is it that among you there is no other willing to devote himself to death?"

He did not wait long for a reply. Zhang Yi stepped to the front.

"Zhang He is a most famous leader in Wei and valorous beyond all compare. You are not a match for him," said Zhuge Liang.

"If I fail, may my head fall at the tent door," said Zhang Yi.

"Since you wish to go, I accept you. Each of you shall have ten thousand veterans. You will hide in the valleys till the enemy come up, and you will let them pass. Then you will fall upon their rear. If Sima Yi comes, you must divide the army, Zhang Yi to hold the rear and Wang Ping to check the advance. But they will fight desperately, and I must find a way to aid you."

When they had gone, Jiang Wei and Liao Hua were called, and Zhuge Liang said, "I am going to give you a silken bag. You are to proceed secretly into those mountains in front. When you see that Zhang Yi and Wang Ping are in great straits with the enemy, then open the bag and you will find a plan of escape."

After this he gave secret instructions to four other generals---Hu Ban, Wu Yi, Ma Zheng, and Zhang Ni---to observe the enemy and, if the enemy seemed confident of victory, to retire, fighting at intervals, till they saw Guan Xing come up, when they could turn and fight their best.

Then calling Guan Xing, he said to them, "Hide in the valleys with five thousand troops till you see a red flag flutter out, and then fall on the enemy."

Zhang He and Dai Ling hurried along like a rain squall till they were suddenly confronted by Ma Zheng, Zhang Ni, Wu Yi, and Hu Ban. Zhang He dashed toward his enemy, and then they retired, stopping at intervals to fight. The Wei army pursued for about seven miles.

It was the sixth moon and very hot, so that soldiers and horses sweated profusely. When they had gone ten miles farther, the soldiers and horses were panting and nearly spent. Then Zhuge Liang, who had watched the fighting from a hill, gave the signal for Guan Xing to emerge and join battle. Ma Zheng, Zhang Ni, Hu Ban, and Wu Yi all led on their troops. Zhang He and Dai Ling fought well, but they could not extricate themselves and retire.

Presently, with a roll of drums, Wang Ping and Zhang Yi came out and made for the rear to cut the retreat.

"Why do you not fight to death?" shouted Zhang He to his generals when he saw the new dangers.

The soldiers of Wei dashed this way and that, but were stayed at every attempt. Then there was heard another roll of drums, and Sima Yi came up in the rear. He at once signaled to his generals to surround Wang Ping and Zhang Yi.

"Our minister is truly wonderful. The battle goes just as he foretold," cried Zhang Yi. "He will surely send help now, and we will fight to the death."

Thereupon the Shu force were divided into two parties. Wang Ping led one army to hold up Zhang He and Dai Ling; Zhang Yi led the other division to oppose Sima Yi. On both sides the fighting was keen and continued all the day.

From their station on a hill, Jiang Wei and Liao Hua watched the battle. They saw that the Wei force was very strong and their side was in danger and slowly giving way.

"Now surely is the moment to open the bag," said Jiang Wei.

So the bag was opened, and they read the letter. It said:

"If Sima Yi comes and Wang Ping and Zhang Yi seem hard pressed, you are to divide forces and go off to attack Sima Yi's camp, which will cause him to retire, and then you can attack him as his army is in disorder. The actual capture of the camp is not of great moment."

So Jiang Wei and Liao Hua divided the force and started for the enemy's camp.

Now Sima Yi had really feared that he would fall victim to some ruse of Zhuge Liang, so he had arranged for messengers and news to meet him at intervals along the road.

Sima Yi was pressing his troops to fight when a messenger galloped up to report: "The soldiers of Shu are making for the main camp by two directions."

Sima Yi was frightened and changed color. He turned on his generals, saying, "I knew Zhuge Liang would plan some trick, but you did not believe me. You forced me to pursue, and now the whole scheme has gone astray."

Thereupon he gathered in his army and turned to retire. The troops went hurriedly and got into disorder. Zhang Yi came up behind, causing huge damage to the Wei army. Zhang He and Dai Ling, having but few troops left, sought refuge among the hills. The victory was to Shu, and Guan Xing came up helping in the rout wherever there appeared a chance to strike.

Sima Yi, defeated, hurried to the camp. But when he reached it, the army of Shu had already left. He gathered in his broken army and abused his generals as the cause of his failure.

"You are all ignorant of the proper way to wage war, and think it simply a matter of valor and rude strength. This is the result of your unbridled desire to go out and give battle. For the future no one of you will move without definite orders, and I will apply strict military law to any who disobey."

They were all greatly ashamed and retired to their quarters. In this fight the losses of Wei were very heavy, not only in soldiers, but in horses and weapons.

Zhuge Liang led his victorious army to their camp. He intended to advance again, when a messenger arrived from Capital Chengdu with the sad news that Zhang Bao had died. When they told Zhuge Liang he uttered a great cry, blood gushed from his mouth and he fell in a swoon. He was raised and taken to his tent, but he was too ill to march and had to keep his bed. His generals were much grieved.

A later poet sang:

Fierce and valiant was Zhang Bao,
Striving hard to make a name;
Sad the gods should interfere
And withhold a hero's fame!
Zhuge Liang wept his end
In the western winds blowing.
For he knew the warrior gone,
This grieving is beyond knowing.

Zhuge Liang's illness continued. Ten days later he summoned to his tent Dong Jue and Fan Jian, and said, "I feel void and am too ill to carry on, and the best thing for me is to return into Hanzhong and get well. You are to keep my absence perfectly secret, for Sima Yi will certainly attack if he hears."

Zhuge Liang issued orders to break up the camp that night, and the army retired into Hanzhong forthwith. Sima Yi only heard of it five days later, and he knew that again he had been outwitted.

"The man appears like a god and disappears like a demon. He is too much for me," sighed Sima Yi.

Sima Yi set certain generals over the camp and placed others to guard the commanding positions, and he also marched homeward.

As soon as the Shu army was settled in Hanzhong, Zhuge Liang went to Chengdu for treatment. The officials of all ranks came to greet him and escort him to his palace. The Latter Ruler also came to inquire after his condition and sent his own physicians to treat him. So gradually he recovered.

In Beginning Prosperity, eighth year and seventh month (AD 230), Cao Zhen, the Grand Commander in Wei, had recovered, and he sent a memorial to his master, saying,

"Shu has invaded more than once and threatened Changan. If this state be not destroyed, it will ultimately be our ruin. The autumn coolness is now here. The army is in good form, and it is the time most favorable for an attack on Shu. I desire to take Sima Yi as colleague and march into

Hanzhong to exterminate this wretched horde and free the borders from trouble."

Personally, the Ruler of Wei approved, but he consulted Liu Ye, saying, "Cao Zhen proposes an attack on Shu. How about that?"

Liu Ye replied, "The Grand Commander speaks well. If that state be not destroyed, it will be to our hurt. Your Majesty should give effect to his desire."

The Ruler of Wei nodded.

When Liu Ye went home, a crowd of officers flocked to inquire, saying, "We heard the Emperor has consulted you about an expedition against Shu: What think you?"

"No such thing," said Liu Ye. "Shu is too difficult a country to invade. It would be a mere waste of humans and weapons."

They left him. Then Yang Jin went into the Emperor and said, "It is said that yesterday Liu Ye advised Your Majesty to fall upon Shu. Today when we talked with him, he said Shu could not be attacked. This is treating Your Majesty with indignity, and you should issue a command to punish him."

Wherefore Cao Rui called in Liu Ye and asked him to explain.

Liu Ye replied, "I have studied the details. Shu cannot be attacked."

Cao Rui laughed.

In a short time Yang Jin left.

Then Liu Ye said, "Yesterday I advised Your Majesty to attack Shu. That being a matter of state policy should be divulged to no person. The essential of a military move is secrecy."

Then Cao Rui understood, and thereafter Liu Ye was held in greater consideration.

Ten days later Sima Yi came to court, and Cao Zhen's memorial was shown him.

Sima Yi replied, "The moment is opportune. I do not think there is any danger from Wu."

Cao Zhen was created Minister of War, General Who Conquers the West, and Commander-in-Chief of the Western Expedition; Sima Yi was made Grand Commander, General Who Conquers the West, and was second in command; and Liu Ye was made Instructor of the Army. These three then left the court, and the army of four hundred thousand troops marched to Changan, intending to dash to Saber Pass and attack Hanzhong. The army was joined by Guo Huai and Sun Li.

The defenders of Hanzhong brought the news to Zhuge Liang, then quite recovered and engaged in training his army and elaborating the "Eight Arrays". All was in an efficient state and ready for an attack on Changan.

When Zhuge Liang heard of the intended attack, he called up Zhang Ni and Wang Ping and gave orders: "You are to lead one thousand troops to Chencang and garrison that road so as to check the Wei army."

The two replied, "It is said the Wei army numbers four hundred thousand, though they pretend to have eight hundred thousand. But they are very numerous, and a thousand troops is a very small force to meet them."

Zhuge Liang replied, "I would give you more, but I fear to make it hard for the soldiers. If there be a failure, I shall not hold you responsible. I send you thus; you may be sure there is a meaning in it. I observed the stars yesterday, and I see there will be a tremendous rain this month. The army of Wei may consist of any number of legions, but they will be unable to penetrate into a mountainous country. So there is no need to send a large force. You will come to no harm, and I shall lead the main body into Hanzhong and rest for a month while the enemy retreats. Then I shall smite them. My strong army needs only one hundred thousand to defeat their worn four hundred thousand. Do not say any more, but get off quickly."

This satisfied Wang Ping and Zhang Ni, and they left, while Zhuge Liang led the main body out toward Hanzhong. Moreover, every station was ordered to lay in a stock of wood and straw and grain enough for a whole month's use, ready against the autumn rains. A month's holiday was given, and food and clothing were issued in advance. The expedition was postponed for the present.

When Cao Zhen and Sima Yi approached Chencang and entered the city, they could not find a single house.

They questioned some of the people near, who

said, "Zhuge Liang had burned everything before he left."

Then Cao Zhen proposed to advance along the road, but Sima Yi opposed, saying that the stars foretold much rain.

"I have watched the Heaven, and the stars' movement signals long rains. If we get deep in a difficult country and are always victorious, it is all very well. But if we lose, we shall not get out again. Better remain in this city and build what shelter we can against the rains."

Cao Zhen followed his advice. In the middle of the month the rain began, and came down in a deluge so that the surrounding country was three feet under water. The equipment of the soldiers was soaked, and the soldiers themselves could get no place to sleep. For a whole month the rain continued. The horses could not be fed, and the soldiers grumbled incessantly. They sent to Luoyang, and the Ruler of Wei himself ceremonially prayed for fine weather, but with no effect.

Minister Wang Su sent up a memorial:

"The histories say that when supplies have to be conveyed a long distance, the soldiers are starved; if they have to gather brushwood before they can cook, then the army is not full fed. This applies to ordinary expeditions in an ordinary country. If, in addition, the army has to march through a difficult country and roads have to be cut, the labor is doubled. Now this expedition is hindered by rain and steep and slippery hills; movement is cramped and supplies can only be maintained with difficulty. All is most unpropitious to the army.

"Cao Zhen has been gone over a month and has only got half through the valley. Road making is monopolizing all energies, and the fighting soldiers have to work on them. The state of affairs is the opposite to ideal, and the fighting soldiers dislike it.

"I may quote certain parallels. King Wu of Zhou attacked the last king of Shang Dynasty; he went through the pass, but returned. In recent times Emperors Cao and Pi, attacking Sun Quan, reached the river, and went no farther. Did they not recognize limitations and act accordingly? I pray Your Majesty remember the grave difficulties caused by the rain and put an end to this expedition. By and by another occasion will arise for using force, and in the joy of overcoming difficulties the people will forget death."

The Ruler of Wei could not make up his mind, but two other memorials by Yang Fu and Hua Xin followed, and then he issued the command to return, which was sent to Cao Zhen and Sima Yi.

Cao Zhen and Sima Yi had already discussed the abandonment of the expedition.

Cao Zhen had said, "We have had rain for a whole month, and the soldiers are downhearted and think only of getting home again. How can we stop them?"

Sima Yi replied, "Return is best."

"If Zhuge Liang pursue, how shall we repulse him?"

"We can leave an ambush."

While they were discussing this matter, the Emperor's command arrived. Whereupon they faced about and marched homeward.

Now Zhuge Liang had reckoned upon this month of rain and so had had his troops camped in a safe place. Then he ordered the main army to assemble at Red Slope and camp there.

He summoned his officers to his tent and said, "In my opinion the enemy must retire, for the Ruler of Wei will issue such an order. To retreat needs preparation, and if we pursue, we will fall in their trap. So we will let them retire without molestation. Some other plan must be evolved."

So when Wang Ping sent news of the retreat of the enemy, the messenger carried back the order not to pursue.

It is only lost labor to cover retreat
When your enemy does not pursue.

By what means Zhuge Liang intended to defeat Wei will be told in the next chapter.

Chapter 100

Raiding A Camp, The Shu Soldiers Defeat Cao Zhen;
Contesting Array Battles, Zhuge Liang Shames Sima Yi.

When the Shu officers got to know that the Wei army had gone but they were not to pursue, they were inclined to discontent and went in a body to the Prime Minister's tent and said, "The rain has driven the enemy away. Surely it is the moment to pursue."

Zhuge Liang replied, "Sima Yi is an able leader who would not retreat without leaving an ambush to cover it. If we pursue we shall fall victims. Let him go in peace, and I shall then get through the Xie Valley and take Qishan, making use of the enemy's lack of defense."

"But there are other ways of taking Changan," said they. "Why only take Qishan?"

"Because Qishan is the first step to Changan, and I want to gain the advantage of position. And every transportation from the West Valley Land must come this way. It rests on River Wei in front and is backed by the Xie Valley. It gives the greatest freedom of movement and is a natural maneuvering ground. That is why I want it."

They bowed to his wisdom.

Then Zhuge Liang dispatched Wei Yan, Zhang Ni, Du Qiong, and Chen Shi for Gu Valley; and he sent Ma Dai, Wang Ping, Zhang Yi, and Ma Zheng for the Xie Valley; all were to meet at the Qishan Mountains. He led the main army himself, with Guan Xing and Liao Hua in the van.

When the Wei army retreated, Cao Zhen and Sima Yi remained in the rear superintending the movement. They sent a reconnoitering party along the old road to Chencang, and they returned saying no enemy was to be seen. Ten days later the leaders, who had commanded in the ambush, joined the main body saying that they had seen no sign of the enemy.

Cao Zhen said, "This continuous autumn rain has rendered all the plank trails[xvii] impassable. How could the soldiers of Shu know of our retreat?"

"They will appear later," said Sima Yi.

"How can you know?"

"These late five dry days they have not pursued, because they think we shall have left a rearguard in ambush. Therefore they have let us get well away. But after we have gone, they will try to occupy Qishan."

Cao Zhen was not convinced.

"Why do you doubt?" asked Sima Yi. "I think Zhuge Liang will certainly advance by way of the two valleys, and you and I should guard the entrances. I give them ten days, and if they do not appear, I will come to your camp painted in the face to own my mistake."

"If the army of Shu do appear, I will give you the

girdle and the steed that the Emperor gave me," replied Cao Zhen.

And they split their force, Cao Zhen taking up his station on the west of Qishan in the Xie Valley, and Sima Yi going to the east in the Gu Valley.

As soon as the camp was settled, Sima Yi led a cohort into hiding in the valley. The remainder of the force was placed in detachments on the chief roads.

Sima Yi disguised himself as a soldier and went among the soldiers to get a private survey of all the camps.

In one of them he happened upon a junior officer who was complaining, saying, "The rain has drenched us for days, and they would not retire. Now they have camped here for a wager. They have no pity for us soldiers."

Sima Yi returned to his tent and assembled his officers.

Hauling out the grumbler, Sima Yi said to him, angrily, "The state feeds and trains soldiers a thousand days for one hour's service. How dare you give vent to your spleen to the detriment of discipline?"

The man would not confess, so his comrades were called to bear witness. Still he would not own up.

"I am not here for a wager, but to overcome Shu," said Sima Yi. "Now you all have done well and are going home, but only this fellow complains and is guilty of mutinous conduct."

Sima Yi ordered the lictors to put him to death, and in a short time they produced his head.

The others were terrified, but Sima Yi said, "All you must do your utmost to guard against the enemy. When you hear a bomb explode, rush out on all sides and attack."

With this order they retired.

Now Wei Yan, Zhang Ni, Chen Shi, and Du Qiong, with twenty thousand troops, entered the Gu Valley. As they were marching, Adviser Deng Zhi came.

"I bear an order from the Prime Minister. As you go out of the valley, beware of the enemy," said Deng Zhi.

Chen Shi said, "Why is the Prime Minister so full of doubts? We know the soldiers of Wei have suffered severely from the rain and must hasten home. They will not lay any ambush. We are doing double marches and shall gain a great victory. Why are we to delay?"

Deng Zhi replied, "You know the Prime Minister's plans always succeed. How dare you disobey his orders?"

Chen Shi smiled, saying, "If he was really so resourceful, we should not have lost Jieting."

Wei Yan, recalling that Zhuge Liang had rejected his plan, also laughed, and said, "If he had listened to me and gone out through Ziwu Valley, not only Changan but Luoyang too would be ours. Now he is bent on taking Qishan. What is the good of it? He gave us the order to advance and now he stops us. Truly the orders are confusing."

Then said Chen Shi, "I will tell you what I will do. I shall take only five thousand troops, get through the Gu Valley, and camp at Qishan. Then you will see how ashamed the Prime Minister will look."

Deng Zhi argued and persuaded, but to no avail: The willful leader hurried on to get out of the valley. Deng Zhi could only return as quickly as possible and report.

Chen Shi proceeded. He had gone a few miles when he heard a bomb, and he was in an ambush. He tried to withdraw, but the valley was full of the enemy and he was surrounded as in an iron cask. All his efforts to get out failed. Then there was a shout, and Wei Yan came to the rescue. Wei Yan saved his comrade, but Chen Shi's five thousand troops was reduced to about five hundred, and these wounded. The Wei soldiers pursued, but two other divisions of Zhang Ni and Du Qiong prevented the pursuit, and finally the army of Wei retired.

Chen Shi and Wei Yan who had criticized Zhuge Liang's powers of prevision no longer doubted that he saw very clearly. They regretted their own shortsightedness.

When Deng Zhi told his chief of the bad behavior of Chen Shi and Wei Yan, Zhuge Liang only laughed.

Said he, "Wei Yan has been disposed to disobey and resent. However, I value his valor, and so I have employed him. But he will do real harm some day."

Then came a messenger, who reported, "Chen Shi had fallen into an ambush and lost more than four thousand troops. He has led his remained five hundred horse back to the gorge."

Zhuge Liang sent Deng Zhi back again to Gu Valley to console with Chen Shi and so keep him from actual mutiny.

Then Zhuge Liang called to his tent Ma Dai and Wang Ping, and said, "If there are any troops of Wei in the Xie Valley, you are to go across the mountains, marching by night and concealing yourselves by day, and make for the east of Qishan. When you arrive, make a fire as a signal."

Next he gave orders to Ma Zheng and Zhang Ni, saying, "You are to follow the by-roads to the west of Qishan. You are also to march by night and conceal by day. Then you are to join up with Ma Dai and Wang Ping. The four of you shall make a joint attack on Cao Zhen's camp. I shall lead the army through the valley and attack the camp in the center."

After the four Generals left, Guan Xing and Liao Hua also received secret orders.

The armies marched rapidly. Not long after starting, two other detachments led by Hu Ban and Wu Yi received secret orders and left the main body.

The doubts about the coming of the Shu army made Cao Zhen careless, and he allowed his soldiers to become slack and rest. He only thought of getting through the allotted ten days, when he would have the laugh against his colleague.

Seven of the days had passed, when a scout reported a few odd men of Shu in the valley. Cao Zhen sent Qin Liang with five thousand troops to reconnoiter and keep them at a distance.

Qin Liang he led his troops to the entrance of the valley. As soon as he arrived, the enemy retired. Qin Liang went after them, but they had disappeared. He was perplexed and puzzled, and while trying to decide, he told the troops to dismount and rest.

But almost immediately he heard a shout, and ambushing troops appeared in front of him. He jumped on his horse to look about him, and saw a great cloud of dust rising among the hills. He disposed his troops for defense, but the shouting quickly came nearer, and then Hu Ban and Wu Yi appeared advancing towards him. Retreat was impossible for Guan Xing and Liao Hua had blocked the road.

The hills were on both sides, and from the hill-tops came shouts of "Dismount and yield!"

More than half did surrender. Qin Liang rode out to fight, but he was slain by Liao Hua.

Zhuge Liang put the Wei soldiers who had come over to his side in one of the rear divisions. With their dress and arms, he disguised five thousand of his own troops so that they looked like his enemies, and then he sent this division---under Guan Xing, Liao Hua, Wu Yi, and Hu Ban---to raid Cao Zhen's camp. Before they reached the camp, they sent one of their number ahead as a galloper to tell Cao Zhen that there had been only a few men of Shu and they had all been chased out of sight, and so lull him into security.

This news satisfied Cao Zhen.

But just then a trusty messenger from Sima Yi came with a message: "Our troops have fallen into an ambush, and many have been killed. Do not think any more about the wager: That is canceled. But take most careful precautions."

"But there is not a single soldier of Shu near," said Cao Zhen.

He told the messenger to go back. Just then they told him Qin Liang's army had returned, and he went out to meet them. Just as he got near, someone remarked that some torches had flared up in the rear of his camp. He hastened thither to see. As soon as he was out of sight, the four leaders waved on their troops and dashed up to the camp. At the same time Ma Dai and Wang Ping came up behind, and Ma Zheng and Zhang Yi came out.

The soldiers of Wei were trapped and helpless. They scattered and fled for life. Cao Zhen, protected by his generals, fled away eastward. The enemy chased them closely. As Cao Zhen fled there arose a great shouting, and up came an army at full speed. Cao Zhen thought all was lost, and his heart sank, but it was Sima Yi, who drove off the pursuers.

Though Cao Zhen was saved, he was almost too ashamed to show his face.

Then said Sima Yi, "Zhuge Liang has seized Qishan, and we cannot remain here. Let us go to River Wei, whence we may try to recover our lost ground."

"How did you know I was in danger of defeat?" asked Cao Zhen.

"My messenger told me that you said there was not a single soldier of Shu near, and I knew Zhuge Liang would try to seize your camp. So I came to your help. The enemy's plan succeeded, but we will say no more about that wager. We must both do our best for the country."

But the fright and excitement made Cao Zhen ill, and he took to his bed. And while the army were in such a state of disorder, Sima Yi was afraid to advise a return. They camped at River Wei.

After this adventure Zhuge Liang hastened back to Qishan. After the soldiers had been feasted and services recognized, the four discontented leaders---Wei Yan, Chen Shi, Du Qiong, and Zhang Ni---came to the tent to apologize.

"Who caused the loss?" said Zhuge Liang.

Wei Yan said, "Chen Shi disobeyed orders and rushed into the valley."

"Wei Yan told me to," said Chen Shi.

"Would you still try to drag him down after he rescued you?" said Zhuge Liang. "However, when orders have been disobeyed, it is useless to try and gloze it over."

Zhuge Liang sentenced Chen Shi to death, and he was led away. Soon they brought his head into the presence of the assembled generals. Zhuge Liang spared Wei Yan as there was yet work for him to accomplish.

After this, Zhuge Liang prepared to advance. The scouts reported that Cao Zhen was ill, but was being treated by doctors in his tent.

The news pleased Zhuge Liang, and he said to his officers, "If Cao Zhen's illness is slight, they will surely return to Changan. They must be delayed by his serious sickness. He stays on so that his soldiers may not lose heart. Now I will write him such a letter that he will die."

Then he called up the soldiers of Wei who had yielded, and said to them, "You are Wei troops, and your families are all over there: It is wrong for you to serve me. Suppose I let you go home?"

They thanked him, falling prostrate and weeping.

Then Zhuge Liang continued, "Friend Cao Zhen and I have a compact, and I have a letter for him which you shall take. The bearer will be well rewarded."

They received the letter and ran home to their own tents, where they gave their Commander-in-Chief the letter. Cao Zhen was too ill to rise, but he opened the cover and read:

"The Prime Minister of Han, Zhuge Liang, to the

Minister of War, Cao Zhen:

"You will permit me to say that a leader of an army should be able to go and come, to be facile and obdurate, to advance and retire, to show himself weak or strong, to be immovable as mountains, to be inscrutable as the operations of nature, to be infinite as the universe, to be everlasting as the blue void, to be vast as the ocean, to be dazzling as the lights of heaven, to foresee droughts and floods, to know the nature of the ground, to understand the possibilities of battle arrays, to conjecture the excellencies and defects of the enemy.

"Alas! One of your sort, ignorant and inferior, rising impudently in heaven's vault, has had the presumption to assist a rebel to assume the imperial style and state at Luoyang, to send some miserable soldiers into Xie Valley. There they happened upon drenching rain. The difficult roads wearied both soldiers and horses, driving them frantic. Weapons and armors littered the countryside, swords and spears covered the ground. You, the Commander-in-Chief, were heart-broken and cowed, your generals fled like rats. You dare not show your faces at home, nor can you enter the halls of state. The historians' pens will record your defeats; the people will recount your infamies: 'Sima Yi is frightened when he hears of battle fronts, Cao Zhen is alarmed at mere rumors.' My soldiers are fierce and their steeds strong; my great generals are eager as tigers and majestic as dragons. I shall sweep the Middle Land bare and make Wei desolate."

Cao Zhen's wrath rose as he read. At the end it

filled his breast. And he died that evening. Sima Yi sent his coffin to Luoyang on a wagon.

When the Ruler of Wei heard of the death of Cao Zhen, he issued an edict urging Sima Yi to prosecute the war, to raise a great army, and to fight with Zhuge Liang.

Sima Yi sent a declaration of war one day in advance, and Zhuge Liang replied that he would fight on the morrow.

After the envoy had left, Zhuge Liang said, "Cao Zhen must have died!"

He called Jiang Wei by night to receive secret orders. He also summoned Guan Xing and told him what to do.

Next morning the whole force marched to the bank of River Wei and took up a position in a wide plain with the river on one flank and hills on the other. The two armies saluted each other's appearance with heavy flights of arrows. After the drums had rolled thrice the Wei center opened at the great standard and Sima Yi appeared, followed by his officers. Opposite was Zhuge Liang, in a four-horse chariot, waving his feather fan.

Sima Yi addressed Zhuge Liang, "Our master's ascension of the Throne was after the manner of King Yao, who abdicated in favor of King Shun. Two emperors have succeeded and have their seat in the Middle Land. Because of his liberality and graciousness, my lord has suffered the rule of Shu and Wu lest the people should suffer in a struggle. You, who are but a plowman from Nanyang, ignorant of the ways of Heaven, wish to invade us, and you should be destroyed. But if you will examine your heart and repent of your fault and retire, then each may maintain his own borders, and a settled state of three kingdoms will be attained. Thus the people may be spared distress, and you will save your life."

Zhuge Liang smiled and replied, "Our First Ruler entrusted to me the custody of his orphan son: Think you that I shall fail to exert myself to the uttermost to destroy rebels against his authority? Your soldiers of the Cao family will soon be exterminated by Han. Your ancestors were servants of Han and for generations ate of their bounty. Yet, instead of giving grateful service, you assist usurpers. Are you not ashamed?"

The flush of shame spread over Sima Yi's face, but he replied, "We will try the test of battle. If you can conquer, I pledge myself to be no longer a leader of armies. But if you are defeated, then you will retire at once to your own village and I will not harm you."

"Do you desire a contest of generals, or of weapons, or of battle array?" asked Zhuge Liang.

"Let us try a contest of battle array," replied Sima Yi.

"Then draw up your array that I may see," said Zhuge Liang.

Sima Yi withdrew within the line and signaled to his officers with a yellow flag to draw up their troops.

When he had finished, he rode again to the front,

saying, "Do you recognize my formation?"

"The least of my generals can do as well," said Zhuge Liang, smiling. "This is called the 'Disorder-in-Order' formation."

"Now you try while I look on," said Sima Yi.

Zhuge Liang entered the lines and waved his fan. Then he came out and said, "Do you recognize that?"

"Of course. This is the 'Eight Arrays'."

"Yes; you seem to know it. But dare you attack?"

"Why not, since I know it?" replied Sima Yi.

"Then you need only try."

Sima Yi entered the ranks and called to him three generals---Dai Ling, Zhang Hu, and Yue Chen---to whom he said, "That formation consists of eight gates---Birth, Exit, Expanse, Wound, Fear, Annihilation, Obstacle, and Death. You will go in from the east at the Gate of Birth, turn to the southwest and make your way out by the Gate of Annihilation. Then enter at the north, at the Exit Gate, and the formation will be broken up. But be cautious."

They started with Zhang Hu leading, Dai Ling next, and Yue Chen in rear, each with thirty horsemen. They made their way in at the Gate of Birth amid the applause of both sides. But when they had got within they found themselves facing a wall of troops and could not find a way out. They hastily led their men round by the base of the line toward the southwest to rush out there. But they were stopped by a flight of arrows. They became confused and saw many gates, but they had lost their bearings. Nor could they aid each other. They dashed hither and thither in disorder, but the formation was as if gathering clouds and rolling mists. Then a shout arose, and each one was seized and bound.

They were taken to the center, where Zhuge Liang sat in his tent, and the three leaders with their ninety men were ranged in front.

"Indeed you are prisoners. Are you surprised?" said Zhuge Liang, smiling. "But I will set you free to return to your leader, and tell him to read his books again, and study his tactics, before he comes to try conclusions with me. You are pardoned, but leave your weapons and horses here."

So they were stripped of their arms and armors and their faces inked. Thus were they led on foot out of the array. Sima Yi lost his temper at sight of his people thus put to shame.

Said he, "After this disgrace, how can I face the other officers in the Middle Land?"

He gave the signal for the army to fall on and attack the enemy, and, grasping his sword, led his brave generals into the fray and commanded the attack. But just as the two armies came to blows, Guan Xing came up fromt the southwest, his drums rolling and troops shouting, and attacked. Sima Yi told off a division from the rear to oppose Guan Xing, and again turned to urge on his main body.

Then the army of Wei was thrown into confusion by another attack from Jiang Wei, who came up silently and joined in the battle. Thus three sides of the Wei army were attacked by three different divisions of the enemy, and Sima Yi decided to retire. However, this was difficult. The soldiers of Shu hemmed him in and came closer every moment. At last, by a desperate push, he cut an alley toward the south and freed his army. But he had lost six or seven out of every ten of his soldiers.

The Wei army withdrew to the south bank of River Wei and camped. They strengthened their position and remained entirely on the defensive.

Zhuge Liang mustered his victorious army and returned to Qishan.

Now Li Yan sent an officer, General Gou An, from Baidicheng with a convoy of grain. Gou An was a drunkard and loitered on the road so that he arrived ten days late.

Zhuge Liang, angry at the delay, upbraided him, saying, "This grain is of the utmost importance to the army and you delay it. Three days' delay ought to mean the death penalty. What can you say to this delay of ten?"

Gou An was sentenced to death and hustled out.

But Yang Yi ventured to intervene, saying, "Gou An is a servant of Li Yan, and Li Yan has sent large supplies of all sorts from the West River Land. The road is long and difficult. If you put this man to death, perhaps others will not undertake transport duty."

Zhuge Liang then bade the executioners loose the offender, give him eighty blows, and let him go.

This punishment filled Gou An's heart with bitter resentment, and, in the night, he deserted to the enemy, he and his half dozen personal staff. He was taken before Sima Yi and told the tale of his wrongs.

"Your tale may be true, but it is hard to trust it," said Sima Yi. "Zhuge Liang is full of guile. However, you may render me a service, and if you do, I will ask the Ruler of Wei that you may be allowed to serve him and obtain a post for you."

"Whatever you ask, I will do the best I can," replied the deserter.

"Then go to Chengdu and spread a lying report that Zhuge Liang is angry with the powers there and means to make himself emperor. This will get him recalled, and that will be a merit to you."

Gou An accepted the treacherous mission. In Chengdu he got hold of the eunuchs, and told them his lying tale that the Prime Minister was too proud of his services and was about to use his sweeping powers to usurp the Throne.

The eunuchs became alarmed for their own safety and told the Emperor all these things.

"In such a case what am I to do?" asked the Latter Ruler.

"Recall him to the capital," said the eunuchs, "and take away his military powers so that he cannot rebel."

The Latter Ruler issued an edict recalling the army.

But Jiang Wan stepped forward and said, "The Prime Minister has rendered many great services since he led out the army. Wherefore is he recalled?"

"I have a private matter to consult him about," said the Latter Ruler. "I must see him personally."

So the edict was issued and sent to Zhuge Liang. The messenger was at once received as soon as he reached Qishan.

"The Emperor is young, and there is some jealous persons by his side," said Zhuge Liang sadly. "I was just going to achieve some solid success. Why am I recalled? If I go not, I shall insult my Prince. If I retire, I shall never get such a chance again."

"If the army retire, Sima Yi will attack," said Jiang Wei.

"I will retire in five divisions. Thus today this camp goes. Supposing that there are a thousand soldiers in the camp, then I shall have two thousand cooking places prepared, or if there are three thousand soldiers, then four thousand cooking plates shall be got ready, and so on, increasing the cooking arrangements as the troops are sent away."

Yang Yi said, "In the days of old, when Sun Bin[xviii] was attacking Pang Juan, Sun Bin decreased the cooking arrangements as the soldiers were increased. Why do you reverse this, O Prime Minister?"

"Because Sima Yi is an able leader and would pursue if he knew we were retreating. But he would recognize the probability of an ambush; and if he sees an increase in the cooking arrangements in a camp, he will be unable to conclude whether the troops have gone or not, and he will not pursue. Thus I shall gradually withdraw without loss."

The order for retreat was given.

Confident of the effect that Gou An's lying report would produce, Sima Yi waited for the retreat of the Shu army to begin. He was still waiting when the scouts told him the enemy's camps were empty. Wishing to make sure, he rode out himself with a small reconnoitering party and inspected the empty camps. Then he bade them count the stoves. Next day he paid a second visit to another empty camp, and again the cooking stoves were counted. The count showed an increase of a half.

"I felt sure that Zhuge Liang would have more troops ready. He has increased the cooking arrangements, and so, if we pursue, he will be ready for us. No; we also will retire and await another opportunity."

So there was no pursuit, and Zhuge Liang did not lose a soldier on his retreat to Hanzhong.

By and by, people came in from the River Lands to say that the retreat was a fact, and that only the cooking arrangements had been increased, not the soldiers.

Sima Yi knew that he had been tricked, and looking up the sky, he sighed, "Zhuge Liang imitated the ruse of Sun Bin to rouse my suspicion.

His thinking is superior to mine."

And Sima Yi set out for Changan.

When players of equal skill are matched,
Then victory hovers between;
Perhaps your opponent's a genius,
So put on your lowliest mien.

What happened when Zhuge Liang returned to Chengdu will be told next.

Chapter 101

**Going Out From Longshang, Zhuge Liang Dresses As A God;
Dashing Toward Saber Pass, Zhang He Falls Into A Snare.**

By means of the artifice just described, Zhuge Liang withdrew his army safely into Hanzhong, while Sima Yi retreated upon Changan. Zhuge Liang distributed the rewards for success and then went to Capital Chengdu for audience.

"Your Majesty recalled me just as I was about to advance upon Changan. What is the important matter?" said the Prime Minister.

For a long time the Latter Ruler made no reply.

Presently he said, "I longed to see your face once more, that is the only reason."

Zhuge Liang replied, "I think my recall was not on your own initiative. Some slanderous persons has hinted that I cherished ulterior objects."

The Latter Ruler, who indeed felt guilty and ill at ease, made no reply.

Zhuge Liang continued, "Your late father laid me under an obligation which I am pledged to fulfill to the death. But if vile influences are permitted to work at home, how can I destroy the rebels without?"

"The fact is I recalled you because of the talk of

the eunuchs. But I understand now and am unutterably sorry," said the Latter Ruler.

Zhuge Liang interrogated the eunuchs and thus found out the base rumors that had been spread abroad by Gou An. He sent to arrest this man, but Gou An had already fled and gone over to Wei. The eunuchs who had influenced the Emperor were put to death, and all the other eunuchs who were involved were expelled from the Palace.

The Prime Minister also upbraided Jiang Wan and Fei Yi for not having looked into the matter and set the Son of God right. The two Ministers bowed their heads and admitted their fault.

Zhuge Liang then took leave of the Latter Ruler and returned to the army. He wrote to Li Yan to see to the necessary supplies and began preparations for a new expedition.

Yang Yi said, "The soldiers are wearied by the many expeditions, and the supplies are not regular. I think a better plan would be to send half the army to Qishan for three months, and at the end of that time exchange them for the other half, and so on alternately. For example, if you have two hundred thousand troops, let one hundred thousand go into the field and one hundred thousand remain. In this way, using ten legions and ten legions, their energies will be conserved and you can gradually work toward the Middle Land."

"I agree with you," said Zhuge Liang. "Our attack is not a matter to be achieved in haste. The suggestion for an extended campaign is excellent!"

Wherefore the army was divided, and each half

went out for one hundred days' service at a time, when it was relieved by the other half. Full penalties were provided for any laxity and failure to maintain the periods of active service.

In the spring of the ninth year of Beginning Prosperity, the Shu army once more took the held against Wei. In Wei it was the fifth year of Calm Peace (AD 231).

When the Ruler of Wei heard of this new expedition, he called Sima Yi and asked his advice.

"Now that my friend Cao Zhen is no more, I am willing to do all that one man can to destroy the rebels against Your Majesty's authority," said Sima Yi.

Cao Rui was gratified by this ready offer, and honored Sima Yi with a banquet. Next day an edict was issued for the army to move. The Ruler of Wei, riding in his state chariot, escorted Sima Yi out of the city, and, after the farewells, the Commander took the road to Changan, where the force was gathering. There was assembled a council of war.

Zhang He offered his services, saying, "I volunteer to guard Yongcheng and Meicheng against the Shu army."

But Sima Yi said, "Our vanguard army is not strong enough to face the enemy's whole force. Moreover, to divide an army is not generally a successful scheme. The better plan will be to leave a guard in Shanggui and send all the others to Qishan. Will you undertake the Leadership of the

Van?"

Zhang He consented, saying, "I have always been most loyal and will devote my energies entirely to the service of the state. So far I have not had an adequate opportunity to prove my sincerity. But now that you confer upon me a post of such responsibility, I can only say that no sacrifice can be too great for me, and I will do my utmost."

So Zhang He was appointed Van Leader, and then Guo Huai was set over the defense of the counties of West Valley Land. Other generals were distributed to other posts, and the march began toward Qishan.

The spies reported: "The main force of Shu is directed toward Qishan, and the Leaders of the Van are Wang Ping and Zhang Ni. The route chosen for their march is from Chencang across San Pass and to the Xie Valley."

Hearing this, Sima Yi said to Zhang He, "Zhuge Liang is advancing in great force and certainly intends to reap the wheat in West Valley Land for his supply. You get sufficient troops to hold Qishan, while Guo Huai and I go to Tianshui and foil the enemy's plan to gather the wheat."

So Zhang He took forty thousand troops to hold Qishan, and Sima Yi set out westwards to the West Valley Land.

When Zhuge Liang reached Qishan and had settled his army in camp, he saw that the bank of River Wei had been fortified by his enemy.

"That must be the work of Sima Yi," remarked

Zhuge Liang to his generals. "But we have not enough food in camp. I have written to Li Yan to send grain, but it has not yet arrived. The wheat in West Valley Land is now just ripe, and we will go and reap it."

Leaving Wang Ping, Zhang Ni, Hu Ban, and Wu Yi to guard for the camps, Zhuge Liang, with Wei Yan, Jiang Wei, and several other generals, went over to Lucheng. The Governor of that city knew he could not offer any real defense, so he opened the gates and yielded.

After calming the people, Zhuge Liang asked, "Where is the ripe wheat to be found?"

The Governor replied, "Longshang is the place."

So Zhang Yi and Ma Zheng were left to guard the city, and the remainder of the army went to Longshang.

But soon the leading body returned to say, "Sima Yi has already occupied that city."

"He guessed what I intended to do!" said Zhuge Liang, taken aback.

Zhuge Liang then retired, bathed and put on another dress. Next he bade them bring out three four-wheeled chariots, all exactly alike, that were among the impedimenta of the army. They had been built in Shu some time before.

Jiang Wei was told off to lead a thousand troops as escort for one chariot, and five hundred drummers were appointed to accompany it. The chariot with its escort and drummers was sent away behind the city. In like manner two other chariots were equipped and sent east and west of the city under Ma Dai and Wei Yan. Each chariot was propelled by a team of twenty-four men, all dressed in black, barefooted and with loosened hair. Each one of the team also had in hand a sword and a black seven-starred flag.

While the chariots were taking up their positions, thirty thousand soldiers were ordered to prepare wagons and sickles to cut and carry away the grain.

Next Zhuge Liang selected twenty-four good soldiers, whom he dressed and armed like those sent away with the three chariots. These were to push his own chariot. Guan Xing was told to dress up as the God of Clouds and to walk in front of Zhuge Liang's chariot holding a black seven-starred flag. These preparations complete, Zhuge Liang mounted, and the chariot took the road toward the Wei camp.

The appearance of a chariot with such attendants more than startled the enemy's scouts, who did not know whether the apparition was that of a human or a demon. They hastened to their Commander and told him.

Sima Yi came out himself and saw the cavalcade, and its central figure being Zhuge Liang, dressed as a Taoist mystic, with headdress, white robe, and a feather fan. Around the chariot were twenty-four hair-loosened beings, each with a sword in hand; and leading was a being as a heaven-sent god with the seven-starred flag.

"Some of Zhuge Liang's odd doings," said he.

And Sima Yi ordered two thousand troops, saying, "Chase as fast as you can, and bring in the chariot, escort, and the seated figure."

The soldiers went out to do their bidding. But as soon as they appeared, the chariot retired and took a road leading to the Shu camp. Although the Wei soldiers were mounted, they could not come up with the cavalcade. What they did meet with was a chilly breeze and a cold mist that rolled about them.

They found it uncanny and halted, saying one to another, "How extraordinary it is that we have been pressing on and yet we got no nearer. What does it mean?"

When Zhuge Liang saw that the pursuit had ceased, he had his chariot pushed out again to the front and passed within sight of the halted troops. At first they hesitated, but presently took up the pursuit once more. Whereupon the chariot again retired, proceeding slowly, but always keeping out of reach. And thus more than seven miles were covered and the chariot was still not captured.

Again the soldiers halted, puzzled and perplexed at this incomprehensible chase. But as soon as they stopped, the chariot came again toward them and they retook pursuit.

Sima Yi now came up with a strong force. But he also halted, and said to his generals, "This Zhuge Liang is a master in the arts of necromancy and juggling and Eight Gates and knows how to call up the Deities of Six Layers to his aid. I know this trick of his: It is the 'Ground Rolling' in the 'Book of Six Layers Deities', and it is vain to pursue."

So they ceased following. But then a roll of drums came from the left side as if a body of troops were approaching. Sima Yi told off some companies to repel them, but there only came into view a small force, and in their midst was a party of men dressed in black, the exact counterpart of the cavalcade he had first sent to pursue. In the chariot sat another Zhuge Liang just like the one that had just disappeared.

"But just now he was sitting in that other chariot, which we chased for fifteen miles. How can he be here?" said Sima Yi.

Shortly after they heard another roll of the drums, and as the sound died away there appeared another body of men, with a chariot in the midst, exactly like the last and also carrying a sitting figure of Zhuge Liang.

"They must be heaven-sent soldiers," said Sima Yi.

The soldiers were now feeling the strain of these weird appearances and began to get out of hand. They dared not stay to fight such beings, and some ran away. But before they had gone far, lo! another roll of drums, another cohort and another chariot with a similar figure seated therein.

The soldiers of Wei were now thoroughly frightened, and even Sima Yi himself began to feel doubtful whether these appearances should be ascribed to humans or devils. He realized, however, that he was in the midst of dangers as he did not know the number of the Shu soldiers, and he and his troops ran away helter-skelter, never stopping till they reached Shanggui. They entered the city and closed the gates.

Having thus driven off the Wei soldiers, Zhuge Liang proceeded to reap and gather the wheat in Longshang, which was carried into Lucheng and laid out to dry.

Sima Yi remained shut up within the walls for three days. Then, as he saw his enemies retiring, he sent out some scouts, who presently returned with a Shu soldier they had captured. The prisoner was questioned.

"I was of the reaping party," said the man. "They caught me when I was looking for some horses that had strayed."

"What wonderful soldiers were they of yours that one saw here lately?" asked Sima Yi.

The man replied, "Zhuge Liang was with one party of them, the others were led by Jiang Wei, Ma Dai, and Wei Yan. There was a thousand of fighting soldiers with each chariot and five hundred drummers. Zhuge Liang was with the first party."

"His comings and goings are not human," said Sima Yi sadly.

Then Guo Huai came, and he was called to a council.

Said Guo Huai, "I hear the soldiers of Shu in Lucheng are very few, and they are occupied with gathering the grain. Why not smite them?"

Sima Yi told him his last experience of his opponent's wiles.

"He threw dust in your eyes that time," said Guo Huai with a smile. "However, now you know. What is the good of more talk? Let me attack the rear, while you lead against the front, and we shall take the city and Zhuge Liang too."

An attack was decided upon.

In Lucheng, while the soldiers were still busy with the wheat, Zhuge Liang called up his generals, and said, "The enemy will attack tonight. There is a suitable place for an ambush in the newly reaped fields, but who will lead for me?"

Four generals---Jiang Wei, Wei Yan, Ma Dai, and Ma Zheng---offered themselves, and he posted them, each with two thousand troops, outside the four corners of the city. They were to await the signal and then converge. When these had gone, Zhuge Liang led out a small party of one hundred soldiers and hid in the newly reaped fields.

In the meantime Sima Yi was drawing near. It was dusk when he stood beneath the walls of Lucheng.

Said he to his officers, "If we attacked by daylight, we should find the city well prepared. So we will take advantage of the darkness. The moat is shallow here, and there shall be no difficulty in crossing it."

The troops bivouacked till the time should come to attack. About the middle of the first watch Guo Huai arrived, and his force joined up with the others. This done, the drums began to beat, and the city was quickly surrounded. However, the defenders maintained such a heavy discharge of arrows, bolts and stones from the walls that the besiegers dared not close in.

Suddenly from the midst of the Wei army came the roar of a bomb, soon followed by others from different places. The soldiers were startled, but no one could say whence the sounds had proceeded. Guo Huai went to search the wheat fields, and then the four armies from the corners of the city converged upon the Wei army. At the same time the defenders burst out of the city gates, and a great battle began. Wei lost many troops.

After heavy fighting Sima Yi extricated his army from the battle and made his way to a hill, which he set about holding and fortifying, while Guo Huai got round to the rear of the city and called a halt.

Zhuge Liang entered the city and sent his troops to camp again at the four corners of the walls.

Guo Huai went to see his chief, and said, "We have long been at grips with these soldiers and are unable to drive them off. We have now lost another fight. Unless something is done, we shall not get away at all."

"What can we do?" asked Sima Yi.

"You might write to Yongzhou and Liangzhou to send their forces to our help. I will try my fortune against Saber Pass and cut off Zhuge Liang's retreat and supplies. That should bring about discontent and mutiny, and we can attack when we see the enemy in confusion."

The letters were sent, and soon Sun Li came leading the troops of Yongzhou and Liangzhou, foot and horse, of two hundred thousand. The new arrivals were sent to help Guo Huai in the attack on Saber Pass.

After many days had passed without sight of the enemy, Zhuge Liang thought it was time to make another move.

Calling up Jiang Wei and Ma Dai, he said, "The soldiers of Wei are well posted on the hills and refuse battle because, firstly, they think that we are short of food, and, secondly, they have sent an army against Saber Pass to cut off our supplies. Now each of you will take ten thousand troops and garrison the important points about here to show them that we are well prepared to defend ourselves. Then they will retire."

After these two had gone, Yang Yi came to see Zhuge Liang about the change of troops then due.

Yang Yi said, "O Prime Minister, you have ordered the troops to be alternated every one hundred days. Now the time is due, and the replacing troops have already left Hanzhong and that dispatches from the leading divisions have come in. Here we have eighty thousand troops, of which forty will be due for relief."

"There is the order; carry it out," replied Zhuge Liang.

So the forty thousand home-going soldiers prepared to withdraw.

Just then came the news: "Sun Li has arrived with

reinforcements of two hundred thousand troops from Yongzhou and Liangzhou. Guo Huai and Sun Li have gone to attack Saber Pass, and Sima Yi is leading an army against Lucheng."

In the face of such important news, Yang Yi went to discuss with Zhuge Liang.

Said Yang Yi, "The Wei army are advancing against our critical points. Should you, O Prime Minister, postpone for a time the withdrawal of the field troops in order to strengthen our defense? You can wait for the new troops to arrive first."

Zhuge Liang replied, "I must keep faith with the soldiers. Since the order for the periodical exchange of troops has been issued, it must be carried out. Beside, the soldiers due for relief are all prepared to start, their expectations have been roused and their relatives await them. In the face of yet greater difficulties I would still let them go."

So orders were given for the time-expired soldiers to march that day. But when the legionaries heard it, a sudden movement of generosity spread among them.

And they said, "Since the Prime Minister cares for us so much, we do not wish to go, but will prefer to remain to fight the Wei army to death."

"But you are due for home. You cannot stay here," said Zhuge Liang.

They reiterated that they all wished to stay instead of going home.

Zhuge Liang was glad and said, "Since you wish to

stay and fight with me, you can go out of the city and camp ready to encounter the army of Wei as soon as they arrive. Do not give them time to rest or recover breath, but attack vigorously at once. You will be fresh and fit, waiting for those fagged with a long march."

So they gripped their weapons and joyfully went out of the city to array themselves in readiness.

Now the Yongzhou and Liangzhou troops had traveled by double marches, and so were worn out and needed rest. But while they were pitching their tents, the troops of Shu fell upon them lustily, leaders full of spirit, soldiers full of energy. The weary soldiers could make no proper stand, and retired. The troops of Shu followed, pressing on them till corpses littered the whole plain and blood flowed in runnels.

It was a victory for Zhuge Liang, and he came out to welcome the victors and led them into the city and distributed rewards.

Just then arrived an urgent letter from Li Yan, then at Baidicheng, and when Zhuge Liang had torn it open he read:

"News has just come that Wu has sent an envoy to Luoyang and entered into an alliance with Wei whereby Wu is to attack us. The army of Wu has not yet set out, but I am anxiously awaiting your plans."

Doubts and fears crowded in upon Zhuge Liang's mind as he read. He summoned his officers.

"As Wu is coming to invade our land, we shall

have to retire quickly," said he. "If I issue orders for the Qishan force to withdraw, Sima Yi will not dare to pursue while we are camped here."

The Qishan force broke camp and marched in two divisions under Wang Ping, Zhang Ni, Hu Ban, and Wu Yi. Zhang He watched them go, but was too fearful of the movement being some ruse to attempt to follow. He went to see Sima Yi.

"The enemy have retired, but I know not for what reason."

"Zhuge Liang is very crafty, and you will do well to remain where you are and keep a careful lookout. Do nothing till their grain has given out, when they must retire for good," said Sima Yi.

Here General Wei Ping stepped forward, saying, "But they are retreating from Qishan. We should seize the occasion of their retreat to smite them. Are they tigers that you fear to move? How the world will laugh at us?"

But Sima Yi was obstinate and ignored the protest.

When Zhuge Liang knew that the Qishan troops had got away safely, he called Yang Yi and Ma Zheng and gave them secret orders to lead ten thousand of bowmen and crossbowmen out by the Wooden Path of Saber Pass and place them in ambush on both sides of the road.

Said he, "If the soldiers of Wei pursue, wait till you hear a bomb. When you hear the bomb, at once barricade the road with timber and stones so as to impede them. When they halt, shoot at them with the bows and the crossbows."

Wei Yan and Guan Xing were told to attack the rear of the enemy.

These orders given, the walls of Lucheng were decorated lavishly with flags, and at various points within the city were piled straw and kindling wood ready to make some smoke as though there were cooking activities in the city. The soldiers were sent out along the road toward Saber Pass.

The spies of Wei returned to headquarters to report: "A large number of Shu soldiers have left, but we do not know how many remain within the city."

In doubt, Sima Yi went himself to look, and when he saw the smoke rising from within the walls and the fluttering flags, he said, "The city is deserted!"

He sent men in to confirm this, and they said the place was empty.

"Then Zhuge Liang is really gone. Who will pursue?"

"Let me," replied Zhang He.

"You are too impulsive," said Sima Yi.

"I have been Leader of the Van from the first day of this expedition. Why not use me today, when there is work to be done and glory to be gained?"

"Because the utmost caution is necessary. They are retreating, and they will leave an ambush at every possible point."

"I know that, and you need not be afraid."

"Well; you wish to go and may, but whatever happens you must be prepared for."

"A really noble man is prepared to sacrifice self for country. Never mind what happens."

"Then take five thousand troops and start. Wei Ping shall follow with twenty thousand of horse and foot to deal with any ambush that may discover itself. I will follow later with three thousand to help where need be."

So Zhang He set out and advanced quickly.

Ten miles out he heard a roll of drums, and suddenly appeared from a wood a cohort led by Wei Yan, who galloped to the front, crying, "Whither would you go, O rebel leader?"

Zhang He swiftly turned and engaged Wei Yan, but after some ten passes Wei Yan fled. Zhang He rode after Wei Yan along the road for ten miles and then stopped to observe. As he saw no ambush, he turned again and resumed the pursuit. All went well till he came to a slope, when there arose shouts and yells and another body of soldiers came out.

"Zhang He, do not run away!" cried this leader, who was Guan Xing.

Guan Xing galloped close, and Zhang He did not flee. They fought, and after half a score of passes Guan Xing seemed to have the worst of the encounter and fled. Zhang He followed. Presently they neared a dense wood. Zhang He was fearful of entering in, so he sent forward scouts to search the thickets. They could find no danger, and Zhang

He again pursued.

But quite unexpectedly Wei Yan, who had formerly fled, got round ahead of Zhang He and now appeared again. The two fought a half score bouts and again Wei Yan ran. Zhang He followed, but Guan Xing also got round to the front by a side road and so stopped the pursuit of Zhang He. Zhang He attacked furiously as soon as he was checked, this time so successfully that the troops of Shu threw away their war-gear and ran. The road was thus littered with spoil, and the Wei soldiers could not resist the temptation to gather it. They slipped from their horses and began to collect the arms.

The maneuvers just described continued, Wei Yan and Guan Xing one after the other engaging Zhang He, and Zhang He pressing on after each one, but achieving nothing. And as evening fell the running fight had led both sides close to the Wooden Path.

Then suddenly Wei Yan made a real stand, and he rode to the front, yelling, "Rebel! I have despised fighting you, but you have kept pursuing me. Now we will fight to the death!"

Zhang He was furious and nothing loath, so he came on with his spear to meet Wei Yan, who was flourishing his sword. They met; yet again, after some ten bouts, Wei Yan threw aside weapons, armor, helmet and all his gear, and led his defeated company sway along the Wooden Path.

Zhang He was filled with the lust to kill, and he could not let Wei Yan escape. So he set out after Wei Yan, although it was already dark. But suddenly lights appeared, and the sky became aglow, and at the same time huge boulders and great bulks of timber came rolling down the slopes and blocked the way.

Fear gripped Zhang He, and he cried, "I have blundered into an ambush!"

The road was blocked in front and behind and bordered by craggy precipices. Then, rat-tat-tat! came the sound of a rattle, and therewith flew clouds of arrows and showers of bolts. Zhang He, his more than one hundred generals, and his whole pursuing army perished in the Wooden Path.

With myriad shining bolts the air was filled,
The road was littered with brave soldiers killed;
The force to Saber Pass faring perished here;
The tale of valor grows from year to year.

Soon the second army of Wei under Wei Ping came up, but too late to help. From the signs they knew that their comrades had been victims of a cruel trick, and they turned back.

But as they faced about, a shout was heard, and from the hilltops came, "I, Zhuge Liang, am here!"

Looking up they saw his figure silhouetted against a fire.

Pointing to the slain, Zhuge Liang cried, "I have gone hunting in this wood. Only instead of slaying a horse, I have killed a deer. But you may go in peace, and when you see your Commander, tell him that he will be my quarry one day!"

The soldiers told this to Sima Yi when they returned.

Sima Yi was deeply mortified, saying, "Letting friend Zhang He die is my fault!"

And when he returned to Luoyang, the Ruler of Wei wept at the death of his brave leader and had his body searched and honorably buried.

Zhuge Liang had no sooner reached Hanzhong than he prepared to go on to Capital Chengdu and see his lord.

But Li Yan, who was in the capital, said to the Latter Ruler, "Why does the Prime Minister return, for I have kept him fully supplied with all things needed for the army?"

Then the Latter Ruler sent Fei Yi into Hanzhong to inquire why the army had retired.

When Fei Yi had arrived and showed the cause of his coming, Zhuge Liang was greatly surprised.

Zhuge Liang showed the letter from Li Yan, saying, "Li Yan wrote to warn that East Wu was about to invade the country."

Fei Yi said, "Li Yan memorialized to the Throne, saying he had sent you supplies and knew not why Your Excellency returned."

So Zhuge Liang inquired carefully, and then it came out that Li Yan had failed to find sufficient grain to keep the army supplied, and so had sent the first lying letter to the army that it might retire before the shortage showed itself. His memorial to the Throne was designed to cover the former fault.

"The fool has ruined the great design of the state just to save his own skin!" cried Zhuge Liang bitterly.

He summoned the offender and sentenced him to death.

But Fei Yi interceded, saying, "O Prime Minister, the First Ruler had loved and trusted Li Yan with his son. Please forgive him this time."

And so Li Yan's life was spared.

However, when Fei Yi made his report in Chengdu, the Latter Ruler was wroth and ordered Li Yan to suffer death.

But this time Jiang Wan intervened, saying, "Your late father named Li Yan as one of the guardians of your youth."

And the Latter Ruler relented. However, Li Yan was stripped of all ranks and relegated to Zitong.

Zhuge Liang went to Chengdu and appointed Li Teng, Li Yan's son, as High Counselor.

Preparations then began for another expedition. Plans were discussed, provisions were accumulated, weapons put in order, and officers and soldiers kept fit and trained. By his kindness to the people, Zhuge Liang waited for three years before beginning marching, and in the two River Lands people's hearts filled with joys.

And the time passed quickly.

In the second month of the twelfth year (AD 234), Zhuge Liang presented a memorial, saying, "I have been training the army for three years. Supplies are ample, and all is in order for an expedition. We may now attack Wei. If I cannot destroy these rebels, sweep away the evil hordes, and bring about a glorious entry into the capital, then may I never again enter Your Majesty's presence."

The Latter Ruler replied, "The empire has settled on a tripod, and Wu and Wei trouble us not at all. Why not enjoy the present tranquillity, O Father Minister?"

"Because of the mission left me by your father. I am ever scheming to destroy Wei, even in my dreams. I must strive my best and do my utmost to regain you the Middle Land and restore the glory of the Hans."

As Zhuge Liang said this, a voice cried, "An army may not go forth, O Prime Minister!"

Qiao Zhou had raised a last protest.

Zhuge Liang's sole thought was service,
Himself he would not spare;
But Qiao Zhou had watched the starry sky,
And read misfortune there.

The next chapter will give the arguments against fighting.

Chapter 102

Sima Yi Occupies The Banks Of River Wei; Zhuge Liang Constructs Mechanical Bullocks And Horses.

Qiao Zhou, who protested against the war, was Grand Historian. He was also an astrologer.

He opposed the war, saying, "My present office involves the direction of the observations on the Astrological Terrace, and I am bound to report whether the aspect forebodes misfortune or promises happiness. Not long since, several flights of thousands of birds came from the south, plunged into River Han and were drowned. This is an evil augury. Moreover, I have studied the aspect of the sky, and the 'Wolf' constellation is influencing the aspect of the planet Venus. An aura of prosperity pervades the north. To attack Wei will not be to our profit. Again, the people in Chengdu say that the cypress trees moan in the night. With so many evil omens, I wish that the Prime Minister should not go forth to war, but remain at home to guard what we have."

"How can I?" said Zhuge Liang. "His Late Majesty laid upon me a heavy responsibility, and I must exert myself to the utmost in the endeavor to destroy these rebels. The policy of a state cannot be changed because of inauspicious signs."

Zhuge Liang was not to be deterred. He instructed the officials to prepare the Great Bovine Sacrifice in the Dynastic Temple. Then, weeping, he prostrated himself and made this declaration:

"Thy servant Zhuge Liang has made five expeditions to Qishan without gaining any extension of territory. His fault weighs heavily upon him. Now once again he is about to march, pledged to use every effort of body and mind to exterminate the rebels against the Han House, and to restore to the dynasty its glory in the Middle Land. To achieve this end, he would use the last remnant of his strength and could die content."

The sacrifice ended, he took leave of the Latter Ruler and set out for Hanzhong to make the final arrangements for his march. While so engaged, he received the unexpected news of the death of Guan Xing. He was greatly shocked, and fainted. When he had recovered consciousness, his officers did their utmost to console him.

"How pitiful! Why does Heaven deny long life to the loyal and good? I have lost a most able general just as I am setting out and need him most."

As all are born, so all must die;
People are as gnats against the sky;
But loyalty or piety
May give them immortality.

The armies of Shu numbered three hundred forty thousand strong, and they marched in five divisions, with Jiang Wei and Wei Yan in the van, and when they had reached Qishan, Li Hui, the Commissary General, was instructed to convey stores into the Xie Valley in readiness.

In Wei they had recently changed the style of the year period to "Green Dragon", because a green dragon had been seen to emerge from Mopo Well. The year of the fighting was the second year (AD 234).

The courtiers said to the Ruler of Wei, "The commanders of the passes report thirty or so legions advancing in five divisions from Shu upon Qishan."

The news distressed the Ruler of Wei, who at once called in Sima Yi and told him of the invasion.

Sima Yi replied, "The aspect of the sky is very auspicious for the Middle Land. The Wolf star has encroached upon the planet Venus, which bodes ill for the River Lands. Thus Zhuge Liang is pitting his powers against Heaven, and will meet defeat and suffer death. And I, by virtue of Your Majesty's good fortune, am to be the instrument of destruction. I request to name four leaders to go with me."

"Who are they? Name them," said the Ruler of Wei.

"They are the four sons of Xiahou Yuan: Xiahou Ba, Xiahou Wei, Xiahou Hui, and Xiahou He. Xiahou Ba and Xiahou Wei are trained archers and cavaliers; Xiahou Hui and Xiahou He are deep strategists. All four desire to avenge the death of their father. Xiahou Ba and Xiahou Wei should be Leaders of the Van; Xiahou Hui and Xiahou He should be Marching Generals, to discuss and arrange plans for the repulse of our enemy."

"You remember the evil results of employing the

Dynastic Son-in-Law Xiahou Mao: He lost his army and is still too ashamed to return to court. Are you sure these are not of the same kidney?"

"They are not like Xiahou Mao in the least."

The Ruler of Wei granted the request and named Sima Yi as Commander-in-Chief with the fullest authority. When Sima Yi took leave of the Ruler of Wei, he received a command in Cao Rui's own writing:

"When you, Noble Sir, reach the banks of River Wei and have well fortified that position, you are not to give battle. The army of Shu, disappointed of their desire, will pretend to retire and so entice you on, but you will not pursue. You will wait till their supplies are consumed and they are compelled to retreat, when you may smite them. Then you will obtain the victory without distressing the army unduly. This is the best plan of campaign."

Sima Yi took it with bowed head. He proceeded forthwith to Changan. When he had mustered the forces assembled from all western counties, they numbered four hundred thousand, and they were all camped on River Wei. In addition, fifty thousand troops were farther up the stream preparing nine floating bridges. The two Leaders of the Van, Xiahou Ba and Xiahou Wei, were ordered to cross the river and camp, and in rear of the main camp on the east a solid earth rampart was raised to guard against any surprises from the rear.

While these preparations were in progress, Guo Huai and Sun Li came to the new camp.

Guo Huai said, "With the troops of Shu at Qishan, there is a possibility of their dominating River Wei, going up on the plain, and pushing out a line to the northern hills whereby to cut off all highways in the West Valley Land."

"You say well," said Sima Yi. "See to it. Take command of all the West Valley Land forces, occupy Beiyuan, and make a fortified camp there. But adopt a defensive policy. Wait till the enemy's food supplies get exhausted before you think of attack."

So Guo Huai and Sun Li left to carry out these orders.

Meanwhile Zhuge Liang made five main camps at Qishan, and between Xie Valley and Saber Pass he established a line of fourteen large camps. He distributed the troops among these camps as for a long campaign. He appointed inspecting officers to make daily visits to see that all was in readiness.

When he heard that the army of Wei had camped in Beiyuan, he said to his officers, "They camp there fearing that our holding this area will sever connection with West Valley Land. I am pretending to look toward Beiyuan, but really my objective is River Wei. I am going to build a hundred or more large rafts and pile them with straw, and I have five thousand of marines to manage them. In the darkness of the night I shall attack Beiyuan. Sima Yi will come to the rescue. If he is only a little worsted, I shall cross the river with the rear divisions, then the leading divisions will embark on the rafts, drop down the river, set fire to the floating bridges, and attack the rear of the enemy. I shall lead an army to take the gates of the first camp. If we can get the south bank of the river, the campaign will become simple."

Then the generals took orders and went to prepare.

The spies carried information of the doings of the troops of Shu to Sima Yi, who said to his generals, "Zhuge Liang has some crafty scheme, but I think I know it. He proposes to make a show of taking Beiyuan, and then, dropping down the river, he will try to burn our bridges, throw our rear into confusion, and then attack our camps."

So he gave Xiahou Ba and Xiahou Wei orders: "You are to listen for the sounds of battle about Beiyuan. If you hear the shouting, you are to march down to the river, to the hills on the south, and lay an ambush against the troops of Shu as they arrive."

Zhang Hu and Yue Chen were to lead two other forces, of two thousand of bowmen each, and lie in hiding on the north bank near the bridges to keep off the rafts that might come down on the current and keep them from touching the bridges.

Then he sent for Guo Huai and Sun Li, and said, "Zhuge Liang is coming to Beiyuan to cross the river secretly. Your new force is small, and you can hide half way along the road. If the enemy cross the river in the afternoon, that will mean an attack on us in the evening. Then you are to simulate defeat and run. They will pursue. You can shoot with all your energy, and our marines and land troops will attack at once. If the attack is in great force, look out for orders."

All these orders given, Sima Yi sent his two sons Sima Shi and Sima Zhao to reinforce the front camp, while he led his own army to relieve Beiyuan.

Zhuge Liang sent Wei Yan and Ma Dai to cross River Wei and attack Beiyuan, while the attempt to set fire to the bridges was confided to Hu Ban and Wu Yi. The general attack on the Wei camp by River Wei was to be made by three divisions: The front division under Wang Ping and Zhang Ni, the middle division under Jiang Wei and Ma Zheng, the rear division under Liao Hua and Zhang Yi. The various divisions started at noon and crossed the river, where they slowly formed up in battle order.

Wei Yan and Ma Dai arrived Beiyuan about dusk. The scouts having informed the defenders of their approach, Sun Li abandoned his camp and fled. This told Wei Yan that his attack was expected, and he turned to retire. At this moment a great shouting was heard, and there appeared two bodies of the enemy under Sima Yi and Guo Huai bearing down upon the attackers from left and right. Wei Yan and Ma Dai fought desperately to extricate themselves, but many of the soldiers of Shu fell into the river and drowned. The others scattered. However, Wu Yi came up and rescued the force from entire destruction, and moved across the river to make camp.

Hu Ban set half his troops to navigate the rafts down the river to the bridges. But Zhang Hu and Yue Chen stationed near the bridges shot clouds of arrows at them, and the Shu leader, Hu Ban, was wounded. He fell into the river and was drowned.

The crews of the rafts jumped into the water and got away. The rafts fell into the hands of the soldiers of Wei.

At this time the front division under Wang Ping and Zhang Ni were ignorant of the defeat of their Beiyuan army, and they went straight for the camps of Wei. They arrived in the second watch.

They heard loud shouting, and Wang Ping said to Zhang Ni, "We do not know whether the cavalry sent to Beiyuan has been successful or not. It is strange that we do not see a single soldier of the enemy. Surely Sima Yi has found out the plan and prepared to frustrate the attack. Let us wait here till the bridges have been set on fire and we see the flames."

So they halted. Soon after, a mounted messenger came up with orders: "The Prime Minister bade you retire immediately, as the attack on the bridges has failed."

Wang Ping and Zhang Ni attempted to withdraw, but a bomb exploded and the troops of Wei, who had taken a by-road to their rear, at once attacked. A great fire started also. A disorderly battle ensued, from which Wang Ping and Zhang Ni eventually forced their ways out, but only with great loss.

And when Zhuge Liang collected his army at Qishan once more he found, to his sorrow, that he had lost more than ten thousand troops.

Just at this time Fei Yi arrived front Chengdu.

Zhuge Liang received him and, after the

ceremonies were over, said, "I would trouble you, Sir, to carry a letter for me into East Wu. Will you undertake the mission?"

"Could I possibly decline any task you laid upon me?" said Fei Yi.

So Zhuge Liang wrote a letter and sent it to Sun Quan. Fei Yi took it and hastened to Capital Jianye, where he saw Sun Quan, the Ruler of Wu, and presented this letter:

"The Hans have been unfortunate, and the line of rulers has been broken. The Cao party have usurped the seat of government and still hold the command. My late master, Emperor Bei, confided a great task to me, and I must exhaust every effort to achieve it. Now my army is at Qishan, and the rebels are on the verge of destruction on River Wei. I hope Your Majesty, in accordance with your oath of alliance, will send a leader against the north to assist by taking the Middle Land, and the empire can be shared. The full circumstances cannot be told, but I hope you will understand and act."

Sun Quan was pleased at the news and said to the envoy, "I have long desired to set my arm in motion, but have not been able to arrange with Zhuge Liang. After this letter I will lead an expedition myself, and go to Juchao and capture Xincheng of Wei. Moreover, I will send Lu Xun and Zhuge Jin to camp at Miankou and Jiangxia, and take Xiangyang. I will also send another army under Sun Shao and Zhang Cheng into Guangling to capture Huaiyang. The total number will be three hundred thousand troops, and they shall start at once."

Fei Yi thanked him and said, "In such a case the Middle Land will fall forthwith."

A banquet was prepared. At this, Sun Quan said, "Whom did the Prime Minister send to lead the battle?"

Fei Yi replied, "Wei Yan was the chief leader."

"A man brave enough, but crooked. One day he will work a mischief unless Zhuge Liang is present. But surely Zhuge Liang knows."

"Your Majesty's words are to the point," said the envoy. "I will return at once and lay them before Zhuge Liang."

Fei Yi quickly took leave and hastened to Qishan with his news of the intended expedition of Wu against Wei with three hundred thousand troops in three directions.

"Did the Ruler of Wu say nothing else?" asked Zhuge Liang.

Then Fei Yi told him what had been said about Wei Yan.

"Truly a comprehending ruler," said Zhuge Liang, appreciatively. "But I could not be ignorant of this. However, I value Wei Yan because he is very bold."

"Then Sir, you ought to decide soon what to do with him."

"I have a scheme of my own."

Fei Yi returned to Chengdu, and Zhuge Liang resumed the ordinary camp duties of a leader.

When Zhuge Liang was in a council with his commanders, suddenly a certain Wei leader came and begged to be allowed to surrender. Zhuge Liang had the man brought in and questioned him.

"I am a leader, Zheng Wen by name. General Qin Lang and I are old colleagues. Recently Sima Yi transferred us and, showing great partiality for my colleague, appointed him Leader of the Van and threw me out like a weed. I was disgusted and left, and I wish to join your ranks if you will accept my service."

Just at that moment a soldier came in to say that Qin Lang with a company had appeared in front of the tents and was challenging Zheng Wen.

Said Zhuge Liang, "How does this man stand with you in fighting skill?"

"I should just kill him," said Zheng Wen.

"If you were to slay him, that would remove my doubts."

Zheng Wen accepted the proposer with alacrity, mounted his horse, and away he went. Zhuge Liang went out to see the fight. There was the challenger shaking his spear and reviling his late friend as rebel and brigand and horse-thief.

"Traitor! Give me back my horse you stole!" cried Qin Lang, galloping toward Zheng Wen as soon as he appeared.

Zheng Wen whipped up his horse, waved his sword, and went to meet the attack. In the first bout he cut down Qin Lang. The Wei soldiers then ran away. The victor hacked off the head of his victim and returned to lay it at Zhuge Liang's feet.

Seated in his tent, Zhuge Liang summoned Zheng Wen and burst out: "Take him away and behead him!"

"I have done nothing wrong!" cried Zheng Wen.

"As if I do not know Qin Lang! The man you have just killed was not Qin Lang. How dare? you try to deceive me?"

Zheng Wen said, "I will own up. But this was his brother Qin Ming."

Zhuge Liang smiled.

"Sima Yi sent you to try this on for some reason of his own, but he could not throw dust in my eyes. If you do not tell the truth, I will put you to death."

Thus caught, the false deserter confessed and begged his life.

Zhuge Liang said, "You can save your life by writing a letter to Sima Yi telling him to come to raid our camp. I will spare you on this condition. And if I capture Sima Yi, I will give you all the credit and reward you handsomely."

There was nothing for it but to agree, and the letter was written. Then Zheng Wen was placed in confinement.

But Fan Jian asked, "How did you know this was only a pretended desertion?"

"Sima Yi looks to his people," replied Zhuge Liang. "If he made Qin Lang a leading general, Qin Lang was certainly a man of great military skill and not the sort of man to be overcome by this fellow Zheng Wen in the first encounter. So Zheng Wen's opponent certainly was not Qin Lang. That is how I knew."

They congratulated him on his perspicacity. Then Zhuge Liang selected a certain persuasive speaker from among his officers and whispered certain instructions in his ear. The officer at once left and carried the letter just written to the Wei camp, where he asked to see the Commander-in-Chief. He was admitted, and the letter was read.

"Who are you?" said Sima Yi.

"I am a man from the Middle Land, a poor fellow stranded in Shu. Zheng Wen and I are fellow villagers. Zhuge Liang has given Zheng Wen a Van Leadership as a reward for what he has done, and Zheng Wen got me to bring this letter to you and to say that he will show a light tomorrow evening as a signal, and he hopes you will lead the attack yourself. Zheng Wen will work from the inside in your favor."

Sima Yi took great pains to test the reliability of these statements, and he examined the letter minutely to see if it bore any signs of fabrication, but he found it was Zheng Wen's writing.

Presently he ordered in refreshments for the bearer of the letter, and then he said, "We will fix today at the second watch for the raid, and I will lead in person. If it succeeds, I will give you a good appointment as a reward."

Taking leave, the soldier retraced his steps to his own camp and reported the whole interview to Zhuge Liang.

Zhuge Liang held his sword aloft toward the North Star, took the proper paces for an incantation, and prayed.

This done, he summoned Wang Ping, Zhang Ni, Wei Yan, Ma Dai, Ma Zheng, and Jiang Wei, to whom he gave certain instructions. When they had gone to carry them out, he ascended a hill, taking with him a few score guards only.

Sima Yi had been taken in by Zheng Wen's letter and intended to lead the night raid. But the elder of his sons, Sima Shi, expostulated with his father.

"Father, you are going on a dangerous expedition on the faith of a mere scrap of paper," said his son. "I think it imprudent. What if something goes unexpectedly wrong? Let some general go in your place, and you come up in rear as a reserve."

Sima Yi saw there was reason in this proposal, and he finally decided to send Qin Lang, with ten thousand troops, and Sima Yi himself would command the reserve.

The night was fine with a bright moon. But about the middle of the second watch the sky clouded over, and it became very black, so that a man could not see his next neighbor.

"This is providential," chuckled Sima Yi.

The expedition duly started, soldiers with gags, and horses with cords round their muzzles. They moved swiftly and silently, and Qin Lang made straight for the camp of Shu.

But when he reached it and entered, and saw not a soldier, he knew he had been tricked. He yelled to his troops to retire, but lights sprang up all round, and attacks began from four sides. Fight as he would, Qin Lang could not free himself.

From behind the battle area Sima Yi saw flames rising from the camp of Shu and heard continuous shouting, but he knew not whether it meant victory for his own army or to his enemy. He pressed forward toward the fire. Suddenly, a shout, a roll of drums, and a blare of trumpets close at hand, a bomb that seemed to rend the earth, and Wei Yan and Jiang Wei bore down upon Sima Yi, one on each flank. This was the final blow to him. Of every ten soldiers of Wei, eight or nine were killed or wounded, and the few others scattered to the four winds.

Meanwhile Qin Lang's ten thousand troops were falling under arrows that came in locust-flights, and their leader was killed. Sima Yi and the remnant of his army ran away to their own camp.

After the third watch the sky cleared. Zhuge Liang from the hill-top sounded the gong of retreat. This obscurity in the third watch was due to an incantation called Concealing Method. The sky became clear, because Zhuge Liang performed another incantation to have the Deities of Six Layers sweep away the few floating clouds that still persisted.

The victory was complete. The first order on Zhuge Liang's return to camp was to put Zheng Wen to death.

Next he considered new plans for capturing the south bank. Every day be sent a party to offer a challenge before the camps of the enemy, but no one accepted.

One day Zhuge Liang rode in his small chariot to the front of the Qishan Mountains, keenly scanned the course of River Wei and carefully surveyed the lie of the land. Presently he came to a valley shaped like a bottle-gourd, large enough to form a hiding place for a whole thousand soldiers in the inner recess, while half as many more could hide in the outer. In rear the mountains were so close that they left passage only for a single horseman. The discovery pleased the general mightily, and he asked the guides what the place was called.

They replied, "It is called Shangfang Valley, and nicknamed Gourd Valley."

Returning to his camp, he called up two leaders named Du Rui and Hu Zhong and whispered into their ears certain secret orders. Next he called up a thousand craftspeople and sent them into the Gourd Valley to construct "wooden oxen and running horses" for the use of the troops. Finally he set Ma Dai with five hundred troops to guard the mouth of the Gourd Valley and prevent all entrance and exit.

Zhuge Liang said, "People from outside cannot enter, from inside cannot exit. I will visit the valley at irregular intervals to inspect the work. A plan for the defeat of Sima Yi is being prepared here and must be kept a profound secret."

Ma Dai left to take up the position. The two generals, Du Rui and Hu Zhong, were superintendents of the work in the Gourd Valley. Zhuge Liang came every day to give instructions.

One day Yang Yi went to Zhuge Liang and said, "The stores of grain are all at Saber Pass, and the labor of transport is very heavy. What can be done?"

Zhuge Liang replied, smiling, "I have had a scheme ready for a long time. The timber that I collected and bought in the River Lands was for the construction of wooden transport animals to convey grain. It will be very advantageous, as they will require neither food nor water and they can keep on the move day and night without resting."

All those within hearing said, "From old days till now no one has ever heard of such a device. What excellent plan have you, O Prime Minister, to make such marvelous creatures?"

"They are being made now after my plans, but they are not yet ready. Here I have the sketches for these mechanical oxen and horses, with all their dimensions written out in full. You may see the details."

Zhuge Liang then produced a paper, and all the generals crowded round to look at it. They were all greatly astonished and lauded, "The Prime Minister is superhuman!"

A few days later the new mechanical animals were complete and began work. They were quite life-like and went over the hills in any desired direction. The whole army saw them with delight. They were but in charge of Right General Gao Xiang and a thousand soldiers to guide them. They kept going constantly between Saber Pass and the front carrying grain for the use of the soldiers.

Along the Saber Pass mountain roads
The running horses bore their loads,
And through Xie Valley's narrow way
The wooden oxen paced each day.
O generals, use these means today,
And transport troubles take away.

Sima Yi was already sad enough at his defeat, when the spies told him of these wooden bullocks and horses of new design which the soldiers of Shu were using to convey their grain.

This troubled him still more, and he said to his generals, "I knew the transportation from the River Lands was difficult; therefore, I shut the gates and remained on the defensive waiting for the enemy to be starved. With this device, they may never be compelled to retreat for want of food."

Then he called up Zhang Hu and Yue Chen and gave orders: "Each of you with five hundred troops will goes to the Xie Valley by by-roads. When you see the Shu soldiers transport their grain by, you are to let them through, but only to attack at the end and capture four or five of the wooden horses and bullocks."

So a thousand soldiers went on this service disguised as soldiers of Shu. They made their way along the by-ways by night and hid. Presently the wooden convoy came along under the escort of Gao Xiang. Just as the end of it was passing, they made a sudden rush, and captured a few of the "animals" which the soldiers of Shu abandoned. In high glee they took them to their own camp.

When Sima Yi saw them, he had to confess they were very life-like. But what pleased him most was that he could imitate them now that he had models.

"If Zhuge Liang can use this sort of thing, it would be strange if I could not," said he.

He called to him many clever craftspeople and made them then and there take the machines to pieces and make some exactly like them. In less than half a month, they had completed a couple of thousand after Zhuge Liang's models, and the new mechanical animals could move. Then Sima Yi placed Cen Wei, General Who Guards the Frontiers, in charge of this new means of transport, and the "animals" began to ply between the camp and the West Valley Land. The Wei soldiers were filled with joys.

Gao Xiang returned to camp and reported the loss of a few of his wooden oxen and horses.

"I wished him to capture some of them," said Zhuge Liang, much pleased. "I am just laying out these few, and before long I shall get some very solid help in exchange."

"How do you know, O Prime Minister?" said his officers.

"Because Sima Yi will certainly copy them; and when he has done that, I have another plan ready to play on him."

Some days later Zhuge Liang received a report that the enemy were using the same sort of wooden bullocks and horses to bring up supplies from Xizhou.

"Exactly as I thought," said be.

Calling Wang Ping, he said, "Dress up a thousand soldiers as those of Wei, and find your way quickly and secretly to Beiyuan. Tell them that you are escort for the convoy, and mingle with the real escort. Then suddenly turn on them so that they scatter. Next you will turn the herd this way. By and by you will be pursued. When that occurs, you will give a turn to the tongues of the wooden animals, and they will be locked from movement. Leave them where they are and run away. When the soldiers of Wei come up, they will be unable to drag the creatures and equally unable to carry them. I shall have soldiers ready, and you will go back with them, give the tongues a backward turn and bring the convoy here, The enemy will be greatly astonished."

Next he called Zhang Ni and said, "Dress up five hundred soldiers in the costume of the Deities of the Six Layers so that they appear supernatural. Fit them with demon heads and wild beast shapes, and let them stain their faces various colors so as to look as strange as possible. Give them flags and swords and bottle-gourds with smoke issuing from combustibles inside. Let these soldiers hide among the hills till the convoy approaches, when they will start the smoke, rush out suddenly and drive off the wooden animals. No one will dare pursue such uncanny company."

When Zhang Ni had left, Wei Yan and Jiang Wei were called.

"You will take ten thousand troops, go to the border of Beiyuan to receive the wooden transport creatures and defend them against attack."

Then another five thousand under Zhang Yi and Liao Hua was sent to check Sima Yi if he should come, while a small force under Ma Dai and Ma Zheng was sent to bid defiance to the enemy near their camp on the south bank.

So one day when a convoy was on its way from the West Valley Land, the scouts in front suddenly reported some soldiers ahead who said they were escort for the grain. Commander Cen Wei halted and sent to inquire. It appeared the newcomers were really the soldiers of Wei, however, and so he started once more.

The newcomers joined up with his own troops. But before they had gone much farther, there was a yell, and the men of Shu began to kill, while a voice shouted, "Wang Ping is here!"

The convoy guard were taken aback. Many were killed, but the others rallied round Cen Wei and made some defense. However, Wang Ping slew

Cen Wei, and the others ran this way and that, while the convoy was turned toward the Shu camp.

The fugitives ran off to Beiyuan and reported the mishap to Guo Huai, who set out hot foot to rescue the convoy. When he appeared, Wang Ping gave the order to turn tongues, left the wooden animals in the road, and ran away. Guo Huai made no attempt to pursue, but tried to put the wooden animals in motion toward their proper destination. But he could not move them.

He was greatly perplexed. Then suddenly there arose the roll of drums all round, and out burst two parties of soldiers. These were Wei Yan and Jiang Wei's troops, and when they appeared Wang Ping's soldiers faced about and came to the attack as well. These three being too much for Guo Huai; he retreated before them. Thereupon the tongues were turned back again and the wooden herd set in motion.

Seeing this, Guo Huai came on again. But just then he saw smoke curling up among the hills and a lot of extraordinary creatures burst out upon him. Some held swords and some flags, and all were terrible to look at. They rushed at the wooden animals and urged them away.

"Truly these are supernatural helpers," cried Guo Huai, quite frightened.

The soldiers also were terror-stricken and stood still.

Hearing that his Beiyuan troops had been driven off, Sima Yi came out to the rescue. Midway along the road, just where it was most precipitous, a cohort burst out upon him with fierce yells and bursting bombs. Upon the leading banners he read Han General Zhang Yi and Han General Liao Hua.

Panic seized upon his army, and they ran like winds.

In the field the craftier leader on the convoy makes a raid,
And his rival's life endangers by an ambush subtly laid.

If you would know the upshot, read the next chapter.

Chapter 103

**In Gourd Valley, Sima Yi Is Trapped;
In Wuzhang Hills, Zhuge Liang Invokes The Stars.**

Heavily smitten in the battle, Sima Yi fled from the field a lonely horseman. Seeing a thick wood in the distance, he made for its shelter.

Zhang Yi halted the rear division while Liao Hua pressed forward after the fugitive, whom he could see threading his way among the trees. And Sima Yi indeed was soon in fear of his life, dodging from tree to tree as his pursuer neared. Once Liao Hua was actually close enough to slash at his enemy, but Liao Hua missed the blow and his sword struck a tree; and before he could pull his sword out of the wood, Sima Yi had got clear away. When Liao Hua got through into the open country, he did not know which way to go. Presently he noticed a golden helmet lying on the ground to the east, just lately thrown aside. He picked it up, hung it on his saddle, and went away eastward.

But the crafty fugitive, having flung away his helmet thus on the east side of the wood, had gone away west, so that Liao Hua was going away from his quarry. After some time Liao Hua fell in with Jiang Wei, when he abandoned the pursuit and rode with Jiang Wei back to camp.

The wooden oxen and running horses having been

driven into camp, their loads were put into the storehouse. The grain that fell to the victors amounted to ten thousand carts or more.

Liao Hua presented the enemy's helmet as proof of his prowess in the field, and received a reward of the first grade of merit. Wei Yan went away angry and discontented; Zhuge Liang noticed this, but he said nothing.

Very sadly Sima Yi returned to his own camp. Bad news followed, for a messenger brought letters telling of an invasion by three armies of Wu. The letters said that forces had been sent against them, and the Ruler of Wei again enjoined upon his Commander-in-Chief a waiting and defensive policy. So Sima Yi deepened his moats and raised his ramparts.

Meanwhile, when the South Land marched against the Middle Land, Cao Rui sent three armies against the invaders: Liu Shao led that to save Jiangxia; Tian Du led the Xiangyang force; Cao Rui himself, with Man Chong, went into Hefei. This last was the main army.

Man Chong led the leading division toward Lake Chaohu. Thence, looking across to the eastern shore, he saw a forest of battleships, and flags and banners crowded the sky. So he returned to the main army and proposed an attack without loss of time.

"The enemy think we shall be fatigued after a long march, and so they have not troubled to prepare any defense. We should attack this night, and we shall overcome them."

"What you say accords with my own ideas," said the Ruler of Wei.

Then the Ruler of Wei told off the cavalry leader, Zhang Qiu, to take five thousand troops and try to burn out the enemy with combustibles. Man Chong was also to attack from the eastern bank.

In the second watch of that night, the two forces set out and gradually approached the entrance to the lake. They reached the marine camp unobserved, burst upon it with a yell, and the soldiers of Wu fled without striking a blow. The troops of Wei set fires going in every direction and thus destroyed all the ships together with much grain and many weapons.

Zhuge Jin, who was in command, led his beaten troops to Miankou, and the attackers returned to their camp much elated.

When the report came to Lu Xun, he called together his officers and said, "I must write to the Emperor to abandon the siege of Xincheng, that the army may be employed to cut off the retreat of the Wei army while I will attack them in front. They will be harassed by the double danger, and we shall break them."

All agreed that this was a good plan, and the memorial was drafted. It was sent by the hand of a junior officer, who was told to convey it secretly. But this messenger was captured at the ferry and taken before the Ruler of Wei.

Cao Rui read the dispatch, then said with a sigh, "This Lu Xun of Wu is really very resourceful."

The captive was put into prison, and Liu Shao was told off to defend the rear and keep off Sun Quan's army.

Now Zhuge Jin's defeated soldiers were suffering from hot weather illnesses, and at length he was compelled to write and tell Lu Xun, and ask that his army be relieved and sent home.

Having read this dispatch, Lu Xun said to the messenger, "Make my obeisance to the General, and say that I will decide."

When the messenger returned with this reply, Zhuge Jin asked what was doing in the Commander-in-Chief's camp.

The messenger replied, "The soldiers were all outside planting beans, and the officers were amusing themselves at the gates. They were playing a game of skill, throwing arrows into narrow-necked vases."

Alarmed, Zhuge Jin himself went to his chief's camp.

Said he, "Cao Rui himself leads the expedition, and the enemy is very strong. How do you, O Commander, meet this pressing danger?"

Lu Xun replied, "My messenger to the Emperor was captured, and thus my plans were discovered. Now it is useless to prepare to fight, and so we had better retreat. I have sent in a memorial to engage the Emperor to retire gradually."

Zhuge Jin replied, "Why delay? If you think it best to retire, it had better be done quickly."

"My army must retreat slowly, or the enemy will come in pursuit, which will mean defeat and loss. Now you must first prepare your ships as if you meant to resist, while I make a semblance of an attack toward Xiangyang. Under cover of these operations we shall withdraw into the South Land, and the enemy will not dare to follow."

So Zhuge Jin returned to his own camp and began to fit out his ships as if for an immediate expedition, while Lu Xun made all preparations to march, giving out that he intended to advance upon Xiangyang.

The news of these movements were duly reported in the Wei camps. When the leaders heard it, they wished to go out and fight. But the Ruler of Wei knew his opponent better than they and would not bring about a battle.

So he called his officers together and said to them, "This Lu Xun is very crafty. Keep careful guard, but do not risk a battle."

The officers obeyed.

A few days later the scouts brought in news: "The three armies of Wu have retired!"

The Ruler of Wei doubted and sent out some of his own spies, who confirmed the report.

When he thus knew it was true, he consoled himself with the words, "Lu Xun knows the art of war even as did Sun Zi and Wu Qi[xix]. The subjugation of the southeast is not for me this time."

Thereupon Cao Rui distributed his generals among the various vantage points and led the main army back into Hefei, where he camped ready to take advantage of any change of conditions that might promise success.

Meanwhile Zhuge Liang was at Qishan, where he intended to make a long sojourn. He made his soldiers mix with the people in Wei and share in the labor of the fields, and the crops---the soldiers one-third, the people two-third. He gave strict orders against any encroachment on the property of the farmers, and so they and the soldiers lived together very amicably.

Then Sima Yi's son, Sima Shi, went to his father and said, "These soldiers of Shu have despoiled us of much grain, and now they are mingling with the people of Qishan and tilling the fields along the banks of River Wei as if they intended to remain there. This would be a calamity for us. Why do you not appoint a time to fight a decisive battle with Zhuge Liang?"

His father replied, "I have the Emperor's orders to act on the defensive and may not do as you suggest."

While they were thus talking, one reported that Wei Yan had come near and was insulting the army and reminding them that he had the helmet of their leader. And he was challenging them. The generals were greatly incensed and desired to accept the challenge, but the Commander-in-Chief was immovable in his decision to obey his orders.

"The Holy One says: 'If one cannot suffer small things, great matters are imperiled.' Our plan is to defend."

So the challenge was not accepted, and there was no battle. After reviling them for some time, Wei Yan went away.

Seeing that his enemy was not to be provoked into fighting, Zhuge Liang gave orders to Ma Dai to build a strong stockade in the Gourd Valley and therein to excavate pits and to collect large quantities of inflammables. So on the hill they piled wood and straw in the shape of sheds, and all about they dug pits and buried mines. When these preparations were complete, Ma Dai received instructions to block the road in rear of Gourd Valley and to lay an ambush at the entrance.

"If Sima Yi comes, let him enter the valley, and then explode the mines and set fire to the straw and the wood," said Zhuge Liang. "Also, set up seven star flags at the mouth of the valley and arrange a night signal of seven lamps on the hill."

After Ma Dai had gone, Wei Yan was called in, and Zhuge Liang said to him, "Go to the camp of Wei with five hundred troops and provoke them to battle. The important matter is to entice Sima Yi out of his stronghold. You will be unable to obtain a victory, so retreat that he may pursue. You are to make for the signal, the seven star flags by day or the seven lamps at night. Thus you will lead him into the Gourd Valley, where I have a plan prepared for him."

When Wei Yan had gone, Gao Xiang was summoned.

"Take small herds, forty or fifty at a time, of the

wooden oxen and running horses, load them up with grain and lead them to and fro on the mountains. If you can succeed in getting the enemy to capture them, you will render a service."

So the transport wooden cattle were sent forth to play their part in the scheme, and the remainder of the Qishan soldiers were sent to work in the fields.

He gave orders to his generals, saying, "If the enemy under other leaders come to attack, you are to flee the field. Only in the case Sima Yi comes in person, you are to attack most vigorously the south bank of the river and cut off the retreat."

Then Zhuge Liang led his army away to camp next to the Gourd Valley.

Xiahou Hui and Xiahou He went to their chief, Sima Yi, and said, "The enemy have set out camps and are engaged in field work as though they intended to remain. If they are not destroyed now, but are allowed to consolidate their position, they will be hard to dislodge."

"This certainly is one of Zhuge Liang's ruses," said the chief.

"You seem very afraid of him, Commander," retorted they. "When do you think you can destroy him? At least let us two brothers fight one battle that we may prove our gratitude for the Emperor's kindness."

"If it must be so, then you may go in two divisions," said Sima Yi.

As the two divisions, five thousand troops each,

were marching along, they saw coming toward them a number of the transport wooden animals of the enemy. They attacked at once, drove off the escort, captured them, and sent them back to camp. Next day they captured more, with soldiers and horses as well, and sent them also to camp.

Sima Yi called up the prisoners and questioned them.

They told him, saying, "The Prime Minister understood that you would not fight, and so had told off the soldiers to various places to work in the fields, and therefore provide for future needs. We had been unwittingly captured."

Sima Yi set them free and bade them begone.

"Why spare them?" asked Xiahou He.

"There is nothing to be gained by the slaughter of a few common soldiers. Let them go back to their own and praise the kindliness of the Wei leaders. That will slacken the desire of their comrades to fight against us. That was the plan by which Lu Meng captured Jingzhou."

Then he issued general orders that all Shu prisoners should be well treated and sent away free. However, he kept rewarding those of his army who had done well.

As has been said, Gao Xiang was ordered to keep pretended convoys on the move, and the soldiers of Wei attacked and captured them whenever they saw them. In half a month they had scored many successes of this sort, and Sima Yi's heart was cheered. One day, when he had made new captures of soldiers, he sent for them and questioned them again.

"Where is Zhuge Liang now?"

"He is no longer at Qishan, but in camp about three miles from the Gourd Valley. He is gathering a great store of grain there."

After he had questioned them fully, he set the prisoners free.

Calling together his officers, he said, "Zhuge Liang is not camped on Qishan, but near the Gourd Valley. Tomorrow you shall attack the Qishan camp, and I will command the reserve."

The promise cheered them, and they went away to prepare.

"Father, why do you intend to attack the enemy's rear?" asked Sima Shi.

"Qishan is their main position, and they will certainly hasten to its rescue. Then I shall make for the valley and burn the stores. That will render them helpless and will be a victory."

The son exclaimed his admiration for the plan.

Sima Yi began to march out, with Zhang Hu and Yue Chen following as the reserves.

From the top of a hill Zhuge Liang watched the Wei soldiers march and noticed that they moved in companies from three to five thousand, observing the front and the rear carefully as they marched. He guessed that their object was the Qishan camp.

So he sent strict orders to his generals: "If Sima Yi leads in person, you are to go off and capture the Wei camp and the south bank of River Wei."

They received and obeyed his orders.

When the troops of Wei had got near and made their rush toward the camp of Shu in Qishan, the troops of Shu ran up also, yelling and pretending to reinforce the defenders. Sima Yi, seeing the Shu troops rushing to rescure Qishan, suddenly marched his center army's guards with his two sons, changed his direction, and turned off for the Gourd Valley. Here Wei Yan was expecting him; and as soon as he appeared, Wei Yan galloped up and soon recognized Sima Yi as the leader.

"Sima Yi, stay!" shouted Wei Yan as he came near.

He flourished his sword, and Sima Yi set his spear. The two warriors exchanged a few passes, and then Wei Yan suddenly turned his steed and bolted. As he had been ordered, he made direct for the seven star flags, and Sima Yi followed, the more readily as he saw the fugitive had but a small force. The two sons of Sima Yi rode with him, Sima Shi on the left, Sima Zhao on the right.

Presently Wei Yan and his troops entered the mouth of the valley. Sima Yi halted a time while he sent forward a few scouts.

They returned and reported: "Not a single Shu soldier is seen, but a many straw houses are on the hills."

Sima Yi said, "This must be the store valley!"

He led his army in eagerly. But when he had got well within, Sima Yi noticed that kindling wood was piled over the straw huts; and as he saw no sign of Wei Yan, he began to feel uneasy.

"Supposing soldiers seize the entrance. What then?" said he to his sons.

As he spoke there arose a great shout, and from the hillside came many torches, which fell all around them and set fire to the straw, so that soon the entrance to the valley was lost in smoke and flame. They tried to get away from the fire, but no road led up the hillside. Then fire-arrows came shooting down, and the earth-mines exploded, and the straw and firewood blazed high as the heavens. The fire caused strong winds, and the winds aided the fire; and the valley became a fiery stove.

Sima Yi, scared and helpless, dismounted, clasped his arms about his two sons, and wept, saying, "My sons, we three are doomed!"

As they stood weeping, a fierce gale suddenly sprang up, black clouds gathered, a peal of thunder followed, and rain poured down in torrents, speedily extinguishing the fire all through the valley. The mines no longer exploded, and all the fiery contrivances ceased to work mischief.

"If we do not break out now, what better chance shall we have?" cried Sima Yi, and he led the soldiers to make a dash for the outlet.

As they broke out of the valley, they came upon reinforcements under Zhang Hu and Yue Chen, and so were once more safe. Ma Dai was not strong enough to pursue, and the soldiers of Wei got safely to the river.

But there they found their camp in the possession of the enemy, while Guo Huai and Sun Li were on the floating bridge struggling with the troops of Shu. Sima Yi charged up hastily, and the troops of Shu retreated, whereupon Sima Yi crossed the river and ordered the bridges burned. He then occupied the north bank.

The Wei army attacking the Qishan camp were greatly disturbed when they heard of the defeat of their Commander-in-Chief and the loss of the camp on River Wei. The troops of Shu took the occasion to strike with greater vigor, and so gained a great victory. The beaten army suffered heavy loss. Those who escaped fled across the river.

When Zhuge Liang from the hill-top saw that Sima Yi had been inveigled into the trap by Wei Yan, he rejoiced exceedingly; and when he saw the flames burst forth, he thought surely his rival was done for. Then, unhappily for him, Heaven thought it well to send down torrents of rain, which quenched the fire and upset all his calculations.

Soon after, the scouts reported the escape of his victims.

Zhuge Liang sighed, saying, "Human proposes; God disposes. We cannot wrest events to our will."

Fierce fires roared in the valley,
But the rain quenched them.
Had Zhuge Liang's plan but succeeded,
Where had been the Jins?

From the new camp on the north bank of the river, Sima Yi issued an order: "The south shore has been lost. If any of you proposes going out to battle again, he shall be put to death!"

Accordingly no one spoke of attacking, but all turned their energies toward defense.

Guo Huai went to the general to talk over plans.

He said, "The enemy have been carefully spying out the country. They are certainly selecting a new position for a camp."

Sima Yi said, "If Zhuge Liang goes out to Wugong Hills, and thence eastward along the hills, we shall be in grave danger. If he goes westward along River Wei, and halts on the Wuzhang Hills, we need feel no anxiety."

They decided to send scouts to find out the movements of their enemy. Presently the scouts returned to say that Zhuge Liang had chosen the Wuzhang Hills.

"Our great Emperor of Wei has remarkable fortune," said Sima Yi, clapping his hand to his forehead.

Then he confirmed the order to remain strictly on the defensive till some change of circumstances on the part of the enemy should promise advantage.

After his army had settled into camp on the Wuzhang Hills, Zhuge Liang continued his attempts to provoke a battle. Day after day, parties went to challenge the army of Wei, but they resisted all provocation.

One day Zhuge Liang put a dress made of deer hide in a box, which he sent, with a letter, to his rival. The insult could not be concealed, so the generals led the bearer of the box to their chief. Sima Yi opened the box and saw the deer hide dress. Then he opened the letter, which read something like this:

"Friend Sima Yi, although you are a Commander-in-Chief and lead the armies of the Middle Land, you seem but little disposed to display the firmness and valor that would render a contest decisive. Instead, you have prepared a comfortable lair where you are safe from the keen edge of the sword. Are you not very like a deer? Wherefore I send the bearer with a suitable gift, and you will humbly accept it and the humiliation, unless, indeed, you finally decide to come out and fight like a warrior. If you are not entirely indifferent to shame, if you retain any of the feelings of a tiger, you will send this back to me and come out and give battle."

Sima Yi, although inwardly raging, pretended to take it all as a joke and smiled.

"So he regards me as a deer," said he.

He accepted the gift and treated the messenger well. Before the messenger left, Sima Yi asked him a few questions about his master's eating and sleeping and hours of labor.

"The Prime Minister works very hard," said the messenger. "He rises early and retires to bed late. He attends personally to all cases requiring punishment of over twenty of strokes. As for food, he does not eat more than a few pints of grain daily."

"Indeed, Zhuge Liang eats little and works much," remarked Sima Yi to his generals. "Can he last long?"

The messenger returned to his own side and reported to Zhuge Liang, saying, "Sima Yi took the whole episode in good part and shown no sign of anger. He only asked about the Prime Minister's hours of rest, and food, and such things. He said no word about military matters. I told him that you ate little and worked long hours, and then he said, 'Can he last long?' That was all."

"He knows me," said Zhuge Liang, pensively.

First Secretary Yang Yong presently ventured to remonstrate with his chief.

"I notice," said Yang Yong, "that you check the books personally. I think that is needless labor for a Prime Minister to undertake. In every administration the higher and subordinate ranks have their especial fields of activity, and each should confine his labors to his own field. In a household, for example, the male plows and the female cooks, and thus operations are carried on without waste of energy, and all needs are supplied. If one individual strives to attend personally to every matter, he only wearies himself and fails to accomplish his end. How can he possibly hope to perform all the various tasks well?

"And, indeed, the ancients held this same opinion, for they said that the high officers should attend to the discussion of ways and means, and the lower should carry out details. Of old, Bing Ji[xx] was moved to deep thought by the panting of an ox, but inquired not about the corpses of certain brawlers which lay about the road, for this matter concerned the magistrate. Chen Ping[xxi] was ignorant of the figures relating to taxes, for he said these were the concern of the tax controllers. O Prime Minister, you weary yourself with minor details and sweat yourself everyday. You are wearing yourself out, and Sima Yi has good reason for what he said."

"I know---I cannot but know," replied Zhuge Liang with tears in his eyes. "But this heavy responsibility was laid upon me, and I fear no other will be so devoted as I am."

Those who heard him wept. Thereafter Zhuge Liang appeared more and more harassed, and military operations did not speed.

On the other side the officers of Wei resented bitterly the insult that had been put upon them when their leader had been presented with the deer hide dress.

They wished to avenge the taunt, and went to their general, saying, "We are reputable generals of the army of a great state. How can we put up with such insults from these soldiers of Shu? We pray you let us fight them."

"It is not that I fear to go out," said Sima Yi, "nor that I relish the insults, but I have the Emperor's command to hold on and may not disobey."

The officers were not in the least appeased.

Wherefore Sima Yi said, "I will send your request to the Throne in a memorial. What think you of that?"

They consented to await the Emperor's reply, and a messenger bore to the Ruler of Wei, in Hefei, this memorial:

"I have small ability and high office. Your Majesty laid on me the command to defend and not fight till the army of Shu had suffered by the flux of time. But Zhuge Liang has now sent me a gift of a deer hide dress, and my shame is very deep. Wherefore I advise Your Majesty that one day I shall have to fight in order to justify your kindness to me and to remove the shameful stigma that now rests upon my army. I cannot express the degree to which I am urged to this course."

Cao Rui read it and turned questioningly to his courtiers seeking an explanation.

Said he, "Sima Yi has been in obstinate defense: Why does he want to attack now?"

Commander Xin Pi replied, "Sima Yi has no desire to give battle. This memorial is because of the shame put upon the officers by Zhuge Liang's gift. They are all in a rage. He wishes for an edict to pacify them."

Cao Rui understood and gave to Xin Pi an

authority ensign and sent him to the River Wei camp to make known that it was the Emperor's command not to fight.

Sima Yi received the messenger with all respect, and it was given out that any future reference to offering battle would be taken as disobedience to the Emperor's especial command in the edict.

The officers could but obey.

Sima Yi said to Xin Pi, "Noble Sir, you interpreted my own desire correctly!"

It was thenceforward understood that Sima Yi was forbidden to give battle.

When it was told to Zhuge Liang, he said, "This is only Sima Yi's method of pacifying his army."

Wei Jiang asked, "How do you know, O Prime Minister?"

"Sima Yi has never had any intention of fighting. So he requested the edict to justify his strategy. It is well known that a general in the field takes no command from any person, not even his own prince. Is it likely that he would send a thousand miles to ask permission to fight if that was all he needed? The officers were bitter, and so Sima Yi got the Emperor to assist him in maintaining discipline. All this is meant to slacken our soldiers."

Just at this time Fei Yi came from Capital Chengdu. He was called in to see the Prime Minister, and Zhuge Liang asked the reason for his coming.

He replied, "The Ruler of Wei, Cao Rui, hearing that Wu has invaded his country at three points, has led a great army to Hefei and sent three armies under Man Chong, Tian Du, and Liu Shao, to oppose the invaders. The stores and fight-material of Wu have been burned, and the army of Wu have fallen victims to sickness. A letter from Lu Xun containing a scheme of attack fell into the hands of the enemy, and the Ruler of Wu has marched back into his own country."

Zhuge Liang listened to the end; then, without a word, he fell in a swoon. He recovered after a time, but he was broken.

He said, "My mind is all in confusion. This is a return of my old illness, and I am doomed."

Ill as he was, Zhuge Liang that night went forth from his tent to scan the heavens and study the stars. They filled him with fear.

He returned and said to Jiang Wei, "My life may end at any moment."

"Why do you say such a thing?"

"Just now in the Triumvirate constellation the Guest Star was twice as bright as usual, while the Host Star was darkened; the supporting stars were also obscure. With such an aspect I know my fate."

"If the aspect be as malignant as you say, why not pray in order to avert it?" replied Jiang Wei.

"I am in the habit of praying," replied Zhuge Liang, "but I know not the will of God. However, prepare me forty-nine guards and let each have a black flag. Dress them in black and place them outside my tent. Then will I from within my tent invoke the Seven Stars of the North. If my master-lamp remain alight for seven days, then is my life to be prolonged for twelve years. If the lamp goes out, then I am to die. Keep all idlers away from the tent, and let a couple of guards bring me what is necessary."

Jiang Wei prepared as directed.

It was then the eighth month, mid-autumn, and the Milky Way was brilliant with scattered jade. The air was perfectly calm, and no sound was heard. The forty-nine men were brought up and spaced out to guard the tent, while within Zhuge Liang prepared incense and offerings. On the floor of the tent he arranged seven lamps, and, outside these, forty-nine smaller lamps. In the midst he placed the lamp of his own fate.

This done, he prayed:

"Zhuge Liang, born into an age of trouble, would willingly have grown old in retirement. But His Majesty, Liu Bei the Glorious Emperor, sought him thrice and confided to him the heavy responsibility of guarding his son. He dared not do less than spend himself to the utmost in such a task, and he pledged himself to destroy the rebels. Suddenly the star of his leadership has declined, and his life now nears its close. He has humbly indited a declaration on this silk piece to the Great Unknowable and now hopes that He will graciously listen and extend the number of his days that he may prove his gratitude to his prince and be the savior of the people, restore the old state of the empire and establish eternally the Han sacrifices. He dares not make a vain prayer: This is from his heart."

This prayer ended, in the solitude of his tent Zhuge Liang awaited the dawn.

Next day, ill as he was, he did not neglect his duties, although he spat blood continually. All day he labored at his plans, and at night he paced the magic steps, the steps of seven stars of Ursa Major and Ursa Minor.

Sima Yi remained still on the defensive.

One night as he sat gazing up at the sky and studying its aspect, he suddenly turned to Xiahou Ba, saying, "A leadership star has just lost position: Surely Zhuge Liang is ill and will soon die. Take a reconnoitering party of one thousand to the Wuzhang Hills and find out. If you see signs of confusion, it means that Zhuge Liang is ill. I shall take the occasion to smite hard."

Xiahou Ba left with an army.

It was the sixth night of Zhuge Liang's prayers, and the lamp of his fate still burned brightly. He began to feel a secret joy. Presently Jiang Wei entered and watched the ceremonies. He saw Zhuge Liang was loosening his hair, his hand holding a sword, his heels stepping on Ursa Major and Ursa Minor to hold the leadership star.

Suddenly a great shouting was heard outside, and Wei Jiang was about to send someone to inquire when Wei Yan dashed in, crying, "The Wei soldiers are upon us!"

In his haste Wei Yan had knocked over and extinguished the Lamp of Fate.

Zhuge Liang threw down the sword and sighed, saying, "Life and death are foreordained. No prayers can alter them."

Stunned, Wei Yan fell to the earth and craved forgiveness. Jiang Wei got angry and drew his sword to slay the unhappy general.

Nought is under man's control,
Nor can he with fate contend.

The next chapter will unfold what happened.

Chapter 104

A Falling Star: The Prime Minister Ascends To Heaven;
A Wooden Statue: The Commander-In-Chief Is Terrified.

The unhappy Wei Yan did not suffer the edge of the sword, for Zhuge Liang stayed the stroke, saying, "It is my fate---not his fault."

So Jiang Wei put up his sword.

Zhuge Liang spat a few mouthfuls of blood, then sank wearily upon his couch.

Said he, "Sima Yi thinks I am dead, and he sent these few troops to make sure. Go and drive them off."

Wei Yan left the tent and led out a small party to drive away the troops of Wei, who fled as they appeared. He chased them to more than seven miles and returned. Then Zhuge Liang sent Wei Yan to his own camp and bade him keep a vigilant lookout.

Presently Jiang Wei came in, went up to the sick man's couch, and asked how he felt.

Zhuge Liang replied, "My death is very near. My chief desire has been to spend myself to the utmost to restore Han to its glory and to regain the Middle Land. But Heaven decrees it otherwise. My end is not far away. I have written a book in twenty-four chapters, 104,112 words, treating the Eight Needfuls, the Seven Cautions, the Six Fears, and the Five Dreads of war. But among all those about me there is no one fit to receive it and carry on my work save you. I pray you not to despise it."

He gave the treatise to Jiang Wei, who received it sobbing.

"I have also a plan for a multiple crossbow, which I have been unable to execute. The weapon shoots ten bolts of eight inches length at every discharge. The sketches are quite ready, and the weapons can be made according to them."

Jiang Wei took the papers with a deep bow.

The dying man continued, "There is no part of Shu that causes anxiety, save the Yinping Mountains. That must be carefully guarded. It is protected naturally by its lofty precipices, but it will surely be the cause of great losses."

Next Zhuge Liang sent for Ma Dai, to whom he gave certain whispered instructions, and then said, "You are to follow out my instructions after my death."

Soon after, Yang Yi entered the tent and went to the couch. He received a silken bag containing certain secret orders.

As Zhuge Liang gave it to him, he said, "After my death, Wei Yan will turn traitor. When that happens and the army is in danger, you will find herein what to do."

Just as these arrangements were finished, Zhuge

Liang fell into a swoon, from which he did not revive till late in the evening. Then he set himself to compose a memorial to the Latter Ruler.

When this reached the Latter Ruler, he was greatly alarmed and at once sent Chief Secretary Li Fu to visit and confer with the dying minister.

Li Fu traveled quickly to the Wuzhang Hills and was led to the tent of the Commander-in-Chief. He delivered the Latter Ruler's command and inquired after the sick man's welfare.

Zhuge Liang wept, and he replied, "Unhappily I am dying and leaving my task incomplete. I am injuring my country's policy and am in fault to the world. After my death you must aid the Emperor in perfect loyalty, and see that the old policy is continued, and the rules of government maintained. Do not lightly cast out the people I have employed. My plans of campaign have been confided to Jiang Wei, who can continue my policy for the service of the state. But my hour draws near, and I must write my testament."

Li Fu listened, and then took his leave.

Zhuge Liang made one final effort to carry out his duties. He rose from his couch, was helped into a small carriage, and thus made a round of inspection of all the camps and posts. But the cold autumn wind chilled him to the bone.

"I shall never again lead the army against the rebels," said he. "O Azure Heaven, when will this regret end?"

Zhuge Liang returned to his tent. He became

rapidly weaker and called Yang Yi to his bedside.

Said he, "Ma Dai, Wang Ping, Liao Hua, Zhang Yi, Zhang Ni may be depended on to the death. They have fought many campaigns and borne many hardships; they should be retained in the public service. After my death let everything go on as before, but the army is to be gradually withdrawn. You know the tactics to be followed, and I need say little. My friend Jiang Wei is wise and brave; set him to guard the retreat."

Yang Yi received these orders, weeping.

Next, writing materials were brought in and the dying minister set himself to write his testament. It is here given in substance:

"Life and death are the common lot, and fate cannot be evaded. Death is at hand, and I desire to prove my loyalty to the end. I, thy servant Zhuge Liang, dull of parts, was born into a difficult age, and it fell to my lot to guide military operations. I led a northern expedition, but failed to win complete success. Now sickness has laid hold upon me and death approaches, so that I shall be unable to accomplish my task. My sorrow is inexpressible.

"I desire Your Majesty to cleanse your heart and limit your desires, to practice self-control and to love the people, to maintain a perfectly filial attitude toward your late father and to be benevolent to all the world. Seek out the recluse scholars that you may obtain the services of the wise and good; repel the wicked and depraved that your moral standard may be exalted.

"To my household belong eight hundred mulberry trees and a hundred acres of land; thus there is ample provision for my family. While I have been employed in the service of the state, my needs have been supplied from official sources, but I have not contrived to make any additions to the family estate. At my death I shall not leave any increased possessions, even an excess roll of silk, that may cause Your Majesty to suspect that I have wronged you."

Having composed this document, the dying man turned again to Yang Yi, saying, "Do not wear mourning for me, but make a large coffer and therein place my body, with seven grains of rice in my mouth. Place a lamp at my feet and let my body move with the army as I was wont to do. If you refrain from mourning, then my leadership star will not fall, for my inmost soul will ascend and hold it in place. So long as my star retains its place, Sima Yi will be fearsome and suspicious.

"Let the army retreat, beginning with the rearmost division; send it away slowly, one camp at a time. If Sima Yi pursues, array the army and offer battle, turn to meet him and beat the attack. Let him approach till he is very near and then suddenly display the wooden image of myself that I have had carved, seated in my chariot in the midst of the army, with the generals right and left as usual. And you will frighten Sima Yi away."

Yang Yi listened to these words intently. That night Zhuge Liang was carried into the open and gazed up at the sky.

"That is my star," said he, pointing to one that

seemed to be losing its brilliancy and to be tottering in its place. Zhuge Liang's lips moved as if he muttered a spell. Presently he was borne into his tent and for a time was oblivious of all about him.

When the anxiety caused by this state of coma was at its height, Li Fu arrived.

He wept when he saw the condition of the great leader, crying, "I have foiled the great designs of the state!"

However, presently Zhuge Liang's eyes reopened and fell upon Li Fu standing near his couch.

"I know your mission," said Zhuge Liang.

"I came with the royal command to ask also who should control the destinies of the state for the next century," replied Li Fu. "In my agitation I forgot to ask that."

"After me, Jiang Wan is the most fitting man to deal with great matters."

"And after Jiang Wan?"

"After him, Fei Yi."

"Who is next after Fei Yi?"

No reply came, and when they looked more carefully, they perceived that the soul of the Prime Minister had passed.

Thus died Zhuge Liang, on the twenty-third day of

the eighth month in the twelfth year of Beginning Prosperity, at the age of fifty and four (AD 234).

The poet Du Fu wrote some verses on his death.

A bright star last night falling from the sky,
This message gave, "The Master is no more."
No more in camps shall bold men tramp at his command;
At court no statesman ever will fill the place he held;
At home, his clients miss their patron kind;
Sad for the army, who were lonely in this world.
In the green wood stones and creeks are crying,
No more of his lute, birds have hushed singing.

And Bai Juyi also wrote a poem:

Within the forest dim the Master lived obscure,
Till, thrice returning, there the prince his mentor met.
As when a fish the ocean gains, desire was filled
Wholly the dragon freed could soar aloft at will.
As king's son's guardian none more zealous was;
As minister, most loyally he wrought at court.
His war memorials still to us are left,
And, reading them, the tears unconscious fall.

Now in past days, Commander Liao Li in Changshui had a high opinion of his own abilities and thought himself perfectly fitted to be Zhuge Liang's second. So he neglected the duties of his proper post, showed discontent and indiscipline, and was constantly slandering the minister. Thereupon Zhuge Liang degraded him and transferred him to Minshan.

When Liao Li heard of Zhuge Liang's death, he shed tears and said, "Then, after all, I shall remain a barbarian!"

Li Yan also grieved deeply at the sad tidings, for he had always hoped that Zhuge Liang would restore him to office and so give him the opportunity of repairing his former faults. After Zhuge Liang had died, he thought there was no hope of reemployment, and so he died.

Another poet, Yuan Weizhi, also wrote in praise of the great adviser.

He fought disorder, helped a weak king;
Most zealously he kept his master's son.
In state-craft he excelled Guan Zhong, Yue Yi,
In war-craft he overpassed Wu Qi, Sun Zi.
With awe the court his war memorials heard,
With majesty his Eight Arrays were planned.
Virtue and wisdom both filled in his heart,
For thousand autumns, his fame would still stay.

Heaven grieved and earth mourned on the night of Zhuge Liang's death. Even the moon was dimmed, as Zhuge Liang's soul returned to Heaven.

As the late commander had directed, Jiang Wei and Yang Yi forbade the mourning of his death. His body was placed in the coffer as he had wished, and three hundred of his trusted leaders and soldiers were appointed to watch it.

Secret orders were given to Wei Yan to command the rearguard, and then, one by one, the camps were broken up and the army began its homeward march.

Sima Yi watched the skies. One night a large red star with bright rays passed from the northeast to the southwest and dropped over the camps of Shu. It dipped thrice and rose again. Sima Yi heard also a low rumbling in the distance.

He was pleased and excited, and said to those about him, "Zhuge Liang is dead!"

At once he ordered pursuit with a strong force. But just as he passed his camp gates, doubts filled his mind and he gave up the plan.

"Zhuge Liang is a master of mysteries: He can get aids from the Deities of the Six Layers. It may be that this is but a ruse to get us to take the field. We may fall victims to his guile."

So he halted. But he sent Xiahou Ba with a few dozen scouts to reconnoiter the enemy's camps.

One night as Wei Yan lay asleep in his tent, he dreamed a dream. In his vision two horns grew out of his head. When he awoke he was much perplexed to explain his dream.

Marching General Zhao Zhi came to see him, and Wei Yan said, "You are versed in the Book of Changes. I have dreamed that two horns grew upon my head, and would trouble you to expound the dream and tell me its portent."

Zhao Zhi thought a moment and replied, "It is an auspicious dream. Dragon and Jilin both have horns on the head. It augurs transformation into an ascending creature."

Wei Yan, much pleased, said, "If the dream proves true as you said, I will thank you with very generous gifts."

Zhao Zhi left and presently met Fei Yi, who asked whence he came.

"From the camp of our friend Wei Yan. He dreamed that he grew horns upon his head, and I have given him an auspicious interpretation. But really it is inauspicious. However, I did not wish to annoy him."

"How do you know it is inauspicious?"

"The word for horn is composed of two parts, 'knife' above and 'use' below, and so means that there is a knife upon his head. It is a terrible omen."

"Keep it secret," said Fei Yi.

Then Fei Yi went to the camp of Wei Yan, and when they were alone, he said, "The Prime Minister died last night in the third watch. He left certain final orders, and among them, that you are to command the rearguard to keep Sima Yi at bay while the army retreats. No mourning is to be worn. Here is your authority, so you can march forthwith."

"Who is acting in place of the late minister?" asked Wei.

"The chief command has been delegated to Yang Yi, but the secret plans of campaign have been entrusted to Jiang Wei. This authority was issued from Yang Yi."

Wei Yan replied, "Though the Prime Minister is dead, I am yet alive. Counselor Yang Yi is only a civil officer and unequal to this post. He ought to conduct the coffin home while I lead the army against Sima Yi. I shall achieve success, and it is wrong to abandon a whole plan of campaign because of the death of one man, even if that be the Prime Minister."

"The Prime Minister's orders were to retire, and these orders are to be obeyed."

"If the Prime Minister had listened to me, we should now have been at Changan. I am the Van Leader, General Who Conquers the West, and Lord of Nanzheng. I am not going to act as rearguard for any civil official," said Wei Yan, angry.

"It may be as you say, General, but you must not do anything to make us ridiculous. Let me go back to Yang Yi and explain, and I may be able to persuade him to pass on to you the supreme military authority he holds."

Wei Yan agreed, and Fei Yi went back to the main

camp and told Yang Yi what had passed.

Yang Yi replied, "When near death the Prime Minister confided to me that Wei Yan would turn traitor. I sent him the authority to test him, and now he has discovered himself as the Prime Minister foretold. So I will direct Jiang Wei to command the rearguard."

The coffer containing the remains of Zhuge Liang was sent on in advance, and Jiang Wei took up his post to cover the retreat.

Meanwhile Wei Yan sat in his tent waiting for the return of Fei Yi and was perplexed at the delay. When the suspense became unbearable, he sent Ma Dai to find out the reason.

Ma Dai returned and told him: "Jiang Wei is covering the retreat, and that most of the army has already gone."

Wei Yan was furious.

"How dare he play with me, the pedantic blockhead?" cried he. "But he shall die for this!"

Turning to Ma Dai, Wei Yan said, "Will you help me?"

Ma Dai replied, "I have long hated Yang Yi; certainly I am ready to attack him."

So Wei Yan broke camp and marched southward.

By the time Xiahou Ba had reached the Shu camps, they were all empty, and he hastened back with this news.

"Then Zhuge Liang is really dead! Let us pursue," said Sima Yi, much irritated at being misled.

"Be cautious," said Xiahou Ba. "Send an subordinate leader first."

"No; I must go myself this time."

So Sima Yi and his two sons hastened to the Wuzhang Hills. With shouts and waving flags, they rushed into the camps, only to find them quite deserted.

Sima Yi said to his sons, "You are to bring up the remaining force with all speed, whereas I will lead the vanguard."

Sima Yi hastened in the wake of the retreating army. Coming to some hills, he saw them in the distance and pressed on still harder. Then suddenly a bomb exploded, a great shout broke the stillness, and the retiring army turned about and came toward him, ready for battle. In their midst fluttered a great banner bearing the words, Prime Minister of Han, Lord of Wuxiang, Zhuge Liang.

Sima Yi stopped, pale with fear. Then out from the army came some score of generals of rank, and they were escorting a small carriage, in which sat Zhuge Liang as he had always appeared, in his hand the feather fan.

"Then Zhuge Liang is still alive!" gasped Sima Yi. "And I have rashly placed myself in his power."

As he pulled round his horse to flee, Jiang Wei shouted, "Do not try to run away, O rebel! You have fallen into one of the Prime Minister's traps and had better stay!"

The soldiers, seized with panic, fled, throwing off all their gear. They trampled each other down, and many perished. Their leader galloped fifteen miles without pulling rein. When at last two of his generals came up with him, and had stopped his flying steed by catching at the bridle, Sima Yi clapped his hand to his head, crying, "Have I still a head?"

"Do not fear, Commander, the soldiers of Shu are now far away," they replied.

But he still panted with fear, and only after some time did he recognize that his two companions were Xiahou Ba and Xiahou Hui. The three found their way by by-roads to their own camp, whence scouts were sent out in all directions.

In a few days the natives brought news: "The Shu army had really gone, and as soon as the retiring army entered the valley, they raised a wailing for the dead and hoisted white flags. Zhuge Liang was really dead, and Jiang Wei's rearguard consisted of only one thousand troops. The figure in the carriage was only a wooden image of the Prime Minister."

"While he lived, I could guess what he would do; dead, I was helpless!" said Sima Yi.

The people had a saying that "A dead Zhuge Liang can scare off a live Sima Yi."

In the depth of night a brilliant star
Fell from the northern sky;
Doubts stayed Sima Yi
When he would pursue
His dead, but fearsome enemy.
And even now the western people,
With scornful smile, will say
"Oh, is my head on my shoulder still?
It was nearly lost today."

Now indeed Sima Yi knew that his rival was no more, so he retook the pursuit. But when he reached the Red Hills, the Shu army had marched too far away.

As he took the homeward road, he said to his officers, "We can now sleep in comfort."

As they marched back, they saw the camps of their enemies, and were amazed at their skillful arrangement.

"Truly a wonderful genius!" sighed Sima Yi.

The armies of Wei returned to Changan. Leaving officers to guard the various strategic points, Sima Yi himself went on to Luoyang to see the audience.

Yang Yi and Jiang Wei retired slowly and in good order till they neared the Plank Trail, when they donned mourning garb and began to wail for their dead. The soldiers threw themselves on the ground and wailed in sorrow. Some even wailed themselves to death.

But as the leading companies entered upon the Plank Trail, they saw a great blaze in front, and, with a great shout, a cohort came out barring the way. The leaders of the retreating army were taken aback and sent to inform Yang Yi.

The regiments of Wei are nowhere near,
Then who are these soldiers that now appear?

The next chapter will tell who they were.

Chapter 105

The Lord of Wuxiang Leaves A Plan In The Silken Bag;
The Ruler of Wei Removes The Bronze Statue With The Dew Bowl.

Yang Yi sent forward a man to find out what force this was that stood in his way, and the scout returned to say they were soldiers of Shu led by Wei Yan. Wei Yan had burned the Plank Trail and now barred the way.

Then said Yang Yi, "Just before his death the Prime Minister foretold that this man would one day turn traitor, and here it has come to pass. I did not expect to meet it thus, but now our road of retreat is cut, and what is to be done?"

Then replied Fei Yi, "He certainly has slandered us to the Emperor and said that we were rebelling, and therefore he has destroyed the wooden roads in order to prevent our progress first. Therefore, we must memorialize to the Throne the truth about him and then plan his destruction."

Jiang Wei said, "I know a by-way hereabout that will lead us round to the rear of these covered roads. True it is precipitous and dangerous, but it will take us to our destination. It is called the Chashan Mountain Path."

So they prepared a memorial and turned off in order to follow the narrow mountain road.

Meanwhile in Chengdu the Latter Ruler of Shu was troubled; he lost his appetite and was sleepless. Then he dreamed that the Silky Hills that protected his capital was rived and fell. This dream troubled him till morning, when he called in his officers of all ranks to ask them to interpret his vision.

When he had related his dream, Qiao Zhou stood forth and said, "Last night I saw a large red star fall from the northeast to the southwest. Surely it forebodes a misfortune to the First Minister. Your Majesty's dream corresponds to what I saw."

The Latter Ruler's anxiety increased. Presently Li Fu returned and was summoned into the Latter Ruler's presence.

Li Fu bowed his head and wept, saying, "The Prime Minister is dead!"

He repeated Zhuge Liang's last messages and told all that he knew.

The Latter Ruler was overcome with great sorrow, and wailed, crying, "Heaven smites me!"

And he fell over and lay upon his couch. They led him within to the inner chambers; and when Empress Wu, the Empress Dowager, heard the sad tidings, she also wailed without ceasing. And all the officers were distressed and wept, and the common people showed their grief.

The Latter Ruler was deeply affected, and for many days could hold no court. And while thus prostrate with grief, they told him that Wei Yan had sent up a memorial charging Yang Yi with rebellion. The astounded courtiers went to the Latter Ruler's chamber to talk over this thing, and Empress Wu was also there. The memorial was read aloud. It was much like this:

"I, thy Minister and General, Wei Yan, General Who Conquers the West and Lord of Nanzheng, humbly and with bowed head write that Yang Yi has assumed command of the army and is in rebellion. He has made off with the coffin of the late Prime Minister and wishes to lead enemies within our borders. As a precaution, and to hinder his progress, I have burned the Plank Trail and now report these matters."

The Latter Ruler said, "Wei Yan is a valiant warrior and could easily have overcome Yang Yi. Why then did he destroy the Plank Trail?"

Empress Wu said, "The First Ruler used to say that Zhuge Liang knew that treachery lurked in the heart of Wei Yan, and he wished to put Wei Yan to death; he only spared Wei Yan because of his valor. We should not believe too readily this tale of his that Yang Yi has rebelled. Yang Yi is a scholar and a civil officer, and the late Prime Minister placed him in a position of great responsibility, thereby proving that he trusted and valued Yang Yi. If we believe this statement, surely Yang Yi will be forced to go over to Wei. Nothing should be done without due meditation."

As they were discussing this matter, an urgent memorial came from Yang Yi, and opening it, they read:

"I, Yang Yi, leader of the retreating army, humbly and with trepidation, present this memorial. In his last moments the late Prime Minister made over to me the charge of the great enterprise, and bade me carry out his plan without change. I have respected his charge. I ordered Wei Yan to command the rearguard with Jiang Wei as his second. But Wei Yan refused obedience and led away his own army into Hanzhong. Then he burned the Plank Trail, tried to steal away the body of the late Commander-in-Chief, and behaved altogether unseemly. His rebellion came upon me suddenly and unexpectedly. I send this memorial in haste."

The Empress Dowager listened to the end.

Then, turning to the officers, she said, "What is your opinion now?"

Jiang Wan replied, "Yang Yi is hasty and intolerant, but he has rendered great services in supplying the army. He has long been a trusted colleague of the late Prime Minister, who, being near his end, entrusted to him the conduct of affairs. Certainly he is no rebel. On the other hand, Wei Yan is bold and ambitious and thinks himself everybody's superior. Yang Yi is the only one who has openly been of different opinion, and hence Wei Yan hates him. When he saw Yang Yi placed over his head in command of the army, Wei Yan refused his support. Then Wei Yan burned the Plank Trail in order to cut off Yang Yi's retreat, and maligned him, hoping to bring about his fall. I am ready to guarantee Yang Yi's fealty to the extent of my whole house, but I would not answer for Wei Yan."

Dong Yun followed, "Wei Yan has always been conceited and discontented. His mouth was full of hate and resentment, and only fear of the late Prime Minister held him in check. The Prime Minister's death gave him his opportunity, and he turned traitor. This is certainly the true state of the case. Yang Yi is able, and his employment by the late Prime Minister is proof of his loyalty."

"If this is true and Wei Yan is really a rebel, what should be done?" asked the Latter Ruler.

Jiang Wan said, "I think the late Prime Minister has framed some scheme by which to get rid of Wei Yan. If Yang Yi had not felt secure, he would scarcely have set out to return through the valleys. Your Majesty may feel sure that Wei Yan will fall into some trap. We have received, almost at the same time, two memorials from two men, each bringing against the other a charge of rebellion. Let us wait."

In a short time another memorial arrived from Wei Yan, who accused Yang Yi of rebellion. The Latter Ruler was reading it, when a messenger from Yang Yi was announced with yet another memorial labeling Wei Yan a rebel. The court received several more memorials from both sides blaming each other, and the officials did not know what to do.

Just then Fei Yi arrived. He was summoned into the royal presence and told the story of Wei Yan's revolt.

The Latter Ruler replied, "In that case I should do well to send Dong Yun with the ensigns of authority to mediate the situation and attempt to persuade Wei Yan with kind words."

So Dong Yun left on this mission.

At this time Wei Yan was camped at Nangu Valley, which was a commanding position. He thought his plan was succeeding well. It had not occurred to him that Yang Yi and Jiang Wei could get past him by any by-way.

On the other hand, Yang Yi, thinking that Hanzhong was lost, sent He Ping with three thousand troops on in front while he followed with the coffin.

When He Ping had got to the rear of Nangu Valley, they announced their presence with rolling drums. The scouts quickly told Wei Yan, who at once armed himself, took his sword, and rode out to confront He Ping. When both sides were arrayed, He Ping rode to the front and began to revile his opponent.

"Where is that rebel Wei Yan?" cried He Ping.

"You aided that traitor Yang Yi!" cried Wei Yan, no way backward with his tongue. "How dare you abuse me?"

He Ping waxed more indignant.

"You rebelled immediately after the late chief's death, before even his body was cold. How could you?"

Then shaking his whip at the followers of Wei Yan, He Ping cried, "And you soldiers are Shu people. Your fathers and mothers, wives and children, and your friends are still in the land. Were you treated unkindly that you have joined a traitor and aid his wicked schemes? You ought to have returned home and waited quietly the rewards that would have been yours."

The soldiers were touched by his words. They cheered, and more than a half ran away.

Wei Yan was now raging. He whirled up his sword and galloped forward straight for He Ping, who went to meet him with his spear ready. They fought several bouts, and then He Ping rode away as if defeated. Wei Yan followed, but He Ping's troops began to shoot and Wei Yan was driven backward. As he got near his own ranks, Wei Yan saw many generals leaving their companies and going away. He rode after them and cut some of them down. But this did not stay the movement; they continued to go. The only steady portion of his own army was that commanded by Ma Dai. They stood their ground.

"Will you really help me?" said Wei Yan. "I will surely remember you in the day of success."

The two then went in pursuit of He Ping, who fled before them. However, it was soon evident that He Ping was not to be overtaken, and the pursuers halted. Wei Yan mustered his now small force.

"What if we go over to Wei?" said Wei Yan.

"I think your words unwise," said Ma Dai. "Why should we join anyone? A really strong person would try to carve out his own fortune and not be ready to crook the knee to another. You are far more able and brave than any leader in the River Lands. No one would dare to stand up to you. I pledge myself to go with you to the seizure of

Hanzhong, and thence we will attack the West River Land."

So they marched together toward Nanzheng, where Jiang Wei stationed. From the city wall Jiang Wei saw their approach and marked their proud, martial look. He ordered the drawbridge to be raised and sent to tell his colleague, Yang Yi.

As they drew near, both Wei Yan and Ma Dai shouted out, "Surrender!"

In spite of the smallness of their following, Jiang Wei felt that Ma Dai acting with Wei Yan was a dangerous combination, and he wanted the advice of Yang Yi.

"Wei Yan is valorous, and he is having the help of Ma Dai. How shall we repel them?" asked Jiang Wei.

Yang Yi replied, "Just before his death, the Prime Minister gave me a silken bag, which he said I was to open when Wei Yan's mutiny reached a critical point. It contains a plan to rid ourselves of this traitor, and it seems that now is the moment to see what should be done."

So Yang Yi opened the bag and drew forth the letter it held. On the cover he read, "To be opened when Wei Yan is actually arrayed opposite you."

Said Jiang Wei, "As this has all been arranged for, I had better go out, and when his line is formed then you can come forth."

Jiang Wei donned his armor, took his spear, and rode out, with three thousand troops. They marched out of the city gates with the drums beating. The array completed, Jiang Wei took his place under the great standard and opened with a volley of abuse.

"Rebel Wei Yan, the late Prime Minister never harmed you. Why have you turned traitor?"

Wei Yan reined up, lowered his sword and replied, "Friend Jiang Wei, this is no concern of yours. Tell Yang Yi to come."

Now Yang Yi was also beneath the standard, but hidden. He opened the letter, and the words therein seemed to please him, for he rode forward blithely.

Presently he reined in, pointed to Wei Yan and said, "The Prime Minister foresaw your mutiny and bade me be on my guard. Now if you are able thrice to shout, 'Who dares kill me?', then you will be a real hero, and I will yield to you the whole of Hanzhong."

Wei Yan laughed.

"Listen, you old fool! While Zhuge Liang lived I feared him somewhat. But he is dead and no one dares stand before me. I will not only shout the words thrice, but a myriad times. Why not?"

Wei Yan raised his sword, shook his bridle, and shouted, "Who dares kill me?"

He never finished. Behind him someone shouted savagely, "I dare!" and at the same moment Wei Yan fell dead, cut down by Ma Dai.

This was the denouement, and was the secret entrusted to Ma Dai just before Zhuge Liang's death. Wei Yan was to be made to shout these words and slain when he least expected it. Yang Yi knew what was to happen, as it was written in the letter in the silken bag. A poem says:

Zhuge Liang foresaw when freed from his restraint
Wei Yan would traitor prove. The silken bag
Contained the plan for his undoing. We see
How it succeeded when the moment came.

So before Dong Yun had reached Nanzheng, Wei Yan was dead. Ma Dai joined his army to Jiang Wei's, and Yang Yi wrote another memorial, which he sent to the Latter Ruler.

The Latter Ruler issued an edict: "Wei Yan had paid the penalty of his crime. He should be honorably buried in consideration of his former services."

Then Yang Yi continued his journey and in due time arrived at Chengdu with the coffin of the late Prime Minister. The Latter Ruler led out a large cavalcade of officers to meet the body at a point seven miles from the walls, and he lifted up his voice and wailed for the dead, and with him wailed all the officers and the common people, so that the sound of mourning filled the whole earth.

By royal command the body was borne into the city to the palace of the Prime Minister, and his son Zhuge Zhan was chief mourner.

When next the Latter Ruler held a court, Yang Yi bound himself, and confessed he had been in fault.

The Latter Ruler bade them loose his bonds and said, "Noble Sir, the coffin would never have reached home but for you. You carried out the orders of the late Prime Minister, whereby Wei Yan was destroyed and all was made secure. This was all your doing."

Yang Yi was promoted to be the Instructor of the Center Army, and Ma Dai was rewarded with the rank that Wei Yan had forfeited.

Yang Yi presented Zhuge Liang's testament, which the Latter Ruler read, weeping. By a special edict it was commanded that soothsayers should cast lots and select the site for the tomb of the great servant of the state.

Then Fei Yi said to the Latter Ruler, "When nearing his end, the Prime Minister commanded that he should be buried on Dingjun Mountain, in open ground, without sacrifice or monument."

This wish was respected, and they chose a propitious day in the tenth month for the interment, and the Latter Ruler followed in the funeral procession to the grave on the Dingjun Mountain. The posthumous title conferred upon the late Prime Minister was Zhuge Liang the Loyally Martial, and a temple was built in Mianyang wherein were offered sacrifices at the four seasons.

The poet Du Fu wrote a poem:

To Zhuge Liang stands a great memorial hall,
In cypress shade, outside the Chengdu Wall,
The steps thereto are bright with new grass springing,
Hiding among the branches orioles are singing.
The people and army asked for his wisdoms,
Upon the throne, built for the father, sat the son.
But ere was compassed all his plans conceived
He died; and heroes since for him have ever grieved.

Another poem by the same author says:

Zhuge Liang's fair fame stands clear to all the world;
Among king's ministers he surely takes
Exalted rank; for when the empire cleft
In three, a kingdom for his lord he won
By subtle craft. Throughout all time he stands
A shining figure, clear against the sky.
Akin was he to famous Yi Yin, Lu Wang,
Yet stands with chiefs, like Xiao He, Cao Shen;
The fates forbade that Han should be restored,
War-worn and weary, yet he steadfast stood.

Evil tidings came to the Latter Ruler on his return to his capital. He heard that Quan Zong had marched out with a large army from Wu and camped at the entrance to Baqiu. No one knew the object of this expedition.

"Here is Wu breaking their oath just as the Prime Minister has died," cried the Latter Ruler. "What can we do?"

Then said Jiang Wan, "My advice is to send Wang Ping and Zhang Ni to camp at Baidicheng as a measure of precaution, while you send an envoy to Wu to announce the death and period of mourning. He can there observe the signs of the times."

"The envoy must have a ready tongue," said the Latter Ruler.

One stepped from the ranks of courtiers and offered himself. He was Zong Yu, a man of Nanyang, a Military Adviser. So he was appointed as envoy with the commissions of announcing the death of the Prime Minister and observing the conditions.

Zong Yu set out for Capital Jianye, arrived and was taken in to the Emperor's presence. When the ceremony of introduction was over and the envoy looked about him, he saw that all were dressed in mourning.

But Sun Quan's countenance wore a look of anger, and he said, "Wu and Shu are one house. Why has your master increased the guard at Baidicheng?"

Zong Yu replied, "It seemed as necessary for the west to increase the garrison there as for the east to have a force at Baqiu. Neither is worth asking about."

"As an envoy you seem no way inferior to Deng Zhi," said Sun Quan, smiling.

Sun Quan continued, "When I heard that your Prime Minister Zhuge Liang had gone to heaven, I wept daily and ordered my officers to wear mourning. I feared that Wei might take the occasion to attack Shu, and so I increased the garrison at Baqiu by ten thousand troops that I might be able to help you in case of need. That was my sole reason."

Zong Yu bowed and thanked the Ruler of Wu.

"I would not go back upon the pledge between us," said Sun Quan.

Zong Yu said, "I have been sent to inform you of the mourning for the late Prime Minister."

Sun Quan took up a gold-tipped arrow and snapped it in twain, saying, "If I betray my oath, may my posterity be cut off!"

Then the Ruler of Wu dispatched an envoy with incense and silk and other gifts to be offered in sacrifice to the dead in the land of Shu.

Zong Yu and the envoy took leave of the Ruler of Wu and journeyed to Chengdu, where they went to the Latter Ruler.

Zong Yu made a memorial, saying, "The Ruler of Wu has wept for our Prime Minister and put his court into mourning. The increased garrison at Baqiu is intended to safeguard us from Wei, lest they take the occasion of a public sorrow to attack. And in token of his pledge, the Ruler of Wu broke an arrow in twain."

The Latter Ruler was pleased and rewarded Zong Yu. Moreover, the envoy of Wu was generously treated.

According to the advice in Zhuge Liang's testament, the Latter Ruler made Jiang Wan Prime Minister and Chair of the Secretariat, while Fei Yi became Deputy Prime Minister and Deputy Chair of the Secretariat. Wu Yi was made Commander of the Flying Cavalry and Commander of Hanzhong; Jiang Wei, General Who Upholds the Han, Lord of Pingxiang, Commander-in-Chief, and Commander of Hanzhong.

Now as Yang Yi was senior in service to Jiang Wan, who had thus been promoted over his head, and as he considered his services had been inadequately rewarded, he was discontented and spoke resentfully.

He said to Fei Yi, "If when the Prime Minister died I had gone over to Wei, with the whole army, I should not have been thus left out in the cold."

Fei Yi secretly reported this speech to the Latter Ruler, who was angered and threw Yang Yi into prison.

The Latter Ruler intended putting him to death, but Jiang Wan interceded, saying, "Yang Yi had followed the late Prime Minister in many campaigns and had had many good services. Your Majesty should not put him to death, but take away his rank."

And Yang Yi was reprieved. However, he was

degraded and sent into Hanjia in Hanzhong, where he committed suicide through shame.

In the thirteenth year of Beginning Prosperity of Shu, the same year being the third year of Green Dragon of Wei, and the fourth year of Domestic Peace of Wu (AD 235), there were no military expeditions. In Wei, Sima Yi was created Grand Commander, with command over all the forces of Wei, and he departed for Luoyang.

The Ruler of Wei, at Xuchang, made preparations to build himself a palace complex. At Luoyang he also built the Hall of Sunrise, the Hall of the Firmament, and the Hall of Complete Patterns, all lofty and of beautiful designs. He also raised a Hall of Beautiful Passions, a Green Flageolet Tower, and a Phoenix Tower. He also dug a Nine Dragons Pool. Over all these works he placed Doctorate Scholar Ma Jun as superintendent of their building.

Nothing was spared that would contribute to the beauty of these buildings. The beams were carved, the rafters were painted, the walls were of golden bricks, and the roofs of green tiles. They glittered and glowed in the sunlight. The most cunning craftspeople in the world were sought, many thousands of them, and myriads of ordinary workers labored day and night on these works for the Emperor's glory and pleasure. But the strength of the people was spent in this toil, and they cried aloud and complained unceasingly.

Moreover, the Ruler of Wei issued an edict to carry earth and bring trees for the Fragrant Forest Park, and he employed officers of state in these labors, carrying earth and transporting trees.

The Minister of Works, Dong Xun, ventured upon a remonstrance, sending a memorial:

"From the beginning of Rebuilt Tranquillity Era, a generation ago, wars have been continuous and destruction rife. Those who have escaped death are few, and these are old and weak. Now indeed it may be that the palaces are too small and enlargement is desired, but would it not be more fitting to choose the building season so as not to interfere with cultivation? Your Majesty has always valued many honorable officers, letting them wear beautiful headdresses, clad in handsome robes, and riding in decorated chariots to distinguish them from the common people. Now these officers are being made to carry timber and bear earth, to sweat and soil their feet. To destroy the glory of the state in order to raise a useless edifice is indescribable folly. Confucius the Teacher said that princes should treat ministers with polite consideration, and ministers should serve princes with loyalty. Without loyalty, without propriety, can a state endure?

"I recognize that these words of mine mean death, but I am of no value, a mere bullock's hair, and my life is of no importance, as my death would be no loss. I write with tears, bidding the world farewell.

"Thy servant has eight sons, who will be a burden to Your Majesty after his death. I cannot say with what trepidation I await my fate."

"Has the man no fear of death?" said Cao Rui, greatly angered.

The courtiers requested the Emperor to put Dong Xun to death, but Cao Rui remembered his rectitude and proven loyalty and only degraded him, adding a warning to put to death those who would remonstrate.

A certain Zhang Mao, in the service of the Heir Apparent, also ventured upon a remonstrance. Cao Rui put him to death immediately.

Then Cao Rui summoned his Master of Works, Ma Jun, and said, "I have built high terraces and lofty towers with intent to hold intercourse with gods and goddesses, that I may obtain from them the elixir of life."

Then Ma Jun replied, "Of the four and twenty emperors of the line of Latter Han, only Emperor Wu[xxii] enjoyed the throne very long and really attained to old age. That was because he drank of the essence of the brilliancy of the sun and the brightness of the moon. In the Palace at Changan is the Terrace of Cypress Beams, upon which stands the bronze figure of a man holding up a Dew Bowl, whereinto distills, in the third watch of the night, the vapor from the great constellation of the north. This liquid is called Celestial Elixir, or Sweet Dew. If mingled with powdered jade and swallowed, it restores youth to the aged."

"Take workers to Changan immediately and bring hither the bronze figure to set up in the Fragrant Forest Park," said the Ruler of Wei.

As the Ruler of Wei commanded, they took ten thousand workers to Changan, and they built a scaffold around the figure. Then they attached ropes to haul it down. The terrace being two hundred feet high and the pedestal ten cubits in circumference, Ma Jun bade his laborers first detach the bronze image. They did so and brought it down. Its eyes were moist as with tears, and the workers were affrighted.

Then suddenly beside the terrace sprang up a whirlwind, with dust and pebbles flying thick as a shower of rain, and there was a tempestuous roar as of an earthquake. Down fell the pedestal, and the platform crumbled, crushing a thousand people to death.

However, the bronze figure and the golden bowl were conveyed to Luoyang and presented to the Emperor.

"Where is the pedestal?" asked the Ruler of Wei.

"It is too heavy to transport," replied the Ma Jun. "It weighs a million and half of pounds."

Wherefore the Ruler of Wei ordered the pillar to be broken up and the metal brought, and from this he caused to be cast two figures which he named Saints of Wengzhong. They were placed outside the gate of the Board of War. A pair of dragons and a pair of phoenixes were also cast, the dragons forty feet high and the birds thirty. These were placed in front of the Hall of Audience.

Moreover, in the Fragrant Forest Park the Ruler of Wei planted wonderful flowers and rare trees, and he also established a menagerie of strange animals.

Yang Fu, Assistant Imperial Guardian, remonstrated with the Emperor on these extravagances in a memorial:

"As is well known, King Yao preferred his humble thatched cottage, and all the world enjoyed tranquillity; King Yu contented himself with a small modest palace, and all the empire rejoiced. In the days of Yin and Zhou Dynasties the hall of the ruler stood three feet above the usual height and its area was nine mats. The sage emperors and illustrious kings had no decorated chambers in lofty palaces built with the wealth, and by the strength, of a worn-out and despoiled people.

"Emperor Jie built a jade chamber and elephant stables; Emperor Zhou erected a surpassingly beautiful palace complex and a Deer Terrace. But these lost the empire. King Ling of Chu built beautiful palaces, but he came to an evil end. The First Emperor of Qin made the Epang Palace, but calamity fell upon his son, for the empire rebelled and his house was exterminated in the second generation.

"All those who have failed to consider the means of the people and given way to sensuous pleasures have perished. Your Majesty has the examples of Kings Yao, Yu, Shun, and Tang on the one hand, and the warnings of Kings Jie, Zhou, Ling, and the First Emperor on the other. To seek only self-indulgence and think only of fine palaces will surely end in calamity.

"The prince is the first and the head; his ministers are his limbs; they live or die together, they are involved in the same destruction. Though I am timorous, yet if I dared forget my duty, or failed to speak firmly, I should be unable to move Your Majesty. Now I have prepared my coffin and bathed my body ready for the most condign punishment."

But the Ruler of Wei disregarded this memorial and only urged on the rapid completion of the terrace. Thereon he set up the bronze figure with the golden bowl. Moreover, he sent forth a command to select the most beautiful women in the empire for his garden of delight. Many memorials were presented, but the Ruler of Wei heeded them not.

Now the Consort of the Ruler of Wei was of the Mao family of Henei. In earlier days, when he was a prince, he had loved her exceedingly, and when he succeeded to the throne she became Empress Mao. Later he favored Lady Guo, and his Consort Mao was neglected. Lady Guo was beautiful and clever, and the Ruler of Wei delighted in her. He neglected state affairs for her society and often spent a month at a time in retirement with her. Every day there was some new gaiety.

In the spring, when the plants in the Fragrant Forest Park were in flower, the Ruler of Wei and Lady Guo came to the garden to enjoy them and to feast.

"Why not invite the Empress?" asked Lady Guo.

"If she came, nothing would pass my lips," replied the Ruler of Wei.

He gave orders that his Consort should be kept in ignorance of these rejoicings.

But when a month passed without the appearance of the Emperor, Empress Mao and her ladies went to the Blue Flower Pavilion to entertain themselves. Hearing music, she asked who was providing it, and they told her that the Emperor and Lady Guo were feasting in the grounds.

That day Empress Mao returned to her palace filled with sorrow. Next day she went out in her carriage and saw the Emperor on a verandah.

"Yesterday Your Majesty was walking in the north garden, and you had plenty of music too," said she, smiling.

Cao Rui was wroth and sent for all the attendants.

He upbraided them with disobedience, saying, "I had forbidden you to tell things to the Empress, and you disobeyed my command."

With this he put them all to death. Empress Mao feared and returned to her palace.

Then an edict appeared forcing Empress Mao to commit suicide and raising Lady Guo to be Empress in her place. And no officer dared to utter a remonstrance.

Just after this the Imperial Protector of Youzhou, Guanqiu Jian, sent in a memorial, saying: "Gongsun Yuan of Liaodong has risen in revolt, assumed the style of Prince of Yan[xxiii], and adopted a reign title of Extending Han. Gongsun Yuan has built himself a Palace, established an administration of his own, and is disturbing the whole north with plundering."

A council met to consider this memorial.

Within, officials labor at ignoble tasks, and mean,
Without, the glint of weapons on the border may be seen.

How the insurgents were attacked will be related in the next chapter.

Chapter 106

Suffering Defeat, Gongsun Yuan Meets His Death;
Pretending Illness, Sima Yi Deceives Cao Shuang.

This Gongsun Yuan was a grandson of Gongsun Du the Warlike, and a son of Gongsun Kang in Liaodong. In the twelfth year of Rebuilt Tranquillity, when Cao Cao was pursuing Yuan Xi and Yuan Shang[xxiv], who had fled eastward, Gongsun Kang had captured them, beheaded them, and sent their heads to Cao Cao. For this service Gongsun Kang received the title of Lord of Xiangping. After Gongsun Kang's death, as his two sons---Gongsun Huang and Gongsun Yuan---were young, his brother Gongsun Gong took the chiefship; and Cao Pi, beside confirming the lordship, gave him the rank of General of the Flying Cavalry.

In the second year of Calm Peace (AD 228), the second son, Gongsun Yuan, being now grown up, well-educated and trained in military exercises, obstinate and fond of fighting, took away his uncle's power and ruled the heritage of his father. Cao Rui conferred upon him the title of General Who Wields Ferocity, and made him Governor of Liaodong.

Then the Ruler of Wu, Sun Quan, anxious to secure Gongsun Yuan's support, sent two envoys, Zhang Mi and Xu Yan, with gifts of gold and gems and pearls and offered Gongsun Yuan the title of Prince of Yan. Fearing that the Middle Land would resent any dallying with Wu, Gongsun Yuan slew the Wu envoys and sent the heads to the Ruler of Wei. For this proof of fealty, Cao Rui gave him the title of Grand General and the Dukedom of Yuelang.

However, Gongsun Yuan was dissatisfied, and his thoughts turned toward independence. He took council with his officers and proposed to style himself Prince of Yan and to adopt a reign-title of Extending Han, the first year.

One general, Jia Fan, opposed this and said, "My lord, the central authorities have treated you well and honored you. I fear that Sima Yi is too skillful a leader for rebellion to succeed. You see even Zhuge Liang cannot defeat him. How much less can you?"

Gongsun Yuan's reply was to condemn Jia Fan to death. However, Adviser Lun Zhi ventured upon further remonstrance.

"Jia Fan spoke well. The Sacred One says that extraordinary phenomena presage the destruction of a state. Now this time portents are not wanting, and wonders have been seen. A dog, dressed in red and wearing a turban, went up to the roof and walking like a man. Moreover, while a certain person living in a village south of the city was cooking his food, he saw a child in the pan, boiled to death. A great cave opened near the market place and threw out a large, fleshy body completely human save that it lacked limbs. Swords could not cut it; arrows could not penetrate it. No one knew what to call it; and when they consulted the soothsayers, they obtained the reply, 'Incomplete shape, silent mouth: A state is near destruction.' These prodigies are all inauspicious. Flee from evil and strive to walk in fair fortune's way. Make no move without most careful thought."

This second remonstrance enraged Gongsun Yuan still more, and he sent Lun Zhi to death with Jia Fan. Both were executed in the public place.

Gongsun Yuan then prepared to make a bid for empire. He raised an army of one hundred fifty thousand, appointed Bei Yan as Commander, and Yang Zuo as Leader of the Van. This army set out for the Middle Land.

Ruler of Wei was alarmed at the report of this rising, and sent for Sima Yi.

Sima Yi was not greatly perturbed, and said, "My forty thousand troops will be equal to the task."

The Ruler of Wei replied, "The task is heavy, for your troops are few and the road is long."

"The strength of an army is not in numbers, but in strategy. Aided by Your Majesty's good fortune, I shall certainly be able to bring this fellow Gongsun Yuan a captive to your feet."

"What do you think will be the rebel's plan?" asked the Ruler of Wei.

"His high plan would be flight before our army can arrive; his middle plan would be defending his position in Liaodong; his low plan would be to try to hold Xiangping. In the last case I shall certainly capture him."

"How long will the expedition take?"

"We have to cover one thousand five hundred miles which will take a hundred days. Attack will consume another hundred. The return will need a hundred, and with sixty days to rest we shall take a year."

"Suppose during that year we are attacked by Wu or Shu."

"My plans provide for that. Your Majesty need have no anxiety."

The Ruler of Wei being thus reassured, formally ordered Sima Yi to undertake the expedition.

Hu Zun was appointed to lead the van. Hu Zun went and camped in Liaodong. The scouts hastened to tell Gongsun Yuan, who sent Bei Yan and Yang Zuo to camp at Liaosui with eighty thousand troops. They surrounded their camp with a wall seven miles in circumference and placed thorny barriers outside the rampart. It seemed very secure.

Hu Zun saw these preparations and sent to tell his chief. Sima Yi smiled.

"So the rebel does not want to fight, but thinks to weary my soldiers," said Sima Yi. "Now I am disposed to think that most of his army is within that wall, so that his stronghold is empty and undefended. I will make a dash at Xiangping. He will have to go to its rescue, and I will smite him on the way. I should score a great success."

So Sima Yi hastened to Xiangping along unfrequented ways.

Meanwhile Bei Yan and Yang Zuo, the two generals within the walled camp, discussed their plans.

Yang Zuo said, "When the Wei army comes near, we will not fight. They will have come a long march and their supplies will be short, so that they cannot hold out long. When they retreat, we shall find our opportunity. These were the tactics Sima Yi used against Zhuge Liang on River Wei, and Zhuge Liang died before the end of the expedition. We will try similar means."

Presently the scouts reported that the Wei army had marched south.

Bei Yan at once saw the danger and said, "They are going to attack Xiangping, which they know has few troops. If that base be lost, this position is useless."

So they broke up their camp and followed the enemy.

When Sima Yi heard it, he rejoiced, saying, "Now they will fall into the snare I have laid for them."

Sima Yi sent Xiahou Ba and Xiahou Wei to take up position on the River Ji. They were to attack if the army of Liaodong came near them. They had not long to wait. As soon as Bei Yan and his army approached, Xiahou Ba and Xiahou Wei exploded a bomb, beat the drums, waved their flags, and came out, one force on each side. Bei Yan and Yang Zuo made a fight but soon fled to Shoushan Mountain, where they fell in with Gongsun Yuan and joined the main army. Then they turned to give battle to the Wei army.

Bei Yan rode to the front and reviled the enemy, shouting, "You rebels! Do not try trickery, but dare you fight in the open?"

Xiahou Ba rode out to accept the challenge, and after a few bouts Bei Yan fell. In the confusion caused by the death of their leader, Xiahou Ba urged on his troops and drove Gongsun Yuan back to Xiangping, and Gongsun Yuan took refuge in the city.

The city was surrounded. It was autumn, and the rain fell day after day without ceasing. At the end of the month, the plain was under three feet of water, so that the grain boats sailed straight from River Ji to the city walls. The besiegers suffered much from the floods.

Pei Jing, Commander of the Left, went to Sima Yi and asked, "The rain keeps pouring down, and tents cannot be pitched on mud. May the army be moved to camp on the higher ground?"

But Sima Yi flouted the suggestion.

"How can the army move away just when success is in sight? The rebels will be conquered now any day. If any other speaks about drawing off, he will be put to death."

Pei Jing agreed and went away.

Soon after, Chou Lian, Commander of the Right, came to see his chief and repeated the suggestion, saying, "The soldiers are suffering from the rains. O Commander, let them camp on the hills."

Sima Yi got angry and said, "I have sent the command, and you are against it!"

And he ordered Chou Lian to be executed. His head was suspended at the camp gate as a warning to others. The soldiers dared to complain any more.

Then Sima Yi ordered the south camp to be abandoned, and the army marched seven miles south, thus allowing the soldiers and people in the city to come out to gather fuel and pasture their cattle.

The attacking army could not understand this move, and General Chen Qun spoke about it.

"When you besieged Shangyong, O Commander, you attacked all round at eight points, and the city fell in eight days. Meng Da was taken, and you won a great success. Now your forty thousand troops have borne their armors many days over long marches and you do not press the attack, but keep them in the mud and mire and let the enemy gather supplies and feed their cattle. I do not know what your intention may be."

"Sir," replied the Commander-in-Chief, "I see you are ignorant of war after all. You do not understand the different conditions. Meng Da then had ample supplies and few troops, while we were under exactly opposite conditions. So we had to attack vigorously and at once. The suddenness of the attack defeated the enemy. But look at present conditions. The Liaodong troops are many and we few; they are on the verge of starvation, and we are full fed. Why should we force the attack? Our line is to let the soldiers desert and capture the city. Therefore I leave a gate open and the road free that they may run away."

Chen Qun then understood and acknowledged the correctness of the strategy. Sima Yi sent to Luoyang to hasten supplies, that there should be no shortage.

However, the war was not supported in the capital, for when the messenger arrived and the Ruler of Wei summoned his courtiers, they said, "In Liaodong the rain has been continuous for a month, and the soldiers are in misery. Sima Yi ought to be recalled, and the war renewed at a more convenient season."

The Ruler of Wei replied, "The leader of our army is most capable and best able to decide upon what should be done. He understands the conditions and is teeming with magnificent plans. He will certainly succeed. Wherefore, Noble Sirs, wait a few days and let us not be anxious about the result."

So Cao Rui heeded not the voice of the dissentients, but took care that provisions were sent.

After a few days the rain ceased, and fine, clear weather followed. That night Sima Yi went out of his tent that he might study the sky. Suddenly he saw a very large and bright star start from a point over Shoushan Mountain and travel over toward

Xiangping, where it fell. The soldiers were rather frightened at this apparition, but the leader rejoiced.

"Five days from now Gongsun Yuan will be slain where that star fell," said he. "Therefore attack with vigor."

They opened the attack the next morning at dawn, throwing up banks and sapping the walls, setting up stone-throwing machines and rearing ladders. When night came the attack did not cease. Arrows fell in the city like pelting rain.

Within the city, grain began to run short, and soon there was none. They slaughtered bullocks and horses for food. The soldiers began to be mutinous and no longer fought with any spirit. There was talk of slaying Gongsun Yuan and yielding the city.

Gongsun Yuan was disheartened and frightened, and decided to sue for peace. He sent his Prime Minister Wang Jian and Imperial Censor Liu Fei out of the city to beg Sima Yi to allow him to submit. These two had to be let down from the walls by ropes, as no other means of exit were possible.

Wang Jian and Liu Fei found their way to Sima Yi and said, "We pray you, O Commander, retire seven miles and allow the officers to come forth and surrender."

"Why did not Gongsun Yuan himself come?" said Sima Yi. "He is rude."

He put the two envoys to death and sent their

heads back into the city.

Gongsun Yuan was still more alarmed, but he resolved to make one more attempt. This time he sent High Counselor Wei Yin as his envoy. Sima Yi received this messenger sitting in state in his tent with his officers standing right and left. Wei Yin approached on his knees, and when he reached the door of the tent recited his petition.

"I pray you, O Commander, turn your thunderous wrath from us. We will send the son of our leader, Gongsun Xiu, the Heir Apparent, as hostage and all the officers shall appear before you bound with cords."

Sima Yi replied, "There are five possible operations for any army. If you can fight, fight; if you cannot fight, defend; if you cannot defend, flee; if you cannot flee, surrender; if you cannot surrender, die. These five courses are open to you, and a hostage would be useless. Now return and tell your master."

Wei Yin put his hands over his head and fled like a rat. He went into the city and related what had happened to him.

The Gongsuns, father and son, resolved to flee. They chose a thousand of mounted troops, and in the dead of night opened the south gate and got out. They took the road to the east and were rejoiced to find it clear.

All went well for a distance of three miles, when a bomb exploded. This was followed by a roll of drums and the blare of trumpets; and a cohort stood in the way. The leader was Sima Yi, supported by his two sons---Sima Shi and Sima Zhao.

"Stop, O rebel!" cried the sons.

But Gongsun Yuan lashed his steed to a gallop. Then Hu Zun, Xiahou Ba, Xiahou Wei, Zhang Hu, and Yue Chen, with their troops, came up and quickly surrounded them so that they were helpless. Gongsun Yuan saw that escape was impossible, so he came with his son, dismounted, and offered surrender.

Sima Yi hardly looked at the two men, but he turned to his officers and said, "That night the star fell to this land, and today, five days later, the omen becomes true."

They all felicitated him, saying, "The Commander is superhuman!"

Gongsun Yuan and Gongsun Xiu were slain where they stood. Then Sima Yi turned to resume the siege of Xiangping; but before he had reached the walls, Hu Zun's army had entered. Sima Yi went in and was received with great respect, the people burning incense as he passed. He went to the residence, and then the whole of the Gongsun Yuan's clan, and all who had assisted in his rising, were beheaded. They counted heads to the number of seventy.

The city taken and the rebels destroyed, Sima Yi issued a proclamation in order to restore confidence among the people.

Certain persons told him, "Jia Fan and Lun Zhi had been against the revolt and had therefore suffered death."

So Sima Yi honored their tombs and conferred ranks upon their children. The contents of the treasury were distributed among the soldiers as rewards, and then the army marched back to Luoyang.

One night the Ruler of Wei was suddenly awakened by a chill blast that extinguished all the lights, but he saw the form of the late Empress Mao, with a score or two of other Palace attendants, coming toward the bed whereon he lay, and as they approached they demanded his life. He was very frightened and fell ill so that he was like to die.

So the two officers, Liu Fang and Sun Zu, were set over the privy council, and he summoned his brother Cao Yu, the Prince of Yan, to the capital to make him Regent Marshal to assist the Heir Apparent, Cao Fang. However, Cao Yu being modest and retiring by nature, declined these high offices and their responsibilities.

The Ruler of Wei then turned to his two confidants, Liu Fang and Sun Zu, inquired of them, saying, "Who of the family is a suitable person to support the Heir Apparent?"

As Liu Fang and Sun Zu had both received many favors from Cao Zhen, they replied, "None is so fit as Cao Shuang, the son of Cao Zhen."

The Ruler of Wei approved their choice, and thus Cao Shuang became a great person.

Then Liu Fang and Sun Zu memorialized, saying, "As Cao Shuang has been chosen, Cao Yu, the Prince of Yan, should be ordered to leave the capital and return to Yan, his own place."

The Ruler of Wei consented and issued an edict, which these two bore to Cao Yu, saying, "The edict in the Emperor's own hand bids you return to your own domain at once, and you are not to return to court without a special command."

Cao Yu wept, but he left forthwith.

Thereupon Cao Shuang was created Regent Marshal and Court Administrator.

But the Ruler of Wei's illness advanced rapidly, and he sent messenger with authority ensign to call Sima Yi into the Palace. As soon as he arrived, he was led to the Emperor's chamber.

"I feared lest I should not see you again," said the Ruler of Wei. "But now I can die content."

The general bowed and said, "On the road they told me the sacred person was not perfectly well. I grieved that I had not wings to hasten hither. But I am happy in that I now behold the dragon countenance."

The heir, Cao Fang, was summoned to the Emperor's bedside and also Cao Shuang, Liu Fang, Sun Zu, and certain others.

Taking Sima Yi by the hand, the dying Emperor said, "When Liu Bei lay dying at Baidicheng, he confided his son, so soon to be an orphan, to the care of Zhuge Liang, who labored in this task to the very end and whose devotion only ceased with death. If such conduct is possible in the mere remnant of a dying dynasty continued in a small state, how much more may I hope for it in a great country! My son is only eight years of age, and incapable of sustaining the burden of rulership. Happily for him he has ample merit and experience around him in the persons of yourself and his relatives. He will never lack friends for my sake."

Turning to the young prince, he continued, "My friend Sima Yi is as myself, and you are to treat him with the same respect and deference."

Cao Rui bade Sima Yi lead the young prince forward. The boy threw his arms around Sima Yi's neck and clung to him.

"Never forget the affection he has just shown," said Cao Rui, weeping. And Sima Yi wept also.

The dying man swooned; although he could not speak, his hand still pointed to his son, and soon after he died. Cao Rui had reigned thirteen years and was thirty-six years of age. His death took place in the first month of the third year of Spectacular Beginning (AD 239).

No time was lost in enthroning the new Emperor, the supporters being Sima Yi and Cao Shuang. The new ruler's name was Cao Fang. However, he was Cao Rui's son only by adoption. He had been brought up in the Palace secretly, and no one knew his real origin.

The posthumous title of Emperor Rui the Knowledgeable was conferred upon the late ruler, and he was buried in the Gaoping Tombs. Empress

Guo was given the title of Empress Dowager.

The new reign was styled Right Beginning Era, the first year (AD 239). Sima Yi and Cao Shuang conducted the government, and in all matters Cao Shuang treated Sima Yi with deference and took no steps without his knowledge.

Cao Shuang was no stranger at court. Cao Rui had respected him for his diligence and care and had been very fond of him, He had had the freedom of the Palace all his life. He had a host of five hundred clients and retainers. Among them were five wholly light and foppish. Their names were He Yan, Deng Yang, Li Sheng, Ding Mi, and Bi Gui. Deng Yang was a descendant of Commander Deng Yu of Han[xxv]. Beside these five there was another named Huan Fan, Minister of Agriculture, a man of good parts, who had the sobriquet of "Bag of Wisdom". These six were Cao Shuang's most trusted companions and confidants.

One day He Yan said, "My lord, you should not let your great powers slip into the hands of any other, or you will repent it."

Cao Shuang replied, "Sima Yi as well as I received the late Emperor's sacred trust, and I mean to be true."

He Yan said, "When your father and this Sima Yi were winning their victories in the west, your father suffered much from this man's temper, which ultimately brought about his death. Why do you not look into that?"

Cao Shuang seemed suddenly to wake up.

Having entered into an intrigue with the majority of the officers about the court, then one day he presented to the Ruler of Wei a memorial, saying, "Sima Yi should be promoted to the rank of Guardian of the Throne for his great merits and services."

The promotion was made, and consequently Sima Yi, now a civil officer, let the whole military authority fall into the hands of Cao Shuang.

Having thus far succeeded, Cao Shuang next appointed his brothers to high military posts: Cao Xi as Commander of the Center Army; Cao Xun, Commander of the Imperial Guards; Cao Yan, Commander of the Cavalry. Each commanded three thousand of the Palace guards, with right to go in and out of the Palace at will. Moreover, three of his friends---He Yan, Deng Yang, and Ding Mi---were created Chairs of three boards; Bi Gui, Commander of Capital District; and Li Sheng, Governor of Henan. These five and their patron were close associates in all concerns of state.

Cao Shuang gathered about him larger and still larger numbers of supporters, till Sima Yi gave out that he was ill and remained in seclusion. His two sons also resigned their offices.

Cao Shuang and his friends now gave themselves up to dissipation, spending days and nights in drinking and music. In their dress and the furniture of their table they copied the Palace patterns. Tribute in the shape of jewels and curios went to the residence of Cao Shuang before it entered the Emperor's palace, and his complex swarmed with beautiful damsels. Minister Zhang Dang of the Inner Bureau toadied to Cao Shuang so far as to select eighteen of the late Emperor's handmaids and send them to the now powerful minister. Cao Shuang also chose for him a chorus of two score well-born ladies who were skilled in music and dancing. Cao Shuang also built for himself beautiful towers and pavilions and made to himself vessels of gold and silver, the work of the most expert craftspeople, whom he kept constantly employed.

Now He Yan heard of Guan Lu's great skill in divination and sent to Pingyuan to invite him to discuss about the Book of Changes.

When the soothsayer arrived, Deng Yang was of the company to meet him, and he said to Guan Lu, "You call yourself a skillful diviner, but your speech does not resemble the language of the Book of Changes. How is that?"

Guan Lu replied, "An interpreter does not use the language of the original."

He Yan laughed, saying, "Certainly good words are not wearisome. But cast a lot for me, and tell me whether I shall ever arrive at the highest office or not, for I have dreamed repeatedly that many blue flies settled on my nose."

Guan Lu replied, "Gao Kai and Gao Yuan aided King Shun; Duke Zhou assisted the young Emperor Cheng of Zhou Dynasty; all these were kindly and modest and enjoyed great happiness. You, Sir, have come to high honors and wield great powers, but those who esteem you are few and those who fear you, many. You are not careful to walk in the way of good fortune. Now the nose is an eminence. If an eminence retains its characteristic, thereby it remains in honor. But is it not that blue flies gather to foul objects and the lofty fears a fall? I would wish you to give of your abundance for the good of the poor and avoid walking in the wrong road. Then indeed may you reach the highest dignity, and the blue flies will disperse."

"This is mere senile gossip," said Deng Yang.

"The gift of age is to see that which is yet to come; the gift of gossip is to perceive what is not said," replied Guan Lu. Thereupon he shook out his sleeves and went away.

"He is very mad, really," said his two hosts.

Guan Lu went home. When he saw his uncle, Guan Lu gave him an account of the interview.

His uncle was alarmed at the probable consequences, and said, "Why did you anger them? They are too powerful for you to offend."

"What is there to fear? I have been talking to two dead men."

"What do you mean?"

"Deng Yang's gait is that of one whose sinews are loosed from his bones, and his pulse is unsteady. When he would stand, he totters as a man without limbs. This is the aspect of a disembodied soul. He Yan looks as if his soul was about to quit its habitation. He is bloodless, and what should be solid in him is mere vapor. He looks like rotten wood. This is the aspect of a soul even now in the dark valley. Both these men will certainly soon die a violent death, and none need fear them."

His uncle left, cursing him for a madman.

Cao Shuang and his five friends were devoted to hunting and were often out of the city. Cao Xi, a brother of Cao Shuang, remonstrated with him about this and pointed out the dangers of such frequent absence on these excursions.

"You are in an exalted position and yet you are constantly being out hunting. If anyone took advantage of this to work you evil, you might have to be exceedingly regretful."

Cao Shuang only showed anger and replied, "The whole military authority is in my hands, and what is there to fear?"

Huan Fan, Minister of Agriculture, also reasoned with him, but Cao Shuang would not listen.

About this time the style of the reign was changed from Right Beginning, the tenth year, to Domestic Calm, the first year (AD 249).

Now ever since Cao Shuang had enjoyed the monopoly of military authority, he had never heard the truth about the state of health of the man he had maneuvered out of power. But when the Ruler of Wei appointed Li Sheng to the Imperial Protectorship of Qingzhou, Cao Shuang bade Li Sheng go to take leave of Sima Yi, at the same time to find out the true state of his health.

So Li Sheng proceeded to the residence of the

High Minister and was announced.

Sima Yi saw through the device at once and told his sons, saying, "This is Cao Shuang's wish to find out my real condition."

And he bade them play their parts in the scene he arranged, before the visitor was admitted.

Sima Yi threw aside his headdress, so letting his hair fall in disorder, stretched himself upon his couch, tumbled the bed ding into confusion, got a couple of servant girls to support him, and then told his servants to lead in the visitor.

Li Sheng came in and went up to the sick man, saying, "It is a long time since I have seen you, and I did not know you were so seriously ill. His Majesty is sending me to Qingzhou, and I have come to pay my respects to you and bid you farewell."

"Ah, Bingzhou is in the north; you will have to be very careful there," said Sima Yi feigning that he had not heard.

"I am going as Imperial Protector of Qingzhou, not Bingzhou," said Li Sheng.

"Oh, you have just come from Bingzhou."

"Qingzhou, in Huashang Mountains."

"Just back from Qingzhou, eh?" said Sima Yi, smiling.

"How very ill the Imperial Guardian is!" said Li Sheng to the servants.

"The Minister is deaf," said they.

"Give me paper and a pen," said Li Sheng.

Writing materials were brought, when Li Sheng wrote what he wished to say and put it before his host.

"My illness has made me very deaf. Take care of yourself on the way," said Sima Yi.

Looking up, he pointed to his mouth. One of the girls brought some broth and held the cup for him to drink. He put his lips to the cup, but spilled the broth all over his dress.

"I am very weak and ill," said he, "and may die at any moment. My sons are but poor things, but you will instruct them. When you see the Regent Marshal, you will ask him to take care of them for me, will you not?"

At this point Sima Yi fell back on the couch, panting, and Li Sheng took his leave.

Li Sheng told Cao Shuang what he had seen, and Cao Shuang rejoiced, thinking his rival could not last long.

"If the old man died, I should not be the one to grieve," said Cao Shuang.

But no sooner had Li Sheng gone than Sima Yi rose from his couch and said to his sons, "Li Sheng will take a full account of this to Cao Shuang, who will not fear me any more. But wait till Cao Shuang goes on his next hunting trip, and we will see what can be done."

Soon after this, Cao Shuang proposed to the Ruler of Wei, Cao Fang, to visit the Gaoping Tombs where his father lay and perform the filial sacrifices in person. So they went, a goodly company of officers in the train of the imperial chariot, and Cao Shuang with all his brothers and his friends went with the guards.

Huan Fan, Minister of Agriculture, entreated him to remain in the city for fear of plots and risings.

"Your Lordship are in charge of the capital security, and you and your brothers should not leave the city together. Suppose there were a revolt, what then?"

But Cao Shuang asked angrily and rudely, "Who would dare make trouble? Hold your wild tongue!"

And he went with the Emperor.

His departure rejoiced the heart of Sima Yi, who at once began quietly to muster his trusty friends and henchmen and put the finishing touches to the plot for the overthrow of his rival.

Now terminates his forced inaction,
He must destroy the hostile faction.

Cao Shuang's fate will appear in the next chapter.

Chapter 107

The Ruler of Wei Hands Over The Power To Sima Yi;
Jiang Wei Is Defeated At Ox Head Hills.

Sima Yi was very pleased to hear that Cao Shuang and his party were to follow the Ruler of Wei on a visit to the tombs combined with a hunt, for it meant that the whole enemy faction left the city. Accordingly, Cao Shuang and his three brothers Cao Xi, Cao Xun, Cao Yan, and his friends He Yan, Deng Yang, Ding Mi, Bi Gui, Li Sheng, and others left the capital with the Emperor.

As soon as they left, Sima Yi entered with his authority as Imperial Guardian, gave Gao Rou, Minister of the Interior, provisional command of the army and sent him to seize the camp of Cao Shuang. A similar command was given to Wang Guan, Supervisor of the Palace, to replace Cao Xi as Commander of the Center Army and to occupy his camp.

Having secured his position thus, Sima Yi and his supporters went to the palace of the Empress Dowager.

They said to her, "Cao Shuang has betrayed the trust placed in him by the late Emperor and has ruined the government. His fault must be expiated."

Empress Guo replied, "What can be done in the

absence of the Son of Heaven?"

"I have prepared plans for the destruction of these base ministers and will see to it that no trouble happens to yourself."

The Empress was much alarmed, but could only act as she was directed and agree. So two of Sima Yi's supporters, Commander Jiang Ji and High Minister Sima Fu, copied out the memorial he had prepared, and it was sent to the Ruler of Wei by the hand of an eunuch. Then the arsenals were seized.

Soon the news of the rising came to the knowledge of the family of Cao Shuang, and his wife, Lady Liu, came out from the inner apartments and summoned Pan Ju, Commander of the Gates.

She inquired, "The Master is outside, and Sima Yi is revolting: What does it mean?"

"Your Ladyship need feel no alarm. Let me go and find out the truth," said Pan Ju.

Thereupon Pan Ju, at the head of a several dozen bowmen, went up on the wall and looked around. At that moment Sima Yi was crossing the court, and Pan Ju bade his men shoot. Sima Yi could not pass.

But Sun Qiao, one of his generals, said, "You must not shoot at the Imperial Guardian; he is on public service."

Thrice Sun Qiao urged his chief not to let the men shoot, and so Pan Ju desisted. Sima Yi went across guarded by his son Sima Zhao. Then he went out of the city and camped on River Luo at the Floating Bridge.

When the revolution began, one of Cao Shuang's officers, Lu Zhu by name, took counsel with Military Adviser Xin Chang.

"Now that this revolt has begun, what should we do?"

"Let us go to the Emperor with what troops we have," replied Xin Chang.

"Perhaps the best course," replied Lu Zhu.

And Xin Chang went into the inner chamber to get ready to start. There he met his sister, Xin Xianying, who asked the meaning of all this haste.

"His Majesty is out on a hunt, and Sima Yi has closed the gates of the city. This is rebellion."

"I do not think so. He only means to slay Cao Shuang, his rival," replied she.

"What will be the outcome of this?" asked her brother.

"Cao Shuang is no match for Sima Yi," replied she.

"If Sima Yi asks us to join him, should we?" asked Xin Chang.

Xin Xianying replied, "You know what a true man should do. When a man is in danger, there is the greater need for sympathy. To be of Cao Shuang's people and desert him in an emergency is the greatest of evils."

This speech decided Xin Chang, who went with Lu Zhu. At the head of a some twenty horsemen, they forced the gate and got out of the city.

When their escape was reported to Sima Yi, he thought that Huan Fan would surely try to follow their example, so he sent to call him. However, on the advice of his son, Huan Fan did not answer the summons, but decided to flee. He got into his carriage and drove hastily to the South Gate. But the gate was barred. The Commander of the Gate, Si Fan, was an old dependant of Huan Fan.

Huan Fan pulled out from his sleeve a slip of bamboo and said, "The Empress's command: Open the gate for me."

"Let me look," said Si Fan.

"What! How dare you, an old servant of mine, behave thus?"

Si Fan let Huan Fan pass.

As soon as he had got outside, Huan Fan shouted to Si Fan, "Sima Yi has raised a revolt, and you had better follow me!"

Si Fan realized that he had made a mistake, and chase after Huan Fan, but failed to come up with him.

"So the 'Bag of Wisdom' has got away too. That is a pity, but what can we do?" said Sima Yi, when they reported the escape.

"The poor horse always hankers after the old stable and manger. Cao Shuang would not know how to use Huan Fan," replied Jiang Ji.

Then Sima Yi called to him Xu Yun and Chen Tai and said, "Go you to Cao Shuang and say that I have no other intention than to take away the military power from him and his brothers."

As soon as they had left, he called Yin Damu and ordered Jiang Ji prepare a letter to be taken to Cao Shuang by Yin Damu.

Said Sima Yi, "You are on good terms with the man and are the fittest person for this mission. Tell him that Jiang Ji and I are concerned solely with the military powers in the hands of himself and his brothers, as we have sworn pointing to River Luo."

So Yin Damu went his way.

Out in the country Cao Shuang was enjoying the hunting, flying his falcons and coursing his hounds. Suddenly came the news of the rising in the city and the memorial against him. He almost fell out of the saddle when they told him. The eunuch handed in the memorial to the Ruler of Wei in the presence of Cao Shuang, who took it and opened it. A minister in attendance was ordered to read it. It said:

"Sima Yi, General Who Conquers the West and Imperial Guardian, with bowed head and trepidation, presents this memorial. On my return from the expedition into Liaodong, His late Majesty summoned Your Majesty, Cao Shuang, myself and certain others to his bedside, took me by the arm and impressed upon us all our duty in the years to be.

"Now Cao Shuang has betrayed the trust placed in him, has disordered the kingdom, usurped power at court, and seized upon power in the regions. He has appointed Zhang Dang, Administrator of the City, to control the court and spy upon Your Majesty. He is surely lying in wait to seize the empire. He has sown dissension in the royal family and injured his own flesh and blood. The whole land is in confusion, and people's hearts are full of fear. All this is opposed to the injunctions of His Late Majesty and his commands to me.

"Stupid and worthless as I am, yet I dare not forget the words of His Late Majesty. My colleagues, Jiang Ji and Sima Fu, agree that Cao Shuang is disloyal at heart, and great military powers should not be entrusted to him or his brothers.

"I have memorialized Her Majesty and obtained her authority to act.

"All military powers have been wrested from the hands of Cao Shuang, Cao Xi, and Cao Xun, leaving them only the simple title of lordships, so that hereafter they may be unable to hinder or control Your Majesty's actions. If there be any obstruction, the matter shall be summarily dealt with.

"Although in ill health, as a precautionary measure I have camped at the Floating Bridge, whence I write this."

When they had made an end of reading, the Ruler of Wei turned to Cao Shuang and said, "In the face of such words what mean you to do?"

Cao Shuang was at a loss and turned to his

younger brother, saying, "What now?"

Cao Xi replied, "I remonstrated with you, but you were obstinate and listened not. So it has come to this. Sima Yi is false and cunning beyond measure. If Zhuge Liang could not get the better of him, could we hope to do so? I see nothing but to yield that haply we may live."

Just at this moment arrived Adviser Xin Chang and Commander Lu Zhu. Cao Shuang asked what tidings they brought.

They replied, "The city is completely and closely surrounded, Sima Yi is camped on the river at the Floating Bridge, and you cannot return. You must decide how to act at once."

Then galloped up Huan Fan, who said, "This is really rebellion. Why not request His Majesty to proceed to Xuchang till regional troops can arrive and deal with Sima Yi?"

Cao Shuang replied, "How can we go to another place when all our families are in the city?"

Said Huan Fan, "Even a fool in this crisis would think only of life. You have the Son of Heaven with you here and command all the forces of the empire. None would dare disobey you, and yet you march quietly to death."

Cao Shuang could not decide to strike a blow for safety; he did nothing but snivel.

Huan Fan continued, "We can reach Xuchang tonight. The stay in Xuchang would be but brief, and there are ample supplies for years. You have forces at your call at the South Pass. You hold the seal of Minister of War, and I have brought it with me. Everything is in your favor. Act! Act at once! Delay is death."

"Do not hurry me," said Cao Shuang. "Let me think it over carefully."

Then came Xu Yun and Chen Tai, the two messengers of Sima Yi, and said, "The Imperial Guardian desires only to strip the military power of the Regent Marshal. If the Regent Marshal yields, he may return peacefully to the city."

Still Cao Shuang hesitated.

Next arrived Yin Damu, saying, "The Imperial Guardian had sworn by River Luo to the singleness of his aim. Here is letter of Minister Jiang Ji. The Regent Marshal should relinquish the military power and return to the Palace in peace."

When Cao Shuang seemed disposed to accept the assurance of Sima Yi, Huan Fan inveighed against it, saying, "You are a dead man if you listen to the voice of these people!"

Night found Cao Shuang still vacillating. As twilight faded into darkness he stood, sword in hand, sad, sighing and weeping. And morning found him still trying to make up his mind.

Huan Fan again urged him to decide upon some course.

"You have had a whole day and a whole night for reflection and must decide," said he.

"I will not fight; I will yield all; being a wealthy man is enough," said Cao Shuang, throwing down his sword.

Huan Fan left the tent wailing.

"Cao Zhen might boast of his abilities, but his sons are mere cattle," said he, weeping copiously.

The two messengers, Xu Yun and Chen Tai, bade Cao Shuang offer his seal of office to Sima Yi, and it was brought.

But First Secretary Yang Zong clung to it and would not give it up, saying, "Alas! That you, my lord, should resign your powers and make such a pitiful surrender. For surely you will not escape death in the eastern market place."

"The Imperial Guardian will surely keep faith with me," said Cao Shuang.

The seal was borne away, and Cao Shuang's generals and soldiers, thus released from the bonds of discipline, dispersed and the hosts melted away. When the Cao brothers reached the Floating Bridge, they were ordered to go to their dwellings, and they went. Their supporters were imprisoned to await the edicts of the Emperor.

Cao Shuang and his friends, so lately all-powerful, entered the city alone, without even a servant following.

As Huan Fan approached the bridge, Sima Yi, from horseback, pointed his whip disdainfully at him and said, "What brought you to this?"

Huan Fan made no reply, but with head bent followed the others.

It was decided to request the Emperor to declare the hunt at an end and order a return to the city. Cao Shuang, Cao Xi, and Cao Xun were confined in their own house, the gate whereof was fastened with a huge lock, and soldiers were set to guard it round about. They were sad and anxious, not knowing what would be their fate.

Then Cao Xi said, "We have but little food left. Let us write and ask for supplies. If Sima Yi sends us food, we may be sure he does not intend harm."

They wrote, and a hundred carts of supplies were sent.

This cheered them, and Cao Shuang said, "Our lives are safe in the hands of Sima Yi!"

Sima Yi had Zhang Dang arrested and put to the question.

Zhang Dang said. "I am not the only one who has tried to subvert the government. He Yan, Deng Yang, Li Sheng, Ding Mi, and Bi Gui are all involved in the plot."

So they were arrested and, when interrogated, confessed that a revolt had been arranged for the third month. Sima Yi had them locked in one long wooden collar.

The Commander of the Gates, Si Fan, testified: "Huan Fan has imposed upon me with a pretended command from Her Majesty and so has escaped out of the city. Beside he has said the Imperial

Guardian was a rebel."

Then said Sima Yi, "When a person maligns another and is false, the punishment for such a crime as he imputes falls upon his own head."

Huan Fan and those with him were thrown into prison.

Presently Cao Shuang and his brothers, all persons connected with them, and their clans were put to death in the market place. All the treasures of their houses was sent to the public treasury.

Now there was a certain woman of the Xiahou family who had been wife to Wen Shu, a second cousin of Cao Shuang. Early left a childless widow, her father wished her to marry again. Lady Xiahou refused and cut off her ears as a pledge of constancy. However, when the Caos were all put to death, her father arranged another marriage for her; whereupon she cut off her nose. Her own people were chagrined at her obstinate determination.

"For whom are you keeping your vow?" said they. "Man is but as the light dust upon the tender grass, and what is the good of mutilating your body?"

The woman replied, weeping, "I have heard that honorable persons do not break a vow of chastity for the sake of wealth, and the hearts of righteous persons are constant unto death regardless of all losses. While the house of Cao enjoyed prosperity, I remained faithful; how much more should I be true now that it has fallen upon evil days? Can I act like a mere beast of the field?"

The story of her devotion came to the ears of Sima Yi, who praised her conduct and allowed her to adopt a son to rear as her own and so continue the family.

A poem says:

What is a man to be mindful of?
A grain of dust on a blade of grass;
Such virtue as Lady Xiahou had
Stands out sublime as the ages pass.
This fair young wife of gentle mien
Dared all to maintain her purpose high.
What people though strong in the flush of life
Have equaled her in constancy?

After Cao Shuang had suffered death, Jiang Ji said to Sima Yi, "Xin Chang and Lu Zhu and others who had been of his party had forced the gate and joined the rebels. Yang Zong had opposed the surrender of the seal of the late minister. They deserve punishment."

However, no action was taken against them.

"They are righteous people who serves their master faithfully," said Sima Yi, and he even confirmed these men in their offices.

Xin Chang sighed, "Had I not listened to the advice of my sister, I would have walked in the way of unrighteousness."

A poet has praised his sister, Xin Xianying.

You call him lord and take his pay,
Then stand by him when danger nears."
Thus to her brother spoke Xin Xianying,
And won fair fame though endless years.

A general amnesty was extended to all Cao Shuang's partisans, and no officer was removed or dismissed for having supported the late order of things. All were left in possession of their property, and soon all was tranquillity.

However, it is to be noted that He Yan and Deng Yang met the unhappy end that Guan Lu had foretold for them.

The seer Guan Lu was deeply read
In all the lore of the ancient sages.
Thus he could see events to come
As clear as those of former ages.
And he perceived the soul of He Yan,
Already in the vale of gloom.
And knew the outer shell of Deng Yang
Was hastening to an early tomb.

After his recovery of power, Sima Yi was made Prime Minister and received the Nine Dignities. Sima Yi refused these honors, but the Ruler of Wei insisted and would take no denial. His two sons were made assistants to their father, and all state affairs fell under the control of these three.

However, Sima Yi remembered that one man, Xiahou Ba, a member of the Cao clan, still commanded at Yongzhou. In his position Xiahou Ba might be a real danger, and he must be removed. So an edict was issued calling him to Capital Luoyang to discuss affairs.

Upon receiving this call, Xiahou Ba was shocked. But instead of obeying this call, he declared himself a rebel, and he had a force of three thousand troops to support him. As soon as this was known, Guo Huai marched to suppress the malcontent. The two armies were soon face to face, and Guo Huai went to the front and began to revile his opponent.

"How could you rebel against the ruling house, you who are of the same clan as our great founder, and you who have always been treated generously?"

Xiahou Ba replied, "My forefathers served the state right well, but who is this Sima Yi that he has put to death my kinspeople and would now destroy me? What is his aim, if it be not to usurp the Throne? If I can cut him off and so frustrate his design, I shall at least be no traitor to the state."

Guo Huai rode forward to attack, and Xiahou Ba advanced to the encounter. They fought some ten bouts, and then Guo Huai turned and fled. But this was only a feint to lead on his enemy, for ere Xiahou Ba had gone far, he heard a shout behind him and turned to see Chen Tai about to attack. At the same moment Guo Huai turned again, and thus Xiahou Ba was between two fires. He could effect nothing, so he fled, losing many troops. Soon he decided that his only course was to flee to Hanzhong and to surrender to the Ruler of Shu.

Wherefore he went into Hanzhong to see if haply the Latter Ruler would accept his services. When Jiang Wei heard of his desire to surrender, he had doubts of Xiahou Ba's sincerity. However, after due inquiry Jiang Wei was satisfied and allowed the renegade from Wei to enter the city. After making his obeisance, Xiahou Ba, with many tears, told the story of his wrongs. Jiang Wei expressed sympathy.

Said Jiang Wei, "In the ancient time Wei Zi[xxvi] left the court of King Zhou in disgust, and this act has assured to him everlasting honor. You may be able now to assist in the restoration of the House of Han, and you will then stand no whit inferior to any person of antiquity."

A banquet was ordered, and while it was being prepared the host talked of affairs in Capital Luoyang.

Said Jiang Wei, "The Simas are now most powerful and in a position to carry out any scheme they planned. Think you that they have any intentions against Shu?"

"The old traitor has enough to do with his rebellion; he has no leisure to trouble about any outside matters. However, two other young leaders in Wei have lately come to the front, and if Sima Yi sent them against Shu and Wu, it might go ill with you both."

"And who are these two?"

"One is named Zhong Hui, a man of Changsha. He is a son of the former Imperial Guardian Zhong Yao. As a mere boy he was noted for being bold and smart. His father used to take him and his brother, Zhong Yu, to court. Zhong Hui was seven and his brother a year older. Emperor Pi noticed one day that the elder boy was sweating and asked him the reason. Zhong Yu replied, 'Whenever I am frightened, the sweat pours out.' Then Emperor Pi said to the other boy, 'You do not seem frightened.' And Zhong Hui replied, 'I am so frightened that the sweat cannot come out.' The Emperor was discerned the extraordinary ability of the boy. A little later Zhong Hui was always studying books on war and tactics, and became an able strategist, so that he won admiration from both Sima Yi and Jiang Ji. Zhong Hui is being a secretary in the Palace.

"The second man is Deng Ai from Yiyang. He was left an orphan very early, but he was ambitious and enterprising. If he saw lofty mountains or wide marshes, he always looked for those points where soldiers might be stationed or depots of provisions made or combustibles laid. People ridiculed him, but Sima Yi saw there was much to admire and employed the young man on his staff. Deng Ai had an impediment in his speech, so that he called himself 'Deng-eng-eng-Ai', and Sima Yi used to make fun of him and asked him one day how many there were of him since he called himself 'Deng-eng-eng-Ai'. Deng Ai at once replied, 'There is only one phoenix when they say 'O Phoenix! O Phoenix!" This ready repartee shows the quickness of his intellect, and you may well be on your guard against him and the other, for they are to be feared."

"I do not think them worth even talking about," replied Jiang Wei.

Jiang Wei took Xiahou Ba to Chengdu and presented him to the Latter Ruler.

Jiang Wei said, "Sima Yi had slain Cao Shuang, and he wanted to bait Xiahou Ba, who yielded to Shu. Now the Simas, father and sons, are holding the supreme power, the young Ruler Cao Fang is a weakling, and Wei's fortune is near its end. For many years in Hanzhong, our troops have been well trained, and our stores and depots filled with ample supplies. Now I wish to lead an expedition, using Xiahou Ba as guide, to conquer the Middle Land and to reestablish the House of Han in its old capital. This is how I could show my gratitude to Your Majesty and fulfill the desire of the late Prime Minister."

But Fei Yi, Chair of the Secretariat, opposed any expedition, saying, "We have lately lost by death two trusty ministers, Jiang Wan and Dong Yun, and there is no one left fit to take care of the government. The attempt should be postponed; no hasty move should be made."

"Not so," replied Jiang Wei. "Life is short. Our days flash by as the glint of a white horse across a chink in the door. We are waiting and waiting. Are we never to try to restore Han to its old glory?"

"Remember the saying of the wise Sun Zi: 'Know thyself and know thine enemy, then is victory sure.' We are not the equals of the late Prime Minister, and where he failed, are we likely to succeed?"

Jiang Wei said, "I would enlist the aid of the Qiangs. I have lived near them in Longshang and know them well. With their help, even if we do not gain the whole empire, we can at least conquer and hold all west of Changan."

The Latter Ruler here closed the discussion, saying, "Sir, as you desire to conquer Wei, do your best. I will not damp your enthusiasm."

Thus the Latter Ruler's consent was given. Then Jiang Wei left the court and betook himself, with Xiahou Ba, into Hanzhong to prepare for a new expedition.

"We will first send an envoy to the Qiangs to make a league with them," said Jiang Wei. "Then we will march out by the Xiping Pass to Yongzhou, where we will build up two ramparts in Qushan in Qushan Mountains and garrison them. The position is a point of vantage. Then we will send supplies beyond the pass by land and waterways, and advance gradually, according to the plan devised by the late Prime Minister."

In the autumn of the year (AD 249) they sent the two Shu generals, Li Xin and Gou Ai, with fifteen thousand troops, to construct the two ramparts in Qushan in Qushan Mountains, of which Gou Ai was to hold the eastern and Li Xin the western.

When the news reached Yongzhou, the Imperial Protector, Guo Huai, sent a report to Luoyang and also dispatched Chen Tai with a force of fifty thousand troops to oppose the troops of Shu. When that army arrived, Li Xin and Gou Ai led their troops to meet it. But their armies were too weak to stand such a large force, and they once more retired into the city. Chen Tai ordered his army to lay siege and occupy the road that led to Hanzhong, so that supplies were cut off.

After some days, and when the soldiers of Shu began to feel the pinch of hunger, Guo Huai came to see what progress his general was making.

At sight of the position he rejoiced exceedingly, and when he returned to camp he said to Chen Tai, "In this high country the city must be short of water, which means that the besieged must come out for supplies. Let us cut off the streams that supply them, and they will perish of thirst."

So the Wei soldiers were set to work to divert the streams above the city, and the besieged were soon distressed. Li Xin led out a strong force to try to seize the water sources and fought stubbornly, but was at length worsted and driven back within the walls. After that Li Xin and Gou Ai joined their forces and made another attempt to go out and fight. But the Yongzhou troops surrounded them, and a melee ensured until Li Xin and Gou Ai fought their way back to the city.

Meanwhile the soldiers were parched with thirst.

Gou Ai discussed the circumstance with Li Xin, saying, "I do not understand the delay of Commander Jiang Wei's reinforcements."

Li Xin said, "Let me try to fight my way out and get help."

So the gates were opened, and Li Xin rode out with some twenty horsemen. These were opposed and had to fight every inch of the way, but eventually Li Xin won though severely wounded. All his followers had fallen.

That night a strong north wind brought a heavy fall of snow, and the besieged were thus temporarily relieved from the water famine. They melted the snow and prepared food.

Li Xin, severely wounded, made his way west along the hill paths. After two days he fell in with Jiang Wei.

He dismounted, prostrated himself, and told his story: "Qushan had been surrounded and cut off water supplies. By luck it snowed, and our soldiers were partly relieved. But the situation was very urgent."

"The delay is not due to my slackness. The Qiang allies we depended upon have not come," said Jiang Wei.

Jiang Wei sent an escort with the wounded Li Xin to conduct him to Chengdu, where his wounds could be treated.

Turning to Xiahou Ba, Jiang Wei asked, "The Qiangs do not come, and the Wei army is besieging Qushan. General, do you have any plan to propose?"

Xiahou Ba replied, "If we wait for the coming of the Qiangs, it looks as if we shall be too late to relieve Qushan. It is very probable that Yongzhou has been left undefended, wherefore I propose that you go toward Ox Head Hills and work round to the rear of Yongzhou, which will cause the Wei army to fall back to relieve Yongzhou and so relieve our force."

"The plan appears excellent," replied Jiang Wei. And he set out.

When Chen Tai knew that Li Xin had escaped, he said to his chief, "Now that this man has got out, he will tell Jiang Wei of the danger and Jiang Wei will conclude that our efforts are concentrated on the ramparts and will endeavor to attack our rear. Therefore I suggest, General, that you go to River Yao and stop the supplies of our enemies, while I go to the Ox Head Hills and smite them. They will retreat as soon as they know their supplies are threatened."

So Guo Huai marched secretly to River Yao, while Chen Tai went to the hills.

When the Shu army led by Jiang Wei came near the Ox Head Hills, they heard a great shouting in front, and the scouts came in to report that the road was barred. Jiang Wei himself rode out to look.

"So you intended to attack Yongzhou, did you?" shouted Chen Tai. "But we know it and have been watching for you a long time."

Jiang Wei rode forth to attack. Chen Tai advanced with a flourish of his sword, and they engaged. Chen Tai soon ran away. Then the soldiers of Shu came forward and fell on, driving the soldiers of Wei back to the summit of the hills. But they halted there, and Jiang Wei encamped at the foot of the hills, whence he challenged the enemy every day. But he could gain no victory.

Seeing no result after some days of this, Xiahou Ba said, "This is no place to remain in. We can get no victory and are tempting fate by remaining open to a surprise. I think we should retire till some better plan can be tried."

Just then it was reported: "The supplies road by River Yao has fallen into the hands of Guo Huai!"

Shocked with the news, Jiang Wei bade Xiahou Ba march away first, and he covered the retreat. Chen Tai pursued in five divisions along five different roads, but Jiang Wei got possession of the meeting point and held them all in check, finally forcing them back on the hills. But from this position Chen Tai ordered his troops to shoot heavy discharges of arrows and stones so that Jiang Wei was forced to abandon his position. He went to River Yao, where Guo Huai led his force out to attack. Jiang Wei went to and fro smiting where he could, but he was surrounded and only got out by a desperate effort and after suffering more than half of his force.

Jiang Wei hastened toward Yangping Pass, but fell in with another body of the enemy, at the head of which he saw a fierce, youthful leader, who at once rode out furiously to attack. This leader had a round face, long ears, and a square mouth with thick lips. Below his left eye was a large hairy mole. It was the elder son of Sima Yi. He was General of the Flying Cavalry, Sima Shi.

"Simpleton! How dare you stand in my way?" yelled Jiang Wei, as he rode forward with his spear set.

Sima Shi met the attack, and a few bouts were fought before Sima Shi fled. Jiang Wei came off victor and so was free to continue his way. Presently he reached the pass and was welcomed within its sheltering walls. Sima Shi soon followed and attacked the Pass after his arrival, but those within the ramparts replied with the multiple crossbows which threw ten bolts at each discharge. For the army of Shu had made these engines of war after the design left by Zhuge Liang.

Owing to superior weapons, Shu defeated Wei,
Wei would never recover what was lost that day.

What befell Sima Shi will be told in the next chapter.

Chapter 108

**In The Snow, Ding Feng Wins A Victory;
At A Banquet, Sun Jun Executes A Secret Plan.**

As has been said, Jiang Wei, in his retreat, fell in with a force under Sima Shi, barring his road. It came about thus. After Jiang Wei invaded Yongzhou, Guo Huai had sent a flying messenger to the capital, and the Ruler of Wei summoned Sima Yi for advice. It had then been decided to send reinforcements to Yongzhou, and fifty thousand troops had marched, led by the son of the Prime Minister. On the march Sima Shi had heard that the Shu army had been beaten back, and he had concluded they were weak. So he decided to meet them on the road and give battle. Near the Yangping Pass, however, the roads had been lined with troops armed with the multiple crossbows designed by Zhuge Liang. Since Zhuge Liang's death, large numbers of these weapons had been made, and the bolts from them, which went in flights of ten, were poisoned. Consequently the Wei losses were very heavy, and Sima Shi himself barely escaped with life. However, eventually he returned to Luoyang.

From the walls of Qushan, the Shu general, Gou Ai, watched anxiously for the expected help. As it came not, he ultimately surrendered. And Jiang Wei, with a loss of twenty to thirty thousand soldiers, marched back into Hanzhong.

In the third year of Domestic Calm (AD 251), in

the eighth month, Sima Yi fell ill. His sickness increased rapidly, and, feeling that his end was near, he called his two sons to his bedside to hear his last words.

"I have served Wei many years and reached the highest rank possible among ministers. People have suspected me of ulterior aims, and I have always felt afraid of that. After my death the government will be in your hands, and you must be doubly careful."

Sima Yi passed away even as he said these last words. The sons informed the Ruler of Wei, who conferred high honors upon the dead and advanced his sons, Sima Shi to the rank of Regent Marshal with the leadership of the Chairs of the Boards, and Sima Zhao to the rank of Commander of the Flying Cavalry.

Meanwhile in the South Land, the Ruler of Wu, Sun Quan, had named his son Sun Deng as his heir. His mother was Lady Xu. But Sun Deng died in the fourth year of the Red Crow Era (AD 241). So the second son Sun He was chosen his successor. His mother was Lady Wang. A quarrel arose between Sun He and Princess Quan, who maligned him and intrigued against him, so that he was set aside. Sun He died of mortification. Then the third son Sun Liang was named the Heir Apparent. His mother was Lady Pan.

At this time old officials like Lu Xun and Zhuge Jin were dead, and the business of the government, great and small, was in the hands of Zhuge Ke, son of Zhuge Jin.

In the first year of Grand Beginning Era (AD 251),

on the first of the eighth month, a great storm passed over Wu. The waves rose to a great height, and the water stood eight feet deep over the low-lying lands. The pines and cypresses, which grew at the cemetery of the Imperial Ancestors of Wu, were uprooted and carried to the South Gate of Jianye, where they stuck, roots upward, in the road.

Sun Quan was frightened and fell ill. In the early days of the next year his illness became serious, whereupon he called in Imperial Guardian Zhuge Ke and Regent Marshal Lu Dai to hear the declaration of his last wishes. Soon after he died, at the age of seventy-one. He had reigned for twenty-four years. In Shu-Han calendar it was the fifteenth year of Long Enjoyment (AD 252).

A hero, green-eyed and purple-bearded,
He called forth devotion from all.
He lorded the east without challenge
Till death's one imperative call.

Zhuge Ke immediately placed his late lord's son Sun Liang on the throne, and the opening of the new reign was marked by the adoption of the style Great Prosperity Era, the first year (AD 252). A general amnesty was proclaimed. The late ruler received the posthumous style of Sun Quan the Great Emperor and was buried in Jiangling.

When these things were reported in the Wei capital, Sima Shi's first thought was to attack the South Land.

But his plans were opposed by Chair of the Secretariat Fu Gu, saying, "Remember what a strong defense to Wu is the Great River. The country has been many times attacked by our ancestors, but never conquered. Rather let us all hold what we have till the time be expedient to possess the whole empire."

Sima Shi replied, "The way of Heaven changes thrice in a century, and no three-part division is permanent. I wish to attack Wu."

Sima Zhao, his brother, was in favor of attack, saying "The occasion is most opportune. Sun Quan is newly dead, and the present ruler is a child."

An expedition was decided upon. Wang Chang, General Who Conquers the South, was sent with one hundred thousand troops against Nanjun. Guanqiu Jian, General Who Guards the South, was given one hundred thousand troops to go against Wuchang. Hu Zun, General Who Conquers the East, led one hundred thousand troops against Dongxing. They marched in three divisions. Sima Zhao was made Commander-in-Chief of the campaign.

In the winter of that year, the tenth month, Sima Zhao marched the armies near to the Wu frontiers and camped. Sima Zhao called together Wang Chang, Guanqiu Jian, Hu Zun, and various other commanders to decide upon plans.

He said, "The county of Dongxing is most important to Wu. They have built a great rampart, with walls right and left to defend Lake Chaohu from an attack in the rear. You gentlemen will have to exercise extreme care."

Then he bade Wang Chang and Guanqiu Jian each to take ten thousand troops and place themselves right and left, but not to advance till Dongxing had been captured. When that city had fallen, these two were to go forward at the same time. Hu Zun was to lead the van. The first step was to construct a floating bridge to storm the rampart. The two walls should then be captured.

News of the danger soon came to Wu, and Zhuge Ke called a council to take measures.

Then said Ding Feng, General Who Pacifies the North, "Dongxing is of the utmost importance as its loss would endanger Wuchang."

"I agree with you," said Zhuge Ke. "You say just what I think. You should lead three thousand marines up the river in thirty ships, while on land Lu Ju, Tang Zi, and Liu Zang will follow in three directions with ten thousand troops each. The signal for the general attack will be a cluster of bombs."

Ding Feng received the command, and, with three thousand marines and thirty battleships, he sailed in the Great River to Dongxing.

Hu Zun, the Van Leader of Wei, crossed on the floating bridge, took and camped on the rampart. He then sent Huan Jia and Han Zong to assault the left and right flanking forts, which were held by the Wu Generals Quan Yi and Liu Lue. These forts had high walls and strong, and made a good resistance, so that the Wei force could not overcome. But Quan Yi and Liu Lue dared not venture out to attack so strong a force as was attacking them.

Hu Zun made a camp at Xutang. It was then the depth of winter and intensely cold. Heavy snow fell. Thinking that no warlike operations were possible in such weather, Hu Zun and his officers made a great feast.

In the midst of the feasting came one to report: "Thirty ships are coming in the river."

Hu Zun went out to look and saw them come into the bank. He made out a hundred troops on each.

As they were so few, he returned to the feast and told his officers, "Only three thousand sailors. There is nothing to be alarmed at."

Giving orders to keep a careful watch, they all returned to enjoy themselves.

Ding Feng's ships were all drawn up in line. Then he said to his officers, "Today there is indeed a grand opportunity for a brave soldier to distinguish himself. We shall need the utmost freedom of movement, so throw off your armor, leave your helmets, cast aside your long spears, and reject your heavy halberds. Short swords are the weapons for today."

From the shore the soldiers of Wei watched the Wu marines with amusement, taking no trouble to prepare against an attack. But suddenly a cluster of bombs exploded, and simultaneously with the roar Ding Feng sprang ashore at the head of his troops. They dashed up the bank and made straight for the Wei camp.

The soldiers of Wei were taken completely by surprise and were helpless. Han Zong grasped one of the halberds that stood by the door of the commander's tent, but Ding Feng stabbed him in the breast, and he rolled over. Huan Jia went round and came up on the left. Just as he poised his spear to thrust, Ding Feng gripped it under his arm. Huan Jia let go and turned to flee, but Ding Feng sent his sword flying after him and caught him in the shoulder. He turned and was thrust through by Ding Feng's spear.

The three companies of Wu marines went to and fro in the camp of Wei slaying as they would. Hu Zun mounted a horse and fled. His troops ran away across the floating bridge, but that gave way and many were thrown into the water and drowned. Dead bodies lay about on the snow in large numbers. The spoil of military gear that fell to Wu was immense.

Sima Zhao, Wang Chang, and Guanqiu Jian, seeing the Dongxing front had been broken, decided to retreat.

Zhuge Ke marched his army to Dongxing, and he made great feastings and distribution of rewards in celebration of victory.

Then he said to his leaders, "Sima Zhao has suffered a defeat and retreated to the north. It is time to take the Middle Land!"

So he told his officers that this was his intention, and also sent away letters to Shu to engage the aid of Jiang Wei, promising that the empire should be divided between them when they had taken it.

An army of two hundred thousand troops was told off to invade the Middle Land. Just as it was starting, a stream of white vapor was seen emerging from the earth, and as it spread it gradually enveloped the whole army so that people could not see each other.

"It is a white rainbow," said Jiang Yan, "and it bodes ill to the army. I advise you, O Imperial Guardian, to return and not march against Wei."

"How dare you utter such ill-omened words and blunt the keenness of my army?" cried Zhuge Ke, angrily.

He bade the lictors take Jiang Yan out and put him to death. But Jiang Yan's colleagues interceded for him, and he was spared, but he was stripped of all rank. Orders were issued to march quickly.

Then Ding Feng offered a suggestion, saying, "Wei depends on Xincheng for the defense of its passes. It would be a severe blow to Sima Shi if Xincheng falls."

Zhuge Ke welcomed this suggestion and gave orders to march on Xincheng. They came up and found the city gates closed, wherefore they began to besiege the city. The Commander in the city, Zhang Te, saw the legions of Wu at the walls, held a strict defense.

A hasty messenger was sent to Luoyang, and Secretary Yu Song told the Prime Minister, Sima Shi.

Yu Song said, "Zhuge Ke is laying siege to Xincheng. The city should not try to repulse the attack, but simply hold out as long as possible. When the besiegers have exhausted their provisions, they will be compelled to retire. As they retreat, we can smite them. However, it is necessary to provide against any invasion from Shu."

Accordingly Sima Zhao was sent to reinforce Guo Huai so as to keep off Jiang Wei, while Guanqiu Jian and Hu Zun kept the army of Wu at bay.

For months the army of Zhuge Ke battered at Xincheng without success. He urged his generals to strenuous efforts, threatening to put to death anyone who was dilatory. At last his attacks looked like succeeding, for the northeast corner of the wall seemed shaken.

Then Zhang Te, the Commander of Xincheng, thought of a device. He sent a persuasive messenger with all the register documents to Zhuge Ke.

And the messenger said, "It is a rule in Wei that if a city holds out against attack for a hundred days and reinforcement has not arrived, then its commander may surrender without penalty to his family. Now Xincheng has held out for over ninety days, and my master hopes you will allow him to withstand the few days necessary to complete the hundred, when he will yield. Here are all register documents that he desires to tender first."

Zhuge Ke had no doubts that the story was genuine. He ordered the army to retreat temporarily, and the defenders enjoyed a rest. But all Zhang Te really desired was time wherein to strengthen the weak angle of the wall. As soon as the attacks ceased, the defenders pulled down the houses near the corner and repaired the wall with the material.

As soon as the repairs were complete, Zhang Te threw off all pretense and cried from the wall, "I have half a year's provisions yet and will not surrender to any curs of Wu!"

The defense became as vigorous as before the truce. Zhuge Ke was enraged at being so tricked, and urged on the attack. But one day one of the thousands of arrows that flew from the rampart struck him in the forehead, and he fell. He was borne to his tent, but the wound inflamed, and he became very ill.

Their leader's illness disheartened the troops, and, moreover, the weather became very hot. Sickness invaded the camp, so that soldiers and leaders alike wished to go home.

When Zhuge Ke had recovered sufficiently to resume command, he urged on the attack, but the generals said, "The soldiers are sick and unfit for battle."

Zhuge Ke burst into fierce anger, and said, "The next person who mentions illness will be beheaded."

When the report of this threat got abroad, the soldiers began to desert freely. Presently Commander Cai Lin, with his whole company, went over to the enemy. Zhuge Ke began to be alarmed and rode through the camps to see for himself. Surely enough, the soldiers all looked sickly, with pale and puffy faces.

The siege had to be raised, and Zhuge Ke retired into his own country. But scouts brought the news of retreat to Guanqiu Jian who led the Wei's grand army to follow and harass Zhuge Ke's march and inflicted a severe defeat.

Mortified by the course of events, after his return Zhuge Ke did not attend court held by the Ruler of Wu, but pretended illness.

Sun Liang, the Ruler of Wu, went to the residence to see his general, and the officers came to call. In order to silence comment, Zhuge Ke assumed an attitude of extreme severity, investigating everyone's conduct very minutely, punishing rigorously any fault or shortcoming and meting out sentences of banishment, or death with exposure, till everyone walked in terror. He also placed two of his own cliques---Zhang Yue and Zhu En---over the royal guards, making them the teeth and claws of his vengeance.

Now Sun Jun was a son of Sun Gong and a great grandson of Sun Jing, brother of Sun Jian. Sun Quan loved him and had put him in command of the guards. Sun Jun was enraged at being superseded by Zhang Yue and Zhu En, the two creatures of Zhuge Ke.

Minister Teng Yin, who had an old quarrel with Zhuge Ke, said to Sun Jun, "This Zhuge Ke is as cruel as he is powerful. He abuses his authority, and no one is safe against him. I also think he is aiming at something yet higher and you, Sir, as one of the ruling family ought to put a stop to it."

"I agree with you, and I want to get rid of him," replied Sun Jun. "Now I will obtain an edict condemning him to death."

Both went in to see the Ruler of Wu, Sun Liang, and they laid the matter before him.

"I am afraid of him, too," replied Sun Liang. "I have wanted to remove him for some time, but have found no opportunity. If you would prove your loyalty, you would do it for me."

Then said Teng Yin, "Your Majesty can give a banquet and invite him, and let a few braves be ready hidden behind the curtains. At a signal, as the dropping of a wine cup, they might jump out and slay him, and all further trouble would be avoided."

Sun Liang agreed.

Zhuge Ke had never been to court since his return from the unfortunate expedition. Under a plea of indisposition he had remained moping at home. One day he was going out of his reception room when he suddenly saw coming in a person dressed in the mourning white.

"Who are you?" said he, rather roughly.

The person seemed too terror-stricken to reply or resist when he was seized.

They questioned him, and he said, "I was in mourning for my father newly dead, and had come into the city to seek a priest to read the liturgy. I had entered by mistake, thinking it was a temple."

The gate wardens were questioned. They said, "There are scores of us at the gate, which is never unwatched. We have not seen a man enter."

Zhuge Ke raged and had the mourner and the gate wardens put to death. But that night he was restless and sleepless. By and by he heard a rending sound that seemed to come from the reception hall, so he arose and went to see what it was. The great main beam had broken in two.

Zhuge Ke, much disturbed, returned to his chamber to try once more to sleep. But a cold wind blew, and, shivering in the chilly air, he saw the figures of the mourner and the gate wardens he had put to death. They advanced toward him holding their heads in their hands and seemed to threaten him. He was frightened, and fell in a swoon.

Next morning, when washing his face, the water seemed tainted with the smell of blood. He bade the maid throw it away and bring more; it made no difference, the odor was still there. He was perplexed and distressed. Then came a messenger with an invitation to a royal banquet. He had his carriage prepared. As he was passing through the gate, a yellow dog jumped up and caught hold of his garment and then howled lugubriously.

"The dog even mocks me!" said he, annoyed, and he bade his attendants take it away.

Then he set out for the Palace. Before he had gone far, he saw a white rainbow rise out of the earth and reach up to the sky. While he was wondering what this might portend, his friend Zhang Yue came up and spoke a word of warning.

"I feel doubtful about the real purpose of this banquet," said Zhang Yue, "and advise you not to go."

Zhuge Ke gave orders to drive home again. But before he had reached his own gate, the two conspirators---Sun Jun and Teng Yin---rode up and asked, "O Imperial Guardian, why are you turning back?"

"I feel unwell and cannot see the Emperor today," replied Zhuge Ke.

They replied, "This court is appointed to be held especially to do honor to you and the army. You have not yet reported, and there is a banquet for you. You may be ill, but you really must go to court."

Zhuge Ke yielded, and once more set his face toward the Palace. Sun Jun and Teng Yin went with him, and his friend Zhang Yue followed. The banquet was spread when he arrived, and after he had made his obeisance he went to his place.

When the wine was brought in, Zhuge Ke, thinking it might be poisoned, excused himself from drinking, saying, "I am currently ill, and I cannot drink wine."

"Will you have some of the medicated wine brought from your own residence?" said Sun Jun.

"Yes; I could drink that," replied he.

So a servant was sent for a supply that he might drink with the other guests.

After several courses, the Ruler of Wu made an excuse and left the banquet hall. Sun Jun went to the foot of the hall and changed his garments of ceremony for more homely garb, but underneath these he put on armor.

Then suddenly he raised his keen sword and ran up the hall, shouting, "The Emperor has issued an edict to slay a rebel!"

Zhuge Ke, startled so that he dropped his cup, laid his hand upon his sword. But he was too late; his head rolled to the floor. His friend Zhang Yue drew his sword and rushed at the assassin, but Sun Jun evaded the full force of the blow and was only wounded in the left finger. Sun Jun slashed back at Zhang Yue and wounded him in the right arm. Then the braves dashed in and finished Zhang Yue.

The braves were then sent to arrest Zhuge Ke's family, while the bodies of Zhuge Ke and Zhang Yue were hastily rolled in matting, thrown into a cart, taken to the outside of the south gate, and tossed into a rubbish pit.

While Zhuge Ke was absent in the palace, his wife sat in the women's quarters at home feeling strangely unquiet.

Presently a maid came in and, when she drew near, his wife said, "Why does your clothing smell of blood?"

To her horror the maid suddenly transformed into a weird creature with rolling eyes and gritting teeth, that went dancing about the room and leaping till it touched the roof-beams, shrieking all the time, "I am Zhuge Ke, and I have been slain by that bastard Sun Jun!"

By this time the whole family were frightened and began wailing. And a few minutes later the residence was surrounded by a crowd of armed guards sent to murder the inmates, whom they bound, carried off to the market place, and put to the sword. These things occurred in the tenth month of the second year of Great Prosperity (AD 253).

When Zhuge Jin lived, he saw his son's ability display prominently, and he often sighed, saying, "This son will not safeguard the family."

Others had also predicted an early death. Zhang Qi, High Minister in Wei, used to say to Sima Shi, "Zhuge Ke will die soon."

And when asked why, Zhang Qi replied, "Can a person live long when his dignity endangers that of his lord?"

After the conspiracy, Sun Jun became Prime Minister in place of his victim. He was also placed in command of all the military forces, and became very powerful. The control of all matters was in his hands.

In Chengdu, when the letter of Zhuge Ke asking help from Jiang Wei arrived, Jiang Wei had audience with the Latter Ruler and requested authority to raise an army against the north.

The army fought, but fought in vain,
Success may crown a new campaign.

Who were victorious will appear in the next chapter.

Chapter 109

A Ruse Of A Han General: Sima Zhao Is Surrounded;
Retribution For The House Of Wei: Cao Fang Is Dethroned.

It was the autumn of the sixteenth year of Long Enjoyment (AD 253), and Jiang Wei's army of two hundred thousand was ready to march against the north. Liao Hua and Zhang Yi were Leaders of the Van; Xiahou Ba was Army Strategist; Zhang Ni was in command of the commissariat. The army marched out by the Yangping Pass.

Discussing the plan of campaign with Xiahou Ba, Jiang Wei said, "Our former attack on Yongzhou failed, so this time they will doubtless be even better prepared to resist. What do you suggest?"

Xiahou Ba replied, "Nanan is the only well-provided place in all Longshang. If we take that, it will serve as an excellent base. Our former ill-success was due to the non-arrival of the Qiangs. Let us therefore send early to tell them to assemble at Longyou, after which we will move out at Shiying and march to Nanan by way of Dongting."

"You spoke well," said Jiang Wei.

He at once sent Xi Zheng as his envoy, bearing gifts of gold and pearls and silk to win the help of the King of the Qiangs, whose name was Mi Dang. The mission was successful: King Mi Dang accepted the presents and sent fifty thousand troops to Nanan under the Qiang General Ehe Shaoge.

When Guo Huai heard of the threatened attack, he sent a hasty memorial to Capital Luoyang.

Sima Shi at once asked his leaders, "Who will go out to meet the army from the west?"

Xu Zi volunteered, and as Sima Shi had a high opinion of his capacity, he appointed Xu Zi as Leader of the Van. The brother of the Prime Minister, Sima Zhao, went as Commander-in-Chief.

The Wei army set out for West Valley Land, reached Dongting, and there fell in with Jiang Wei. When both sides were arrayed Xu Zi, who wielded a mighty splitter-of-mountains ax as his weapon, rode out and challenged. Liao Hua went forth to accept, but after a few bouts he took advantage of a feint and fled.

Then Zhang Yi set his spear and rode forth to continue the fight. He also soon fled and returned within his own ranks. Thereupon Xu Zi gave the signal to fall on in force, and the army of Shu lost the day. They retired ten miles, Sima Zhao also drew off his troops, and both sides encamped.

"Xu Zi is very formidable. How can we overcome him?" asked Jiang Wei.

"Tomorrow make pretense of defeat and so draw them into an ambush," replied Xiahou Ba.

"But remember whose son this Sima Zhao is," said

Jiang Wei. "Sima Zhao cannot be a novice in war. If he sees a likely spot for an ambush, he will halt. Now the troops of Wei have cut our transportation many times. Let us do the same to them, and we may slay this Xu Zi."

He called in Liao Hua and Zhang Yi and gave them secret orders, sending them in different directions. Then he laid iron thorns along all the approaches and planted thorny barriers as if making a permanent defense. When the troops of Wei came up and challenged, the troops of Shu refused battle.

The scouts reported to Sima Zhao: "The Shu supplies are coming up along the rear of Iron Cage Mountain, and they are using the wooden oxen and running horses as transport. The Shu army are building permanent defenses and are awaiting the arrival of their allies the Qiang tribes."

Then said Sima Zhao to Xu Zi, "We formerly defeated the army of Shu by cutting off supplies, and we can do that again. Let five thousand troops go out tonight and occupy the road."

About the middle of the first watch Xu Zi marched across the hills. When he came to the other side, he saw a couple of hundred soldiers driving a hundred or so heads of mechanical animals laden with grain and forage. His army rushed down upon them with shouts, and the troops of Shu, seeing that their road was impassable, abandoned their supplies and ran away. Xu Zi took possession of the supply train, which he sent back to his own camp under the escort of half his troops. With the other half he set out in pursuit.

About three miles away, the road was found blocked with carts set across the track. Some of his soldiers dismounted to clear the way. But as they did so, the brushwood on both sides burst into a blaze. Xu Zi at once drew off his force and turned to retire, but coming to a defile he found the road again blocked with wagons, and again the brushwood began to burn. He made a dash to escape, but before he could get clear a bomb roared, and he saw the troops of Shu coming down on him from two directions. Liao Hua and Zhang Yi from left and right fell on Xu Zi with great fury, and the troops of Wei were wholly defeated. Xu Zi himself got clear, but without any following.

He struggled on till he and his steed were almost spent with fatigue. Presently he saw another company of the enemy in his way, and the leader was Jiang Wei. Before he could make any resistance, Jiang Wei's spear thrust him down, and as Xu Zi lay on the ground he was cut to pieces.

Meanwhile those troops of Wei who had been sent to escort to camp the convoy of supplies which they had seized were captured by Xiahou Ba. They surrendered. Xiahou Ba then stripped them of their weapons and clothing and therein disguised some of his own soldiers. Holding aloft banners of Wei, these disguised soldiers made for the Wei camp. When they arrived, they were mistaken by those in the camp for comrades, and the gates were thrown open. They rushed in and began to slay. Taken wholly by surprise, Sima Zhao leaped upon his steed and fled. But Liao Hua met him and drove him back. Then appeared Jiang Wei in the path of retreat, so that no road lay open. Sima Zhao made off for the hills, hoping to be able to hold out on the Iron Cage Mountain.

Now there was only one road up the hill, which rose steeply on all sides. And the hill had but one small spring of water, enough to serve a hundred people or so, while Sima Zhao's force numbered six thousand. Their enemies had blocked the only road of escape. This one fountain was unequal to supplying the needs of the beleaguered army, and soon they were tormented with thirst.

In despair, Sima Zhao looked up to heaven and sighed, saying, "Death will surely come to me here!"

The host of Wei on Iron Cage Mountain
Were once fast held by Jiang Wei's skill;
When Pang Juan first crossed the Maling Hills,
His strategy was reckoned fine
As Xiang Yu at the Nine Mountains;
Both bent opponents to their will.

In this critical situation Secretary Wang Tao reminded his leader of what Geng Gong had done in ancient time, saying, "O General, why do you not imitate Geng Gong, who, being in great need, prostrated himself and prayed at a well, wherefrom he afterwards was supplied with sweet water?"

So the leader went to the summit of the hill and knelt beside the spring and grayed thus:

"The humble Sima Zhao received a command to repulse the army of Shu. If he is to die here, then may this spring cease its flow, when he will end his own life and let his soldiers yield to the enemy. But if his allotted span of life be not reached, then, O Blue Vault, increase the flow of water and save the lives of this multitude."

Thus he prayed; and the waters gushed forth in plenty, so that they all quenched their thirst and lived.

Jiang Wei had surrounded the hill, holding the army thereon as in a prison.

He said to his officers, "I have always regretted that our great Prime Minister was unable to capture Sima Yi in the Gourd Valley, but now I think his son is doomed to fall into our hands!"

However, news of the dangerous position of Sima Zhao had come to Guo Huai, who set about a rescue.

Chen Tai said to him, "Jiang Wei has made a league with the Qiangs, and they have arrived to help him. If you go away to rescue Sima Zhao, the Qiangs will attack from the rear. Therefore I would propose to send someone to the tribespeople to try to create a diversion and get them to retire. If they are disposed of, you may go to the rescue of Sima Zhao."

Guo Huai saw there was much reason in this, and told Chen Tai to take a force of five thousand troops and go to the camp of the King of the Qiangs. When Chen Tai reached the camp, he threw off his armor and entered weeping and crying that he was in danger of death.

He said, "Guo Huai sets himself up as superior to everyone and is trying to slay me. Therefore I have come to offer my services to you. I know all the secrets of the Wei army, and, if you will, this very night I can lead you to their camp. I have friends in the camp to help, and you can destroy it."

King Mi Dang was taken with the scheme, and sent his General Ehe Shaoge to go with Chen Tai. The deserters from Wei were placed in the rear, but Chen Tai himself rode with the leading body of the Qiangs. They set out at the second watch and soon arrived. They found the gates open, and Chen Tai rode in boldly. But when Ehe Shaoge and his troops galloped in, there suddenly arose a great cry as soldiers and horses went tumbling into great pits. At the same time Chen Tai came round in the rear and attacked, while Guo Huai appeared on the flank. The Qiangs trampled each other down, and many were killed. Those who escaped death surrendered, and the leader, Ehe Shaoge, committed suicide in a pit.

Guo Huai and Chen Tai then hastened back into the camp of the Qiangs. Mi Dang, taken unprepared, rushed out of his tent to get to horse, but was made prisoner. He was taken before Guo Huai, who hastily dismounted, loosed the prisoner's bonds, and soothed him with kindly words.

"Our government has always regarded you as a loyal and true friend," said Guo Huai. "Why then are you helping our enemies?"

Mi Dang sank to the ground in confusion, while Guo Huai continued, "If you will now raise the siege of Iron Cage Mountain and drive off the troops of Shu, I will memorialize the Throne and obtain a substantial reward for you."

Mi Dang agreed. He set out forthwith, his own army leading and the army of Wei in the rear. At the third watch he sent on a messenger to tell Jiang Wei of his coming. And the Shu leader was glad. Mi Dang was invited to come. On the march the soldiers of Wei had mingled with the Qiangs, and many of them were in the forefront of the army.

As they drew near the camp, Jiang Wei gave order: "The army are to camp outside. Only the King can enter the gate."

Mi Dang went up toward the gate with a hundred or more followers, and Jiang Wei with Xiahou Ba went to welcome him. Just as they met, before Mi Dang could say a word, the Wei generals dashed on past him and set on to slay. Jiang Wei was taken aback, leaped on his steed and fled, while the mixed force of troops of Wei and Qiangs drove the camp defenders before them and sent them flying.

When Jiang Wei leaped upon his steed at the gate, he had no weapon in his hand, only his bow and quiver hung at his shoulder. In his hasty flight the arrows fell out and the quiver was empty, so when he set off for the hills with Guo Huai in pursuit, Jiang Wei had nothing to oppose to the spears of his pursuers. As they came near he laid hands upon his bow and made as if to shoot. The string twanged and Guo Huai blenched. But as no arrow went flying by, Guo Huai knew Jiang Wei had none to shoot. Guo Huai therefore hung his spear, took his bow and shot. Jiang Wei caught the arrow as it flew by and fitted it to his bowstring. He waited till Guo Huai came quite near, when he pulled the string with all his force and sent the arrow flying straight at Guo Huai's face. Guo Huai fell even as the bowstring sang.

Jiang Wei pulled up and turned to finish his fallen enemy, but the soldiers of Wei were nearly upon him, and he had only time to snatch up Guo Huai's spear and ride off. Now that Jiang Wei was armed and their own leader wounded, the soldiers of Wei had no more desire to fight. They picked up their general and carried him to camp. There the arrow-head was pulled out, but the flow of blood could not be stanched, and Guo Huai died.

Sima Zhao descended from the hill as soon as Jiang Wei moved away, and pursued some distance before returning.

Xiahou Ba forced his way out and rejoined Jiang Wei as soon as he could, and they marched away together. The losses of Shu in this defeat were very heavy. On the road they dared not halt to muster or reform, but went helter-skelter into Hanzhong. In that campaign, though the Shu army were defeated, they had killed Xu Zi and Guo Huai on the other side and had damaged the prestige of Wei. Thus Jiang Wei's achievement made up for his offense.

After rewarding the Qiangs for their help, Sima Zhao led his army back to Capital Luoyang, where he joined his brother Sima Shi in administering the government. They were too strong for any of the officers to dare opposition, and they terrorized Cao Fang, the Ruler of Wei, so that he shook with fright whenever he saw Sima Shi at court, and felt as if needles were being stuck into his back.

One day, when the Ruler of Wei was holding a court, Sima Shi came into the hall wearing his sword. Cao Fang hastily left his Dragon Throne to receive him.

"What does this mean? Is this the correct etiquette for a prince when his minister approaches?" said Sima Shi, smiling. "I pray Your Majesty remember your dignity and listen while the ministers address the Throne."

Court business then proceeded. Sima Shi decided every question without reference to the Ruler of Wei; and when Sima Shi retired, he stalked haughtily down the hall and went home, followed by his escort, which numbered thousands of horse and foot.

When the Ruler of Wei left the court, only three followed him to the private apartments. They were Minister Xiahou Xuan, Secretary Li Feng, and High Minister Zhang Qi. Zhang Qi was the father of his consort, Empress Zhang. Sending away the servants, Cao Fang and these three went into a private chamber.

Seizing his father-in-law's hand, Cao Fang began to weep, saying, "That man Sima Shi treats me as a child and regards the officers of state as if they were so many straws. I am sure the throne will be his one day."

And he wept bitterly.

Said Li Feng, "Do not be so sad, Sire. I am but a

poor sort of person. But if Your Majesty will give me authority, I will call together all the bold people in the country and slay this man."

"It was from fear of this man that my brother Xiahou Ba was forced to go over to Shu," said Xiahou Xuan. "If Sima Shi were destroyed, my brother could return. I belong to a family related to the rulers of the state for many generations, and I cannot sit still while a wretch ruins the government. Put my name in the command as well, and we will work together to remove him."

"But I am afraid we can not overcome him," said Cao Fang.

They wept and said, "We pledge ourselves to work together for the destruction of the tyrant, and to show our gratitude to Your Majesty!"

Cao Fang them stripped himself of his innermost garment, gnawed his finger till the blood flowed, and with his finger-tip traced a command in blood.

He gave it to his father-in-law, Zhang Qi, saying, "My ancestor, Emperor Cao, put to death Dong Cheng for just such a matter as this, so you must be exceedingly careful and maintain the greatest secrecy."

"Oh, why use such ill-omened words?" cried Li Feng. "We are not like Dong Cheng, and Sima Shi cannot compare to the Founder. Have no doubts."

The three conspirators took leave and went out carrying the edict with them. Beside the Donghua Gate of the Palace, they saw Sima Shi coming to meet them wearing a sword. Following him were many armed guards. The three ministers took the side of the road to let the party go by.

"Why are you three so late in leaving the Palace?" asked Sima Shi.

"His Majesty was reading, and we stayed with him," said Li Feng.

"What was he reading?"

"The histories of the Xia, Shang, and Zhou dynasties."

"What questions did the Emperor ask as he read those books?"

"He asked about Yi Yin[xxvii] and how he upheld the Shang; and the Duke of Zhou[xxviii], how he acted when he was regent. And we told His Majesty that you were both Yi Yin and the Duke Zhou to him."

Sima Shi smiled grimly and said, "Why did you compare me with those two when in your hearts you think me a rebel like Wang Mang and Dong Zhuo?"

"How should we dare when we are your subordinates?" said the three ministers.

"You are a lot of flatterers," said Sima Shi, angrily. "And what were you crying about in that private chamber with the Emperor?"

"We did no such thing."

"Your eyes are still red: You cannot deny that."

Xiahou Xuan then knew that the secrecy had been

showed, so he broke out into a volley of abuse, crying, "Well, we were crying because of your conduct, because you terrorize over the Emperor and are scheming to usurp the Throne!"

"Seize him!" roared Sima Shi.

Xiahou Xuan threw back his sleeves and struck at Sima Shi with his fists, but the lictors pulled him back. Then the three were searched, and on Zhang Qi was found the blood-stained garment of the Emperor. They handed it to their chief, who recognized the object of his search, the secret edict. It said:

"The two Sima brothers have stolen away all my authority and are plotting to take the Throne. The edicts I have been forced to issue do not represent my wishes, and hereby all officers, civil and military, may unite to destroy these two and restore the authority of the Throne. These ends achieved, I will reward those who help to accomplish them."

Sima Shi, more angry than ever, said, "So you wish to destroy me and my brother. This is too much!"

He ordered his followers to execute the three on the public ground by waist-bisection and to destroy their whole clans.

The three reviled without ceasing. On the way to the place of execution, they ground their teeth with rage, spitting out the pieces they broke off. They died muttering curses.

Sima Shi then went to the rear apartments of the

Palace, where he found the Emperor talking with his Consort.

Just as he entered, she was saying to the Emperor, "The Palace is full of spies, and if this comes out, it will mean trouble for me."

Sima Shi strode in, sword in hand.

"My father placed Your Majesty on the throne, a service no less worthy than that of Duke Zhou; I have served Your Majesty as Yi Yin served his master. Now is kindness met by enmity and service regarded as a fault. Your Majesty has plotted with two or three insignificant officials to slay me and my brother. Why is this?"

"I had no such intention," said Cao Fang.

In reply Sima Shi drew the garment from his sleeve and threw it on the ground.

"Who did this?"

Cao Fang was overwhelmed: His soul flew beyond the skies, his spirit lied to the ninth heaven.

Shaking with fear, he said, "I was forced into it. How could I think of such a thing?"

"To slander ministers by charging them with rebellion is an aggravated crime," said Sima Shi.

Cao Fang knelt at his feet, saying, "Yes; I am guilty. Forgive me."

"I beg Your Majesty to rise: The laws must be

respected!"

Pointing to Empress Zhang, Sima Shi said, "She is of the Zhang house and must die!"

"Spare her!" cried Cao Fang, weeping bitterly.

But Sima Shi was obdurate. He bade the lictors lead her away, and she was strangled with a white silk cord at a Palace gate.

Now I recall another year; and lo!
An empress borne away to shameful death.
Barefooted, weeping bitterly she shrieks
"Farewell," torn from her consort's arms.
History repeats itself; time's instrument,
Sima Shi avenges this on Cao Cao's heirs.

The day after these events, Sima Shi assembled all the officers and addressed them thus: "Our present lord is profligate and devoid of principle; familiar with the vile and friendly with the impure. He lends a ready ear to slander and keeps good people at a distance. His faults exceed those of the Prince of Changyi[xxix] of old, and he has proved himself unfit to rule. Wherefore, following the precedents of Yi Yin[xxx] and Huo Guang, I have decided to put him aside and to set up another, thereby to maintain the sanctity of the ruler and ensure tranquillity. What think you, Sirs?"

They all agreed, saying, "General, you are right to play the same part as Yi Yin and Huo Guang, thereby acting in accordance with Heaven and fulfilling the desire of humankind. Who dares dispute it?"

Then Sima Shi, followed by the whole of the officials, went to the Palace of Everlasting Peace and informed the Empress Dowager of his intention.

"Whom do you propose to place on the throne, General?" she asked.

"I have observed that Cao Ju, Prince of Pengcheng, is intelligent, benevolent, and filial. He is fit to rule the empire."

She replied, "He is my uncle, and it is not convenient. However, there is Cao Mao, Duke of Gaogui, and grandson of Emperor Pi. He is of mild temperament, respectful, and deferential, and may be set up. You, Sir, and the high officers of state might favorably consider this."

Then spoke one, saying, "Her Majesty speaks well: Cao Mao should be raised to the throne."

All eyes turned toward the speaker, who was Sima Fu, uncle of Sima Shi.

The Duke of Gaogui was summoned to the capital.

The Empress called Cao Fang into her presence in the Hall of Principles and blamed him, saying, "You are vicious beyond measure, a companion of lewd men and a friend of vile women. You are unfitted to rule. Therefore resign the imperial seal and revert to your status of Prince of Qi[xxxi]. You are forbidden to present yourself at court without special command."

Cao Fang, weeping, threw himself at her feet. He gave up the seal, got into his carriage and went away. Only a few faithful ministers restrained their tears and bade him farewell.

Cao Cao, the mighty minister of Han,
Oppressed the helpless; little then thought he
That only two score swiftly passing years
Would bring like fate to his posterity.

The Emperor-elect Cao Mao was the grandson of Emperor Pi, and son of Cao Lin, Prince of Donghai. When Cao Mao was nearing the capital, all the officers attended to receive him at the Nanye Gate, where an imperial carriage awaited him. He hastily returned their salutations.

"The ruler ought not to return these salutations," said Grand Commander Wang Su.

"I also am a minister and must respond," replied he.

They conducted him to the carriage to ride into the Palace, but he refused to mount it, saying, "Her Majesty has commanded my presence; I know not for what reason. How dare I enter the Palace in such a carriage?"

He went on foot to the Hall, where Sima Shi awaited him. He prostrated himself before Sima Shi. Sima Shi hastily raised him and led him into the presence.

The Empress Dowager said, "In your youth I noticed that you bore the impress of majesty. Now you are to be the Ruler of the Empire. You must be respectful and moderate, diffusing virtue and benevolence. You must do honor to your ancestors---the former emperors."

Cao Mao modestly declined the proposed honor, but he was compelled to accept it. He was led out of the presence of the Empress Dowager and placed in the seat of empire in the Hall of Principles.

The style of the reign was changed from Domestic Calm, the sixth year, to Right Origin, the first year (AD 254). An amnesty was granted. Honors were heaped upon Sima Shi, who also received the golden axes, with the right to proceed leisurely within the precincts, to address the Throne without using his name, and to wear arms at court. Many other officers also received promotions.

But in the spring of the second year of Right Origin, it was reported at court that Guanqiu Jian, General Who Guards the East, and Wen Qin, Imperial Protector of Yangzhou, were raising armies with the declared design of restoring the deposed emperor.

Sima Shi disconcerted.

If ministers of Han have always faithful been,
Wei leaders, too, prove their loyalty are keen.

How this new menace was met will appear in the next chapter.

Chapter 110

Riding Alone, Wen Yang Repulses A Brave Force;
Following The River, Jiang Wei Defeats The Enemy.

It has been said that in the second year of Right Origin (AD 256) Guanqiu Jian, of the South of River Huai, General Who Guards the East, was commanding the forces in River Huai when he heard the news Sima Shi deposed Cao Fang.

He was moved to great anger, and his eldest son, Guanqiu Dian, fomented his father's wrath, saying, "Father, you are chief of all this region. With this Sima Shi in such a position, the country is in danger, and you cannot sit still and look on."

"My son, you speak well!" replied Guanqiu Jian.

Whereupon he requested Wen Qin, Imperial Protector of Yangzhou, to come and consult with him. This Wen Qin had been a client of Cao Shuang's, and he hastened at the call of the general. When he arrived, he was led into the private apartments, and, the salutations at an end, the two began to talk over the situation. Presently the host began to weep, and his visitor asked the cause of his tears.

"Think you that this conduct of Sima Shi does not tear my heart? He has deposed the Emperor and now holds in his grip all authority of the state.

Things are all upside down."

Wen Qin replied, "You are the chief of this region. If you are willing to play the part, you ought to take arms and slay this rebel. I will help you, regardless of consequences. My second son, Wen Yang, is a good warrior and a man of great valor. Moreover, he hates Sima Shi and wishes to avenge on the Sima brothers the death of Cao Shuang. He would make an excellent Leader of the Van."

Guanqiu Jian was delighted to get such ready and willing support, and the two poured a libation in pledge of mutual good faith. Then, pretending that they held an edict from the Empress Dowager, they summoned all the officers to Shouchun, where they built an altar on the west side and sacrificed a white horse, smearing their lips with its blood in token of their oath.

They made this declaration:

"Sima Shi is a rebel and devoid of rectitude. We have a secret edict commanding us to muster the forces of the South of River Huai and put down this rebellion."

Thus supported, Guanqiu Jian led sixty thousand troops to Xiangcheng, where he camped, while his fellow-conspirator Wen Qin took twenty thousand troops to the front to go to and fro lending help where it was needed. Letters were sent all through the counties and territories calling for assistance.

Now that mole below the left eye of Sima Shi used to pain at times, and he decided to have it removed. The surgeon excised it, closed and dressed the wound, and the patient rested quietly in his palace till it should heal.

It was at this time that he received the disquieting news of opposition to his authority. Whereupon he called in Grand Commander Wang Su to discuss the matter.

Said Wang Su, "When Guan Yu was most famous, Sun Quan sent Lu Meng to capture Jingzhou by surprise. What did Lu Meng do? He first won over the officers of Guan Yu by taking care of their families and thus broke the power of his enemy like a tile. Now the families of all the officers in the South of River Huai are here in the Middle Land. Treat them well, at the same time taking care that they do not get away, and you will be irresistible."

"Your words are good," said Sima Shi. "However, I cannot go out to war till I have recovered. Yet, to send another is to take great risks, and I shall feel insecure."

There was also present Secretary Zhong Hui, who here interposed, saying, "The forces of the South of River Huai and Chu[xxxii] are very formidable. If you send another, there is danger whatever happens; and if your leader makes a serious mistake, your whole policy will fail."

"No one but myself can succeed," cried Sima Shi, starting from his couch. "I must go."

So, in spite of illness, he resolved to lead in person. He left his brother in charge of affairs at Luoyang and set out, traveling in a padded carriage.

Zhuge Dan, General Who Guards the East, was given command over all the forces of Yuzhou and ordered to march from Anfeng and to take possession of Shouchun. Hu Zun, General Who Conquers the East, with the Qingzhou forces, was sent to bar any retreat at Qiaosong. Wang Ji, Imperial Protector of Yuzhou and Army Inspector, was sent to capture Chennan.

To his camp at Xiangyang, Sima Shi summoned all his officers to a council.

Minister Zheng Mao spoke first, saying, "Guanqiu Jian is fond of laying plans, but slow to come to any decision. His fellow-conspirator Wen Qin is bold, but imprudent. Now this scheme of theirs is too large for their minds. But as their soldiers are full of spirit, they should not be engaged lightly. We should remain on the defensive till their ardor has burned out. This is what Zhou Yafu[xxxiii] of old time did."

But Army Inspector Wang Ji objected, saying, "This is not a rising of the people, nor of the soldiers, but is the work of Guanqiu Jian. The people are merely his tools and cannot help themselves. The rebellion will go to pieces as soon as an army approaches the region."

"I agree with you," replied Sima Shi.

Then he advanced upon River Ying and camped by the bridge.

Wang Ji said, "The city of Nandun is an excellent camping ground. Occupy it at once, for if not the enemy will do so."

Sima Shi sent Wang Ji to carry out his own plan.

Reports of these movements of the enemy came to Guanqiu Jian in Xiangcheng, and an assembly of officers was called.

The Leader of the Van, Ge Yong, said, "Nandun is an excellent site for a camp, with a river beside it and hills at the rear. If the Wei armies camp there, we shall be unable to dislodge them. Let us occupy it."

So the army set out. But before they drew near, the scouts reported a camp already there. It was incredible, and Guanqiu Jian rode to the front to reconnoiter. He was convinced by the sight of flags and banners over all the plain, fluttering above an orderly array of tents and huts. The sight disconcerted him, and he rode back to the main body not knowing what to do.

Just then a scout came in to say: "Sun Jun of Wu has crossed the river to attack Shouchun."

"If we lose that city, we shall have no base," cried Guanqiu Jian.

That same night he retreated upon Xiangcheng.

Seeing the enemy retreat, Sima Shi called together his officers to talk it over.

Chair of the Secretariat Fu Gu, who was of the expedition, said, "The retirement to Xiangcheng was obviously due to Wu's threatened attack upon Shouchun. General, you should send three armies to attack upon Xiangcheng, Lojia, and Shouchun. The Imperial Protector of Yanzhou, Deng Ai, is a man of tactics; he should be sent against Lojia. Our main army will reinforce them."

His plan was acceptable to Sima Shi, who sent letters to Yanzhou telling Deng Ai to march against Lojia, where Sima Shi himself would soon meet him.

Camped at Xiangcheng, Guanqiu Jian sent spies to Lojia to see what might be happening there, for he feared it would be attacked.

When he spoke of his fears to Wen Qin, the latter said, "General, you need not be anxious. My son Wen Yang and I will answer for its safety. Give us but five thousand troops."

Father and son, with the five thousand troops, went to Lojia.

Before the main body arrived, the scouts reported: "Wei banners are flying on the west of the city. There are about ten thousand troops. In their midst are seen authority ensigns such as white yaks' tails, golden axes, purple umbrellas, and a flag bearing the word Commander. Perhaps Sima Shi himself is at this camp. The troops are pitching the camp rapidly, but it is not yet complete."

When this was reported to Wen Qin, his son Wen Yang, bearing his famous whip of steel, was by his father's side.

"We should attack before they have settled down in camp, Father," said he. "Let us go quickly and attack on two sides."

"When can we start?" said the father.

"Tonight at dusk. You lead half the force round by the south, and I will march the other half round by the north, and we will meet in the third watch at the Wei camp."

The youth who propounded this plan was then eighteen, tall and strong. He wore complete armor and carried at his waist a steel whip. When the hour came to start, he took his spear, swung himself into the saddle and set out.

That night Sima Shi, who had arrived and had at once set about settling into camp, lay on a couch in his tent, for he was still suffering pain from the surgery wound beneath his eye. The tent was surrounded by several hundred armored guards. Deng Ai had not arrived.

About the third watch Sima Shi heard a great shouting and asked what it was.

One replied: "An army has come round from the north and burst into the lines. The leader is too bold for anyone to face."

Sima Shi became much troubled. His heart burned within him, and the excitement caused the wound to open, so that the eyeball protruded and blood flowed freely. The pain became intense, nearly unbearable. In his agony and alarm lest his army should be thrown into confusion, he lay gnawing the bed clothes till they were in rags.

Wen Yang's force lost no time, but attacked as soon as it arrived. He dashed into the camp, slashing and thrusting right and left, and everyone gave way before him. If anyone stayed to oppose, the sharp spear or the terrible whip did its work, and that one fell. But after a time, seeing no sign of his father, Wen Yang grew anxious. And he had to retire several times before the fierce flights of arrows and crossbow bolts as he tried to reach the main tent.

About daylight he heard shouts and thought they must mean the arrival of his father with help. But the shouting came from the north, and his father was to arrive by the south road. He galloped out to get a clearer view, and saw a force sweeping down like a gale of wind.

It was not his father, but a body of the enemy, and the leader was Deng Ai.

Deng Ai rode forward shouting, "Rebel, flee not!"

Wen Yang had no intention to flee. Setting his spear, he rode savagely toward his opponent. They engaged and fought half a hundred bouts without either gaining the advantage. Then, the duel still raging, the Wei army attacked in full force, and Wen Yang's troops began to give way and run, so that soon he found himself alone.

However, he got clear of the fight and went away south. But he was pursued, for more than a hundred Wei generals plucked up courage to follow when he ran away. They pressed on his heels till near the Lojia Bridge, when it seemed that they must catch him. Then he suddenly pulled up his steed, turned and rode in among them, flogging with the terrible steel whip, and wherever it struck there lay warriors and horses in confused heaps. So they left him, and he retook his way in peace.

Then the Wei generals met and said, "Lo! Here is a man who has driven us all backward. But we are many and may not suffer that."

Wherefore they reformed and once again took up pursuit.

"You fools?" cried Wen Yang, as he saw them coming on. "Have you then no regard for your lives?"

Again he fell upon them with the steel whip and slew many, so that the survivors retreated. But yet again they found courage to come on, and yet again, but they had to fall back before the lash of that terrible whip.

Defiance hurled at Cao Cao's mighty host
Arrayed near Long Slope proclaimed Zhao Yun,
A valiant man; and peerless stood he till.
At Lojia another hero faced,
Alone, another host, and Wen Yang's name
Was added to the roll of famous people.

Wen Qin never reached the appointed rendezvous. In the darkness he lost his way among the precipices and gullies, whence he only got out as day dawned. He saw all the signs of a fight and a victory for Wei, but could not discover whither his son had gone. So he returned without fighting, and in spite of pursuit, made his way safely to Shouchun.

Now Commander Yin Damu had accompanied Sima Shi on his expedition, but was no friend of his. He had been of the Cao Shuang's party and bitterly resented the death of his patron. He was watching for a chance to avenge him. Seeing that Sima Shi was ill, he thought to secure his end by making friends with Wen Qin.

So he went in to see the sick Sima Shi, and said, "Wen Qin had no sincere intention to rebel, but was led astray by Guanqiu Jian. If you will let me go and speak with him, he will come over to you at once."

Sima Shi said he might go to try, and Yin Damu put on his armor and rode after Wen Qin. By and by he got near enough to shout.

"Do you not recognize me? I am Yin Damu."

Wen Qin stopped and looked back.

Yin Damu removed his helmet that his face might be clearly seen, and said, "O Imperial Protector, why can you not bear up for a few days?"

Yin Damu implied that Sima Shi was very near death, and he wished Wen Qin to remain at hand. But Wen Qin did not understand. He abused Yin Damu and even threatened that the bowmen should shoot, and Yin Damu could only sorrowfully turn away.

When Wen Qin reached Shouchun and found it occupied by Zhuge Dan, he tried for Xiangcheng. But three armies under Hu Zun, Wang Ji, and Deng Ai came up and attacked at once so that it seemed impossible that his army could hold out long. So he decided to flee to Wu and serve Sun Jun.

Guanqiu Jian, then behind the walls of Xiangcheng, heard that Shouchun had fallen, that his fellow-conspirator Wen Qin had failed and, with three armies against his city, knew that his case was desperate. He mustered all the forces in the city and marched out to try his fortune.

As he went forth, he fell in with Deng Ai. He bade Ge Yong go out to fight, but Ge Yong fell in the first encounter, cut down by Deng Ai himself. The enemy came on in force. Guanqiu Jian fought gallantly, but his army fell into confusion. Then two other armies under Wang Ji and Hu Zun came up, and he was completely surrounded. Nothing could be done, and he fled from the field with a dozen riders and made for Shenxian.

Here Governor Song Bai received him kindly and comforted him with a feast. At the banquet Guanqiu Jian drowned his sorrows in the wine cup till he was helpless, when he was slain by his host. His head was sent to the Wei army as proof of his death, and the rising came to an end. Peace was restored in the South of River Huai.

Sima Shi grew worse. Recovery being hopeless, he called Zhuge Dan to his tent and gave him a seal and conferred upon him the title of General Who Conquers the East, with command of all the forces in Yangzhou, and soon after the army marched back to Xuchang.

The sick man began to have visions. Night after night he was troubled by the apparitions of the three courtiers---Zhang Qi, Li Feng, and Xiahou

Xuan---he had put to death, and he knew that his end was near. He sent for his brother, Sima Zhao, who came and wept by his couch while he listened to his elder brother's last commands.

Said Sima Shi, "The responsibility of power is heavy, but we must bear it: There is no possible relief. You must continue my plans and maintain my policy yourself, and you must be exceedingly careful how you entrust any other with power, lest you bring about the destruction of our whole clan."

Then Sima Shi handed the seal of office to Sima Zhao, weeping the while. Sima Zhao would ask some questions still, but with a deep groan as his eye popped out Sima Shi died. It was the second month of the second year of Right Origin (AD 256).

Sima Zhao put on mourning for his brother and informed the Ruler of Wei, Cao Mao, of the death. By special edict Sima Zhao was ordered to remain at Xuchang so as to guard against any attack from Wu. This order was unpleasing to its recipient, but he felt doubtful what to do.

Sima Zhao took counsel with Zhong Hui, who said, "The death of your brother has disturbed the country. If you remain here, some shifting of power at the capital will surely work to your disadvantage. It will be too late for regrets then."

Wherefore Sima Zhao left Xuchang and camped on River Luo. This move alarmed Cao Mao.

Then Grand Commander Wang Su advised, saying, "Sima Zhao has succeeded the office of his late brother. It is well that Your Majesty should placate him with a new title."

So Cao Mao sent Wang Su with an edict creating Sima Zhao Regent Marshal, with control of the Secretariat. Sima Zhao came to Luoyang to thank the Emperor for these honors and stayed. Henceforward all matters and the whole government were under Sima Zhao's hand.

When news of these things came to Chengdu, Jiang Wei thought the time had come to make another bid for the empire, so he wrote a memorial to the Latter Ruler:

"Sima Shi having just died, his brother, Sima Zhao, who succeeds, will be unable to leave Luoyang until he has consolidated his position. Wherefore I crave permission to attack Wei."

The Latter Ruler agreed and bade him raise an army. So he went into Hanzhong to prepare for the expedition.

However, Zhang Yi, General Who Conquers the West, was opposed to the expedition and said, "Shu is not a big country, and its resources are not too abundant. Thus a far expedition should be avoided. The state policy should rather be the improvement of conditions at home. Thinking well for the soldiers and the people is the way to preserve the country."

"You are mistaken," said Jiang Wei. "Before our great Minister Zhuge Liang emerged from his reed hut in the wilds and undertook the affairs of a state, the three kingdoms were already a fact. Six times he led armies to try to gain the northern portion of the empire, but failed to attain his desire. Unhappily he died leaving his design unaccomplished. But he bequeathed to me the legacy of his intention, and I must be a loyal and worthy executor. If I die in the attempt, I will perish without regret. Now is our opportunity, and if we miss it, shall we find a better?"

"What you say is the real truth," said Xiahou Ba. "Let us send first some light horse out by Baohan to capture Nanan and thereby settle that county."

Then said Zhang Yi, "Procrastination and delay have been hitherto the causes of our failure. We ought to obey the precepts of the books of war, strike where the enemy is unprepared and appear where he does not expect us. A rapid march and a sudden blow will find Wei unready, and we shall succeed."

So Jiang Wei led an army of fifty thousand troops out by Baohan. When he reached River Yao, the spies reported his arrival to Wang Jing, Imperial Protector of Yongzhou, who led out seventy thousand troops against him. Jiang Wei gave certain orders to Zhang Yi and Xiahou Ba, and after they had marched, he drew up the main body by River Yao.

Wang Jing rode out to parley.

"Wu, Shu, and Wei are now actually established as a tripod. Why then have you invaded our borders these many times?"

Jiang Wei replied, "Because Sima Shi deposed his prince without cause, and it behooves the neighboring countries to punish such a crime. Moreover, your country is a rival state."

Then Wang Jing turned and said to four of his generals, Zhang Ming, Hua Yong, Liu Dan, and Zhu Fang, "You see that the enemy is drawn up with a river at his back, so that his troops must conquer or drown. Though Jiang Wei is bold, you four can fight him at the same time and pursue if he retires."

The four rode out two and two. Jiang Wei stood through a few encounters, but then moved backward toward his camp. At this, Wang Jing led on his main body to smite. Jiang Wei fled toward the river.

As he drew near he shouted, "Danger, O Generals! Now do your utmost!"

His generals turned on the foe and fought with such vigor that the Wei army was defeated, and, as they turned away, Zhang Yi and Xiahou Ba fell upon their rear. Soon the Wei army was hemmed in, and Jiang Wei rushed in among the host of Wei and threw them into utter confusion. They trod each other down in the press, and many fell into the river. Dead bodies lay about over several miles.

Wang Jing and a hundred horsemen forced their way out and fled to Didao, where they entered within the walls and barred the gates.

After Jiang Wei had rewarded and feasted his army, he was for attacking Didao, but Zhang Yi was against this.

"General, you have won a great victory, which will bring you fame. If you attempt more, things may go astray, and you will only add legs to your sketch of a serpent."

Said Jiang Wei, "When our army were defeated not long ago, they still desired to overrun the whole north. Now our opponents have been overcome, and that has broken the spirit of their army, and this city can be easily captured. Do not damp the spirit of the soldiers."

So it was decided to attack Didao despite further remonstrances of Zhang Yi.

Chen Tai, General Who Conquers the West and Commander of Yongzhou, was just about to set out to avenge the defeat of Wang Jing when Deng Ai, Imperial Protector of Yanzhou, arrived with his army. Chen Tai welcomed him, and when Deng Ai had said he had come by imperial edict to assist to defeat the army of Shu, Chen Tai asked his plans.

Deng Ai replied, "They are victors on River Yao. If they enlist the aid of the Qiangs to cause a diversion in the West Valley Land and the Land Within the Passes and also obtain the support of the four counties, it will be a misfortune for us. If they do not think of that, but try to take Didao, they will only fritter away their energies against a place too strongly fortified for them to capture. Let us now array our force along the Xiangling Mountain, and then we can advance and smite them. We shall get a victory."

"That is well said!" cried Chen Tai.

Then twenty cohorts of fifty soldiers each were told off to find their way secretly to the southeast of Didao and there hide in the valleys. They were then to display many ensigns and sound trumpets as if they were a very large force, and make huge fires at night, so as to cause anxiety among the enemy. And thus they waited for the troops of Shu to come, while Chen Tai and Deng Ai marched with forty thousand troops against the Shu army.

The army of Shu had marched to Didao and begun the siege around the whole circuit of the walls. At the end of many days the fall of the city seemed no nearer, and Jiang Wei began to fret. He could think of no plan likely to succeed.

One eventide a horseman came in to report: "Two armies are approaching rapidly, and the names on the banners were General Who Conquers the West Chen Tai and Imperial Protector of Yanzhou Deng Ai."

Jiang Wei called in his colleague Xiahou Ba, who said, "I have spoken to you of Deng Ai many times. He is perspicacious, valiant, resourceful, and has always delighted in the study of military topography. As he is coming, we shall have to put forth all our energies."

Jiang Wei replied, "We will attack before he can get a foothold and while his soldiers are fatigued with the march."

So Zhang Yi was left to carry on the siege while the two leaders went out to meet the new armies. Jiang Wei went against Deng Ai, and Xiahou Ba against Chen Tai.

Before Jiang Wei had marched far, the stillness was broken by the roar of a bomb, and at once all about the Shu army arose the rolling of drums and the blare of trumpets, soon followed by flames that shot up to the very sky. Jiang Wei rode to the front and saw the ensigns of Wei all about him.

"I have fallen into a trap set by Deng Ai!" cried he.

He sent orders to Xiahou Ba and Zhang Yi to withdraw immediately while he would cover their retreat. When they had retired, he followed them into Hanzhong, harassed all along the road by the sounds of marching soldiers and glimpses of enemy banners. But these enemies never attacked. It was only after the army had retreated to Saber Pass that Jiang Wei knew all this was make-believe.

He camped in Zhongti. For his services and success on River Yao, Jiang Wei was rewarded with the rank of Regent Marshal. As soon as the ceremonies connected with his promotion were ended, he began again to talk of an expedition against Wei.

Remember enough is as good as a feast,
Having sketched a good snake don't add legs to the beast;
And in fighting remember that others are bold,
And tigers have claws though their teeth may be old.

The result of the new expedition will be told in the next chapter.

Chapter 111

Deng Ai Outwits Jiang Wei;
Zhuge Dan Battles Sima Zhao.

Jiang Wei camped at Zhongti. The army of Wei camped outside Didao. Wang Jing welcomed Chen Tai and Deng Ai and prepared a banquet to celebrate the raising of the siege and also rewarded the army with gifts. Then Chen Tai sent up a memorial to the Ruler of Wei, Cao Mao, eulogizing the magnificent services of Deng Ai, who was rewarded with the title General Who Pacifies the West. For the time, Deng Ai was left in the west. He and Chen Tai placed their men in cantonments in Yongzhou, Liangzhou, and the counties round about.

After Deng Ai had rendered his thanks to the Emperor, Chen Tai spread a great feast in his honor, and in congratulating his guest, said, "Jiang Wei slipped off in the night because he was broken, and he will never dare to return."

"I think he will," replied Deng Ai, smiling. "I can give five reasons why he should."

"What are they?"

"First, although the soldiers of Shu have retired, they have the self-possessed and confident look of holding the victory; our soldiers are really weak and broken. Second, the soldiers of Shu were trained and inspirited by Zhuge Liang and are easy to mobilize; our generals are all of different periods of service, and our army indifferently trained. Third, the Shu soldiers often use boats for traveling, and so they move at leisure and the troops arrive fresh; ours do all their journeys on land, and they arrive fatigued with marching. Fourth, again, Didao, Longxi, Nanan, and Qishan are all places suitable for defense or use as battle fields, and thus the army of Shu can conceal their intentions and strike where they will; we have to remain on guard at many points, thus dividing our forces; when they concentrate, they have only to reckon with a part of our force. And fifth, if they come out by way of Longxi and Nanan, they have the grain of the Qiangs to depend upon; and if they choose Qishan, they have the wheat there. These are the five reasons why they should make another expedition."

Chen Tai was overcome with the clear vision of his new colleague.

"Sir, your foresight is godlike. I think we need feel no anxiety about what the enemy can achieve."

The two leaders became the best of friends in spite of the difference of age. Deng Ai spent his time in training the army, and garrisons were placed at all points where surprise attacks seemed possible.

There was feasting also at Zhongti, and the occasion was taken to discuss a new attack on Wei.

But Assistant Fan Jian opposed. "General, your expeditions have partly failed many times; you have never scored a complete victory. But now on River Yao the army of Wei recognize your superiority, and why should you try again? There is small chance of success, and you risk all you have gained."

Jiang Wei replied, "You all regard only the largeness and population of Wei and the time necessary for conquest, but you do not see five reasons for victory."

The assembly asked what these were.

"First, the fighting spirit of the soldiers of Wei has been badly broken on River Yao, while that of our soldiers, although we retired, is unimpaired. If we attack, we shall certainly succeed. Second, our soldiers can travel in boats and so will not be wearied with marching; their soldiers have to march to meet us. Third, our soldiers are thoroughly trained; theirs are recruits, a mere flock of crows, quite undisciplined. Fourth, when we go out by Qishan, we can seize upon the autumn wheat for food. Finally, they are scattered, having to defend various points, while we can concentrate on any point we wish, and they will find it difficult to bring up reinforcements. If we miss this chance, can we hope for a better?"

Xiahou Ba said, "Deng Ai is young, but he is deep and crafty. He has certainly taken great pains to secure the regions under his charge as General Who Pacifies the West. Victory will not be so easy as it was before."

"Why should I fear him?" cried Jiang Wei, angrily. "You should not laud the spirit of the enemy and belittle that of our own soldiers. But in any case I have made up my mind and shall take West Valley Land."

No one dared to offer any further opposition. Jiang Wei himself led the first army; the others followed in due order; and thus the soldiers of Shu marched out of Zhongti to Qishan.

Before they could reach Qishan, the scouts reported the hills already occupied by the armies of Wei. Jiang Wei rode forward to verify this, and, surely enough, he saw the Wei camps, nine in number, stretching over the hills like a huge serpent, and all arranged to give each other support.

"Xiahou Ba spoke only too well," said he. "The plan of those camps is excellent and only our Zhuge Liang could have laid them out with equal skill."

Returning to his own army, he said to his officers, "They must have known of my coming, and I think Deng Ai is here too. Now from this as base you are to send out daily small reconnoitering parties showing my banner, but different flags and uniforms, blue, yellow, red, white, and black, in turns. While you are thus distracting attention, I will lead the main army by Dongting to attack Nanan."

Bao Su was sent to camp at the mouth of the Qishan Mountains Valley while the main army marched.

As soon as Deng Ai had heard that the enemy would come out at Qishan, he had camped there with his colleague Chen Tai. But when days had passed without anyone coming to fling a challenge, he sent out spies to find out where the Shu army was lurking. They could find nothing, and so Deng

Ai went to the summit of a hill to look around.

He came to the conclusion, saying, "Jiang Wei must not be in this camp. He must be on his way to capture Nanan. Those soldiers in the Shu camp were nothing but a feint, accentuated by the daily change of uniform. Going to and fro for days, the horses look tired, and their leaders are certainly none of the ablest. Therefore, General, I advise an attack here. If that succeeds, the Dongting road can be occupied, and Jiang Wei will be unable to retreat. I think I ought to try to relieve Nanan. I will go by the Wucheng Mountain, and if I occupy that, the enemy will try to take Shanggui. Near that place is a narrow and precipitous valley called Block Valley, just the place for an ambush, where I shall lie in wait till Jiang Wei comes to take the Wucheng Mountain."

Chen Tai replied, "I have been here over twenty years and have never known so much of the military possibilities of the place. You are very wonderful and must carry out your plan."

So Deng Ai marched toward Nanan by double marches. Soon they came to the Wucheng Mountain, where they camped without opposition. He sent his son Deng Zhong and Shi Zuan, each leading five thousand troops, to lie in wait in the Block Valley and not to betray their presence.

In the meantime Jiang Wei was marching between Dongting and Nanan.

Near the Wucheng Mountain, he turned to Xiahou Ba and said, "That hill is our point, and Nanan is close. I fear lest the artful Deng Ai may seize and fortify it."

They hastened, anxious to reach the hill before the enemy. But it was not to be. Presently they heard the roar of bombs and the beating of drums, and then flags and banners appeared, all of Wei. And among them fluttered the leader's standard, bearing two words Deng Ai.

This was a sad disappointment. The army of Shu halted, and veteran soldiers of Wei came rushing down from various points on the hill, too many for the troops of Shu to drive back. So the advance guard was defeated. Jiang Wei went to their help with his central body, but when he got near, the soldiers of Wei had retreated up to the hill.

Jiang Wei went on to the foot of the hill and challenged, but no one came out to accept. The soldiers of Shu began to shout abuse, and kept it up till late in the day, but they failed to provoke a fight. As the army of Shu began to retire, the Wei drums beat furiously, yet no one appeared. Jiang Wei turned about to ascend the hill, but its defenders prevented that by stones thrown from above. He hung on till the third watch, when he tried again. But he failed. Thereupon he went down the hill and halted, bidding his soldiers build a barricade of wood and boulders. The troops of Wei came on again, and the Shu troops scrambled to run to the old camp.

Next day Jiang Wei brought up many transport wagons and placed them on the slope as the nucleus of a camp. But in the night a number of Wei troops came down with torches and set fire to them. A fight ensued, which lasted till dawn.

Seeing that a camp could not be made there, Jiang

Wei retired to consider new plans with Xiahou Ba.

"Since we cannot take Nanan, our next best plan is to try for Shanggui, which is the storehouse of Nanan."

Leaving Xiahou Ba on the hill, Jiang Wei led a force of veteran soldiers and bold officers along the road toward Shanggui. They marched all night, and dawn found them in a deep valley, which the guides said was Block Valley.

"That sounds too much like 'Cut-off Valley'," said Jiang Wei. "And if a force held the mouth, we should be in sorry straits."

While hesitating whether to advance farther or not, the leading troops came back to say: "We have seen a cloud of dust beyond the hills, which seems to indicate a body of soldiers in hiding."

So the order was given to retire. At that moment the armies under Shi Zuan and Deng Zhong came out and attacked. Jiang Wei, alternately fighting and retreating, tried to get away. Then Deng Ai himself appeared, and the Shu army had enemies on three sides. They were in grave danger, but Xiahou Ba came to their rescue, and so Jiang Wei escaped.

Jiang Wei proposed to return to Qishan, but Xiahou Ba said, "We cannot go thither, for Chen Tai has destroyed the force under Bao Su, and he himself was killed. All that was left of that army has gone back into Hanzhong."

It was no longer a question of taking the Dongting road. Jiang Wei sought out by-roads to march along. Deng Ai came in pursuit, and as he pressed hard on the rear, Jiang Wei sent the others on ahead while he covered the retreat.

Soon Chen Tai came out from the hills, and Jiang Wei was surrounded by a shouting body of the enemy. He fought all directions, but could not clear the way. He and his horse were very weary when Zhang Ni, who had heard of his straits, came to his rescue with a body of cavalry. Zhang Ni cut his way in, and Jiang Wei immediately broke the siege and got out. Zhang Ni saved his general, but lost his own life in the melee. Finally Jiang Wei got back into Hanzhong.

From Hanzhong the death of Zhang Ni in battle was reported to the Latter Ruler, who bestowed suitable honors upon his family.

The Shu people blamed Jiang Wei for the serious loss of life of their relatives in the military operations that had just failed, and Jiang Wei, following the precedent in Jieting of the late Lord of Wuxiang, asked that he himself should be degraded in rank, retaining, however, the command. He was put back to General of the Rear Army.

The country being now cleared of the enemy, Chen Tai and Deng Ai prepared a banquet in honor of victory and gave rewards to the soldiers who had fought. Chen Tai sent a memorial to the capital upon the services of Deng Ai, and a special commission of Sima Zhao brought Deng Ai higher rank; the title of lordship was given to his son, Deng Zhong.

At this time the style of the reign in Wei was

changed from Right Origin, the third year, to Gentle Dew Era, the first year (AD 256). Sima Zhao commanded all the military forces and made himself Empire Commander-in-Chief. He assumed great pomp, and whenever he moved outside his palace, he was escorted by three thousand mail-clad guards, beside squadrons of cavalry. All power lay in his hands, and he decided all questions so that the court was rather in his palace than in that of the Emperor.

Plans for taking the final step constantly occupied his thoughts. The question of mounting the throne was openly mooted by Jia Chong, a confidant, who was a son of Commander Jia Kui. Jia Chong was holding the High Counselor office in the Prime Minister's palace.

Jia Chong said, "Sir, all real authority is in your hands, and the country is not tranquil. The only remedy is for you to become actual ruler, and you should find out who are your supporters."

Sima Zhao replied, "This has been in my thoughts a long time. You might be my emissary to the east to find out the feeling there. You can pretend you go to thank the soldiers who took part in the late campaign. That would be a good pretext."

Accordingly Jia Chong traveled into the South of River Huai, where he saw Zhuge Dan, General Who Guards the East. This officer was from Nanyang and a cousin of the late Lord of Wuxiang, Zhuge Liang. Zhuge Dan had gone to Wei for employment, but had received no significant office while Zhuge Liang was the Prime minister of Shu. After Zhuge Liang's death, Zhuge Dan's promotion was rapid. He was now Lord of Gaoping and Commander of the south and east of River Huai.

Jia Chong went to Zhuge Dan to ask him to convey to the army the appreciation of the soldiers' services. Jia Chong was received courteously, and at a banquet, when host and guest were both mellow with wine, Jia Chong set himself to discover Zhuge Dan's feelings.

Jia Chong said, "Lately in Luoyang there has been much talk of the weakness and lack of ability of the Emperor and his unfitness to rule. Now General Sima Zhao comes of a family noted for state service for three generations. His own services and virtues are high as the heavens, and he is the man best fitted to take the rulership of Wei. Is this not your opinion?"

But Zhuge Dan did not favor the suggestion. On the contrary, he broke out angrily, "You are a son of Jia Kui of Yuzhou, and your family have received the bounty of Wei. Yet you dare speak of rebellion!"

Jia Chong said, "I only repeat what people have said."

Zhuge Dan said, "If the state is in difficulty, then one ought to stand up for it even to the death!"

Jia Chong said no more. He soon returned and told Sima Zhao what had been said.

"The rat!" cried Sima Zhao, angrily.

"Zhuge Dan is exceedingly popular there in the South of River Huai; and if he is left too long, he will do harm."

Sima Zhao began to take measures. He wrote privately to Yue Chen, Imperial Protector of Yangzhou, and sent a messenger to Zhuge Dan with an edict making him Minister of Works. This meant that Zhuge Dan had to come to the capital.

But Zhuge Dan knew that Jia Chong had done him mischief, and he interrogated the messenger, who told him that Yue Chen knew all about the matter.

"How does he know?"

"General Sima Zhao sent him a private letter."

The messenger was condemned to death. Then Zhuge Dan placed himself at the head of his personal guard and marched to Yangzhou. The city gates were closed and the drawbridge raised. He summoned the gate, but no one answered.

"How dare this fellow Yue Chen treat me thus?" cried Zhuge Dan.

He ordered his troops to force the gate. Ten of his bold generals dismounted, crossed the moat, and climbed the ramparts, where they slew all who opposed them and opened the gate. The others entered, set fire to the houses, and began to fight their way toward the state residence.

The Imperial Protector sought refuge in a tower, but Zhuge Dan made his way up and reproached his enemy, crying, "Your father, Yue Jing, enjoyed the bounty of Wei. Yet you have not sought to repay the kindness of the Ruling House, but you want to help the rebel Sima Zhao!"

Before Yue Chen was able to answer, Zhuge Dan slew him. Then he sent to Luoyang a memorial detailing Sima Yi's many faults, and made preparations for war. He called up all the militia of the south and east of River Huai, to the total of one hundred thousand, and took over the forty thousand troops who had surrendered on the fall of Yue Chen and gathered supplies. He also sent Adviser Wu Gang to Wu for aid, offering his son Zhuge Jing as a hostage for his good faith.

At this time Sun Jun had died and his brother, Sun Chen, was Prime Minister. Sun Chen was a man of cruel and violent temper and had put many officers to death on his way to power---among them were Grand Commander Teng Yin, General Lu Ju, and Minister Wang Chun. The Ruler of Wu, Sun Liang, although intelligent, was helpless in his hands.

The messenger, Wu Gang, conducted Zhuge Jing to the residence of Sun Chen in Shidou, who asked what he had come for.

Wu Gang explained, "Zhuge Dan is a cousin of the Lord of Wuxiang in Shu. Zhuge Dan had been in service of Wei; and seeing Sima Zhao depose the his prince and oppress good people, he wants to punish the tyrant. But his force is not enough, and he asks for your help. To show his sincerity, he sends his son Zhuge Jing as a token of good faith."

Wu Gang's request was received favorably, and Sun Chen sent seventy thousand troops with a full complement of officers---Quan Yi and Quan Duan as Commanders, Yu Quan as Rear Guard, Tang Zi and Zhu Yi as Leaders of the Van, Wen Qin as

Military Guide. They marched in three directions to attack Wei.

Wu Gang returned to Shouchun report success. Zhuge Dan thought all was going well and prepared the army for a general attack.

In Luoyang, Zhuge Dan's memorial angered Sima Zhao, who wished to set out to revenge the attack at once, but Jia Chong preached caution.

"My lord, you derived your power from your father and brother, and people have not had time to discover your own virtue. If you leave the court and there be a revulsion of feeling against you, you will lose all. Rather request the Empress Dowager and the Son of Heaven to go with you in the expedition, and nothing is to be feared," said Jia Chong.

"That is an excellent plan."

Sima Zhao went into the Palace and proposed it to Her Majesty, saying, "Zhuge Dan is in revolt, and my colleagues and I intend to punish him. I beg that you will accompany the expedition as the late Emperor would have done."

The Empress was afraid, but dared not refuse, and the next day was requested to set out with the Ruler of Wei, Cao Mao.

Cao Mao said, "General, you command all the armies and dispose them as you will. Why do you ask me to go?"

Sima Zhao replied, "Your Majesty is wrong to hesitate. Your ancestors traveled over the empire and wished to unite the whole under one ruler. Wherever there was a worthy opponent, they went to face him. Your Majesty should follow their example and sweep the land clean. Why fear?"

Cao Mao, fearing his minister's terrible power, consented, and an edict was issued for the commands to mobilize two hundred sixty thousand troops of two capitals. Wang Ji, General Who Corrects the South, was in command of the van, and Chen Qian, General Who Pacifies the East, was second in command of the van. Shi Bao, Army Inspector, and Zhou Cai, Imperial Protector of Yangzhou, led the Imperial Escort. The army moved into the South of River Huai like a great flood.

Zhu Yi, the Leader of the Van of Wu, encountered them, and both sides drew up for battle. Zhu Yi rode out and took the challenge, but was overcome by Wang Ji in the third bout and he fled. Tang Zi also rode out, but was also beaten in the third encounter by Wang Ji. Then Wang Ji ordered a full attack. The troops of Wu were broken and retired fifteen miles and camped. Thence they sent tidings of their ill-success to Shouchun.

Zhuge Dan in Shouchun led out his bold and strong soldiers to join forces with Wen Qin and his two sons, Wen Yang and Wen Hu. Then they set out against Sima Zhao.

Now here is a check to the armies of Wu,
And Wei's gallant men advance.

The next chapter will tell how went victory.

Chapter 112

Rescuing Shouchun, Yu Quan Dies Nobly; Attacking Changcheng, Jiang Wei Mobilizes.

Hearing of this threatened attack, Sima Zhao sought advice from two of his officers, High Counselor Pei Xiu and Palace Assistant Zhong Hui.

Zhong Hui said, "The Wu army is helping our enemies for the sake of profit, and hence we can seduce them with an offer of greater profit."

Sima Zhao agreed in this opinion and resolved accordingly. As part of his plan, he sent Shi Bao and Zhou Cai to lay ambushes in different places near Shouchun.

As ordered by Sima Zhao, Wang Ji and Chen Qian commanded an army of veterans on the rear, Cheng Zu led thirty thousand troops out to bring on a battle, while Chen Jun got together many wagons, herds of oxen, droves of horses, donkeys and mules, and heaps of military supplies, all of which he crowded together in the midst of the army. This stuff was meant to be abandoned as soon as the fight began, so that the enemy might be tempted to plunder.

That day, Zhuge Dan led the center army, while Zhu Yi and Wen Qin commanded the left and right armies. The armies being drawn up, Zhuge Dan looked across at his opponents and saw that the center of the Wei army was taken up by a disorderly mass of transport. Presently he led on his troops to attack, and Cheng Zu, as bidden to do, gave way and fled, leaving a large amount of spoil. When the soldiers of Wu saw such huge quantities of booty, theirs for the taking, they lost all desire to fight and scattered to gather the spoil.

While thus occupied, suddenly a bomb exploded and, from left and right, down came Shi Bao and Zhou Cai and the army of Wei upon the spoilers. Zhuge Dan attempted to draw off, but other forces under Wang Ji and Chen Qian appeared, and he was heavily smitten. Then came on Sima Zhao with his army, and Zhuge Dan fled to Shouchun, where he entered and shut the gates. The army of Wei set down to the siege of the city, and the army of Wu retired into camp at Anfeng. The Ruler of Wei, Cao Mao, was lodging at this time in Xiangcheng.

Then said Zhong Hui, "Zhuge Dan has been worsted, but the city wherein he has taken refuge is well supplied, and his allies, the troops of Wu, are not distant. His position is strong. Our soldiers are besieging the city all round, which means that those within will hold out for a long time, or they will make a desperate sortie. Their allies also may fall upon us at the same time, and it would go hard with us. Therefore, I advise that the attack be made only on three sides, leaving the south gate open for them if they wish to flee. If they flee, we can fall on the fugitives. The troops of Wu cannot have supplies for very long. If we sent some light cavalry round by their rear, we might stay their fighting power without a battle."

"You are my Zhang Liang[xxxiv]," said Sima Zhao, stroking the back of his adviser. "Your advice is excellent!"

So Wang Ji, who was on the south of the city, was ordered to withdraw.

But in the Wu camp at Anfeng was much sadness at the want of success.

Sun Chen said to General Zhu Yi, "If we cannot succor Shouchun, how can we hope to overrun the Middle Land? Now and here you have to win a victory or die, for another defeat will mean death."

Zhu Yi went back to his camp and talked with Yu Quan.

Yu Quan said, "The south gate of Shouchun is free, and I will lead therein some of our troops to help Zhuge Dan. Then you challenge the Wei army on one side, and we will come out from the city and attack on the other side."

Zhu Yi thought the plan good, and Quan Yi, Quan Duan, and Wen Qin were willing to go into the city and share in the attack. They were allowed to march in without hindrance as the Wei generals had no orders to stop them.

When this was reported to Sima Zhao, he said, "This is a plan to defeat our army by making a front and rear attack."

So he called Wang Ji and Chen Qian and told them to take five thousand troops to keep the road along which Zhu Yi would come and strike him in rear.

Zhu Yi was advancing toward the city when he heard a shouting in the rear, and soon the attack began from two sides by Wang Ji and Chen Qian. His army was worsted and returned to Anfeng.

When Sun Chen heard of this new defeat, he was very angry.

"What is the use of leaders who always lose?" cried he.

He sentenced Zhu Yi to death, and upbraided Quan Wei, son of Quan Duan, and said, "If you do not drive off this army of Wei, let me never again see your face, nor that of your father."

Then Sun Chen returned to Capital Jianye.

When this was known in the Wei camp, Zhong Hui said to his chief, "Now the city of Shouchun may be attacked, for Sun Chen has gone away, and there is no hope of succor for the besieged."

A vigorous assault began. Quan Wei tried to cut his way through and get into the city. But when he saw Shouchun quite surrounded by the enemy and no hope of success, he gave in and went over to Sima Zhao, by whom he was well received and given the rank of General.

Deeply affected by this kindness, Quan Wei wrote to his father, Quan Duan, and uncle, Quan Yi, advising them to follow his example. He tied the letter to an arrow and shot it over the walls. Quan Yi found the letter, and he and Quan Duan, with their several thousand troops, came out and yielded.

Within the city Zhuge Dan was very sad.

Two advisers, Jiang Ban and Jiao Yi, came to him and said, "The food in the city is short, and the soldiers are many; this can not last long. General, you should let the Wu troops to go out and make a decisive fight with the Wei army."

Zhuge Dan turned on them angrily.

"Why do you tell me to fight when I am set on holding out to the very last? If you say that again, you shall die as traitors!"

"He is lost!" said they, going away. "We can do no other than surrender or we shall die too."

That night Jiang Ban and Jiao Yi slipped over the wall and surrendered. Both were given employment.

Of those left in the city some were for fighting, but no one dared say so.

Meanwhile Zhuge Dan saw the Wei troops build earth walls to anticipate the expected floods of River Huai. This flood had been the only hope of Zhuge Dan, who had trusted to be able to smite the besiegers when it came to destroy the earth wall. However, that autumn was dry, and the river did not swell.

Within the besieged city the food diminished rapidly, and soon starvation stared them in the face. Wen Qin and his sons were defending the citadel, and they saw their soldiers sinking one by one for lack of food till the sight became unbearable.

Wen Qin went to Zhuge Dan with a proposal, saying, "The northern troops should be sent away in order to save food."

His suggestion called forth an outburst of fierce wrath of Zhuge Dan.

"Do you want to kill me that you propose to send the northern soldiers away?"

Wen Qin suffered death. His two sons, Wen Yang and Wen Hu, ran amok with rage. Armed with short swords, they attacked all they met and slew many scores in their desperate anger. The fit over, they dropped down the wall and deserted to the Wei camp.

However, Sima Zhao had not forgotten that Wen Yang had defied and held at bay his whole army once. At first Sima Zhao thought to put Wen Yang to death, but Zhong Hui interposed.

"The real offender was his father, Wen Qin," said Zhong Hui, "but he is dead, and these two come to you in desperation. If you slay those who surrender, you will strengthen the obstinacy of those who remain in the city."

There was reason in this, and so their submission was accepted. They were led to Sima Zhao's tent, and he soothed them with kind words and gave them gifts and lordships, and made them Generals.

After expressing their gratitude, they rode about the city on the horses he had given them, shouting, "We have received great kindness at the hands of Sima Zhao, who not only has pardoned us but given us gifts. Why do you not all yield?"

When their companions heard this, they said one to another. "This Wen Yang was an enemy, and yet he has been well received. How much more may we expect generous treatment?"

The desire to surrender possessed them all. When Zhuge Dan heard it, he was incensed and went round the posts night and day on the watch for any who seemed inclined to go. He put many to death in these efforts to retain his authority.

Zhong Hui heard how things were going in the city and went in to Sima Zhao to say the moment to attack had come. Sima Zhao was only too pleased. He stimulated his troops, and they flocked to the ramparts and assaulted vigorously. Then the commander of the north gate, Zeng Xuan, treacherously opened the gate and let in the Wei soldiers.

When Zhuge Dan heard that the enemy were in the city, he called his guards and tried to escape. He took his way along the smaller streets to the gate, but on the drawbridge he met Hu Fen, who cut him down. His followers were made prisoners.

Wang Ji fought his way to the west gate, where he fell in with the Wu general, Yu Quan.

"Why do you not yield?" shouted Wang Ji.

"Where is the principle for yielding when I have my orders to rescue the city and so far have not succeeded?" Throwing off his helmet, he cried, "The happiest death a man can die is on the battlefield!"

Whirling his sword about, Yu Quan dashed among

his enemies and fought till he fell under many wounds.

Many were they who yielded at Shouchun,
Bowing their heads in the dust before Sima Zhao.
Wu had produced its heroes,
Yet none were faithful to the death like Yu Quan.

When Sima Zhao entered the city, he put to death the whole family of Zhuge Dan. Some of his guards fell into the hands of Sima Zhao alive, and he offered them their lives if they would yield.

They all refused, saying, "We would rather share the fate of our leader."

They were sent out of the city to be beheaded, but orders were given to offer each one his life at the last moment. Thus, before a person was about to receive the fatal blow, that one was asked to yield. Not one accepted, and they all died. In admiration for their fortitude, they were honorably interred by order of Sima Zhao.

The loyal servant flees not in the day of disaster;
Such were they who followed Zhuge Dan to the shades.
Ever and again begins the Song of Life's Brevity.
Faithful unto death were they, even as Tian Heng's people[xxxv].

As has been said, many of the troops of Wu surrendered.

Then said Pei Xiu, "The parents and children of these soldiers are living all over River Huai. If you spare them and they return home, they will foment rebellion by and by. The best way is to bury them."

But Zhong Hui said, "No. When the ancients made war, their policy was to maintain the state as a whole, and so they only put to death the originators of trouble. It would be inhumane to slay all. Rather let them return home as witnesses to your liberal policy."

"That is better advice," said Sima Zhao. So the soldiers of Wu were released and allowed to return home.

Tang Zi dared not return to his own place in Wu for fear of the cruel Sun Chen, so he went over to Wei, taking his company with him. He was well received, and his people were employed over the counties of the three rivers.

The country about River Huai being now quiet, Sima Zhao decided to march homeward.

Just then the news came: "Jiang Wei, the Shu General, is attacking Changcheng and interfering with the supplies."

And so a council was called to discuss this matter.

At this time in Shu, the reign style was changed from Long Enjoyment, the twentieth year, to Wonderful Sight, the first year (AD 258). In Hanzhong Jiang Wei had recruited two generals,

Fu Qian and Jiang Shu, both of whom he loved greatly, and set them to train the army, horse and foot.

Then came the news: "Zhuge Dan has set out to destroy Sima Zhao; Sun Chen of Wu has supported him with a large army; and Sima Zhao has led the army himself, bringing with him the Empress Dowager and the Ruler of Wei."

Jiang Wei said, "The great opportunity has come at last!"

So he asked the Latter Ruler's authority to make another expedition.

But Minister Qiao Zhou heard this with grief, for internal affairs were not well.

Said he, "The court is sunk in dissipation, and the Emperor's confidence is given to that eunuch, Huang Hao. State affairs are neglected for pleasure, which is the Emperor's sole aim. Jiang Wei has led many expeditions and wasted the lives of many soldiers, so that the state is falling."

Qiao Zhou then wrote an essay on "Enemy Kingdoms," which he sent to Jiang Wei.

"When one asks by what means the weak overcame the strong in past times, the answer is that those responsible for the strong state made no struggle against general laxity, while those in power in a weak state took careful steps for improvement. Confusion followed upon laxity and efficiency grew out of diligence, as is the universal rule. King Wen of Zhou[xxxvi] devoted himself to the welfare of his people, and with a small number achieved great results; Gou Jian[xxxvii] sympathized with all, and with a weak force overcame a powerful opponent. These were their methods.

"One may recall that in the past Chu was strong and Han weak when the empire was divided by agreement at the Great Canal[xxxviii]. Then, seeing that his people were satisfied and settled in their minds, Zhang Liang[xxxix] went in pursuit of Xiang Yu and destroyed him.

"But is it necessary to act like King Wen and Gou Jian? Listen to the reply. In the days of Shang and Zhou, when imperial ranks had long existed and the relations between prince and minister were firmly established, even such as the Founder of the Hans could not have carved his way to a throne. But when the dynasty of Qin had suppressed the feudal nobles and set up mere representatives of its own power, and the people were weak and enslaved, the empire was rived asunder, and there succeeded a time of contention, when every bold soul strove with his neighbor.

"But we are now in other times. Since there is not the state of confusion that waited on the end of Qin, but a state of things more nearly like that of the period of the Warring States, in which six kingdoms contended for the mastery, therefore one may play the part of King Wen. If one would found a dynasty, then must that one wait upon time and favorable destiny. With these in his favor, the consummation will follow forthwith, as the armies of Kings Tang[xl] and Wu[xli] fought but one battle. Therefore have real compassion for the people and wait on opportunity. If wars are constant, and a mishap come, even the wisest will be unable to show the way of safety."

"An effusion from the pen of a rotten pedant?" cried Jiang Wei wrathfully as he finished reading, and he dashed the essay on the ground in contempt.

The protest was disregarded, and the army marched.

"In your opinion where should we begin?" asked he of Fu Qian.

Fu Qian replied, "The great storehouse of Wei is at Changcheng, and we ought to burn their grain and forage. Let us go out by the Luo Valley and cross the Shen Ridge. After the capture of Changcheng, we can go on to Qinchuan, and the conquest of the Middle Land will be near."

"What you say just fits in with my secret plans," replied Jiang Wei.

So the army marched to the Luo Valley and crossed the Shen Ridge.

The Commander in Changcheng was Sima Wang, a cousin of Sima Zhao. Huge stores of grain were in the city, but its defenses were weak. So when Sima Wang heard of the approach of the Shu army, he and his two leaders, Wang Zhen and Li Peng, made a camp seven miles from the walls to keep any attack at a distance.

When the enemy came up, Sima Wang and his two generals went forth from the ranks to meet them.

Jiang Wei stood in the front of his army and said,

"Sima Zhao has forced his prince to go with him to war, which plainly indicates that he intends to emulate the deeds of Li Jue and Guo Si. My government has commanded me to punish this fault. Wherefore I say to you yield at once. For if you persist in the way of error, you and yours shall all be put to death!"

Sima Wang shouted back, "You and yours are wholly strangers to any feeling of rectitude. You have repeatedly invaded a superior state's territory. If you do not at once retire, I will see to it that not even a breastplate returns!"

With these words General Wang Zhen rode out, his spear set ready to thrust. From the host of Shu came Fu Qian to take the challenge, and the two champions engaged. After a few encounters Fu Qian tempted his opponent by feigning weakness. Wang Zhen thrust at the opening he gave. Fu Qian evaded the blow, snatched Wang Zhen out of the saddle, and bore him off.

Seeing this, his colleague, Li Peng whirled up his sword and went pounding down toward the captor. Fu Qian went but slowly, thus luring Li Peng into rash pursuit. When Li Peng was near enough, Fu Qian dashed his prisoner with all his strength to the earth, took a firm grip on his four-edged brand, and smote Li Peng full in the face. The blow knocked out an eye, and Li Peng fell dead. Wang Zhen had been already killed by the Shu troops as he lay on the ground. Both generals being dead, the troops of Wei fled into the city and barred the gates.

Jiang Wei gave orders for the army to rest that

night and take the city on the morrow with all vigor.

Next day, at dawn, the assault began. The soldiers, fresh from their rest, vied with each other who should be first on the wall. They shot over the ramparts fire-arrows and firebombs and burned all the buildings on the wall. They next brought up brushwood and piled it against the rampart and set it alight, so that the flames rose high.

When the city seemed about to fall, the defenders set up a howling and a lamentation that could be heard all around. But suddenly a great rolling of drums diverted the attention of the assailants from the city, and they turned their faces to see a great host of Wei soldiers marching up in all the glory of waving banners. Jiang Wei faced about to meet this attack and took his place beneath the great standard.

Presently Jiang Wei made out a youthful-looking leader riding in advance with his spear ready to thrust. He looked scarcely more than twenty years of age, his face was smooth as if powdered, and his lips were crimson. But from them came fierce words.

"Do you recognize General Deng?" cried he.

"So this is Deng Ai," thought Jiang Wei.

Thereupon Jiang Wei set his spear and rode out. Both were adepts in arms and neither gave the other an opening, so that at the end of near half a hundred bouts neither could claim advantage. The youth wielded his spear with perfect skill.

"If I cannot gain the advantage by some ruse, how shall I win?" thought Jiang Wei.

So he turned aside his steed and dashed along a certain road that led to the hills. The youth followed. Presently Jiang Wei slung his spear, laid hands upon his bow, chose with care a feathered arrow, and laid it on the string. But the youth was quick of eye, and as the bowstring sang, he bent his head over the saddle and the arrow passed harmlessly by.

The next time Jiang Wei turned, he saw his pursuer close upon him, and already the spear was threatening his life. But as the youth thrust, Jiang Wei evaded the blow and caught the shaft under his arm. Thus deprived of his weapon, the young man made for his own array.

"What a pity! What a great pity!" cried Jiang Wei, turning to pursue.

He followed the young general close up to the standard.

But just as he came near, a warrior came to the front, shouting, "Jiang Wei, you fool, do not pursue my son when I, Deng Ai, am here!"

Jiang Wei was taken aback; so he had only been contending with Deng Zhong, the son of his real opponent. Although he was astonished at the skill and vigor of the youth, he now knew that a heavier task lay before him and feared lest his steed was then too far spent for the contest.

So he said to Deng Ai, "Seeing things are so, let us both hold off our troops till the morrow, when we will fight."

Deng Ai, glancing around, saw that the place was ill-suited for him, so he agreed to wait, saying, "Let us lead off our armies then, and whoever shall take any secret advantage is a base fellow."

Both sides retired into camp, Deng Ai on the bank of River Wei, and Jiang Wei on the hills.

Deng Ai saw that the army of Shu had the advantage of position, so he wrote off at once to Sima Wang:

"General, we should not give battle, but wait for reinforcements. Meanwhile the soldiers of Shu will be consuming their supply of grain, and we will attack on three sides when they begin to be hungry. I send my son Deng Zhong to you for further help in the defense of the city."

Jiang Wei sent a messenger to the Wei camp to deliver a letter of battle, the contest to take place the next day. Deng Ai openly accepted. But when morning came and Jiang Wei had arrayed his troops, his enemy had not appeared on the field. Nor was there any sign of giving battle, no display of flags or rolling of drums all day.

At nightfall the army of Shu returned to camp, and Jiang Wei sent a letter reproaching his opponent with his failure to keep his word.

Deng Ai treated the bearer of the letter with great courtesy and explained, saying, "I have been indisposed today, but will certainly fight on the morrow."

But the next day passed also without any move on the part of Wei; and the same thing went on for five days.

Then said Fu Qian to his chief, "There is some knavery afoot, and we must be on our guard."

"They must be waiting for reinforcements from Within the Passes that they may attack on three sides," said Jiang Wei. "But now will I send into Wu and get Sun Chen to strike at the same time as I."

Just then scouts came to give the news of the rout of the army of Wu: "Sima Zhao has defeated Shouchun and killed Zhuge Dan. Many in the Wu army have gone over to Wei. Sima Zhao has gone to Luoyang and is planning to march an army to attack Changcheng."

"So our attack on Wei is but a sham!" said Jiang Wei, bitterly. "It is only a picture of a cake."

Four times he missed! He hailed
The fifth occasion joyfully, and failed.

The next chapter will tell the story of the retreat.

Chapter 113

Ding Feng Makes A Plan To Slay Sun Chen; Jiang Wei Arrays A Battle To Defeat Deng Ai.

Fearing lest reinforcements would strengthen his enemy beyond his own power of resistance, Jiang Wei decided to retreat while he could. He sent all his stores and baggage away first with the footmen, and kept the cavalry to cover the retirement.

The spies reported his movements to Deng Ai, who said, "He has gone because he knew that the main army would soon be upon him. Let him go, and do not follow. If we pursue, he will play us some evil trick."

Scouts were sent to keep in touch with the retreating army, and when they returned they reported that preparations of dry woods and straws had been made in the Luo Valley to check any pursuit with fire.

The officers praised the prescience of Deng Ai, "General, your calculation is superhuman!"

When Deng Ai reported these matters to the capital, Sima Zhao was very pleased and confer more rewards.

The Prime Minister of Wu, Sun Chen, was greatly angered by the desertion of so many of his soldiers and officers to Wei, and revenged himself by putting their families to death. The Ruler of Wu,

Sun Liang, disapproved of these acts of cruelty, but he was powerless.

The young Emperor was of an ingenious turn of mind. One day he went to the West Park to eat of the newly ripened plums. He bade one of the eunuchs bring some honey. It was brought, but there were mouse droppings in it. The Ruler of Wu called the storekeeper and blamed him for carelessness.

The storekeeper said, "We are very careful to keep the stores in good order, and the honey cannot not possibly have been fouled in the storehouse."

"Has anyone asked you for honey lately?" asked the Ruler of Wu.

"One of the eunuchs asked for some a few days ago. I refused him."

The Ruler of Wu called the named eunuch and said, "You defiled the honey out of spite."

The man denied it.

"It is very easy to tell," said the Ruler of Wu. "If the dirt has been lying in the honey for some time it will be wet all through."

Then the Ruler of Wu ordered them to cut one of the lumps, and it was quite dry inside. The eunuch then confessed.

This shows the Ruler of Wu was quick-witted. But clever as he was, he could not control his Prime Minister, whose relatives were in command of all the garrisons and armies, so that he was unassailable. His four brothers all had high offices: Sun Ju was General Who Terrifies Distant Regions and Commander of Imperial Guards; Sun En, General Who Shows Prowess; Sun Gan, Imperial Commander; and Sun Kan, Commander of Changshui.

One day the Ruler of Wu, musing over his sorrows and feeling very miserable, began to weep. The officer in charge of the eunuchs, who was an Imperial Brother-in-Law, stood by.

"Sun Chen holds all real power and does as he wishes, while I am despised," said the Ruler of Wu. "Something must be done."

Quan Ji said, "I would think no sacrifice too great if Your Majesty would make use of me."

"If you could muster the Palace guards and help General Liu Cheng to keep the gates, I would go and murder that ruffian. But you must not let anyone know; for if you tell your noble mother, who is a sister of Sun Chen, she will tell her brother, and that would be very serious for me."

"Will Your Majesty give me a command that I may have authority to act when the time comes?" said Quan Ji. "At the critical moment I could show the edict and hold back Sun Chen's supporters."

The command was given, and Quan Ji went home. But he could not keep his secret, and confided the plan to his father, Quan Shang.

His father told his wife, "Sun Chen will be got rid of in three days."

"Oh, he deserves that," said she.

Although she seemed to approve with her tongue, she sent a secret messenger with a letter to the proposed victim.

That same night Sun Chen called in his four leader brothers, and the Palace was surrounded. The conspirators were seized, with Liu Cheng and Quan Shang and all their families.

About dawn the Ruler of Wu was disturbed by a commotion at the gates, and a servant told him, "Sun Chen with his army has surrounded the Inner Palace!"

Sun Liang knew that he had been betrayed. He turned on Empress Quan, who was of the Quan house, and reproached her.

"Your father and brother have upset all my plans!"

Drawing his sword, he was dashing out when his Consort and her people clung to his clothing and held him back.

After putting to death Liu Cheng's and Quan Shang's parties, Sun Chen assembled the officers in the court and addressed them thus: "The Emperor is vicious and weak, depraved and foolish and unfit for his high office. Wherefore he must be deposed. Any of you who oppose will be punished as for conspiracy."

"We shall obey your command, O General!" said the court officiers out of fear.

Only one of those present dared to say a word of

protest.

It was Chair of the Secretariat Huan Yi, who said, "How dare you utter such words? Our Emperor is very intelligent, and I will not support you. I would rather die!"

Sun Chen wrathfully drew his sword and slew Huan Yi.

Then Sun Chen went into the Palace and said to Sun Liang, "O unrighteous and unenlightened Highness, your death would be the only fitting reparation to make to the empire, but out of consideration for your ancestors you are only deposed and degraded to princely rank as Prince of Kuaiji. I will select a worthy successor."

Secretary Li Zong was ordered to bring in the royal seal, which was delivered to Deng Cheng. The deposed ruler retired weeping.

The sage example of the wise Yi Yin
Perverted now to traitor's use we see;
And Huo Guang's faithful services[xlii] *are made*
A cloak to cover vilest treachery.
Even able princes are but toys of fate,
And need our pity, fallen from high estate.

Sun Chen then sent two ministers of the court, Royal Clan Recorder Sun Kai and Secretary Dong Cao, went as envoys to Hulin to request Sun Xiu, Prince of Langye, the sixth son of Sun Quan, to ascend the throne.

The Emperor-elect had had some premonition of

the high honor to which he was now called, for in a dream he saw he ascended into the skies seated on a dragon. Only the dragon seemed to have no tail. He woke up in a fright, and the next day brought the Imperial Envoys, Sun Kai and Dong Cao.

Sun Xiu set out. At Que his carriage was stopped by a venerable old man who claimed to be Gan Xiu and offered felicitations.

"Your Majesty should move faster, for things may change swiftly," said the aged one.

Sun Xiu thanked the old man.

At Busai Pavilion awaited Sun En with a chariot, but Sun Xiu's modesty would not allow him to mount it. He remained in his own simple carriage and therein traveled to the Palace. Officials lined the road to salute him, and he dismounted to return their salutations. Then Sun Chen stood forth and bade them take the newly-elected Emperor by the arm and lead him into the Great Hall, where, after thrice refusing the honor, he at last took his seat in the Dragon Throne and received the jade seal passed from one ruler to another.

When all the officers had made obeisance, there were the usual amnesties, promotions, and honors, and Eternal Tranquillity, the first year (AD 258), was the name of the new reign. Sun Chen was confirmed as Prime Minister, with the Imperial Protectorship of Jingzhou. Moreover, Sun Hao, the son of his elder brother, was created Lord of Wucheng.

Sun Chen, with five persons in his family holding lordships and the whole army under their command, was immensely powerful, able to set up and pull down at will. The new Ruler of Wu, Sun Xiu, secretly feared him; and although outwardly he showed Sun Chen great favor, yet he kept careful watch over Sun Chen, whose arrogance knew no bounds.

In the winter Sun Chen sent into the Palace presents of oxen and wine as birthday gifts. The Ruler of Wu declined them. Sun Chen was very annoyed and took the presents to Zhang Bu's residence, where they two dined together. Zhang Bu was the General of the Left Army.

When warmed with wine, Sun Chen said, "When I deposed the present Prince of Kuaiji, many people urged me to take the throne myself. But I acted magnanimously and set up this present Emperor. Now I suffer the mortification of seeing my presents rejected. You will see what will come of this slight."

Zhang Bu showed sympathy, but the next day he secretly told the Ruler of Wu, and Sun Xiu's fears increased so that he could not rest. Shortly after this, Sun Chen sent a large body of troops under the command of Minister Meng Zong into camp at Wuchang, and Sun Chen armed them from the state arsenals.

Whereupon General Wei Miao and Imperial Guard Shi Shuo secretly memorialized the Ruler of Wu: "Sun Chen has moved the troops outside and provided them with state arms. This action points to rebellion."

Sun Xiu was shocked, and called in Zhang Bu to consult, and he said, "The Veteran General Ding

Feng is an able and trustworthy officer. He should be consulted."

So Ding Feng was called and taken into the Emperor's confidence.

"Have no anxiety," said Ding Feng. "I will find some way of ridding the state of this evil."

"What do you propose?"

"When the winter court is held, and all the officers are assembled, spread a great banquet and invite Sun Chen. I shall be ready to act."

Wei Miao and Shi Shuo were taken into the plot and were to do what was possible outside the Palace, and Zhang Bu saw to arrangements within.

One night a heavy storm came on to blow, which tore up great trees by the roots. However, by daylight it had abated, and that morning an Emperor's messenger arrived bearing an invitation to a banquet in the Palace. Sun Chen rose from his couch, and, as he did so, fell flat on the ground as though he had been pushed from behind. This accident troubled him, and he felt apprehensive, so he called half a score of his trusty guards to act as his escort to the Palace.

As he was leaving home, his family besought him not to go out, saying, "The storm last night and the fall this morning are fearful omens. You should not go to that banquet."

However, he made light of their fears and said, "My brothers are holding the army. Who will dare come near me? But if there is anything amiss, you just give a fire signal from the Prime Minister's residence."

So Sun Chen took his seat, and the carriage set out. When he reached the court, the Ruler of Wu rose from his place to welcome him, and at table Sun Chen sat in the seat of honor. The banquet proceeded.

"There is a fire outside: What does that mean?" said a guest presently.

Sun Chen rose to go out, but the Ruler of Wu said, "There is no danger, and there are plenty of soldiers outside to take care of that."

Just at that moment Zhang Bu entered at the head of thirty armed guards. He rushed up the banquet chamber, shouting, "I hold a command to slay the rebel Sun Chen!"

Instantly the Prime Minister was seized. He fell prostrate before the Ruler of Wu, knocking his head on the ground and crying, "Spare my life! Exile me to Jiaozhou[xliii], where I will do plow work."

"Did you exile any of your victims---Teng Yin, Lu Ju, Wang Chun, and others?" said the Ruler of Wu, angrily.

The order went forth to carry out the execution, and Sun Chen was hustled out and put to death. No single person of his servants raised a hand to help him.

Then Zhang Bu read an edict: "Sun Chen is the only culprit, and no other will be questioned."

Then at Zhang Bu's request, the Ruler of Wu went up on the Tower of the Five Phoenixes. Zhang Bu, Wei Miao, and Shi Shuo brought the brothers of the Prime Minister before Sun Xiu, and he condemned them to death. After this their families were slain, so that many hundreds suffered death. Not content with all these things, the tomb of Sun Jun was broken open and his corpse beheaded.

Magnificent tombs were raised to his victims---Zhuge Ke, Teng Yin, Lu Ju, Wang Chun, and others. Thus at last loyalty was rewarded, and the banished were permitted to return home with full pardon. The conspirators were rewarded.

News of this revolution was sent into Chengdu, and the Latter Ruler sent an envoy into Wu with felicitations. In return, the Ruler of Wu sent Xue Xu as his envoy to Shu.

When Xue Xu returned, the Ruler of Wu questioned about affairs in the west, and Xue Xu said, "All affairs of state are in the hands of a certain eunuch named Huang Hao, and all the courtiers look up to him as to a father. At court plain truth is never heard, and the country people look sallow and starved. The whole country appears on the verge of destruction. The birds on the roof do not know that the building is about to be burned."

"Ah ! If only Zhuge Liang the Martial Lord was still alive---how different all would be!" said Sun Xiu, with a sigh.

Letters were prepared saying that beyond doubt Sima Zhao intended usurpation, and when that came about in Wei, both Wu and Shu would be invaded. Wherefore both should be ready.

On the arrival of these letters, Jiang Wei hastened to seek permission to attempt another expedition. Consent being given, a large army marched into Hanzhong in the winter of the first year of Wonderful Sight (AD 258). Liao Hua and Zhang Yi were appointed Leaders of the Van, Wang Han and Jiang Bin as Commanders of the Left Army, and Jiang Shu and Fu Qian as Commanders of the Right Army, while Jiang Wei and Xiahou Ba led the main column.

Asked what he thought should be the first objective, Xiahou Ba replied, "There is no better fighting ground than Qishan, as the tactics of the late Prime Minister made evident, and it is the only good exit."

So thither three armies marched, and they made three camps at the entrance to the valley. At this time Deng Ai had a training camp at Qishan drilling the Longyou troops.

The scouts told him: "The Shu army have pitched three camps in the valley."

He ascended a hill to see and verify their reports. He seemed pleased when he saw the enemy camp.

"They have just done as I foresaw," said Deng Ai.

Now Deng Ai had carefully considered the topography of the countryside, and so had not interfered with the Shu army when it was on the march or settling into camp. Moreover, he had excavated a subterranean road to the spot where he had thought they would halt, and their left camp had been pitched just on it. Wang Han and Jiang Bin commanded in that camp.

Deng Ai called his son Deng Zhong and Shi Zuan and sent them with ten thousand troops each to attack the left camp, one on each flank. Then he sent Zheng Lun and five hundred troops into the underground road, which opened in rear of the camp of Wang Han and Jiang Bin.

As the newly made camp was not yet well fortified, Wang Han and Jiang Bin exercised great care and kept their troops under arms all night, watching with vigilance. So when the alarm was given, they had but to seize their weapons and go out. But as the two leaders were mounting their steeds, Deng Zhong and Shi Zuan had attacked from without, and Zheng Lun from within. Thus attacked from three sides, soon Wang Han and Jiang Bin found the position untenable and fled.

When Jiang Wei saw that his left camp had been attacked on three sides, he mounted and took his position in front of the center camp.

"Let no one move on pain of death!" he shouted. "Stand still. When the enemy approaches, shoot!"

The right camp was ordered to stand fast. His defense was effective. A dozen of times the troops of Wei came forward, only to be driven back before the arrows and bolts of the defenders. Daylight found the Shu camps still firm, and the Wei troops drew off.

"Jiang Wei has indeed learned of Zhuge Liang," said Deng Ai. "His soldiers stood the night attack without flinching, and the leaders took the chances of battle quite calmly. He is able."

Next day, when Wang Han and Jiang Bin went to confess their fault, Jiang Wei said, "It was less your fault than mine, for I did not clearly recognize the nature of the terrain."

So no penalty was inflicted. The camp was made stronger, and the subterranean passage was filled with the bodies of the slain.

A challenge to battle for the following day was sent to Deng Ai, who accepted it joyfully.

Next day the two armies were arrayed in front of the Qishan Mountains. The troops of Shu arrayed according to the "Eight Formations" designed by Zhuge Liang, which are called Heaven, Earth, Wind, Cloud, Bird, Serpent, Dragon, and Tiger. While the maneuver was in progress, Deng Ai recognized it as the Eight Gates Formation and placed his troops accordingly.

Jiang Wei then gripped his spear and rode out, saying, "You have made a good imitation of my eight, but can you work variations?"

"You call these yours! Did you think that you alone held the secret? Since I have made it, of course I know the variations."

Deng Ai reentered his ranks, gave the signal officers certain orders, and the eight gates were evolved in rapid succession into sixty-four gates. Then he rode to the front again.

"What of my evolution?" asked Deng Ai.

"Not so bad. Would you like to try a surrounding move with me?" replied Jiang Wei.

"Why not?"

The two armies moved in orderly ranks. Deng Ai stood in the midst of his army giving the necessary orders. Then the clash came, but his tactics did not grip. Then Jiang Wei waved a certain signal flag, and his force suddenly assumed the form of a serpent coiled on the ground with Deng Ai in the center. Shouts arose all about him, and Deng Ai could not understand what had happened and began to feel afraid. Gradually the troops of Shu closed in upon him, and he saw no way of escape.

"Deng Ai, you must surrender!" cried the soldiers.

"Indeed a moment of pride had led me into the trap of Jiang Wei!" he sighed.

Suddenly from the northwest a cohort dashed in. To Deng Ai's great joy they were soldiers of Wei, and they forced over the battle array and released him. The leader was Sima Wang.

But although Deng Ai had been rescued, his nine camps were seized by his enemy and he had to retire. He led his army to the south of River Wei and made a camp.

"How did you know exactly where to strike in that maze?" asked Deng Ai of his rescuer.

Sima Wang replied, "In my youth I went to study in Jingzhou and was friendly with Shi Guangyuan and Cui Zhouping. They explained that formation to me. Jiang Wei used what is known as 'The

Serpent Coil', and the only way to break it is to attack the head, which I saw was in the northwest."

Deng Ai replied, "Although I have studied formations, I do not know all the modifications. But since you know about this, we may be able to recover our camps."

"I fear the little I have learned will not be enough to overcome Jiang Wei."

"Tomorrow you shall contend with him, and while his attention is engaged, I will attack the rear of Qishan, and we will recover our camps."

So a force was prepared to attack on the morrow, and Deng Ai sent a letter of challenge to a contest in tactics for the same day. Jiang Wei marked in to accept.

Jiang Wei said to his officers, "In the secret book that I received from the Prime Minister, the variations of the formation are three hundred and sixty-five, corresponding to the circuit of the heavens. This challenge from them is as one going to teach hewing to the God of Carpenters. I think some ruse lies behind this. Can you guess what it is?"

Liao Hua replied, "While they engage your attention in this competition, they intend to attack our rear."

"Just so; that is also my opinion," replied Jiang Wei.

So he prepared a counter-stroke by sending Liao Hua and Zhang Yi to lie in wait at the back of the hills with ten thousand troops.

Next day Jiang Wei led all the troops from the nine camps out and drawn up in front of the hills. Sima Wang came out on the other side and presently rode to the front to parley.

"You have challenged me to a contest. Now draw up your army for me to see," said Jiang Wei.

Sima Wang did so and arrayed the eight diagrams.

"That is what we know as the Octagon," said Jiang Wei. "But it is nothing wonderful, only a sort of array fit for a brigand's raid."

"You also have only stolen another man's tactics," replied his adversary.

"How many modifications of this are there?" asked Jiang Wei.

"Since I have arranged this, naturally I know the variations, of which there are nine nines, making eighty-one."

"Try them."

Sima Wang returned to his array and evolved many, finally riding out and asking his opponent if he recognized them.

"My formation admits of three hundred and sixty-five variations. You are but a frog in a well and know nothing of the deeper mysteries."

Now Sima Wang knew that so many variations were possible, but had not studied them. However, he put on a bold air and said contemptuously, "I do not believe you. Prove it!"

"Go and call Deng Ai," replied Jiang Wei. "I will display them to him."

"General Deng Ai has excellent plans and does not think much of such tactics."

"What plans? I suppose you mean a plan to keep me here while he tries a surprise attack in the rear."

Sima Wang was aghast. He made a sudden dash forward, and a melee began. Jiang Wei made a signal with his whip, and his force poured in from both wings. The troops of Wei were seized with sudden panic, threw down their weapons and fled.

Now Deng Ai had hurried on Zheng Lun to make the first attack. As Zheng Lun turned the corner of the hill, a bomb exploded. At once the drums rolled and an ambush discovered itself. Liao Hua was in command. Neither side stayed to parley, and the leaders engaged in single combat. In the first encounter Liao Hua cut Zheng Lun down.

Deng Ai had not expected such preparation, and he hastened to withdraw. Then Zhang Yi came forth and attacked on the other side. The army of Wei was worsted. Deng Ai fought his way out, but he bore four arrow wounds upon his body. He got to the river, where he found Sima Wang, and they discussed how to get away.

But Sima Wang proposed another form of attack.

"Recently the Ruler of Shu has had a favorite, Eunuch Huang Hao, in whom he places all his trust and with whom he spends his time in one round of pleasure. Let us use the eunuch to sow distrust between the Emperor and his general and so get Jiang Wei recalled. In that way we shall retrieve our defeat."

So Deng Ai assembled his advisers and asked who could go into Shu and get into communication with Huang Hao.

Dang Jun volunteered at once. Deng Ai entrusted gold and pearls and precious things to him, and sent him into Shu to win the treacherous alliance of the eunuch. As Dang Jun went, he also disseminated reports that Jiang Wei was angry and intended to go over to Wei.

These rumors became the common talk in Chengdu, and everyone believed them. Huang Hao carried them to the Emperor, and a messenger was sent to call the general to the capital.

Meanwhile Jiang Wei tried every day to bring the enemy to give battle, but they remained obstinately behind their defenses. Jiang Wei began to think some evil scheme was afoot, when suddenly he was recalled by Imperial Edict. Although ignorant of the reason, he could not disobey; and when he began the retreat, Deng Ai and Sima Wang knew that their plot had succeeded. They broke camp and set out to attack the retreating army.

Because of court intrigues
Yue Yi[xliv] *and Yue Fei*[xlv] *failed.*

How matters went will be told in the next chapter.

Chapter 114

Driving To The South Gate, Cao Mao Plunges Into Death;
Abandoning Stores, Jiang Wei Defeats The Wei Army.

When the order to retreat was given, Liao Hua said, "A leader in the field is independent and need not obey even the command of his prince."

Zhang Yi said, "The country begins to resent these many years of war. Rather take the occasion of the victory you have just won to return and pacify the people."

"It is good," said Jiang Wei.

A systematic and orderly retirement began. The army of Wei, loth to forgo an opportunity, followed, but the absence of the least confusion gave them no chance.

As he saw his enemy disappearing in perfect order, Deng Ai sighed, "Jiang Wei is a worthy inheritor of the warlike methods of Zhuge Liang."

Deng Ai did not pursue but returned to his camp on Qishan.

On his return to Chengdu, Jiang Wei had audience with the Latter Ruler, whereat he inquired, saying, "Your Majesty has commanded me to return for an important reason?"

The Latter Ruler replied, "Because you have been so long on the frontier, Noble Sir. I thought the soldiers must be weary. There was no other reason."

"Your Majesty, thy servant had got his camps on Qishan and was on the eve of complete success. To leave off thus in the middle just played into the hands of our enemies. Surely Deng Ai found means of sowing distrust in me."

The Latter Ruler sat lost in thought, and silent.

Jiang Wei continued, "I am pledged to destroy those rebels and prove my devotion to my country. Your Majesty should not listen to the babble of mean persons till distrust grows in your heart."

"I do not distrust you," said the Latter Ruler after a long pause. "You may return into Hanzhong and await the next favorable opportunity."

Jiang Wei left the court and betook himself into Hanzhong to the army.

Dang Jun went back to the Qishan camp and reported his success.

Deng Ai and Sima Wang rejoiced, saying, "In the River Lands, trouble is not far off when the ruler and his servants do not live in harmony."

They sent Dang Jun to Luoyang to tell his own story to Sima Zhao, who also rejoiced, for he ardently desired to subdue Shu.

On this matter Sima Zhao consulted Jia Chong, Commander of the Center Guard.

"What do you think of an attack upon Shu?"

"Not to be considered," said Jia Chong. "The Emperor does not trust you, and your departure would be the beginning of trouble for you. Last year, when a yellow dragon was seen in the Ningling well and all the officers were felicitating the Emperor upon such a very auspicious occurrence, the Emperor said, 'It is not auspicious; just the reverse. The dragon symbolizes the ruler. To be neither in heaven, nor on earth among the people, but to be in a well, is a dark portent and bodes evil.' He wrote some verses, and one stanza undoubtedly points to you, my lord. It reads:

"The dragon like a prisoner is,
No longer leaps he in the abyss.
He soars not to the Milky Way
Nor can he in the meadows play;
But coiled within a dismal well,
With slimy creatures he must dwell,
Must close his jaws, his claws retract,
Alas! Quite like myself in fact."

The recital of the poem annoyed Sima Zhao.

"This fellow is very like Cao Fang, and if I do not remove him he will hurt me," said he.

"I will see to it for you," said Jia Chong.

In the fifth year of Sweet Dew, in Wei calendar (AD 261), during the fourth month, in summer, Sima Zhao had the effrontery to go to court armed.

However, the Ruler of Wei received him with exaggerated courtesy.

The courtiers said, "The services of the Regent Marshal are so magnificent, and his virtue so high that he should be rewarded with the title 'Duke of Jin' and the Nine Dignities."

Cao Mao hung his head and kept silent.

And Sima Zhao himself said discontentedly, "My father and my brother have all given great services to Wei, and yet I deserves not being a mere Duke of Jin?"

"Should I dare not do what you requested?" said Cao Mao.

"That poem about the Lurking Dragon called us slimy creatures. What sort of politeness is that?" said Sima Zhao.

The Ruler of Wei had nothing to say, and the haughty minister left the chamber, smiling cruelly.

Cao Mao retired, taking with him Minister Wang Jing, Adviser Wang Shen, and General of the Cavalry Wang Ye, and they went to a privy chamber to consult. Cao Mao was very sad.

He said, "There is no doubt that Sima Zhao intends to usurp the throne---everybody knows that. But I will not sit thereon patiently awaiting the indignity of being pushed off. Cannot you gentlemen help me to kill him?"

"He may not be slain," said Wang Jing. "That will not do. In the old state of Lu, King Zhao could not bear with the Ji family, and ran away, thus losing his country. But this Sima Zhao and his family have been in power very long and have innumerable supporters, many of whom are quite independent of any act of his whether loyal or disloyal. They support him under any conditions. Your Majesty's guards are few and weak and incapable---not the ones for any desperate effort. It would be most lamentable if Your Majesty could not bear this trial. The correct course is to wait and not act hastily."

"If I can bear this, what cannot I bear?" said Cao Mao. "But I will do something, and if I die, what matters?"

He went into the private apartments and spoke to the Empress Dowager.

Wang Shen, Wang Jing, and Wang Ye sat outside talking.

"This matter is coming to a head, and unless we want to be put to death and all our loved ones with us, we had better go and warn Sima Zhao," said Wang Shen.

This advice angered Wang Jing, and he said, "The prince's sorrow is the minister's shame, and a shamed minister dies. Dare you contemplate treachery?"

Wang Jing would have nothing to do with this visit to Sima Zhao, but the other two went to the Prime Minister's palace to betray their prince.

Shortly after, Cao Mao appeared, called the officer of the guard, Jiao Bo, and bade him muster his force, as many as he could. Jiao Bo got together about three hundred, and this little force marched out to the beating of a drum as escort to a small carriage, in which sat the Ruler of Wei gripping his sword. They proceeded south.

Wang Jing stepped to the front and prayed Cao Mao to stay his steps and not go.

"To go against Sima Zhao with such a force is driving the sheep into the tiger's jaws. To die such a death is a vain sacrifice. Not that I want to live, but this can do nothing," said Wang Jing.

"Do not hinder me. I have made up my mind," replied the Ruler of Wei, heading toward the Dragon Gate.

Presently Jia Chong came in sight. He was armed and mounted on a fine horse. Beside him rode two generals, Cheng Zu and Cheng Ji, and behind him followed a body of mail-clad guards, who shouted one to another as they rode.

Then Cao Mao held up his sword and cried, "I am the Son of God. Who are you thus breaking into the Forbidden City? Are you come to murder your lawful ruler?"

The soldiers suddenly stopped, for they were Palace guards.

Then Jia Chong shouted to Cheng Ji, saying, "What did Duke Sima Zhao train you for if not for this day's work?"

Cheng Ji took his halberd and turned to Jia Chong, saying, "Death or capture?"

"Duke Sima Zhao said the man had to die," replied Jia Chong.

Cheng Ji rushed toward the carriage.

"Fool! How dare you?" cried the Ruler of Wei.

But the shout was cut short by a thrust from the halberd full in the breast; another thrust, and the point came out at the back, so that Cao Mao lay there dead beside his carriage. Jiao Bo coming up to strike a blow in defense was also slain, and the little escort scattered.

Wang Jing, who had followed, upbraided Jia Chong, shouting, "Rebel and traitor! How dare you kill the Emperor?"

Jia Chong got angry and bade his lictors arrest Wang Jing and stop his tongue.

When they told Sima Zhao, he went into the Palace, but the Emperor was dead. He assumed an air of being greatly shocked and beat his head against the carriage, weeping and lamenting the while. He sent to tell all the officials of high rank.

When Imperial Guardian Sima Fu saw the dead body of the Emperor, he threw himself beside it, his head resting thereon, and wept, saying, "It is my fault that they slew Your Majesty!"

Sima Fu had a coffin brought, and the remains were laid therein and borne to the West Hall. Therein Sima Zhao entered and summoned the chief officers to a council. They came, all but Minister Chen Tai. Sima Zhao noticed his absence and sent the Chair of the Secretariat Xun Yi, his uncle, to call him.

Chen Tai wept aloud, saying, "Gossips often class me and my uncle together. Yet today is my uncle less virtuous than I."

However, Chen Tai obeyed the summons and came, dressed in the coarse white cloth of mourning, and prostrated himself before the bier. Sima Zhao feigned to be grieved also.

"How can this day's work be judged?" said Sima Zhao.

"If only Jia Chong be put to death, that will only be a slight atonement to satisfy the empire," replied Chen Tai.

Sima Zhao was silent and thought long before he spoke. Then he said, "How about a little less severe?"

"That is only the beginning. I know not other punishments less severe."

"Cheng Ji is the ungodly rebel and actual criminal. He should suffer the death of shame---and his family, too," said Sima Zhao.

Thereupon Cheng Ji broke out into abuse of Sima Zhao and reviled him, saying, "It was not my crime: It was Jia Chong who passed on your own orders!"

Sima Zhao bade them cut out his tongue and put him to death. They did so; and Cheng Ji and his brother Cheng Zu were both put to death in the market place, and their families were exterminated.

The Emperor must die," thus spoke Sima Zhao full plain
In Jia Chong's hearing; and the Emperor was slain.
Although they killed Cheng Ji, who dealt the blow,
The author of the crime we all well know.

Wang Jing's whole household were imprisoned. He himself was standing in the courthouse when he saw his mother, Lady Zhao, being brought up a prisoner.

He knocked his head on the ground and wept, saying, "O unfilial son to bring distress upon a gentle mother!"

But his mother laughed.

"Who does not die?" cried she. "The only thing to be feared is not dying the proper death. Who would regret dying like this?"

When next day the family were led out to execution, both mother and son smiled as they went past. But the whole city wept tears of sorrow.

Mother Yuan was famous at the rise of Han,
Mother Zhao was distinguished at the end of Wei,
With purest virtue and unfaltering heart,
With resolution stern she played her part.
Her fortitude was great as Taishan Mountains,
Her life but as the floating down did count,
Like mother like son, their fame never will die,
So long as shall endure the earth and sky.

Imperial Guardian Sima Fu proposed that the body of the late Emperor should receive a royal funeral, and Sima Zhao consented. Jia Chong and those of his party urged Sima Zhao to assume the Throne and replace Wei, but he refused.

"Formerly King Wen had two-thirds of the empire, and yet he supported and served the state of Yin to its end. Wherefore Confucius called him 'Complete of Virtue'. Emperor Cao of Wei would not replace the Hans, nor will I accept an abdication of Wei."

Those who heard this felt that in these words was an implication that he intended to place his own son Sima Yan on the throne, and they ceased to urge him to act.

In the sixth month of that year, Cao Huang, Duke of Changdao, was raised to the throne as Emperor, the period-style being changed to Wonderful Beginning, the first year (AD 260). Cao Huang was a son of Cao Yu, Prince of Yan, and a great grandson of Cao Cao.

Sima Zhao was made Prime Minister and Duke of Jin[xlvi]. Beside, he received gifts of one hundred thousand gold coins and ten thousand rolls of silk. All the officers were promoted or received honors.

When these doings in Wei were told in Shu, Jiang Wei seized upon them as pretext for another war, to punish Wei for the deposition of its ruler. So letters were written calling upon Wu to help, and a memorial was sent to the Throne. The army raised was one hundred fifty thousand, and there were many carts with boxes made to fit them. Liao Hua and Zhang Yi were the Leaders of the Van. Liao Hua was to march to the Ziwu Valley, and Zhang

Yi to the Luo Valley, while Jiang Wei took the Xie Valley road. They marched at the same time and hastened toward Qishan.

Deng Ai was still on the Qishan Mountains training the Wei soldiers when he heard that the Shu armies were once more on the war path. He called his officers together.

And Adviser Wang Guan said, "I have a plan to propose, but I will not tell it openly. However, I have written it down for your consideration."

Deng Ai took the envelop, opened, and read it.

"Though excellent, I fear it is not enough to beguile the leader of Shu," said Deng Ai as he finished reading.

"I am willing to stake my life on it," said Wang Guan, "and I will lead the way."

"Since you have such confidence you may try. You ought certainly to succeed."

So five thousand troops were put under the leadership of Wang Guan, and they set out for the Xie Valley, where they fell in with the scouts of Jiang Wei's force.

Seeing these, their leader, Wang Guan, shouted, "We are deserters. Tell your leader!"

So the scouts told Jiang Wei, who replied, "Hold up the soldiers, letting their leader only come to me."

Wang Guan went forward and kneeled before

Jiang Wei, saying, "I am a nephew of Wang Jing, and I hate Sima Zhao for what he has done to the Emperor and my family, and I wish to join you and my five thousand soldiers with me. I also desire to be sent against the rebel army that I may avenge my uncle."

Then said Jiang Wei, "Since you are sincere in your desertion, I must be sincere in my treatment of you. The one thing my army needs is grain. There is plenty at the border of the River Lands. If you can transport it to Qishan, I can go straightway and take the Qishan camps of Deng Ai."

This reply rejoiced Wang Guan, who saw that Jiang Wei was just going to walk into the trap. So he agreed at once.

"But you will not need five thousand troops to see after the transport. Take three thousand and leave two thousand as guides for me."

Wang Guan, thinking that suspicions would be raised if he refused, took the three thousand of his troops and marched away, and the other two thousand were attached to the army of Shu.

Then Xiahou Ba was announced, and, when he was come in, he said, "O Commander, why have you believed the tale of this Wang Guan? In Wei I never heard that Wang Guan was related to Wang Jing, though it is true I never made particular inquiries. You should look to it, for there is much pretense in his story."

"I know Wang Guan is false," said Jiang Wei, with a smile. "That is why I have taken away many of his force. I am meeting trick with trick."

"How do you know for certain he is a false?"

"Sima Zhao is as crafty as Cao Cao. If he slew all Wang Jing's family, would he have left a nephew and sent that nephew to the pass beyond his own reach with soldiers? You saw this, as did I."

So Jiang Wei did not go out by the Xie Valley, but he set an ambush there ready for any move of Wang Guan. And indeed, within ten days, the ambush caught a man with a letter from Wang Guan to Deng Ai telling him what had come about. From the letter and the bearer thereof, Jiang Wei learned that Wang Guan would divert a convoy of grain to the Wei camps on the twentieth and Deng Ai was to send troops to Yunshan Valley to help.

Jiang Wei beheaded the courier. Then he sent another letter to Deng Ai by a man dressed as a Wei soldier, the date being altered to the fifteenth instead of the twentieth.

As a preparation, Jiang Wei ordered many wagons to be emptied of their grain and laden with inflammables, covered with green cloth. The two thousand Wei soldiers were ordered to show flags belonging to the Shu transport corps. Then Jiang Wei and Xiahou Ba went into the valleys in ambush, while Jiang Shu was ordered to march to the Xie Valley, and Liao Hua and Zhang Yi were sent to capture Qishan.

The letter, apparently from Wang Guan, was sufficient for Deng Ai, and he wrote back to say it was agreed. So on the fifteenth day, Deng Ai led out fifty thousand veteran troops and moved in sight near Yunshan Valley. And the scouts saw endless carts of grain and fodder in the distance zigzagging through the mountains. When Deng Ai got closer, he distinguished the uniforms of Wei.

His staff urged him, saying, "It is getting dark, O General. Hurry to help Wang Guan escort the convoy out of the valley!"

"The mountains ahead are hazardous," said the general. "If by any chance an ambush has been laid, we could hardly escape. We will wait here."

But just then two horsemen came up at a gallop and said, "Just as General Wang Guan was crossing the frontier with the convoy, he was pursued, and reinforcements are urgently needed!"

Deng Ai, realizing the importance of the request, gave orders to press onward. It was the first watch, and a full moon was shining as bright as day. Shouting was heard behind the hills, and he could only conclude it was the noise of the battle in which Wang Guan was engaged.

So Deng Ai dashed over the hills. But suddenly a body of troops came out from the shelter of a grove of trees, and at their head rode the Shu leader, Fu Qian.

"Deng Ai, you are stupid! You have just fallen into the trap set for you by our general. Dismount and prepare for death!"

Deng Ai halted and turned to flee. Then the wagons burst into flame. That flame was a signal, and down came the army of Shu.

He heard shouts all round him, "A thousand ounces of gold for anyone who captures Deng Ai, and a lordship of ten thousand households as well!"

Terrified, Deng Ai dropped his arms, threw aside his armor, slipped from his steed, mingled with the footmen, and with them scrambled up the hills. The generals of Shu only looked for him among the mounted leaders, never guessing that he had got away among the common soldiers. So he was not captured.

Jiang Wei gathered in his victorious army and went to meet Wang Guan and his convoy.

Having made all arrangements, as he thought, complete, Wang Guan was patiently awaiting the development of his scheme.

But suddenly a trusted subordinate came and told him, "The ruse has been discovered, and Deng Ai has already suffered defeat!"

Wang Guan sent out some scouts, and the report was confirmed, with the addition that the Shu armies were coming against him. Moreover, clouds of dust were rising. There was no way of escape, so Wang Guan ordered his troops to set fire to the convoy, and soon huge flames were rising high into the air.

"The case is desperate," cried Wang Guan. "It is a fight to the death!"

He led his force westward, but the army of Shu came in pursuit. Jiang Wei thought Wang Guan would try at all costs to get back to his own side, but instead, Wang Guan went on toward Hanzhong. As his troops were too few to risk a battle, Wang Guan ordered them to burn and destroy all military stations and even the Plank Trail as he went. Fearing the loss of Hanzhong, Jiang Wei made all haste along the by-roads after Wang Guan. Surrounded on all sides, Wang Guan jumped into the Black Dragon River and so died. Those of his soldiers who survived were slain by Jiang Wei.

Though a victory had been won and Wang Guan killed, it was costly. Many wagons and much grain had been lost, and the Plank Trail had been destroyed. Jiang Wei led his army into Hanzhong.

Deng Ai made his way back to Qishan. From there he reported his defeat to the Ruler of Wei and asked for degradation as a penalty. However, Sima Zhao saw that Deng Ai had rendered good services, so he did not degrade the general, but, on the other hand, sent him magnificent gifts, which Deng Ai distributed to the families of the soldiers who had been killed. Sima Zhao also sent him fifty thousand troops as reinforcement lest Shu should attack again.

Jiang Wei set about the restoration of the Plank Trail ready for the next expedition.

Repair the roads for marching feet to tread,
The strife will only cease when all are dead.

The next chapter will tell who won.

Chapter 115

Listening To Slander, The Latter Ruler Recalls His Army;
Living In Farms, Jiang Wei Avoids Disaster.

In the autumn of the fifth year of Wonderful Sight, in Shu-Han calendar (AD 262), Jiang Wei was occupied with preparations for the renewal of an attack: Mending the hill roads, gathering stores, and mobilizing his boats on the waterways of Hanzhong. These things done, he memorized the Throne, asking permission to go again to the attack:

"Although I have not been wholly victorious nor accomplished great things, yet I have put fear into the hearts of the Wei armies. Our soldiers have been long under training, and they must now be used, or the army will go to pieces for lack of exercise. The soldiers are ready to die, the officers prepared for all risks, and I am determined to conquer or perish."

The Latter Ruler did not consent at once.

As he was hesitating, Qiao Zhou stood forth and said, "I have observed the heavens. I have seen the leadership stars in Shu dull and obscured. This expedition will be disastrous, and I hope Your Majesty will not approve."

The Latter Ruler replied, "Let us see the results of this campaign. If it fails, then the war shall cease."

Qiao Zhou tried to dissuade the Latter Ruler two or

three more times, but he failed. In despair he withdrew to his home, and retired on the pretext of illness.

As the final preparations were being made, Jiang Wei said to Liao Hua, "We are pledged to get through to the Middle Land this time. What do you advise to start with?"

"I dare not presume to advise you, General. For years we have been fighting and giving the people no rest. In Deng Ai we find a most formidable and resourceful opponent and an extraordinarily capable man, so that you must exert yourself to the very utmost."

Jiang Wei was annoyed. Said he, "The late Prime Minister made six attempts, all for the state. I have attacked eight times. Was anyone of those attacks to serve my private ends? This time I go to attack Taoyang, and no one shall say me nay. I will punish opposition with death."

Jiang Wei left Liao Hua in charge of the base in Hanzhong and marched with three hundred thousand troops to Taoyang. His movements were reported in the Qishan camps, and Deng Ai's spies confirmed the news.

It happened that Sima Wang was with Deng Ai discussing military matters, and the former, when he heard it, said, "That move is a decoy: He does not mean it. What he really intends is an attack on Qishan."

"However, he has really gone to Taoyang," said Deng Ai.

"How can you know?"

"Formerly Jiang Wei has always opened with a march to those parts of the country where we have stored supplies. Taoyang has no stores, so he thinks we shall not have taken care for its defense as we shall concentrate our efforts on Qishan. But, if he can take that place, he can collect stores there, and get into touch with the Qiang tribespeople and finally work out some grand plan."

"Supposing this true, what should we do?"

"I advise the abandonment of this place and a march in two bodies toward Taoyang. I know a small town called Houxia, eight miles from Taoyang, which is the throat of the place. You go to Taoyang, hide your force, and open the gates. Then act as I shall tell you presently. I will lie in wait at Houxia. We shall score a victory."

Deng Ai gave Shi Zuan the command of the camps in Qishan when the main body left.

Meanwhile Xiahou Ba led the van of the Shu army toward Taoyang. As he drew near, he noticed the place seemed to have no defenses; not a flag staff reared its head. The gates stood wide open.

He was too wary to go straight in however, and said, "Is there any ruse in there?"

His generals said, "We think the city was deserted when they heard your army coming. A few people were running away along the southern road."

Xiahou Ba rode south and saw there that the northwest road, at a little distance from the city, was crowded with fugitives.

"The city is really empty," said Xiahou Ba.

He led the way in all ready to fight, and the troops followed. As they came near to the curtain wall, however, a bomb exploded. At this sound the drums beat, trumpets blared, and flags suddenly appeared. At the same moment the drawbridge rose.

"Caught!" said Xiahou Ba.

As he turned to retire, the arrows and stones flew down in clouds, and under these Xiahou Ba and many of his soldiers lost their lives.

Most able strategist and brave,
Xiahou Ba, outwitted here
By Deng Ai, more prudent still, and slain,
Deserves a pitying tear.

The flights of arrows from the ramparts was followed by a sortie, which broke up the force of Shu entirely, and the troops fled. However, Jiang Wei came up and drove Sima Wang back into the city. The army of Shu camped beside the walls. Jiang Wei was very grieved at the loss of Xiahou Ba.

That night Deng Ai came up secretly and attacked the Shu camp. At the same time the defenders within the city made a sortie. Jiang Wei could not resist the double attack, and left the field. He marched some seven miles and camped.

Twice beaten, the soldiers of Shu were very downcast.

Jiang Wei tried to console them, saying, "Loss or gain is the platitude of war. But I am not worried yet about our recent defeats, for a total victory will surely come in this expedition if all of you strive your best. But remember, no mutiny! He who talks of retreat will suffer death."

Then Zhang Yi said, "With so many troops of Wei here, their camp at Qishan must be undefended. I propose, General, that while you continue the contest here with Deng Ai, I go to try to capture the nine camps. If I succeed, Changan will be at our mercy."

The second division of the army was detached to march on Qishan, and Jiang Wei went down to Houxia to provoke Deng Ai into fighting. The challenge this time was accepted forthwith. Deng Ai led his troops out and engaged with Jiang Wei in a fight, but after thirty bouts without a decision, both retired to their camps.

For days after this, Jiang Wei challenged again and again, but Deng Ai declined and would not fight. The Shu soldiers howled abuse and hurled insults at their opponents, but all without effect.

Then Deng Ai thought within him, "There must be some reason for this persistence. I think they have sent an army to try to seize Qishan while they hold me here. Shi Zuan and the force there are insufficient, and I shall have to go to the rescue."

Deng Ai called his son Deng Zhong, and said, "Hold this place most carefully. Let them challenge as they may, do not go out. Tonight I go to the help of Qishan."

It was night, and Jiang Wei was in his tent, intent upon his plans, when he was disturbed by a great shouting and drumming. They told him Deng Ai had suddenly appeared. The generals asked leave to go out to fight.

"Let no one move!" said Jiang Wei.

The fact was Deng Ai had only made a demonstration at the camp of Shu on his way to reinforce Qishan.

Then Jiang Wei said to his officers, "The attack of Deng Ai was a feint. He has certainly gone to relieve Qishan."

So Jiang Wei decided to go to the aid of Zhang Yi. He left Fu Qian to guard the camp, and he marched away with three thousand troops.

Zhang Yi was then actually attacking the Wei position on Qishan. Shi Zuan had few troops, and it looked as though the defenders must soon give in, when the sudden appearance of Deng Ai made all the difference. The onslaught of Deng Ai's force drove off Zhang Yi, and he was forced to take refuge behind the hills. No road was open to him. When things looked worst, he saw the Wei soldiers suddenly falling back in confusion.

"General Jiang Wei has come!" they told him.

Zhang Yi took the opportunity to return to the attack, and the tables were turned. Deng Ai lost the fight and retired into his camp, which Jiang Wei surrounded and attacked vigorously.

In Chengdu the Latter Ruler fell daily more and more under the malign influence of Huang Hao, who encouraged him in every form of self-indulgence and ministered to every desire for luxury and dissipation. Government was left to look after itself.

At that time High Minister Liu Yang had a very beautiful wife, Lady Hu. One day she went into the Palace to visit the Empress, who kept her there a whole month. Liu Yang was not without suspecting an intrigue with the Latter Ruler and took a brutal revenge. He bound Lady Hu, and made five hundred of his soldiers shame her to the last degree by beating her on the face with their boots. She swooned many times.

The story got to the ears of the Latter Ruler, and he ordered the officials concerned to investigate and decide the crime and its punishment.

The judges found that: "Soldiers are not proper persons to administer a punishment to a woman, and the face is not a portion of the body to be mortified: The author of this crime ought to be put to death."

Wherefore Liu Yang was beheaded.

As time went on the Latter Ruler indulged in unbridled sensuality, and gradually all good people left the government, giving place to the meanest, who soon swarmed there.

Among the sycophants of Huang Hao was Yan Yun, General of the Right Army, whose lack of merit had not stood in the way of preferment.

Hearing of Jiang Wei's defeats at Qishan, Yan Yun got his friend Huang Hao to propose to the Latter Ruler, saying, "Jiang Wei should be recalled as he has not been able to score a decisive victory. Yan Yun can be sent to replace him."

The Latter Ruler agreed, and the edict was issued.

One day, as Jiang Wei was working out his plan of attack on the camps of Wei, three edicts came, all to the same effect, recalling him to the capital. Disobedience being out of the question, Jiang Wei ceased all operations and sent the Taoyang force back first. Then gradually he and Zhang Yi withdrew with the others.

Deng Ai in his camp wondered at the rolling of drums one night, but next day he heard that the Shu camps were empty. However, he suspected some ruse and did not pursue.

Arrived in Hanzhong, the army halted, and Jiang Wei went on to the capital in company with the messenger who had brought his orders. Here he waited ten days, and still the Latter Ruler held no court. He began to suspect mischief.

One day near a Palace gate he met Secretary General Xi Zheng, and asked, "Do you know the reason for my recall?"

"What General! Do you not know? Huang Hao wanted to push Yan Yun into favor, so he intrigued for your recall. Now they have found out Deng Ai is too clever to be tackled, and so they are not fighting any more."

"I shall certainly have to put this eunuch fellow out of the way," said Jiang Wei.

"Hush! You are the successor of the Martial Lord, Zhuge Liang, the man to whom he bequeathed his unfinished task. You are too important to act hastily or indiscreetly. If the Emperor withdrew his support, it would go ill with you."

"Sir, what you say is true," replied Jiang Wei.

However, soon after this Jiang Wei, with a small party, got into the Palace. The Latter Ruler was enjoying himself with Huang Hao in the gardens. They told Huang Hao, who at once hid himself among the rocks by a pond.

Jiang Wei approached his master and prostrated himself, saying, "Why did Your Majesty recall me? I had the enemy in my power at Qishan when the triple edicts came."

The Latter Ruler hummed and hawed, but made no reply. Then Jiang Wei began his real grievance.

"This Huang Hao is wicked and artful and seems to have the last say in everything. The times of the Emperor Ling and the Ten Regular Attendants have returned. Your Majesty may recall Zhang Rang[xlvii] recently or Zhao Gao[xlviii] in the old time. If you will only slay this man, the court will be purified, and you may return gloriously to the home of your fathers."

The Latter Ruler smiled, saying, "Huang Hao is

but a minor servant, one who runs errands for me. If he tried to do as you say, he could not. I always wondered why Dong Yun seemed to hate poor Huang Hao so much. Now you are the same. I pray you, Noble Sir, take no notice of him."

"Unless Your Majesty gets rid of him, evil is very close," said Jiang Wei, beating his head upon the ground.

The Latter Ruler replied, "If you love anyone, you want him to live; if you dislike him, you desire his death. Can you not bear with my one poor eunuch?"

The Latter Ruler bade one of the attendants go and call Huang Hao. When Huang Hao approached the pavilion, the Latter Ruler told him to ask pardon of Jiang Wei.

Huang Hao prostrated himself and wept, saying, "I am always in attendance upon the Sacred One---that is all I do. I never meddle in state affairs. I pray you, General, pay no heed to what people say. If you desire my death, I am in your hands, but pity me."

And tears ran down his cheeks. Jiang Wei went away in ill humor. Outside he sought his friend Xi Zheng and told him what had happened.

"General, you are in grave danger," said Xi Zheng. "And if you fall, the country falls with you."

"Can you advise me?" said Jiang Wei. "How can I secure the state and myself?"

Xi Zheng replied, "There is a place of refuge for

you in the West Valley Land, and that is Tazhong. It is a rich county, and you can make a cantonment there like the Martial Lord did. Request the Emperor to let you go thither. You can gather in corn and wheat for your armies, you can secure all the west of Longyou, you can keep Wei from troubling Hanzhong, you will retain your military authority, so that no one will dare intrigue against you, and you will be safe. Thus you can ensure the safety of the state and yourself. You should lose no time."

"Your speech is gold and jewels!" said Jiang Wei, gratefully.

Without loss of time, Jiang Wei memorialized the Throne and obtained the Latter Ruler's consent. Then he returned to Hanzhong, assembled his officers, and told them his plans.

"Our many expeditions have failed to achieve success owing to lack of supplies. Now I am about to take eighty thousand troops to Tazhong to form a cantonment and grow wheat and corn ready for the next expedition. You are spent with much fighting and may now repose while collecting grain and guarding Hanzhong. The armies of Wei are from home and have to drag their grain over the mountains. They will be worn out with the labor and must soon retire. That will be the time to smite them, and success must be ours."

Hu Ji was set over Hanshou, Wang Han of Yuecheng, Jiang Bin over Hancheng, and Jiang Shu and Fu Qian went to guard the passes. After these arrangements had been made, Jiang Wei went off to Tazhong to grow grain and mature his plans.

Deng Ai heard of these dispositions and discovered that the armies of Shu were distributed in forty camps, each connected with the next like the joints of a huge serpent. He sent out his spies to survey the country, and they made a map which was sent to the capital.

But when the Duke of Jin, Sima Zhao, saw the memorial and the map, he was very angry.

"This Jiang Wei has invaded our country many times, and we have been unable to destroy him. He is the one sorrow of my heart."

Said Jia Chong, "He has carried on the work of Zhuge Liang only too thoroughly, and it is hard to force him back. What you need is some crafty brave to assassinate him, so remove this constant menace of war."

But Assistant Xun Xu said, "That is not the way. Liu Shan, the Ruler of Shu, is steeped in dissipation and has given all his confidence to one favorite, Eunuch Huang Hao. The higher officers of state are concerned solely with their own safety, and Jiang Wei has gone to Tazhong only that he may save his life. If you send an able leader and a strong army, victory is certain. Where is the need for an assassin's dagger?"

"These are excellent words," said Sima Zhao, with a laugh, "but if I would attack Shu, where is the leader?"

"Deng Ai is the ablest leader of the day," said Xun Xu. "Give him Zhong Hui as his second, and the thing is done."

"Exactly what I think!" said Sima Zhao.

So he summoned Zhong Hui and said to him, "I desire to send you as leader against Wu: Can you go?"

"My lord's design is not against Wu, but Shu," was his reply.

"How well you know my inmost thought!" said Sima Zhao. "But how would you conduct an expedition against Shu?"

"Thinking that my lord would desire to attack Shu, I have already prepared plans. Here they are."

He laid out his maps, and thereon were shown the camps, and storehouses, and roads all complete.

Sima Zhao was highly pleased.

"You are an excellent leader," said he. "What say you to going with Deng Ai?"

"The River Lands is large, and there is space for more than one set of operations. Deng Ai can be sent along another line."

Zhong Hui was given the title of General Who Conquers the West and the insignia of a Commander-in-Chief over the forces of the Land Within the Passes and control of the armies of Qingzhou, Xuzhou, Yanzhou, Yuzhou, Jingzhou, and Yangzhou. At the same time a commission with authority ensign was sent to Deng Ai giving him command of the forces beyond the pass, with the title of General Who Conquers the West. And the time for an attack on Shu was settled.

When Sima Zhao was settling the plans in the court, Deng Dun, General of the Front Army, said, "Why are you sending our armies into a distant and dangerous country and thus inviting trouble? Jiang Wei has invaded this country many times, and the wars have cost us many lives. We should rather seek safety in defense."

"I am sending a righteous army against an unrighteous ruler. How dare you oppose my designs?"

Sima Zhao ordered the executioners to put Deng Dun to death forthwith, and they soon returned to lay his head at the foot of the steps. This frightened all those present, and they turned pale.

Sima Zhao said, "It is six years since I conquered the east, and the six years have been spent in preparation. I have long intended to reduce both Wu and Shu. Now I will destroy Shu, and then like a flood I will descend upon Wu and conquer that. That is the method 'destroy Guo to capture Yu'. I can tell very nearly what forces they have in Shu. There are eighty or ninety thousand troops in the garrison of Capital Chengdu, forty or fifty thousand on the frontier, while Jiang Wei has about sixty thousand in his cantonments. Against them we can pit one hundred thousand troops beyond the pass under Deng Ai, enough to hold Jiang Wei and keep him from moving east, and Zhong Hui has two or three hundred thousand veterans within the pass. And they will march in three divisions through Luo Valley and straight into Hanzhong. Liu Shan, the Ruler of Shu, is an oblivious fool with his frontier cities in ruins, the populace and officials quaking with fear. The state will not last long."

The assembly praised this perspicacity.

Zhong Hui marched as soon as he received his seal of office. Lest his real object should be known, he gave out that his force was directed against Wu. To give color to the pretense, he had many large ships built in Qingzhou, Yanzhou, Yuzhou, Jingzhou, and Yangzhou. He also sent Tang Zi along the coastal regions of Dengzhou and Laizhou to collect vessels.

Even his chief, Sima Zhao, was deceived and called him to ask: "I commanded you to invade the Riverlands by land march. Why are you collecting ships?"

Zhong Hui replied, "If Shu hears that we intend to attack the west, they will ask assistance from Wu. So I pretend to attack Wu, and Wu will not dare to move under a year. When Shu is beaten, the ships will be ready and useful for an expedition into the east."

Sima Zhao was pleased. The day chosen for the march was the third day of the seventh month in the fourth year of Wonderful Beginning, in Wei calendar (AD 264). Sima Zhao escorted his leader out of the city for three miles and then took his leave.

Shao Ti, Minister of the Western Affairs, whispered a word of warning.

"My lord has sent Zhong Hui with a large army against Shu. I think he is too ambitious to be trusted with such powers?"

"Think you I do not know?" said Sima Zhao.

"Then why have you sent him alone and without a colleague?"

Sima Zhao said a few words to Shao Ti which put his doubts at rest.

Zhong Hui went alone, although his master knew,
Occasion serving, he would be untrue.

The next chapter will tell the reader what Shao Ti heard.

Chapter 116

On Hanzhong Roads, Zhong Hui Divides The Army;
In Dingjun Mountain, The Martial Lord Shows His Apparition.

The words whispered in the ear of Shao Ti proved Sima Zhao's subtlety.

Said Sima Zhao, "This morning the officers all maintained that Shu should not be attacked, because they are timid. If I let them lead the army, they would surely be defeated. You saw Zhong Hui was set upon his plan, and he is not afraid. Shu must therefore be beaten, and then the Shu people's hearts will be torn. Beaten leaders cannot boast, and the officers of a broken state are no fit guardians of its welfare. When Zhong Hui turns against us, the people of Shu cannot support him. Further, our troops being victors, they will wish to return home and will not follow their leader into revolt. Hence there is nothing to be feared. I know this, as you do, but it must remain our secret."

Shao Ti showed his admiration for Sima Zhao.

In his camp, just prior to his march, Zhong Hui assembled his officers, among them were Army Inspector Wei Guan, Assistant General Hu Lie, Generals Tian Xu, Tian Zhang, Yuan Xing, Qiu Jian, Xiahou Xian, Wang Mai, Huangfu Kai, Gou Ai, and others, some eighty of them.

"Firstly I want a Leader of the Van," said Zhong Hui. "He must be skilled in making roads and repairing bridges."

"I will take that post," said a voice, and the speaker was Xu Yi, son of the Tiger Leader Xu Chu.

"Nobody is fitter!" cried all present.

"You shall have the seal," said Zhong Hui. "You are lithe and strong and have the renown of your father to maintain. Beside, all your colleagues recommend you. Your force shall be five thousand of cavalry and a thousand of footmen. You are to march into Hanzhong in three divisions, the center you will lead through the Xie Valley, the other two passing through the Luo and Ziwu Valleys. You must level and repair the roads, put the bridges in order, bore tunnels and break away rocks. Use all diligence, for any delay will entail punishment."

Xu Yi was told to set out immediately, and his chief would follow with one hundred thousand troops.

In West Valley Land, as soon as Deng Ai received his orders to attack Shu, he sent Sima Wang to keep the Qiangs in check. Next he summoned Zhuge Xu, Imperial Protector of Yongzhou, Wang Qi, Governor of Tianshui, Qian Hong, Governor of Longxi, and Yang Xin, Governor of Jincheng, and soon soldiers gathered in the West Valley Land like clouds.

One night Deng Ai dreamed a dream wherein he was climbing a lofty mountain on the way into

Hanzhong. Suddenly a spring of water gushed out at his feet and boiled up with great force so that he was alarmed.

He awoke all in a sweat and did not sleep again, but sat awaiting the dawn. At daybreak he summoned his guard Shao Yuan, who was skilled in the Book of Changes, told him the dream and asked the interpretation.

Shao Yuan replied, "According to the book, 'water on a mountain' signifies the diagram Jian, whereunder we find that the southwest augurs well, but the northeast is unpropitious. Confucius said of Jian that it meant advantage in the southwest, that is, success, but the northeast spelt failure, that is, there was no road. In this expedition, General, you will overcome Shu, but you will not have a road to return."

Deng Ai listened, growing more and more sad as the interpretation of his dream was unfolded.

Just then came dispatches from Zhong Hui asking him to advance into Hanzhong together. Deng Ai at once sent Zhuge Xu with fifteen thousand troops to cut off Jiang Wei's retreat; and Wang Qi was to lead fifteen thousand troops to attack Tazhong from the left; Qian Hong was to march fifteen thousand troops to attack Tazhong from the right; and Yang Xin with fifteen thousand troops was to block Jiang Wei at Gansong. Deng Ai took command of a force to go to and fro and reinforce whatever body needed help.

Meanwhile in the camp of Zhong Hui, all the officials came out to see him depart. It was a grand sight, the gay banners shutting out the sun, breastplates and helmets glittering. The soldiers were fit and the horses in good condition. They all felicitated the leader.

All save one; for Adviser Liu Shi was silent. He smiled grimly.

Then Grand Commander Wang Xiang made his way through the crowd and said, "Do you think these two---Zhong Hui and Deng Ai---will overcome Shu?"

Said Liu Shi, sighing, "With such brave soldiers and bold leaders and their talents, they will overcome Shu certainly. Only I think neither will ever come back."

"Why do you say that?"

But Liu Shi did not reply; he only smiled. And the question was not repeated.

The armies of Wei were on the march when Jiang Wei heard of the intended attack. He at once sent up a memorial:

Your Majesty need to make defensive arrangements by commanding Zhang Yi, Left Commander of the Flying Cavalry, to guard the Yangping Pass, and Liao Hua, Right Commander of the Flying Cavalry, to guard the Yinping Bridge in Yinping. These two places are the most important points upon which depend the security of Hanzhong. Send also to engage the help of Wu. I, thy humble servant, shall gather soldiers in Tazhong ready for the march."

That year in Shu the reign-style had been changed

from Wonderful Sight, the fifth year, to Joyful Prosperity, the first year (AD 263). When the memorial of Jiang Wei came to the Latter Ruler, it found him as usual amusing himself with his favorite Huang Hao.

He read the document and said to the eunuch, "Here Jiang Wei says that the Wei armies under Deng Ai and Zhong Hui are on the way against us. What shall we do?"

"There is nothing of the sort. Jiang Wei only wants to get a name for himself, and so he says this. Your Majesty need feel no alarm, for we can find out the truth from a certain wise woman I know. She is a real prophetess. May I call her?"

The Latter Ruler consented, and a room was fitted up for the seance. They prepared therein incense, flowers, paper, candles, sacrificial articles and so on, and then Huang Hao went with a chariot to beg the wise woman to attend upon the Latter Ruler.

She came and was seated on the Dragon Couch. After the Latter Ruler had kindled the incense and repeated the prayer, the wise woman suddenly let down her hair, dropped her slippers, and capered about barefoot. After several rounds of this, she coiled herself up on a table.

Huang Hao then said, "The spirit has now descended. Send everyone away and pray to her."

So the attendants were dismissed, and the Latter Ruler entreated the wise woman.

Suddenly she cried out, "I am the guardian spirit of the West River Land. Your Majesty, rejoices in tranquillity; why do you inquire about other matters? Within a few years the land of Wei shall come under you, wherefore you need not be sorrowful."

She then fell to the ground as in a swoon, and it was some time before she revived. The Latter Ruler was well satisfied with her prophesy and gave her large presents. Further, he thereafter believed all she told him. The immediate result was that Jiang Wei's memorial remained unanswered; and as the Latter Ruler was wholly given to pleasure, it was easy for Huang Hao to intercept all urgent memorials from the commander.

Meanwhile Zhong Hui was hastening toward Hanzhong. The Van Leader Xu Yi was anxious to perform some startling exploit, and so he led his force to Nanzheng.

He said to his officers, "If we can take this pass, then we can march directly into Hanzhong. The defense is weak."

A dash was made for the fort, each one vying with the rest to be first. But the Commander of Nanzheng was Lu Xu, and he had had early information of the coming of his enemies. So on both sides of the bridge he posted soldiers armed with multiple bows and crossbows. As soon as the attacking force appeared, the signal was given by a clapper and a terrific discharge of arrows and bolts opened. Many troops of Wei fell, and the army of Xu Yi was defeated.

Xu Yi returned and reported his misfortune. Zhong Hui himself went with a hundred armored horsemen to see the conditions. Again the machine bows let fly clouds of missiles, and Zhong Hui turned to flee.

Lu Xu led out five hundred troops to pursue. As Zhong Hui crossed the bridge at a gallop, the roadway gave, and his horse's hoof went through so that he was nearly thrown. The horse could not free its hoof, and Zhong Hui slipped from his back and fled on foot. As he ran down the slope of the bridge, Lu Xu came at him with a spear, but one of Zhong Hui's followers, Xun Kai by name, shot an arrow at Lu Xu and brought him to the earth.

Seeing this lucky hit, Zhong Hui turned back and signaled to his force to make an attack. They came on with a dash, the defenders were afraid to shoot, as their own troops were mingled with the enemy, and soon Zhong Hui crushed the defense and possessed the pass. The defenders scattered.

The pass being captured, Xun Kai was well rewarded for the shot that had saved his general's life. He was promoted to Assistant General and received presents of a horse and a suit of armor.

Xu Yi was called to the tent, and Zhong Hui blamed him for the lack of care in his task, saying, "You were appointed Leader of the Van to see that the roads were put in repair, and your special duty was to see that the bridges were in good condition. Yet on the bridge just now my horse's hoof was caught, and I nearly fell. Happily Xun Kai was by, or I had been slain. You have been disobedient and must bear the penalty."

The delinquent was sentenced to death.

The other generals tried to beg him off, pleading, "His father is Xu Chu who had rendered good services to the state!"

"How can discipline be maintained if the laws are not enforced?" said Zhong Hui.

The sentence was carried out, and the unhappy Xu Yi's head was exposed as a warning. This severity put fear into the hearts of the officers.

On the side of Shu, Wang Han commanded at Yuecheng, and Jiang Bin was in Hancheng. As the enemy came in great force, they dared not go out to meet them, but stood on the defensive with the gates of the cities closed.

Zhong Hui issued an order, "Speed is the soul of war: No halts."

Li Du was ordered to lay siege to Yuecheng, and Xun Kai was to surround Hancheng. The main army under Zhong Hui would capture the Yangping Pass.

The Shu General Fu Qian commanded at the pass. He discussed plans with Jiang Shu, his second in command, and Jiang Shu was wholly in favor of defense, saying, "The enemy is too strong to think of any other course."

"I do not agree," replied Fu Qian. "They are now fatigued with marching, and we need not fear them. Unless we go out and attack, Yuecheng and Hancheng will fall."

Jiang Shu made no reply. Soon the enemy arrived, and both officers went up to the wall and looked out.

As soon as Zhong Hui saw them, he shouted, "We have here a host of one hundred thousand. If you yield, you shall have higher rank than you hold now. But if you persist in holding out then, when we take the pass, you shall all perish. Jewels and pebbles will share the same destruction!"

This threat angered Fu Qian. He bade Jiang Shu guard the walls, and he went down to give battle, taking three thousand troops. He attacked, and Zhong Hui retreated. Fu Qian pursued. But soon the army of Wei closed up their ranks and counterattacked. Fu Qian turned to retire. But when he reached his own defenses, he saw they flew the flags of Wei---the banners of Shu had gone.

"I have yielded!" cried Jiang Shu from the ramparts.

Fu Qian shouted angrily, "Ungrateful and treacherous rogue! How can you ever face the world again?"

But that did no good. Fu Qian turned to go once more into the battle. He was soon surrounded. He fought desperately, but could not win clear. His troops fell one by one, and when they were reduced to one out of ten, he cried, "Alive I have been a servant of Shu; dead I will be one of their spirits!"

Fu Qian forced his way into the thickest of the fight. Then his steed fell, and as he was grievously wounded, he put an end to his own life.

The loyalty Fu Qian showed in stressful days
Won him a thousand autumns' noble praise;
The base Jiang Shu lived on, a life disgraced,
One would prefer the death that Fu Qian faced.

With the Yangping Pass falling into the hands of Zhong Hui were great booty of grain and weapons. He feasted the army, and that night they rested in the city of Yangan. However, the night was disturbed by sounds as of people shouting, so that Zhong Hui got up and went out thinking there must be an attack. But the sounds ceased, and he returned to his couch. However, he and his army could not sleep.

Next night the same thing happened, shoutings in the southwest. As soon as day dawned scouts went out to search, but they came back to say they had gone three miles and found no sign of any Shu soldier. Zhong Hui did not feel satisfied, so he took a hundred cavalrymen and rode in the same direction to explore.

Presently they happened upon a hill of sinister aspect overhung by angry clouds, while the summit was wreathed in mist.

"What hill is that?" asked Zhong Hui, pulling up to question the guides.

"It is known as the Dingjun Mountain," was the reply. "It is where Xiahou Yuan met his death."

This did not sound cheering at all, and Zhong Hui

turned back to camp greatly depressed. Rounding the curve of a hill, he came full into a violent gust of wind and there suddenly appeared a large body of horse coming down the wind as if to attack.

The whole party galloped off panic-stricken, Zhong Hui leading the way. Many generals fell from their steeds. Yet when they arrived at the pass, not a man was missing, although there were many with bruises and cuts from the falls and many had lost helmets. Everyone had seen phantom horsemen, who did no harm when they came near, but melted away in the wind.

Zhong Hui called the surrendered General Jiang Shu and asked, "Is there any temple to any supernatural being on the Dingjun Mountain?"

"No," replied he, "there is nothing but the tomb of Zhuge Liang."

"Then this must have been a manifestation of Zhuge Liang," said Zhong Hui. "I ought to sacrifice to him."

So he prepared presents and slew an ox and offered sacrifice at the tomb, and when the sacrifice had been completed, the wind calmed, and the dark clouds dispersed. There followed a cool breeze and a gentle shower, and the sky cleared. Pleased with the evidence of the acceptance of their offerings, the sacrificial party returned to camp.

That night Zhong Hui fell asleep in his tent with his head resting on a small table. Suddenly a cool breeze began to blow, and he saw a figure approaching clad in Taoist garb, turban, feather fan, white robe of Taoist cut bound with a black girdle. The countenance of the figure was as refined as jade, the lips a deep red and the eyes clear. The figure moved with the calm serenity of a god.

"Who are you, Sir?" asked Zhong Hui, rising.

"Out of gratitude for your kindly visit this morning, I would make a communication. Though the Hans have declined and the mandate of the Eternal cannot be disobeyed, yet the people of the west, exposed to the inevitable miseries of war, are to be pitied. After you have passed the frontier, do not slay ruthlessly."

Then the figure disappeared with a flick of the sleeves of its robe, nor would it stay to answer any questions.

Zhong Hui awoke and knew that he had been dreaming, but he felt that the spirit of Zhuge Liang the Martial Lord had visited him, and he was astonished.

He issued an order that the leading division of his army should bear a white flag with six words plainly written thereon, Secure the state, comfort the people, so that all might know that no violence was to be feared. If anyone was slain wantonly, then the offender should pay with his own life. This tender care was greatly appreciated, so that the invaders were welcomed in every step. Zhong Hui soothed the people, and they suffered no injury.

Those phantom armies circling in the gleam
Moved Zhong Hui to sacrifice at Zhuge Liang's tomb;
For the Lius had Zhuge Liang wrought unto the end,
Though dead, he would the Han people still defend.

Jiang Wei at Tazhong heard of the invasion and wrote to his three generals---Zhang Yi, Liao Hua, and Dong Jue---to march against the enemy, while he prepared to repulse them if they came to his station.

Soon they came, and he went out to encounter them. Their leader was Wang Qi, Governor of Tianshui.

When near enough, Wang Qi shouted, "Our forces are numbered by millions, our generals by thousands. Two hundred thousand are marching against you, and Chengdu has already fallen. In spite of this you do not yield, wherefore it is evident you do not recognize the divine command!"

Jiang Wei cut short this tirade by galloping out with his spear set. Wang Qi stood three bouts and then fled. Jiang Wei pursued, but seven miles away he met a cohort drawn up across the road. On the banner he read Qian Hong, Governor of Longxi.

"Dead rat! No match for me," said Jiang Wei, smiling.

Despising this antagonist, he led his army straight

on, and the enemy fell back. He drove them before him for three more miles, and then came upon Deng Ai. A battle at once began, and the lust of battle held out in the breast of Jiang Wei for a score of bouts. But neither could overbear the other. Then in the Shu rear arose the clang of gongs and other signs of coming foes.

Jiang Wei retired the way he had come, and presently one came to report: "The Governor of Jincheng, Yang Xin, has destroyed the camps at Gansong."

This was evil tidings. He bade his generals keep his own standard flying and hold Deng Ai while he went to try to recover the camps. On the way he met Yang Xin, but Yang Xin had no stomach for a fight with Jiang Wei and made for the hills. Jiang Wei followed till he came to a precipice down which the enemy were hurling boulders and logs of wood so that he could not pass.

Jiang Wei turned to go back to the battlefield he had just left, but on the way he met the defeated Shu army, for Deng Ai had crushed his generals. Jiang Wei joined them but was surrounded by the Wei forces. Presently he got clear with a sudden rush and hastened to the great camp.

Next came the news: "Zhong Hui has defeated the Yangping Pass; Jiang Shu has surrendered, while Fu Qian has fallen in the field. Hanzhong is now in the possession of Wei. Wang Han of Yuecheng and Jiang Bin of Hancheng has also opened their gates and yielded to the invaders at the loss of Hanzhong. Hu Ji has gone to Chengdu for help."

This greatly troubled Jiang Wei, so he broke camp and set out for Hanzhong. That night the Shu army reached the Frontier River Pass. An army under Yang Xin barred his way, and again Jiang Wei was forced to fight. He rode out in a great rage, and as Yang Xin fled, he shot at him thrice, but his arrows missed.

Throwing aside his bow, he gripped his spear and set off in pursuit, but his horse tripped and fell, and Jiang Wei lay on the ground. Yang Xin turned to slay his enemy now that he was on foot, but Jiang Wei thrust Yang Xin's horse in the head. Other Wei troops came up rescued Yang Xin.

Mounting another steed of his follower, Jiang Wei was just setting out again in pursuit when they reported that Deng Ai was coming against his rear. Realizing that he could not cope with this new force, Jiang Wei collected his troops in order to retreat into Hanzhong.

However, the scouts reported: "Zhuge Xu, Imperial Protector of Yongzhou, is holding Yinping Bridge, our retreat path."

So Jiang Wei halted and made a camp in the mountains. Advance and retreat seemed equally impossible.

He cried in anguish, "Heaven is destroying me!"

Then said Ning Sui, one of his generals, "If our enemies are blocking Yinping Bridge, they can only have left a weak force in Yongzhou. We can make believe to be going thither through the Konghan Valley and so force them to abandon the bridge in order to protect the city. When the bridge is clear, you can make a dash for Saber Pass and plan for a recapture of Hanzhong."

This plan seemed to promise success, so Jiang Wei ordered them to march into the Konghan Valley, making as though they would go to Yongzhou.

When Zhuge Xu, who was at the Yinping Bridge, heard this, he said in great shock, "Yongzhou is my own city, and headquarters of the expedition. If it would be lost, I would be punished!"

So Zhuge Xu set off to its relief by the south road. He left only a small force at the bridge.

Jiang Wei marched along the north road for ten miles till he guessed that Zhuge Xu had abandoned the bridge, when he reversed his course, making the rearguard the van. He dispersed the small force left at the bridge head and burned their camp. Zhuge Xu, as he marched, saw the flames, and he turned back to the bridge, but he arrived too late. The army of Shu had already crossed, and he dared not pursue.

Soon after Jiang Wei crossed the bridge, he saw another force, but this was led by his own generals, Liao Hua and Zhang Yi.

They told him, "The Latter Ruler, firm in his faith in a wise woman, would not send help to defend the frontiers. We heard Hanzhong was threatened, and thus marched there to its rescue, but then Zhong Hui had taken the Yangping Pass. We also heard you were surrounded here, so we came to your help."

The two armies amalgamated and marched

together.

Liao Hua said, "We are attacked all round, and the grain transportation is blocked. It seems to me wisest to retire on the Saber Pass and plan other designs."

But Jiang Wei was doubtful. Then they heard that Deng Ai and Zhong Hui were approaching in ten divisions.

Jiang Wei was disposed to stand, but Liao Hua said, "This country of White Water is laced with by-roads and is too narrow and difficult to fight in with any hope of success. It would be better to retreat to the Saber Pass. If we loss that pass, all paths will be closed to us."

At last Jiang Wei consented, and the march began. But as they neared the pass, they heard drums rolling and saw flags fluttering, which told them that the pass was held.

Hanzhong, that strong defense, is lost;
And storm clouds gather round Saber Pass.

What force was at the pass will be told in the next chapter.

Chapter 117

Deng Ai Gets Through The Yinping Mountains; Zhuge Zhan Falls In The Battlefield Of Mianzhu.

When Dong Jue, General Who Upholds the State, heard of the invasion of Wei in ten divisions, he brought to the frontier twenty thousand troops to Saber Pass. And when the dust showed an approaching army, Dong Jue thought it wise to go to the Pass lest the coming armies should be enemies to be stopped.

But Dong Jue found that the newcomers were Jiang Wei, Liao Hua, and Zhang Yi. He let them pass through. Then he gave them the news from the capital, bad news of the deeds of both the Latter Ruler and Huang Hao. His tears fell as he told the tales.

"But do not grieve," said Jiang Wei. "So long as I live, I will not allow Wei to come and conquer Shu. Now we must defend this pass, and then evolve a strategy."

They kept good guard at Saber Pass, while they discussed future plans.

"Though we are holding this pass, yet Chengdu is well-nigh empty of soldiers," said Dong Jue. "If it was attacked, it would go crack!"

Jiang Wei replied, "The natural defenses of Chengdu are excellent: It is hard to cross over the mountains and climb the steep roads. No one needs fear."

Soon after this, Zhuge Xu appeared at the pass challenging the defenders. Jiang Wei forthwith placed himself at the head of five thousand troops and went down to meet the Wei army. He gained an easy victory, slaying many of the enemy and taking much spoil in horses and weapons.

While Jiang Wei went back to the pass, the defeated Zhuge Xu made his way to Zhong Hui's camp, seven miles away, to confess his failure. His general was very angry.

"My orders to you were to hold Yinping Bridge so as to stop Jiang Wei, and you lost it. Now without any orders you attack and are defeated."

"Jiang Wei played so many deceitful tricks. He pretended to be going to take Yongzhou, and I thought that was very important, so I sent troops to rescue it. Then he meanly got away. I followed to the pass, but never thought he would come out and defeat my troops."

Zhuge Xu pleaded thus, but he was sentenced to die.

Now Wei Guan, Army Inspector, said, "Zhuge Xu is really a subordinate of Deng Ai and, admitting that he is in fault, his punishment should not have been pronounced by you, O Commander."

But Zhong Hui swaggeringly replied, "I have a command from the Emperor and orders from the Prime Minister to attack Shu. If Deng Ai himself offended, I would behead him."

However, other leaders interceded for Zhuge Xu, and Zhong Hui did not put him to death, but sent him a caged prisoner to the capital to be judged. The surviving soldiers were added to Zhong Hui's army.

This insolent speech of Zhong Hui was duly repeated to Deng Ai, who was angry in his turn and said, "His rank and mine are the same. I have held a frontier post for years and sustained many fatigues in the country's service. Who is he that he gives himself such airs?"

His son Deng Zhong endeavored to appease his wrath.

"Father, if you cannot suffer small things, you may upset the grand policy of the state. Unfriendliness with him may do great harm, so I hope you will bear with him."

Deng Ai saw his son was right, and said no more; but he nourished anger in his heart. With a small escort he went to call upon his colleague.

When his coming was announced, Zhong Hui asked his staff, "How many soldiers are following Deng Ai?"

"He has only some twenty horsemen," they replied.

Zhong Hui had a large body of guards drawn up about his tent, and then gave orders that his visitor should be led in. Deng Ai dismounted, and the two men saluted each other. But the visitor did not like the look on the faces of his host's guards. He decided to find out what Zhong Hui was thinking.

"The capture of Hanzhong is a piece of excellent fortune for the state," said Deng Ai. "The capture of Saber Pass can now be accomplished easily."

"What is your own idea, General?" asked Zhong Hui.

Deng Ai tried to evade answering the question, admitting he had no good suggestion. But Zhong Hui pressed him to reply.

Finally he said, "In my simple opinion one might proceed by by-roads from the pass through the Yinping Mountains to Deyang in Hanzhong, and thence make a surprise march to Chengdu. Jiang Wei must go to its defense, and you, General, can take the Saber Pass."

"A very good plan," said Zhong Hui. "You may start forthwith, and I will wait here till I hear news of your success."

They drank, and Deng Ai took his leave. Zhong Hui went back to his own tent filled with contempt for Deng Ai's plan. which he thought impracticable.

"They say Deng Ai is able. I think he is of most ordinary capacity," said he to his officers.

"But why?" said they.

"Because the by-roads by Yinping Mountains are impassable, nothing but lofty cliffs and steep hills. A hundred defenders at a critical point could cut all communications, and Deng Ai's army would starve to death. I shall go by the direct road, and there is no fear about the result. I shall overcome

Shu."

So he prepared scaling ladders and stone-throwing machines and set himself to besiege Saber Pass.

Deng Ai went out to the main gate of the court. While mounting, he said to his followers, "What did Zhong Hui think of me?"

"He looked as though he held a poor opinion of what you had said, General, and disagreed with you, although his words were fair enough."

"He thinks I cannot take Chengdu. So I shall take it!"

He was received at his own camp by Shi Zuan and his son Deng Zhong, and a party of others of his generals, and they asked what the conversation had been about.

"I told Zhong Hui simple truth, but he thinks I am just a common person of no ability to speak of. He regards the capture of Hanzhong as an incomparable feat of arms. Where would he have been if I had not held up Jiang Wei at Tazhong? But I think the capture of Chengdu will beat that of Hanzhong."

That night the camp was broken up, and Deng Ai set his army out upon a long march along the mountainous paths. At twenty miles from Saber Pass they made a camp. The scouts told Zhong Hui of his movement, and Zhong Hui laughed at the attempt.

From his camp Deng Ai sent a letter to Sima Zhao.

Then he called his officers to his tent and asked them, saying, "I am going to make a dash for Chengdu while it is still undefended, and success will mean unfading glory for us all. Will you follow me?"

"We will follow you and obey your orders," cried they all.

So the final dispositions were made. Deng Zhong and three thousand troops went first to improve the road. His troops wore no armor, but they had axes and boring tools. They were to level roads and build bridges.

Next went thirty thousand troops furnished with dry grain and ropes. At every one hundred miles they were to make a post of three thousand.

In autumn of that year, they left Yinping, and in the tenth month they were in most precipitous country of the Yinping Mountains. They had taken twenty days to travel two hundred and fifty miles. They were in an uninhabited country. After garrisoning the various posts on the way, they had only two thousand soldiers left. Before them stood a range named Heaven Cliffs, which no horse could ascend. Deng Ai climbed up on foot to see his son and the troops with him opening up a road. They were exhausted with fatigue and weeping.

Deng Ai asked why they were so sad, and his son replied, "We have found an impassable precipice away to the northwest which we cannot get through. All our labor has been in vain."

Deng Ai said, "We have got over two hundred and fifty miles, and just beyond is Jiangyou. We cannot go back. How can one get tiger cubs except by going into tiger caves? Here we are, and it will be a very great feat to capture Chengdu."

They all said they would go on. So they came to the precipice. First they threw over their weapons; then the leader wrapped himself in blankets and rolled over the edge; next the generals followed him, also wrapped in blankets. Those who had not blankets were let down by cords round the waist, and others clinging to trees followed one after another till all had descended and the Heaven Cliffs was passed. Then they retook their armor and weapons and went on their way.

They came across a stone by the roadside. It bore a mysterious inscription, translated literally it read:

This stone is a message of Zhuge Liang the Prime Minister: Two fires were just founded; armies pass by here. Two soldiers compete; both soon die."[xlix]

Deng Ai was astonished. Presently he bowed before the stone and prayed to the spirit of Zhuge Liang.

"O Martial Lord, immortal! I grieve that I am not thy worthy disciple."

The rugged lofty mountain peaks
Of Yinping, pierce the sky,
The somber crane with wearied wing
Can scarcely over them fly.
Intrepid Deng Ai in blankets wrapped
Rolled down the craggy steep,
His feat Zhuge Liang prophesied
By insight wondrous deep.

Having crossed this great range of mountains without discovery, Deng Ai marched forward. Presently he came to a roomy camp, empty and deserted. He was told that while Zhuge Liang lived, a thousand troops had been kept in garrison at this point of danger, but the Latter Ruler had withdrawn them. Deng Ai sighed at the thought.

He said to his troops, "Now retreat is impossible, there is no road back. Before you lies Jiangyou with stores in abundance. Advance and you live, retreat and you die. You must fight with all your strength."

"We will fight to the death!" they cried.

The leader was now afoot, doing double marches with his two thousand troops toward Jiangyou.

The commander at Jiangyou was Ma Miao. He heard the East River Land had fallen into the hands of the enemy. Though some thing prepared for defense, yet his post had a wide area to cover and guard, and he trusted Jiang Wei would defend the Saber Pass. So he did not take his military duties very seriously, just maintaining the daily drills and then going home to his wife to cuddle up to the stove and drink.

His wife was of the Li family. When she heard of the state of things on the frontier, she said to her husband, "If there is so great danger on the borders, how is it you are so unaffected?"

"The affair is in Jiang Wei's hands and is not my concern," replied he.

"Nevertheless, you finally have to guard the capital, and that is a heavy responsibility."

"O, well! The Emperor trusts his favorite Huang Hao entirely and is sunk in vice and pleasure. Disaster is very near. If the Wei armies get here, I shall yield. It is no good taking it seriously."

"You call yourself a man! Have you such a disloyal and treacherous heart? Is it nothing to have held office and taken pay for years? How can I bear to look upon your face?"

Ma Miao was too ashamed to attempt to reply. Just then his house servants came to tell him that Deng Ai, with his two thousand troops, had found their way along some road and had already broken into the city. Ma Miao was now frightened and hastily went out to find the leader and offer his formal submission.

He went to the Town Hall and bowed on the steps, crying, "I have long desired to come over to Wei. Now I yield myself and my army and all the town."

Deng Ai accepted his surrender and incorporated

his army with his own force. He took Ma Miao into his service as guide.

Then came a servant with the news: "Lady Li has hanged herself!"

Deng Ai asked why she had done it, and Ma Miao told him. Deng Ai, admiring her rectitude, gave orders for an honorable burial. He also went in person to sacrifice. Everyone extolled her conduct.

When the Ruler of Shu had wandered from the way,
And the House of Han fell lower,
Heaven sent Deng Ai to smite the land.
Then did a woman show herself most noble,
So noble in conduct,
That no leader equaled her.

As soon as Jiangyou was taken, the posts along the road by which the army had come were withdrawn, and there was a general rendezvous at this point. This done, they marched toward Fucheng.

General Tian Xu remonstrated, saying, "We have just finished a long and perilous march and are weary and worn out. We ought to repose for a few days to recover."

Deng Ai angrily replied, "Speed is the one important matter in war. Do not encourage any discontent. I will not have it."

Tian Xu was sentenced to death. But as many officers interceded for him, he was pardoned.

The army pressed on toward Fucheng. As soon as they arrived, the officers yielded as if they thought Deng Ai had fallen from the heavens. Some took the news to the capital, and the Latter Ruler began to feel alarmed. He hastily called for Huang Hao, who at once denied the report.

"That is just false rumor. The spirits would not deceive Your Majesty," said Huang Hao.

The Latter Ruler summoned the wise woman to the Palace, but the messengers said she had gone no one knew whither.

And now urgent memorials and letters fell in from every side like a snow storm, and messengers went to and fro in constant streams. The Latter Ruler called a court to discuss the danger, but no one had any plan or suggestion to offer. The courtiers just looked blankly into each other's faces.

Finally Xi Zheng spoke out, "In this extremity Your Majesty should call in the help of the son of the Martial Lord."

This son of Zhuge Liang was named Zhuge Zhan. His mother was born of the Huang family and a daughter of Huang Chenyan. She was singularly plain and extraordinarily talented. She had studied everything, even books of strategy and magic. Zhuge Liang in Nanyang had sought to marry her because of her goodness, and she had studied with him for all their lives. She had survived her husband but a short time, and her last words to her son had been "be loyal and filial".

Zhuge Zhan had been known as a clever lad and had married a daughter of the Latter Ruler, so that he was an Imperial Son-in-Law. His father's rank, Lord of Wuxiang, had descended to him. In the fourth year of Wonderful Sight (AD 261) Zhuge Zhan received the rank of General of the Guard as well. But he had retired when Huang Hao, the eunuch, as first favorite, began to direct state affairs.

As suggested, the Latter Ruler summoned Zhuge Zhan to court, and he said, weeping, "Deng Ai has defeated Fucheng, and the capital is seriously threatened. You must think of your father and rescue me!"

"My father and I owe too much to the First Ruler's and Your Majesty's kindness for me to think any sacrifice too great to make for Your Majesty. I pray that you give me command of the troops in the capital, and I will fight a decisive battle."

So the soldiers, seventy thousand, were placed under Zhuge Zhan's command.

When he had gathered all together, he said, "Who dares be Leader of the Van?"

His son, Zhuge Shang, then nineteen, offered himself, saying, "Since my father commands the army, I volunteer to lead the van!"

Zhuge Shang had studied military books and made himself an adept in the various exercises. So he was appointed, and the army marched to find the enemy.

In the meantime the surrender general, Ma Miao,

had given Deng Ai a very complete map of the country showing the whole sixty miles of road to Chengdu. However, Deng Ai was dismayed when he saw the difficulties ahead of him.

"If they defend the hills in front, I shall fail; for if I am delayed, Jiang Wei will come up, and my army will be in great danger. The army must press on."

He called Shi Zuan and his son Deng Zhong and said, "Lead one army straight to Mianzhu to keep back any Shu soldiers sent to stop our march. I will follow as soon as I can. But hasten; for if you let the enemy forestall you, I will put you to death."

They went. Nearing Mianzhu they met the army under Zhuge Zhan. Both sides prepared for battle. The Shu armies adopted the Eight Diagrams formation and presently, after the usual triple roll of drums, Shi Zuan and Deng Zhong saw their opponents' ranks open in the center, and therefrom emerge a light carriage in which sat a figure looking exactly as Zhuge Liang used to look when he appeared on the battlefield. Everybody knew the Taoist robes and the feather fan. The standard bore his name and titles The Han Prime Minister Zhuge Liang.

The sight was too much for Deng Zhong and Shi Zuan. The cold sweat of terror poured down them, and they stammered out.

"If Zhuge Liang is still alive, that is the end of us!"

They led their army to flee. The troops of Shu came on, and the army of Wei was driven away in defeat and chased a distance of seven miles. Then the pursuers sighted Deng Ai, and they turned and retired.

When Deng Ai had camped, he called the two leaders before him and reproached them for retreating without fighting.

"We saw Zhuge Liang leading the enemy," said Deng Zhong, "So we ran away."

"Why should we fear, even if they bring Zhuge Liang to life again? You ran away without cause, and we have lost. You ought both to be put to death."

However, they did not die, for their fellows pleaded for them, and Deng Ai's wrath was mollified.

Then the scouts came in to say: "The leader of the army is a son of Zhuge Liang, Zhuge Zhan. The Van Leader is Zhuge Zhang's son, Zhuge Shang. They had set up on the carriage the old wooden image of the late strategist."

Deng Ai, however, said to Deng Zhong and Shi Zuan, "This is the critical stage. If you lose the next battle, you will certainly lose your lives with it!"

At the head of ten thousand troops, they went out to battle once more. This time they met the vanguard led by Zhuge Shang, who rode out alone, boldly offering to repulse the leaders of Wei. At Zhuge Zhan's signal the two wings advanced and threw themselves against the Wei line. The center portion of the Wei line met them, and the battle went to and fro many times, till at length the force of Wei, after great losses, had to give way. Both Deng Zhong and Shi Zuan being badly wounded, they fled and the army of Shu pursued and drove the invaders into their camp.

Shi Zuan and Deng Zhong had to acknowledge a new defeat, but, when Deng Ai saw both were severely wounded, he forbore to blame them or decree any penalty.

To his officers Deng Ai said, "This Zhuge Zhan well continues the paternal tradition. Twice they have beaten us and slain great numbers. We must defeat them, and that quickly, or we are lost."

Then Military Inspector Qiu Ben said, "Why not persuade their leader with a letter?"

Deng Ai agreed and wrote a letter, which he sent by the hand of a messenger. The warden of the Shu camp gate led the messenger in to see Zhuge Zhan, who opened the letter and read:

"Deng Ai, General Who Conquers the West, writes to Zhuge Zhan, General of the Guard and Leader of the army in the field.

"Now having carefully observed all the talents of the time, I see not one of them is equal to your most honored father. From the moment of his emergence from his retreat, he said that the country was to be in tripod division. He conquered Jingzhou and Yizhou and Hanzhong and thus established a position. Few have been his equal in all history. He made six expeditions from Qishan, and, if he failed, it was not that he lacked skill---it was the will of Heaven.

"But now this Latter Ruler is dull and weak, and his kingly aura is already exhausted. I have a command from the Son of Heaven to smite Shu with severity, and I already possess the land. Your capital must quickly fall. Why then do you not bow to the will of Heaven and fall in with the desires of people by acting rightly and coming over to our side? I will obtain the rank of Prince of Langye for you, whereby your ancestors will be rendered illustrious. These are no vain words if happily you will consider them."

The letter made Zhuge Zhan furiously angry. He tore it to fragments and ordered the bearer thereof to be put to death immediately. He also ordered the escort to bear the head of the messenger to the camp of Wei and lay it before Deng Ai.

Deng Ai was very angry at this insult and wished to go forth at once to battle. But Qiu Ben dissuaded him.

"Do not go out to battle," said he. "Rather overcome him by some unexpected stroke."

So Deng Ai laid his plans. He sent Wang Qi, Governor of Tianshui, and Qian Hong, Governor of Longxi, to lie in wait in the rear while he led the main body.

Zhuge Zhan happened to be close at hand seeking battle. When he heard the enemy was near, he led out his army eagerly and rushed into the midst of the invaders. Then Deng Ai fled as though worsted, so luring on Zhuge Zhan. But when the pursuit had lasted some time, the pursuers were attacked by those who lay in wait, and the Shu troops were defeated. They ran away into

Mianzhu.

Therefore Deng Ai besieged Mianzhu, and the troops of Wei shouted about the city and watched the ramparts, thus keeping the defenders close shut in as if held in an iron barrel.

Zhuge Zhan was desperate, seeing no way of escape without help from outside. Wherefore he wrote a letter to East Wu begging for assistance, and he gave this letter to Peng He to bear through the besiegers.

Peng He fought his way through and reached Wu, where he saw the Ruler of Wu, Sun Xiu. And he presented the letter showing the wretched plight of Zhuge Zhan and his urgent need.

Then the Ruler of Wu assembled his officers and said to them, "The land of Shu being in danger, I cannot sit and look on unconcerned."

He therefore decided to send fifty thousand troops, over whom he set the Veteran General Ding Feng, with two able assistants---Sun Yin and Ding Fung. Having received his edict, Ding Feng sent away his commanders with twenty thousand troops to Mianzhu, and he himself went with thirty thousand troops toward Shouchun. The army marched in three divisions.

In the city of Mianzhu, Zhuge Zhan waited for the rescue which never came.

Weary of the hopeless delay, he said to his generals, "This long defense is useless. I will fight!"

Leaving his son Zhuge Shang and Chair of the Secretariat Zhang Zun---Zhang Fei's grandson---in the city, Zhuge Zhan put on his armor and led out three thousand troops through three gates to fight in the open. Seeing the defenders making a sortie, Deng Ai drew off and Zhuge Zhan pursued him vigorously, thinking Deng Ai really fled before his force. But there was an ambush, and falling therein he was quickly surrounded as is the kernel of a nut by the shell. In vain he thrust right and shoved left, he only lost his troops in the raining arrows and bolts. The troops of Wei poured in more flights of arrows, so that his army were all shattered. Before long, Zhuge Zhan was wounded and fell.

"I am done," cried he. "But in my death I will do my duty!" He drew his sword and slew himself.

From the city walls his son Zhuge Shang saw the death of his father. Girding on his armor he made to go out to fight.

But Zhang Zun told him, "Young general, do not go out immediately!"

Cried Zhuge Shang, "My father and I and all our family have received favors from the state. My father has died in battle against our enemies, and can I live?"

He whipped his horse and dashed out into the thick of the fight, where he died. A poem has been written extolling the conduct of both father and son.

In skill he was found wanting, not in loyalty,
But the Lord's word had gone forth,
That the Ruler of Shu was to be cut off,
Noble were Zhuge Liang's descendants.

In commiseration of their loyalty, Deng Ai had both father and son buried fittingly. Then he began attacking the city vigorously. Zhang Zun, Huang Chong, and Li Qiu, the defenders, however, held the city desperately, but to no avail for their numbers being small, and the three leaders were slain. This was the end of the defense, and Deng Ai then entered as conqueror. Having rewarded his army, he set out for Chengdu.

The closing days of the Latter Ruler were
As had been those of Liu Zhang.

The next chapter will tell of the defense of Chengdu.

Chapter 118

Weeping At The Ancestral Temple, A Filial Prince Dies;
Marching To The West River Land, Two Leaders Competes.

The news of the fall of Mianzhu and the deaths in battle of Zhuge Zhan and Zhuge Shang, father and son, brought home to the Latter Ruler that danger was very near, and he summoned a council.

Then the officials said, "Panic has seized upon the people, and they are leaving the city in crowds. Their cries shake the very sky!"

Sorely he felt his helplessness. Soon they reported the enemy were actually near the city, and many courtiers advised flight.

"We do not have enough troops to protect the capital. Leave the city and flee south to the seven counties of Nanzhong," said they. "The country is difficult and easily defended. We can get the Mangs to come and help us."

But Minister Qiao Zhou opposed, saying, "No, no, that will not do. The Mangs are old rebels. To go to them would be a calamity."

Then some proposed seeking refuge in Wu: "The people of Wu are our sworn allies, and this is a moment of extreme danger. Let us go thither."

But Qiao Zhou also opposed this, saying, "In the

whole course of past ages no emperor has ever gone to another state. So far as I can see, Wei will presently absorb Wu, and certainly Wu will never overcome Wei. Imagine the disgrace of becoming a minister of Wu and then having to style yourself minister of Wei. It would double the mortification. Do neither. Surrender to Wei, and Wei will give Your Majesty a strip of land where the ancestral temple can be preserved, and the people will be saved from suffering. I desire Your Majesty to reflect well upon this."

The distracted Latter Ruler retired from the council without having come to any decision. Next day confusion had become still worse. Qiao Zhou saw that matters were very urgent and presented a written memorial. The Latter Ruler accepted it and decided to yield.

But from behind a screen stepped out the fifth of the Emperor's sons, Liu Chan, Prince of Beidi.

Liu Chan shouted at Qiao Zhou, "You corrupt pedant, unfit to live among people! How dare you offer such mad advice in a matter concerning the existence of a dynasty? Has any emperor ever yielded to the enemy?"

The Latter Ruler had seven sons in all---Liu Rui, Liu Dao, Liu Zhong, Liu Zan, Liu Chan, Liu Xue, and Liu Ju. But the ablest, and the only one above the common level of people, was this Liu Chan.

The Latter Ruler turned feebly to his son and said, "The ministers have decided otherwise: They advise surrender. You are the only one who thinks that boldness may avail, and would you drench the city in blood?"

The Prince said, "While the First Ruler lived, this Qiao Zhou had no voice in state affairs. Now he gives this wild advice and talks the most subversive language. There is no reason at all in what he says, for we have in the city many legions of soldiers, and Jiang Wei is undefeated in Saber Pass. He will come to our rescue as soon as he knows our straits, and we can help him to fight. We shall surely succeed. Why listen to the words of this dryasdust? Why abandon thus lightly the work of our great forerunner?"

The Latter Ruler became angry at this harangue and turned to his son, saying, "Be silent! You are too young to understand Heaven's will!"

Liu Chan beat his head upon the ground and implored his father to make an effort.

"If we have done our best and defeat yet comes, if parents and children, lords and ministers have set their backs to the wall and died in one final effort to preserve the dynasty, then in the shades of the Nine Golden Springs we shall be able to look the First Ruler in the face, unashamed. But what if we surrender?"

The appeal left the Latter Ruler unmoved.

The Prince cried, "Is it not shameful in one day to throw down all that our ancestors built up with so great labor? I would rather die."

The Latter Ruler, now very angry, bade the courtiers thrust the young man out of the Palace. Then he ordered Qiao Zhou to prepare the formal Act of Surrender. After it had been written, three officers---Adviser Zhang Shao, Imperial Son-in-

Law Commander Deng Liang, and Minister Qiao Zhou---were sent with it and the Hereditary Seal to the camp of Deng Ai to offer submission.

Every day Deng Ai's horsemen rode to the city to see what was afoot. It was a glad day when they returned reporting the hoisting of the flag of surrender. The general had not long to wait. The three messengers soon arrived and presented the letter announcing surrender and the seal therewith. Deng Ai read the letter with great exultation, and took possession of the seal. He treated the envoys courteously, and by their hands sent back a letter to allay any anxiety among the people. In due time they reentered the city and bore this missive to the Latter Ruler, and they told him they had been treated well. The Latter Ruler read the letter with much satisfaction. Then he sent Minister Jiang Xian to order Jiang Wei to surrender.

Then Li Hu, Chair of the Secretariat, carried to the victorious Deng Ai the statistical documents of the resources of the kingdom:

2,800,000 households, 9,140,000 souls, 102,000 active armed soldiers of all ranks, and 40,000 civil employees. Besides, there were granaries with 4,000,000 carts of grain, treasuries with 3,000 pounds of gold and silver and 200,000 rolls of silks of many qualities, and many unenumerated but precious things in the various storehouses.

Li Hu arranged that the ceremony of surrender should take place on the first day of the twelfth month.

The wrath of Prince Liu Chan swelled high as heaven when he heard that his father had actually arranged the date of his abdication.

Girding on his sword, he was setting out for the Palace when his Consort, Lady Cui, stopped him, saying, "My Prince, why does your face bear this look of terrible anger?"

He replied, "The army of Wei is at the gates, and my father has made his Act of Surrender. Tomorrow he and all his ministers are going out of the city to submit formally, and the dynasty will end. But rather than bow the knee to another, I will die and go into the presence of the First Ruler in the realms below."

"How worthy; how worthy!" replied she. "And if my lord must die, I, thy handmaid, prays that she may die first. Then may my Prince depart."

"But why should you die?"

"The Prince dies for his father and the handmaid for her husband. One eternal principle guides us all."

Thereupon she dashed herself against a pillar, and so she died. Then Liu Chan slew his three sons and cut off the head of his Consort that he might sever all ties to life lest he be tempted to live. Bearing the head of the princess in his hand, he went to the Temple of the First Ruler, where he bowed his head, saying, "Thy servant is ashamed at seeing the kingdom pass to another. Therefore has he slain his Consort and his sons that nothing should induce him to live and forego death."

This announcement recited, he made yet another to his ancestors.

"My ancestors, if you have spiritual intelligence, you know the feelings of your descendant."

Then he wept sore till his eyes ran blood, and he committed suicide. The people of Shu grieved deeply for him, and a poet has praised his noble deed.

Both king and courtiers, willing, bowed the knee,
One son alone was grieved and would not live.
The western kingdom fell to rise no more,
A noble prince stood forth, for aye renowned
As one who died to save his forbears' shame.
With grievous mien and falling tears he bowed
His head, declaring his intent to die.
While such a memory lingers none may say
That the Han Dynasty has perished.

When the Latter Ruler knew of the death of his son, he sent people to bury him.

Soon the main body of the Wei army came. The Latter Ruler and all his courtiers to the number of sixty went out three miles from the north gate to bow their heads in submission, the Latter Ruler binding himself with cord and taking a coffin with him.

But Deng Ai with his own hands loosened the bonds and raised the Latter Ruler from the ground. The coffin was burned. Then the victorious leader and the vanquished Emperor returned into the city side by side.

Wei's legions entered Shu,
And the ruler thereof saved his life
At the price of his honor and his throne.
Huang Hao's vicious counsels had brought disaster
Against which Jiang Wei's efforts were vain.
How bright shone the loyalty of the faithful one!
How noble was the grandson of the First Ruler!
Alas! It led him into the way of sorrow.
And the plans of the First Ruler,
Excellent and far-reaching.
Whereby he laid the foundations of a mighty state,
Were brought to nought in one day.

The common people rejoiced at the magnanimity of Deng Ai, and met the returning cavalcade with burning incense and flowers. The title of General of the Flying Cavalry was given to the Latter Ruler and other ranks were given to the ministers who had surrendered.

Deng Ai requested the Latter Ruler to issue one more proclamation from the Palace to reassure the people, and then the conquerors took formal possession of the state and its granaries and storehouses. Two officers---Governor of Yizhou Zhang Shao and Minister Zhang Jung---were sent into the counties and territories to explain the new situation and pacify malcontents, and another messenger was sent to exhort Jiang Wei to yield peaceably. A report of the success was sent to Capital Luoyang.

Huang Hao, the eunuch whose evil counsels had

wrought such ruin to his master, was looked upon as a danger, and Deng Ai decided to put him to death. However, Huang Hao was rich, and he gave bribes to Deng Ai's people, and so he escaped the death penalty.

Thus perished the House of Han. Reflecting on its end a poet recalled the exploits of Zhuge Liang the Martial Lord, and he wrote a poem.

The denizens of tree-tops, apes and birds,
Most lawless of crested things, yet knew
And feared his mordant pen. The clouds and winds
Conspired to aid him to defend his lord.
But nought awaited the leader's precepts, wise
To save; with base content the erstwhile king
Too soon surrendered, yielding all but life.
In gifts Zhuge Liang was peer with
Guan Zhong and Yue Yi,
His hapless death compared with
Zhang Fei's and Guan Yu's;
Sad sight, his temple on the river's brink!
It wrings the heart more than the tearful verse
Of the Liangfu songs he most loved.

In due time Minister Jiang Xian reached the Saber Pass, and gave Jiang Wei the Latter Ruler's command to surrender to the invaders. Jiang Wei was dumb with amazement at the order; his officers ground their teeth with rage and mortification. Their hair stood on end with anger; they drew their swords and slashed at stones in their wrath.

Shouted they, "While we are fighting to our death, the Latter Ruler has yielded!"

The roar of their angry lamentation was heard for miles.

But Jiang Wei soothed them with kindly words, saying, "Generals, grieve not. Even yet I can restore the House of Han!"

"How?" cried they.

And he whispered low in their ears.

The flag of surrender fluttered over the ramparts of Saber Pass, and a messenger went to Zhong Hui's camp. When Jiang Wei and his generals drew near, Zhong Hui went out to meet them.

"Why have you been so long in coming?" said Zhong Hui.

Jiang Wei looked him straight in the face and said, without a tremor, but through falling tears, "The whole armies of the state are under me, and I am here far too soon!"

Zhong Hui wondered about this firm remark, and said nothing more. The two saluted each other and took their seats, Jiang Wei being placed in the seat of honor.

Jiang Wei said, "I hear that every detail of your plans, from the time you left the South of River Huai till now, has been accomplished. The good fortune of the Sima family is owing to you, and so I am the more content to bow my head and yield to you. Had it been Deng Ai, I should have fought to the death, for I would not have surrendered to him!"

Then Zhong Hui broke an arrow in twain, and they two swore close brotherhood. Their friendship became close-knit. Jiang Wei was continued in command of his own army, at which he secretly rejoiced. He sent Jiang Xian back to Chengdu.

As conqueror, Deng Ai arranged for the administration of the newly-gained territory. He made Shi Zuan Imperial Protector of Yizhou and appointed Qian Hong, Yang Xin, and many others to various posts. He also built a tower in Mianzhu in commemoration of his conquest.

At a great banquet, where most of the guests were people of the newly-conquered land, Deng Ai drank too freely and in his cups became garrulous.

With a patronizing wave of his hand, he said to his guests, "You are lucky in that you have had to do with me. Things might well have been otherwise, and you might all have been put to death, if you surrender to other leader!"

The guests rose in a body and expressed their gratitude. Just at that moment Jiang Xian arrived from his visit to Jiang Wei to say that Jiang Wei and his army had surrendered to Zhong Hui. Deng Ai thereupon conceived a great hatred for Zhong Hui, and soon after he wrote to Luoyang a letter something like this:

"I would venture to remark that misleading rumors of war should precede actual attack. Now that Shu has been overcome, the manifest next move is against Wu, and in present circumstances victory would easily follow an attack. But after a great effort, both leaders and led are weary and unfit for immediate service. Therefore of this army twenty thousand Wei troops should be left west of Longyou, and with them twenty thousand Shu troops, to be employed in boiling salt so as to improve the finances. Moreover, ships should be built ready for an expedition down the river. When these preparations shall be complete, then send an envoy into Wu to lay before its ruler the truth about its position. It is possible that matters may be settled without any fighting.

"Further, generous treatment of Liu Shan will tend to weaken Sun Xiu; but if Liu Shan be removed to Luoyang, the people of Wu will be perplexed and doubtful about what may happen to them, and they will not be amenable. Therefore it seems the most fitting to leave the late Ruler of Shu here. Next year, in the winter season, he might be removed to the capital. For the present I would recommend that he be created Prince of Fufeng, and granted a sufficient revenue and suitable attendants. His sons also should receive ducal rank. In this way would be demonstrated that favorable treatment follows upon submission. Such a course would inspire fear of the might of Wei and respect for its virtue, and the result will be all that could be desired."

Reading this memorial, the thought entered the mind of Sima Zhao that Deng Ai was exaggerating his own importance, wherefore he first wrote a private letter and sent it by the hand of Wei Guan to Deng Ai and then caused the Ruler of Wei to issue an edict promoting Deng Ai. The edict ran thus:

"General Deng Ai has performed a glorious exploit, penetrating deeply into a hostile country and reducing to submission a usurping potentate. This task has been quickly performed: The clouds of war have already rolled away, and peace reigns throughout Ba and Shu.

"The merits of Deng Ai surpass those of Bai Qi[l], who subdued the mighty state of Chu, and Han Xin[li], who conquered the state of Zhao. Deng Ai is created Grand Commander, and we confer upon him a fief of twenty thousand homesteads, and his two sons are ennobled, each with a fief of one thousand homesteads."

After the edict had been received with full ceremonies, Wei Guan produced the private letter, which said that Deng Ai's proposals would have suitable consideration in due time.

Then said Deng Ai, "A general in the field may decline to obey even the orders of his prince. My commission was to conquer the west. Why are my plans hindered?"

So he wrote a reply and sent it to the capital by the hand of the envoy. At that time it was common talk at court that Deng Ai intended to rebel; and when Sima Zhao read the letter, his suspicions turned to certainty, and he feared. This was the letter:

"Deng Ai, General Who Conquers the West, has reduced the chief of the revolt to submission, and must have authority to act according as he sees best in order to settle the early stages of administration of the new territory. To await government orders for every step means long delays. According to the Spring and Autumn Annals a high officer, when abroad, has authority to follow his own judgment for the safety of the Throne and the advantage of the state.

"Now seeing that Wu is still unsubdued, all interest centers upon this country, and schemes of settlement should not be nullified by strict adherence to rules and formalities. In war advances are made without thought of reputation, retreats without consideration of avoiding punishment. Though I do not possess the fortitude of the ancients, I shall not be deterred from acting for the benefit of the state by craven and selfish fears for my own reputation."

In his perplexity Sima Zhao turned to Jia Chong for advice.

Said he, "Deng Ai presumes upon his services to be haughty and imperious. His recalcitrance is very evident. What shall I do?"

"Why not order Zhong Hui to reduce him to obedience?" replied Jia Chong.

Sima Zhao accepted the suggestion and issued an edict raising Zhong Hui to Minister of the Interior. After this he made Wei Guan the Inspector of the Forces and set Wei Guan over both armies, with special orders to keep a watch upon Deng Ai and guard against any attempt at insubordination.

The edict sent to Zhong Hui ran as follows:

"Zhong Hui, General Who Conquers the West,

against whose might none can stand, before whom no one is strong, whose virtue conquers every city, whose wide net no one escapes, to whom the valiant army of Shu humbly submitted, whose plans never fail, whose every undertaking succeeds, is hereby made Minister of the Interior and raised to the rank of lordship of a fief of ten thousand families. His two sons also have similar rank with a fief of one thousand families."

When this edict reached Zhong Hui, he called in Jiang Wei and said to him, "Deng Ai has been rewarded more richly than I and is a Grand Commander. But Sima Zhao suspects him of rebellion and has ordered Wei Guan and myself to keep him in order. What does my friend Jiang Wei think ought to be done?"

Jiang Wei replied, "They say Deng Ai's origin was ignoble and in his youth he was a farmer and breeder of cattle. However, he had good luck and has won a great reputation in this expedition. But this is due not to his able plans, but to the good fortune of the state. If you had not been compelled to hold me in check at Saber Pass, he could not have succeeded. Now he wishes the late Ruler of Shu to be created Prince of Fufeng, whereby he hopes to win the goodwill of the people of Shu. But to me it seems that perfidy lies therein. The Duke of Jin suspects him, it is evident."

Zhong Hui complimented him. Jiang Wei continued, "If you will send away your people, I have something to say to you in private."

When this had been done and they two were alone, Jiang Wei drew a map from his sleeve and spread it before Zhong Hui, saying, "Long ago, before he had left his humble cot. Zhuge Liang gave this to the First Ruler and told him of the riches of Yizhou and how well it was fitted for an independent state. Whereupon Chengdu was seized as a first step towards attaining it. Now that Deng Ai has got to the same point, it is small wonder that he has lost his balance."

Zhong Hui asked many questions about the details of the features of the map, and Jiang Wei explained in full. Toward the end, he asked how Deng Ai could be got rid of.

"By making use of the Duke of Jin's suspicions," replied Jiang Wei. "Send up a memorial to say that it looks as if Deng Ai really contemplated rebellion. You will receive direct orders to check the revolt."

So a memorial was sent to Luoyang. It said that Deng Ai aimed at independence, nourished base designs, was making friends with the vanquished, and was about to revolt.

At this news the court was much disturbed. Then to support his charges, Zhong Hui's soldiers intercepted Deng Ai's letters and rewrote them in arrogant and rebellious terms. Sima Zhao was greatly angered and sent Jia Chong to lead an expedition into the Xie Valley, he ordered Zhong Hui to arrest Deng Ai, and he himself directing a great march under the leadership of the Ruler of Wei, Cao Huang, whom he compelled to go with him.

Then said Shao Ti, "Zhong Hui's army outnumbers that of Deng Ai by six to one. You need not go.

You need only order Zhong Hui to arrest Deng Ai."

"Have you forgotten?" said Sima Zhao, smiling. "You said Zhong Hui was a danger. I am not really going against Deng Ai, but against the other."

"I feared lest you had forgotten," said Shao Ti. "I ventured to remind you, but the matter must be kept secret."

The expedition set out.

By this time Zhong Hui's attitude had aroused Jia Chong's suspicions, and he spoke of it to Sima Zhao, who replied, "I have sent you: Should I have doubts about you, too? However, come to Changan and things will clear up."

The dispatch of the army under Sima Zhao was reported to Zhong Hui, who wondered what it might mean. He at once called in Jiang Wei to consult about the seizure of Deng Ai.

Lo! He is victor here, a king must yield;
And there a threatening army takes the field.

The next chapter will relate the plan to arrest Deng Ai.

Chapter 119

The False Surrender: A Wit Scheme Becomes A Vain Plan;
The Abdication: Later Seeds Learns From The Ancient.

Asked to say what was the best plan to secure the arrest of Deng Ai, Jiang Wei said, "Send Wei Guan. If Deng Ai tries to kill Wei Guan, he will manifest the desire of his heart. Then you can destroy him as a traitor."

Hence Wei Guan was sent, with some thirty men, to effect the arrest.

Wei Guan's own people saw the danger of the enterprise and urged him not to go, saying, "Zhong Hui clearly wants Deng Ai to kill you to prove his point!"

But Wei Guan said, "Do not worry. I have a scheme prepared."

Wei Guan first wrote a score or two of letters, all in the same terms, saying:

"Wei Guan has orders to arrest Deng Ai, but no other persons will be dealt with providing they submit quickly. Rewards await those who obey the Imperial Command. However, the punishment for laggards and those who are contumacious will be death to the whole family."

Wei Guan sent these letters to various officers who were serving under Deng Ai. He also prepared two cage carts.

Wei Guan and his small party reached Chengdu about cockcrow and found waiting for him most of the officers to whom he had written. They at once yielded. Deng Ai was still asleep when the party reached his palace, but Wei Guan entered and forced his way into Deng Ai's chamber.

He roared out: "I serve the Son of Heaven's command to arrest Deng Ai and his son!"

The noise awakened the sleeper, who tumbled off his couch in alarm. But before Deng Ai could do anything to defend himself, he was seized, securely bound, and huddled into one of the carts. Deng Ai's son, Deng Zhong, rushed in at the noise, but was also made prisoner and thrust into the other cart. Many generals and attendants in the Palace want to attempt a rescue, but before they had prepared, they saw dust arose outside, and Zhong Hui with an army was close at hand, thus they scattered.

Zhong Hui and Jiang Wei dismounted at the Palace gates and entered.

Zhong Hui, seeing both the Dengs prisoners, struck the elder about the head and face with his whip and insulted him, saying, "Vile cattle breeder! How dare you have your own scheme?"

Nor was Jiang Wei backward. "You fool! See what your good luck has brought you today!" cried he.

And Deng Ai replied in kind. Zhong Hui at once

sent off both the prisoners to Luoyang, and then entered Chengdu in state. He added all Deng Ai's army to his own forces, so that he became very formidable.

"Today I have attained the one desire of my life!" cried Zhong Hui.

Jiang Wei replied, "At the beginning of Han, Han Xin hearkened not to Kuai Tong to establish his own kingdom, and so blundered into trouble at the Weiyang Palace, where he met his fate[lii]. In Yue, High Minister Wen Zhong would not follow Fan Li into retirement on the lakes, and so fell victim to a sword[liii]. No one would say these two---Han Xin and Wen Zhong---were not brilliant, but they did not scent danger early enough. Now, Sir, your merit is great and your prestige overwhelming that of your prince, but why do you risk future dangers? Why not sail off in a boat leaving no trace of your going? Why not go to Emei Mountain[liv] and wander free with Master Red Pine?"

Zhong Hui smiled.

"I do not think your advice much to the point. I am a young man, not forty yet, and think rather of going on than halting. I could not take up a do-nothing hermit's life."

"If you do not, then take heed and prepare for dangers. Think out a careful course, as you are well able to do. You need not trouble any old fool for advice."

Zhong Hui laughed loud and rubbed his hands together with glee.

"How well you know my thoughts, my friend!" said Zhong Hui.

They two became absorbed in the plans for their grand scheme.

But Jiang Wei wrote a secret letter to the Latter Ruler, saying:

"I pray Your Majesty be patient and put up with humiliations for a season, for Jiang Wei, your humble servant, will have the country restored in good time. The sun and moon are all the more glorious when they burst through the dark clouds. The House of Han is not yet done."

While Zhong Hui and Jiang Wei were planning how best to outwit each other, but both being against Wei, there suddenly arrived a letter from Sima Zhao:

"I am at Changan with an army lest there should be any difficulty in disposing of Deng Ai. I need you to come to discuss state affairs."

Zhong Hui divined the real purport at once.

"He suspects," said Zhong Hui. "He knows quite well that my army outnumbers that of Deng Ai many times and I could do what he wishes easily. There is more than that in his coming."

He consulted Jiang Wei, who said, "When the prince suspects a minister, that minister dies. Have we not seen Deng Ai?"

"This decides me," replied Zhong Hui. "Success, and the empire is mine; failure, and I go west into

Shu to be another Liu Bei, but without his mistakes."

Jiang Wei said, "Empress Guo of Wei has just died. You can pretend she left you a command to destroy Sima Zhao, the real murderer of the Emperor. Your talents are quite sufficient to conquer the empire."

"Will you lead the van?" said Zhong Hui. "When success is ours, we will share the spoil."

"The little I can do, I will do most willingly," said Jiang Wei. "But I am not sure of the support of all our subordinates."

"Tomorrow is the fifteenth day of the month, a Feast of Lanterns will be held. We can gather in the Palace for the congratulations. There will be grand illuminations, and we will prepare a banquet for the officers, whereat we can kill all those who will not follow us."

At this, the heart of Jiang Wei leapt with joy. Invitations were sent out in the joint names of the two conspirators, and the feast began. After several courses, suddenly Zhong Hui lifted his cup and broke into wailing.

Everyone asked what was the cause of this grief, and Zhong Hui replied. "The Empress has just died, but before her death she gave me an edict, which is here, recounting the crimes of Sima Zhao and charging him with aiming at the Throne. I am commissioned to destroy him, and you all must join me in the task."

The guests stared at each other in amazement, but

no one uttered a word.

Then the host suddenly drew his sword, crying, "Here is death for those who oppose!"

Not one was bold enough to refuse, and, one by one, they all signed a promise to help. As further security, they were all kept prisoners in the Palace under careful guard.

"They are not really with us," said Jiang Wei. "I venture to request you to bury them all."

"A great pit has been already dug," replied his brother host. "And I have a lot of clubs ready. We can easily club those who disagree and bury them in the pit."

As Jiang Wei and Zhong Hui discussed the matter, General Qiu Jian, a man in the confidence of Zhong Hui, was present. He had once served under Assistant General Hu Lie, who was one of the imprisoned guests, and thus he found means to warn his former chief.

Hu Lie wept and said, "My son, Hu Yuan, is in command of a force outside the city. He will never suspect Zhong Hui capable of such a crime, and I pray you tell him. If I am to die, it will be with less regret if my son can be told."

"Kind master, have no anxiety; only leave it to me," replied Qiu Jian.

He went to Zhong Hui, and said, "Sir, you are holding in captivity a large number of officers, and they are suffering from lack of food and water. Will you not appoint an officer to supply their needs?"

Zhong Hui was accustomed to yield to the wishes of Qiu Jian, and he made no difficulty about this. He told Qiu Jian to see to it himself, only saying, "I am placing great trust in you, and you must be loyal. Our secret must be kept."

"My lord, you may be quite content. I know how to keep a strict watch when necessary."

And Qiu Jian allowed to enter into the place of confinement a trusty confidant of Hu Lie, who gave him a letter to his son Hu Yuan.

When Hu Yuan knew the whole story, he was astonished and told his subordinates, and they were greatly enraged.

They came to their commander's tent to say: "We would rather die than follow a rebel!"

So Hu Yuan fixed upon the eighteenth day of the month to attempt the rescue. He enlisted the sympathy of Wei Guan and got his army ready. He bade Qiu Jian tell his father what was afoot. Hu Lie then told his fellow-captives.

One day Zhong Hui said to Jiang Wei, "Last night I dreamed a dream, that I was bitten by many serpents. Can you expound the vision?"

Jiang Wei replied, "Dreams of dragons and snakes and scaly creatures are exceedingly auspicious."

Zhong Hui was only too ready to accept this interpretation. Then he told Jiang Wei that all was ready and they would put the crucial question to each captive.

"I know they are opposed to us, and you would do well to slay them all, and that right quickly," replied Jiang Wei.

"Good," replied Zhong Hui.

He bade Jiang Wei with several ruffians kill the Wei leaders among the captives. But just as Jiang Wei was starting to carry out these instructions, he was seized with a sudden spasm of the heart, so severe that he fainted. He was raised from the earth and in time revived. Just as he came to, a tremendous hubbub arose outside the Palace. Zhong Hui at once sent to inquire what was afoot, but the noise waxed louder and louder, sounding like the rush of a multitude.

"The officers must be raging," said Zhong Hui. "We would best slay them at once!"

But they told him: "The outside soldiers are in the Palace!"

Zhong Hui bade them close the doors of the Hall of Audience, and he sent his own troops upon the roof to pelt the incoming soldiers with tiles. Many were slain on either side in the melee. Then a fire broke out. The assailants broke open the doors. Zhong Hui faced them and slew a few, but others shot at him with flights of arrows, and he fell and died. They hacked off his head.

Jiang Wei ran to and fro slaying all he met till another heart spasm seized him.

"Failed!" he shrieked, "But it is the will of Heaven!"

He put an end to his own life. He was fifty-nine.

Many hundreds were slain within the Forbidden City. Wei Guan presently ordered that the soldiers were to be led back to their various camps to await the orders of the Duke of Jin.

The soldiers of Wei, burning for revenge of his many invasions, hacked the dead body of Jiang Wei to pieces. They found his gall bladder extraordinarily large, as large as a hen's egg. They also seized and slew all the family of the dead leader.

Seeing that Deng Ai's two enemies on the spot were both dead, his old soldiers bethought themselves of trying to rescue him. When Wei Guan, who had actually arrested Deng Ai, heard this, he feared for his life.

"If Deng Ai lives, I will die in his hand!" said Wei Guan.

Furthermore, General Tian Xu said, "When Deng Ai took Jiangyou, he wished to put me to death. It was only at the prayer of my friends that he let me off. May I not have my revenge now?"

So Wei Guan gave order. At the head of five hundred cavalry, Tian Xu went in pursuit of the cage-carts. He came up with them at Mianzhu and found that the two prisoners had just been released from the carts in which they were being carried to Luoyang. When Deng Ai saw that those coming up were soldiers of his own late command, he took no thought for defense. Nor did Tian Xu waste time in preliminaries. He went up to where Deng Ai was standing and cut him down. His soldiers fell upon the son, Deng Zhong, and slew him also, and thus father and son met death in the same place.

A poem, pitying Deng Ai, was written:

While yet a boy, Deng Ai loved to sketch and plan;
He was an able leader as a man.
The earth could hide no secrets from his eye,
With equal skill he read the starry sky.
Past every obstacle his way he won,
And onward pressed until his task was done.
But foulest murder closed a great career,
His spirit ranges now a larger sphere.

A poem was also composed in pity for Zhong Hui:

Of mother wit Zhong Hui had no scanty share,
And in due time at court did office bear.
His subtle plans shook Sima Zhao's hold on power,
He was well named the Zhang Liang of the hour.
Shouchun and Saber Pass ramparts straight fell down,
When he attacked, and he won great renown.
Ambition beckoned, he would forward press
His spirit homeward wandered, bodiless.

Another poem, in pity of Jiang Wei, runs:

Tianshui boasts of a hero,
Talent came forth from Xizhou,
Lu Wang fathered his spirit,
Zhuge Liang tutored his mind,
Valiant he ever pressed forward,
Nor had a thought of returning,
Grieved were the soldiers of Han
When death rapt his soul from his body.

And thus died all three leaders. Many other generals also perished in the fighting, and with them died Zhang Yi and other officers. Liu Rui, the heir-apparent, and Guan Yi, Lord of Hanshou and grandson of Guan Yu, were also killed by the Wei soldiers. Then followed a time of great confusion and bloodshed, which endured till Jia Chong arrived and restored confidence and order.

Jia Chong set Wei Guan over the city of Chengdu and sent the captive Latter Ruler to Luoyang. A few officers---Fan Jian, Zhang Shao, Qiao Zhou, and Xi Zheng---accompanied the deposed emperor on this degrading journey. Liao Hua and Dong Jue made illness an excuse not to go. They died of grief soon after.

At this time the year-style of Wei was changed from Wonderful Beginning, the fifth year, to Great Glory, the first year (AD 264). In the third month of this year, since nothing could be done to assist Shu to recover its independence, the troops of Wu under Ding Feng were withdrawn and returned to their own land.

Now Secretary Hua Jiao sent up a memorial to Sun Xiu, the Ruler of Wu, saying, "Wu and Shu were as close as are one's lips to one's teeth, and when the lips are gone the teeth are cold. Without doubt Sima Zhao will now turn his thoughts to attacking us, and Your Majesty must realize the danger and prepare to meet it."

Sun Xiu knew that he spoke truly, so he set Lu Kang, son of the late leader Lu Xun, over the army of Jingzhou and the river ports with the title General Who Guards the East; Sun Yin was sent to Nanxu; and Ding Feng was ordered to set up several hundred garrisons along the river banks.

In Shu when Huo Yi, Governor of Jianning, heard that Chengdu had been taken, he dressed himself in white and wailed during three days, facing west toward the capital.

"Now that the capital has fallen and the Ruler of Shu is a captive, it would be well to surrender," said his officers.

Huo Yi replied, "There is a hindrance. I know not how fares our lord, whether he is in comfort or in misery. If his captors treat him generously, then will I yield. But perhaps they will put him to shame; and when the prince is shamed, the minister dies."

So certain persons were sent to Luoyang to find out how fared the Latter Ruler.

Soon after the Latter Ruler reached the capital of Wei, Sima Zhao returned.

Seeing the Latter Ruler at court, Sima Zhao upbraided him, saying, "You deserved death for your vicious courses---corrupt morality, unchecked self-indulgence, contempt of good people, and misgovernment---, which had brought misfortune upon yourself!"

Hearing this, the face of the Latter Ruler turned to the color of clay with fear, and he was speechless.

But the courtiers said, "He has lost his kingdom, he has surrendered without a struggle, and he now deserves pardon."

Thus the Latter Ruler suffered no injury, but was created Duke of Anle. Moreover, he was assigned a residence and a revenue, and he received presents of silk, and servants were sent to wait upon him, males and females in total one hundred. His son Liu Dao and the officers of Shu---Fan Jian, Qiao Zhou, Xi Zheng, and others---were given ranks of nobility. The Latter Ruler expressed his thanks and left.

Huang Hao, whose evil influence had brought the kingdom to nought, and who had oppressed the people, was put to death with ignominy in the public place.

When Huo Yi heard all these things, he came with his officers and yielded submission.

Next day the Latter Ruler went to the residence of Sima Zhao to thank him for his bounty, and a banquet was prepared. At the banquet they performed the music of Wei, with the dances, and the hearts of the officers of Shu were sad. Only the Latter Ruler appeared merry.

Half way through the feast, Sima Zhao said to Jia Chong, "The man lacks feeling. That is what has ruined him. Even if Zhuge Liang had lived, he could not have maintained such a man. It is no wonder that Jiang Wei failed."

Turning to his guest, Sima Zhao said, "Do you never think of Shu?"

"With such music as this, I forget Shu," replied the Latter Ruler.

Presently the Latter Ruler rose and left the table to change dress.

Xi Zheng went over to him and said, "Why did Your Majesty not say you missed Shu? If Your Majesty are questioned again, weep and say that in Shu are the tombs of your forefathers and no day passes that Your Majesty do not grieve to be so far away. The Duke of Jin may let Your Majesty return."

The Latter Ruler promised he would.

When the wine had gone round several more times, Sima Zhao put the same question a second time: "Do you never think of Shu?"

The Latter Ruler replied as he had been told. He also tried to weep, but failed to shed a tear. So he shut his eyes.

"Is not that just what Xi Zheng told you to say?" asked Sima Zhao.

"It is just as you say," was the reply.

They all laughed. But really Sima Zhao was pleased with the frank answer and felt that nothing was to be feared from him.

Laughter loving, pleasure pursuing,
Rippling smiles over a merry face,
Never a thought of his former glory
In his callous heart finds place.
Childish joy in a change of dwelling,
That he feels and that alone;
Manifest now that he was never
Worthy to sit on his father's throne.

The courtiers thought that so grand an exploit as the conquest of the River Lands was worthy of high honor, so they memorialized the Ruler of Wei, Cao Huang, to confer the rank Prince of Jin on Sima Zhao. At that time, Cao Huang ruled in name only, for he had no authority. The whole land was under Sima Zhao, whose will the Emperor himself dared not cross. And so, in due course, the Duke of Jin became Prince of Jin.

After being made Prince of Jin, Sima Zhao posthumously created his father, Sima Yi, the Original Prince and his late elder brother, Sima Shi, the Wonderful Prince.

The wife of Sima Zhao was the daughter of Wang Su. She bore to him two sons, the elder of whom was named Sima Yan. Sima Yan was huge of frame, his flowing hair reached to the ground when he stood up, and both hands hung down below his knees. He was clever, brave, and skilled in the use of arms.

The second son, Sima You, was mild of disposition, a filial son and a dutiful brother. His father loved him dearly. As Sima Shi had died without leaving sons, this youth, Sima You, was regarded as his son, to continue that line of the family.

Sima Zhao used to say: "The empire was really my brother's."

Becoming a prince, it was necessary for Sima Zhao to choose his heir, and he wished to name his younger son Sima You. But Shan Tao remonstrated.

"It is improper and infelicitous to prefer the younger," said Shan Tao.

And Jia Chong, He Zeng, and Pei Xiu followed in the same strain.

"The elder is clever, able in war, one of the most talented people in the state and popular. With such natural advantages he has a great destiny: He was not born to serve."

Sima Zhao hesitated, for he was still unwilling to abandon his desire.

But two other officers---Grand Commander Wang Xiang and Minister of Works Xun Kai---also remonstrated, saying, "Certain former dynasties have preferred the younger before the elder and rebellion has generally followed. We pray you reflect upon these cases."

Finally Sima Zhao yielded and named his elder son Sima Yan as his successor.

Certain officers memorialized: "This year a gigantic figure of a man descended from heaven in Xiangwu. His height was twenty feet and his footprint measured over three feet. He had white hair and a hoary beard. He wore an unlined yellow robe and a yellow cape. He walked leaning on a black-handled staff. This extraordinary man preached, saying, 'I am the king of the people, and now I come to tell you of a change of ruler and the coming of peace.' He wandered about for three days and then disappeared. Evidently this portent refers to yourself, Noble Sir, and now you should assume the imperial headdress with twelve strings of pearls, set up the imperial standard, and have the roads cleared when you make a progress. You should ride in the golden-shafted chariot with six horses. Your consort should be styled 'Empress' and your heir 'Apparent'."

Sima Zhao was greatly pleased. He returned to his palace, but just as he was sitting down, he was suddenly seized with paralysis and lost the use of his tongue. He quickly grew worse. His three chief confidants, Wang Xiang, He Zeng, and Xun Kai, together with many court officials, came to inquire after his health, but he could not speak to them. He pointed toward the heir apparent, Sima Yan, and died. It was the eighth month of that year.

Then said He Zeng, "The care of the empire devolves upon the Prince of Jin: Let us induct the heir. Then we can perform the sacrifices to the late prince."

Thereupon Sima Yan was set up in his father's place. He gave He Zeng the title of Prime Minister; Sima Wang, Minister of the Interior; Shi Bao, Commander of the Flying Cavalry; and conferred many other titles and ranks. The posthumous title of the "Scholar Prince" was conferred upon his late father.

When the obsequies were finished, Sima Yan summoned Jia Chong and Pei Xiu into the Palace, and said, "Cao Cao said that if the celestial mandate rested upon him, he could be no more than King Wen of Zhou, who served as a regent only. Is this really so?"

Jia Chong replied, "Cao Cao was in the service of Han and feared lest posterity should reproach him with usurpation. Wherefore he spoke thus. Nevertheless he caused Cao Pi to become Emperor."

"How did my father compare with Cao Cao?" asked Sima Yan.

"Although Cao Cao was universally successful, yet the people feared him and credited him with no virtue. Cao Pi's rule was marked by strife and lack of tranquillity. No single year was peaceful. Later the Original Prince and Wonderful Prince of your line rendered great services and disseminated compassion and virtue, so that they were beloved. Your late father overcame Shu in the west and was universally renowned. Comparison with Cao Cao is impossible."

"Still Cao Pi succeeded the rule of Han. Can I not

in like manner succeed that of Wei?"

Jia Chong and Pei Xiu bowed low and said, "Cao Pi's action may be taken as a precedent to succeed an older dynasty. Wherefore prepare an abdication terrace to make the great declaration."

Sima Yan resolved to act promptly. Next day he entered the Forbidden City armed with a sword. No court had been held for many days, for Cao Huang was ill at ease and full of dread. When Sima Yan appeared, the Ruler of Wei left his place and advanced to met him. Sima Yan sat down.

"By whose merits did Wei succeed to empire?" he asked suddenly.

"Certainly success was due to your forefathers," replied Cao Huang.

Sima Yan smiled, saying, "Your Majesty is unskilled in debate, inept in war, and unfit to rule. Why not give place to another more able and virtuous?"

Cao Huang's lips refused a reply.

But Zhang Jie, one of the ministers, cried, "You are wrong to speak thus, O Prince. His Majesty's ancestor conquered east and west, north and south, and won the empire by strenuous effort. The present Emperor is virtuous and without fault. Why should he yield place to another?"

Sima Yan replied angrily, "The imperial right lay with the Hans, and Cao Cao coerced them as he did the nobles. In making himself the Prince of Wei, he usurped the throne of Han. Three generations of my forefathers upheld the House of Wei, so that their power is not the result of their own abilities, but of the labor of my house. This is known to all the world, and am I not equal to carrying on the rule of Wei?"

"If you do this thing, you will be a rebel and an usurper," said Zhang Jie.

"And what shall I be if I avenge the wrongs of Han?"

He bade the lictors take Zhang Jie outside and beat him to death, while the Ruler of Wei wept and besought pardon for his faithful minister.

Sima Yan rose and left.

Cao Huang turned to Jia Chong and Pei Xiu, saying, "What should I do? Some decision must be taken."

They replied, "Truth to tell, the measure of your fate is accomplished and you cannot oppose the will of Heaven. You must prepare to abdicate as did Emperor Xian of the Hans. Resign the throne to the Prince of Jin and thereby accord with the design of Heaven and the will of the people. Your personal safety need not cause you anxiety."

Cao Huang could only accept this advice, and the terrace was built. The "mouse" day of the twelfth month was chosen for the ceremony. On that day the Ruler of Wei, dressed in full robes of ceremony, and bearing the seal in his hand, ascended the terrace in the presence of a great assembly.

The House of Wei displaced the House of Han
And Jin succeeded Wei; so turns fate's wheel
And none escape its grinding. Zhang Jie the true
Stood in the way and died. We pity him.
Vain hope with one hand to hide Taishan
Mountains.

The Emperor-elect was requested to ascend the high place, and there received the great salute. Cao Huang then descended, robed himself as a minister and took his place as the first of subjects.

Sima Yan now stood upon the terrace, supported by Jia Chong and Pei Xiu. Cao Huang was ordered to prostrate himself, while the command was recited, and Jia Chong read:

"Forty-five years have elapsed since, in the twenty-fifth year of Rebuilt Tranquillity, the House of Han gave place to the House of Wei. But after forty-five years, the favor of Heaven has now left the latter House and reverts to Jin. The merits and services of the family of Sima reach to the high heavens and pervade the earth. The Prince of Jin is fitted for the high office and to continue the rule. Now His Majesty the Emperor confers upon you the title of Prince of Chenliu. You are to proceed to the city of Jinyong, where you will reside; you are forbidden to come to court unless summoned."

Sadly Cao Huang withdrew with tears in his eyes. Sima Fu, Guardian of the Throne, wept before the deposed Emperor and promised eternal devotion.

"I have been a servant of Wei and will never turn my back upon the House!" said he.

Sima Yan did not take this amiss, and out of admiration he offered Sima Fu the princedom of Anping. But Sima Fu declined the offer.

The new Emperor was now seated in his place, and all the officers made their salutations and felicitated him. The very hills rang with "Wan shui! O King, live forever!"

Thus succeeded Sima Yan, and the state was called Great Jin and a new year-style was changed from Great Glory, the second year, to Great Beginning Era, the first year (AD 265). An amnesty was declared. Since then Wei Dynasty ended.

The kingdom of Wei had ended.
The Founder of the Dynasty of Jin
Took Wei as model; thus the displaced emperor
Was named a prince, when on the terrace high
His throne he had renounced.
We grieve when we recall these deeds.

The new Emperor conferred posthumous rank upon his grandfather, his uncle, and his father: Sima Yi the Original Emperor, Sima Shi the Wonderful Emperor, and Sima Zhao the Scholar Emperor. Sima Yan built seven temples in honor of his ancestors: Sima Jun, the Han General Who Conquers the West; Sima Jun's son, Sima Liang, Governor of Yuzhang; Sima Liang's son, Sima Juan, Governor of Yingchuan; Sima Juan's son,

Sima Fang, Governor of Jingzhao; Sima Fang's son, Sima Yi the Original Emperor; and Sima Yi's sons, Sima Shi the Wonderful Emperor and Sima Zhao the Scholar Emperor.

All these things being accomplished, courts were held daily, and the one subject of discussion was the subjugation of Wu.

The House of Han has gone for aye,
And Wu will quickly follow.

The story of the attack upon Wu will be told next.

Chapter 120

Recommending Du Yu, An Old General Offers New Plans;
Capturing Of Sun Hao, Three Kingdoms Becomes One.

When Sun Xiu, the Ruler of Wu, knew that the House of Wei had fallen before the Jins, he also knew that the usurper's next thought would be the conquest of his own land. The anxiety made him ill, so that he took to his bed and was like to die. He then summoned to his bedside his Prime Minister, Puyang Xing, and his heir, Sun Wan. But they two came almost too late. The dying Ruler, with his last effort, took the Minister by the hand, but could only point to his son. Then he died.

Puyang Xing left the couch and called a meeting of the officers, whereat he proposed to place the heir on his father's throne.

Then Wan Yu, Inspector of the Left Army, rose and said, "Prince Sun Wan is too youthful to rule in such troublous times. Let us confer the throne to Sun Hao, Lord of Wucheng."

Zhang Bu, General of the Left Army, supported his election, saying, "Sun Hao is able and prompt in decision. He can handle the responsibilities of an emperor."

However, Puyang Xing was doubtful and consulted the Empress Dowager.

"Settle this with the officials;" she replied, "I am a widow and know nothing of such matters."

Finally Sun Hao won the day, and in the seventh month he was enthroned as Emperor of Wu, and the first year of his reign was Prosperous Beginning (AD 264). Sun Hao was the son of Sun He, a former Heir Apparent, and grandson of Sun Quan the Great Emperor. The excluded prince, Sun Wan, was consoled with the title of Prince of Yuzhang. Posthumous rank was given to his late father, Sun He the Scholar Emperor, and his mother, Lady He, the Scholar Empress. The Veteran Leader Ding Feng was made Commander of the Right and Left Armies.

However, the year-style was changed to Sweet Dew the very next year. The new ruler soon proved himself cruel and oppressive and day by day grew more so. Sun Hao indulged in every form of vice and chose Eunuch Cen Hun as his confidant and favorite. When Prime Minister Puyang Xing and General Zhang Bu ventured upon remonstrance, both, with all their family, were put to death. Thereafter none dared to speak; the mouth of every courtier was shut tight.

Another year-style, Treasured Paramount, was adopted the next year (266), and the responsibility of the Prime Minister's office was shared by two officers, Lu Kuai the Left and Wan Yu the Right.

At this time the imperial residence was in Wuchang. The people of Yangzhou shouldered heavy tribute and suffered exceedingly. There was no limit to the Ruler's extravagance. The treasury was swept clean, and the income of the royal domain exhausted.

At length Lu Kuai, Left Prime Minister, ventured a memorial, saying:

"No natural calamity has fallen upon the people, yet they starve; no public work is in progress, yet the treasury is empty. I am distressed. The country under the Hans has fallen apart and three states have arisen therefrom. Those ruled by the Caos and the Lius, as the result of their own folly, have been lost in Jin. Foolish I may be, but I would protect the state for Your Majesty against the evils we have seen in the other divisions. This city of Wuchang is not safe as a royal residence. There is a rhyme concerning it, the gist of which is that it is better to drink the water of Jianye than eat the fish of Wuchang, better to die in Jianye than to live in Wuchang. This shows the regard of the people as well as the will of Heaven. Now the public storehouses are nearly empty; they contain insufficient for a year's use. The officers of all grades vex and distress the people and none pity them.

"In former times the Palace women numbered less than a hundred; for years past they have exceeded a thousand. This is an extravagant waste of treasure. The courtiers render no disinterested service, but are split into cliques and cabals. The honest are injured, and the good driven away. All these things undermine the state and weaken the people. I beg Your Majesty to reduce the number of officers and remove grievances, to dismiss the Palace women and select honest officers, to the joy of the people and the tranquillity of the state."

But the Ruler of Wu was displeased, threw the memorial away, and showed his contempt for the Minister's remonstrance by beginning to collect material for the building of a new palace complex to be called the Reflected Light Palace. He even made the officers of the court go into the forest to fell trees for the work.

The Ruler of Wu called in the soothsayer Shang Guang and bade him take the cast and inquire as to the attainment of empire.

Shang Guang cast a lot and replied, "All is propitious, and in the year of the 'mouse' your blue umbrella will enter Luoyang!"

And Sun Hao was pleased.

He said to Minister Hua Jiao, "The former Rulers listened to your words and sent generals to various points and placed defensive camps along the rivers. And over all these was set Ding Feng. Now my desire is to conquer Han and avenge the wrongs of my brother, the Ruler of Shu. What place should be first conquered?"

Hua Jiao replied, "Now that Chengdu has fallen and the Throne there been overturned, Sima Yan will assuredly desire to absorb this southern land. Your Majesty should display virtue and restore confidence to your people. That would be the best plan. If you engage in war, it will be like throwing on hemp to put out a fire---the hemp only adds to the blaze. This is worthy of careful consideration."

But Sun Hao grew angry and said, "I desire to take this opportunity to return to my real heritage. Why do you employ this ill-omened language? Were it not for your long service, now would I slay you and expose your head as a warning."

He bade the lictors hustle Minister Hua Jiao from his presence, and Hua Jiao left the court.

"It is pitiful," said Hua Jiao. "Ere long our silky, beautiful country will pass to another!"

So Hua Jiao retired.

And the Ruler of Wu ordered Lu Kang, General Who Guards the East, to camp his army at Jiangkou in order to attack Xiangyang.

Spies reported this in Luoyang, and it was told the Ruler of Jin. When Sima Yan heard that the army of Wu threatened to invade Xiangyang, he called a council.

Jia Chong stood forth, saying, "I hear the government of Wu, under its present ruler, Sun Hao, is devoid of virtue, and the Ruler of Wu has turned aside out of the road. Your Majesty should send Commander Yang Hu to oppose this army. When internal trouble shall arise, let him attack, and victory will then be easy."

The Ruler of Jin issued an edict ordering Yang Hu to prepare, and so he mustered his troops and set himself to guard the county.

Yang Hu became very popular in Xiangyang. Any of the soldiers of Wu who desired to desert to the other side were allowed to come over. He employed only the fewest possible troops on patrol duty. Instead he set his soldiers to till the soil, and they cultivated an extensive area, whereby the hundred days supplies with which they set out were soon increased to enough for ten years.

Yang Hu maintained great simplicity, wearing the lightest of garments and no armor. His personal escort and servants numbered only about ten.

One day his officers came to his tent and said, "The spies reported great laxity in the enemy's camp. It is time to make an attack!"

But Yang Hu replied, "You must not despise Lu Kang, for he is able and crafty. Formerly his master sent him to attack Xiling, and he slew Bu Chan and many of his generals, before I could save that city. So long as Lu Kang remains in command, I shall remain on the defensive. I shall not attack till there be trouble and confusion among our enemies. To be rash and not await the proper moment to attack is to invite defeat."

They found him wise and said no more. They only kept the boundaries.

One day Yang Hu and his officers went out to hunt, and it happened that Lu Kang had chosen the same day to hunt. Yang Hu gave strict orders not to cross the boundary, and so each hunted only on his own side.

Lu Kang was astonished at the enemy's scrupulous propriety.

He sighed, "The soldiers of Yang Hu have so high a discipline that I may not make any invasion now."

In the evening, after both parties had returned,

Yang Hu ordered an inspection of the slaughtered game and sent over to the other side any that seemed to have been first struck by the soldiers of Wu.

Lu Kang was greatly pleased and sent for the bearers of the game.

"Does your leader drink wine?" asked he.

They replied, "Only fine wines does he drink."

"I have some very old wine," replied Lu Kang, smiling, "and I will give of it to you to bear to your general as a gift. It is the wine I myself brew and drink on ceremonial occasions, and he shall have half in return for today's courtesy."

They took the wine and left.

"Why do you give him wine?" asked Lu Kang's officers.

"Because he has shown kindness, and I must return courtesy for courtesy."

When the gift of wine arrived and the bearers told Yang Hu the story of their reception, he laughed.

"So he knows I can drink," said Yang Hu.

He had the jar opened, and the wine was poured out. One of his generals, Chen Yuan, begged him to drink moderately lest there should be some harm come of it.

"Lu Kang is no poisoner," replied Yang Hu.

And he drank. The friendly intercourse thus

continued, and messengers frequently passed from one camp to the other.

One day the messengers said that Lu Kang was unwell and had been ailing for several days.

"I think he suffers from the same complaint as I," said Yang Hu. "I have some remedies ready prepared and will send him some."

The drugs were taken over to the Wu camp.

But the sick man's officers were suspicious and said, "This medicine is surely harmful: It comes from the enemy."

However, Lu Kang said, "No; old Uncle Yang Hu would not poison a person. Do not doubt."

He drank the decoction. Next day he was much better.

When his staff came to congratulate him, he said, "If our opponents take their stand upon virtue and we take ours upon violence, they will drag us after them without fighting. See to it that the boundaries be well kept and that we seek not to gain any unfair advantage."

Soon after came a special envoy from the Ruler of Wu to urge upon Lu Kang prompt activity.

"Our Emperor sends orders for you to press forward," said the envoy. "You are not to await a Jin invasion."

"You may return, and I will send up a memorial," replied Lu Kang.

So a memorial was written and soon followed the envoy to the capital, which by this time was Jianye. When the Ruler of Wu, Sun Hao, read it, he found therein many arguments against attacking Jin and exhortations to exercise a virtuous rule instead of engaging in hostilities. It angered him.

"They say Lu Kang has come to an understanding with the enemy, and now I believe it!" said the Ruler of Wu.

Thereupon he deprived Lu Kang of his command and took away his commission and degraded him into Marching General. Sun Ji, General of the Left Army, was sent to supersede Lu Kang. And none dared to intervene.

Sun Hao became still more arbitrary and of his own will changed the year-style once more to the Phoenix (AD 269). Day by day his life became more wanton and vicious. The soldiers in every camp murmured with anger and resentment, and at last three high officers---Prime Minister Wan Yu, General Liu Ping, and Minister of Agriculture Lou Xuan---boldly and earnestly remonstrated with the Emperor for his many irregularities. They suffered death. Within ten years more than forty ministers were put to death for doing their duty.

Sun Hao maintained an extravagantly large guard of fifty thousand heavy cavalry, and these soldiers were the terror of everyone.

Now when Yang Hu, on the Jin side of the frontier, heard that his opponent Lu Kang had been removed from his command and that the conduct of the Ruler of Wu had become wholly unreasonable, he knew that the time was near for him to conquer Wu. Wherefore he presented a memorial:

"Although fate is superior to human, yet success depends upon human effort. Now as the geographic difficulties of the South Land are not as those of the River Lands, while the ferocity of Sun Hao exceeds that of Liu Shan, the misery of the people of Wu exceeds that of the dwellers in Shu. Our armies are stronger than ever before, and if we miss this opportunity to bring the whole land under one rule, but continue to weary our army with continual watching and cause the world to groan under the burden of militarism, then our efficiency will decline and we shall not endure."

When Sima Yan read this, he gave orders for the army to move. But three officers---Jia Chong, Xun Xu, and Feng Dan---opposed it, and the orders were withdrawn.

Yang Hu was disappointed at the news and said, "What a pity it is that of ten affairs in the world, one always meets with eight or nine vexations!"

In the fourth year of Universal Tranquillity, in Jin calendar (AD 278), Yang Hu went to court and asked leave to retire on account of ill health.

Before granting him leave to go, Sima Yan asked, "Do you have plans to propose to settle the empire?"

Yang Hu replied, "Sun Hao is a very cruel ruler and could be conquered without fighting. If he were to die and a wise successor sat upon his throne, Your Majesty would never be able to gain possession of Wu."

The Ruler of Jin realized the truth, and he said, "Suppose your army attacked now. What then?"

"I am now too old and too ill for the task," replied Yang Hu. "Some other bold and capable leader must be found."

Yang Hu left the court and retired to his home. Toward the end of the year he was nigh unto death, and the Ruler of Jin went to visit him. The sight of his master at his bedside brought tears to the eyes of the faithful old leader.

"If I died a myriad times, I could never requite Your Majesty," said Yang Hu.

Sima Yan also wept, saying, "My great grief is that I could not take advantage of your abilities to attack Wu. Who now is there to carry out your design?"

Hesitatingly the sick man replied, "I am dying and must be wholly sincere. General Du Yu is equal to the task, and is the one man to attack Wu."

Sima Yan said, "How beautiful it is to bring good people into prominence! But why did you write a memorial recommending certain people and then burn the draft so that no one knew?"

The dying man answered, "I bowed before the officials in open court, but I did not beseech the kindness of the private attendants."

So Yang Hu died, and Sima Yan wailed for him and then returned to his palace. He conferred on the dead leader the posthumous rank of Imperial Guardian and Lord of Juping. The traders closed their shops out of respect to his memory, and all the frontier camps were filled with wailing. The people of Xiangyang, recalling that he loved to wander on the Xian Hills, built there a temple to him and set up a stone and sacrificed regularly at the four seasons. The passers-by were moved to tears when they read Yang Hu's name on the tablet, so that it came to be called "The Stone of Tears".

I saw the fragments of a shattered stone
One spring time on the hillside, when, alone,
I walked to greet the sun. The pines distilled
Big drops of dew unceasing; sadness filled
My heart. I knew this was the Stone of Tears,
The stone of memory of long-past years.

On the strength of Yang Hu's recommendation, Du Yu was made Commander of Jingzhou, and the title of General Who Guards the South was conferred upon him. He was a man of great experience, untiring in study and devoted to the Zuo Volume, the book of commentaries composed by Zuo Qiuming upon the Spring and Autumn Annals. In hours of leisure, a copy of Zuo Volume was never out of his hand; and when he went abroad, an attendant rode in front with the beloved book. He was said to be "Zuo mad".

Du Yu went to Xiangyang and began by being kind to the people and caring for his soldiers. By this time Wu had lost by death both Ding Feng and

Lu Kang.

The conduct of the Ruler of Wu waxed worse and worse. He used to give great banquets whereat intoxication was universal. He appointed Rectors of Feasts to observe all the faults committed by guests, and after these banquets all offenders were punished, some by flaying the face, others by gouging out the eyes. Everyone went in terror of these Rectors.

Wang Jun, Imperial Protector of Yizhou, sent in a memorial advising an attack upon Wu. He said:

"Sun Hao is steeped in vice and should be attacked at once. Should he die and be succeeded by a good ruler, we might meet with serious opposition. The ships I built seven years ago lie idle and rotting: We can use them. I am seventy years of age and must soon die. If any one of these three events happen---the death of Sun Hao, the destruction of these ships, or my death---then success will be difficult to ensure. I pray Your Majesty not to miss the tide."

At the next assembly of officers Sima Yan said to them, "I have decided to act. I have received similar advice from Yang Hu and Wang Jun."

At this arose Minister Wang Hun and said, "I hear Sun Hao intends to march north to the Middle Land and has his army ready. Report says it is formidable and would be hard to defeat. I counsel to await another year till that army has lost its first vigor."

A command to cease warlike preparations was the result of this counsel. The Ruler of Jin betook himself to his private chamber where he engaged in a game of chess with Secretary Zhang Hua as opponent. While at the game, another memorial arrived. It was from Du Yu. It read:

"Formerly Yang Hu explained his plans confidentially to Your Majesty, but did not lay them before the court. The result has been much debate and conflict of opinion. In every project there are pros and cons, but in this the arguments are mostly in favor. The worst that can happen is failure. Since last autumn the proposed attack has become generally known, and, if we stop now, Sun Hao will be frightened and remove the capital to Wuchang, repair his fortifications in the South Land, and move his threatened people out of danger. Then the southern capital cannot be assaulted, nor is there anything left in the countryside to rob. Hence next year's attack will also fail."

Just as the Ruler of Jin finished reading, Zhang Hua pushed aside the board, rose and drew his hands into his sleeves, saying, "Your Majesty's skill in war is almost divine, your state is prosperous, and the army strong. The Ruler of Wu is a tyrant, his people are miserable, and his country mean. Now you can easily conquer him, and I pray that there be no further hesitation!"

"How could I hesitate after your discourse?" said Sima Yan.

Thereupon he returned to the council chamber and issued his commands. Du Yu was made Commander-in-Chief and, with one hundred thousand troops, was to attack Jiangling; Sima

Zhou, Prince of Langye and General Who Guards the East, was to attack Tuzhong; Wang Hun, General Who Conquers the East, to go up against Hengjiang; Wang Rong, General Who Exhibits Prowess, to move against Wuchang; Hu Fen, General Who Pacifies the South, to attack Xiakou. And all divisions, fifty thousand troops each, were under the orders of Du Yu. In addition to the land forces, two large fleets were to operate on the river under Wang Jun, General Who Shows Dragon Courage, and Tang Bin, General Who Possesses Martial Bravery. Marines and lands troops amounted to more than two hundred thousand. A separate force under Yang Ji, General Who Holds the South, was sent away to Xiangyang to coordinate all forces.

The Ruler of Wu was greatly alarmed at the news of such armies and fleets, and he called to him quickly his Prime Minister Zhang Ti, Minister of the Interior He Zhi, and Minister of Works Teng Xun, to consult how to defend his land.

Zhang Ti proposed: "Send Commander of the Flying Chariots Wu Yan to meet the enemy at Jiangling; Commander of the Flying Cavalry Sun Xin to Xiakou; I volunteer to take command of a camp at Niuzhu, together with the General of the Left Army Shen Zong and General of the Right Army Zhuge Xing, ready to lend help at any point."

The Ruler of Wu approved his dispositions and felt satisfied that he was safe by land. But in the privacy of his own apartment he felt miserable, for he realized that no preparations had been made against an attack by water under the Wei leader

Wang Jun.

Then the favorite eunuch Cen Hun asked the Emperor why he bore a sad countenance, and Sun Hao told him of his dread of the enemy navy.

"The armies of Jin are coming, and I have deployed troops for general defense. Only the water front, by which Wang Jun and his several thousand battleships sail east along the tide, makes me feel so worried."

"But I have a scheme that will smash all Wang Jun's ships!" cried Cen Hun.

"What is it?" asked the Ruler of Wu, pleased to hear this.

"Iron is plentiful. Make great chains with heavy links and stretch them across the river at various points. Also forge many massive hammers and arrange them in the stream, so that when the enemy's ships sail down before the wind, they will collide with the hammers and be wrecked. Then they will sail no more."

Blacksmiths were soon at work on the river bank welding the links and forging the hammers. Work went on day and night, and soon all the chains were placed in different points.

As has been said Du Yu was to attack Jiangling, and he sent General Zhou Zhi with eight hundred sailors to sail secretly along the Great River to capture Yuexiang. There they were to make an ambush in the Bashan Mountains and a great show of flags along the bank and among the trees. Drums were to be beaten and bombs exploded during the day and many fires lighted at night to give the appearance of a great army.

So Zhou Zhi sailed to the Bashan Mountains.

Next day Du Yu directed the army and the marine forces in a simultaneous advance.

The scouts reported: "The Ruler of Wu has sent the land force under Wu Yan, the navy under Lu Jing, and the vanguard under Sun Xin!"

Du Yu led his forces forward. The vanguard of Wu, under Sun Xin, came up, and at the first encounter Du Yu's army retired. Sun Xin landed his marines and pursued. But in the midst of the pursuit a signal bomb sounded, and Sun Xin was attacked on all sides by the Jin troops. He tried to retire, but the army he had been pursuing, Du Yu's force, turned back too and joined in the attack. Wu's losses were very heavy, and Sun Xin hastened back to the city. But the eight hundred Jin soldiers of Zhou Zhi mingled with the Wu army at the ramparts and so entered the gates. The Jin soldiers raised signal fires on the walls.

This maneuver amazed Sun Xin, and he said, "The northern troops had surely flown across the river into the city!"

Sun Xin made an effort to escape, but the leader of Jin, Zhou Zhi, unexpectedly appeared and slew him.

Admiral Lu Jing of the Wu fleet of that had accompanied Sun Xin saw on the south shore, in the Bashan Mountains, a great standard bearing the name Jin General Who Guards the South Du Yu.

Lu Jing became alarmed and landed to try to escape, but the Jin General Zhang Shang soon found and slew him.

At his position at Jiangling, Wu Yan heard of these defeats and knew his position was untenable, so he fled. However, he was soon captured and led into the presence of the victorious general.

"No use sparing you," said Du Yu, and he sentenced the prisoner to death.

Thus Jiangling was captured and all the counties along the River Xiang and River Yuan as far as Huangzhou, which surrendered at the first summons.

Du Yu sent out officers to soothe the people of the conquered counties, and they suffered nothing from the soldiery. Next he marched toward Wuchang, and that city also yielded. So the glory of Du Yu became very great. He then summoned his officers to a council to decide upon attacking Capital Jianye.

Hu Fen said, "A one-century rebellion will not be reduced completely at once. The time of the spring rise of waters is near, and our position is precarious. We should do well to await the coming spring."

Du Yu replied, "In the days of old, Yue Yi overcame the powerful state Qi in one battle in Jixi. Our prestige is now high and success certain, easy as the splitting of a bamboo, which seems to welcome the knife after the first few joints have been overcome. We shall meet no great opposition."

So Du Yu gave orders to the various leaders to move in concert against the capital land of Jianye.

Now the Jin leader Wang Jun had gone down the river with his naval force. From his scouts he heard of the iron chains and the hammers that had been laid in the river to hinder his progress. But he only laughed. He constructed great rafts of timber and placed on them straw effigies of soldiers in armors and sent them down river with the current. The defenders of Wu took them for real troops and, alarmed by their numbers, fled in panic. Then the great hammers and chains were dragged away as the rafts drifted on. Moreover, on the rafts they laid great torches many fathoms long, and very thick, made of straw soaked in linseed oil. When the raft was checked by a chain, the torches were lighted and the chains exposed to the heat till they melted and broke asunder. Thus the rafts went down stream conquering wherever they came.

Then the Prime Minister of Wu, Zhang Ti, sent two leaders, General of the Left Army Shen Zong and General of the Right Army Zhuge Xing, to try to check the advance of the armies.

Shen Zong said to his colleague, "The forces above have failed to stop the enemy, and the enemy will surely come here. We shall have to put forth all our strength. If haply we can succeed, the safety of our South Land is assured. But suppose we fight and lose the battle, then is our country lost."

"Sir, you only say what is too true," said Zhuge Xing.

Just as they talked of these matters came reports of the approach of their enemies in irresistible force.

The two leaders were seized with panic and went back to see the Prime Minister.

"Our country is lost!" cried Zhuge Xing. "Why not run?"

"We all know that the land is doomed," replied Zhang Ti. "But if we make no defense, and no one dies for his country, shall we not be shamed?"

Zhuge Xing left, weeping; and Zhang Ti went with Shen Zong to the army. The invaders soon arrived, and the Jin General Zhou Zhi was the first to break into the camp. Zhang Ti resisted stubbornly, but was soon slain in a melee, and Shen Zong was killed by Zhou Zhi. The army of Wu was defeated and scattered.

Jin's army banners waved on Bashan Mountains
And trusty Zhang Ti in Jiangling fighting died;
He accepted not that the kingly grace was spent,
He rather chose to die than shame his side.

The armies of Jin conquered at Niuzhu and penetrated deeply into the country of Wu. From his camp Wang Jun sent a report of his victory to Luoyang, and Sima Yan was pleased.

But Jia Chong again opposed further fighting, saying, "The armies have been long absent, and the soldiers will suffer from the unhealthiness of the southern country. It would be well to call them home."

Zhang Hua spoke against this course, saying, "The Jin army has reached the very home and center of the enemy. Soon Wu courage will fail, and the Ruler of Wu himself will be our prisoner. To recall the army now would be to waste the efforts already made."

The Ruler of Jin inclined to neither side.

Jia Chong turned upon Zhang Hua savagely, saying, "You are wholly ignorant and understand nothing. You are bent upon winning some sort of glory at the expense of our soldiers' lives. Death would be too good for you!"

"Why wrangle?" said Sima Yan. "Zhang Hua agrees with me, and he knows my wishes."

Just at this moment came a memorial from the leader Du Yu also recommending advance, whereupon the Ruler of Jin decided that the army should go on.

The royal mandate duly reached the camp of Wang Jun, and the Jin navy went out to the attack in great pomp. The soldiers of Wu made no defense, but surrendered at once.

When Sun Hao, the Ruler of Wu, heard his armies had surrendered thus, he turned pale, and his courtiers said, "What is to be done? Here the northern army comes nearer every day and our troops just give in."

"But why do they not fight?" said Sun Hao.

The courtiers replied, "The one evil of today is Eunuch Cen Hun. Slay him, and we ourselves will go out and fight to the death!"

"How can a eunuch harm a state?" cried Sun Hao.

"Have we not seen what Huang Hao did in Shu?" shouted the courtiers in chorus.

Moved by sudden fury, the courtiers rushed into the Palace, found the wretched object of their hate and slew him, and even feeding on his palpitating flesh.

Then Tao Jun said, "All my ships are small, but give me large vessels and I will place thereon twenty thousand marines and go forth to fight. I can defeat the enemy."

His request was granted, and the royal guards were sent up the river to join battle, while another naval force went down stream, led by Leader of the Van Zhang Xiang. But a heavy gale came on. The flags were blown down and lay over in the ships, and the marines would not embark. They scattered leaving their leader with only a few score men.

Wang Jun, the leader of Jin, set sail and went down the river.

After passing Three Mountains, the sailing master of his ship said, "The gale is too strong for the fleet to go on. Let us anchor till the storm has moderated."

But Wang Jun would not listen. Drawing his sword, he said, "I wish to capture Capital Shidou[lv], and will not hear of anchoring."

So he compelled the sailing master to continue. On

the way Zhang Xiang, one of the leaders of Wu, came to offer surrender.

"If you are in earnest, you will lead the way and help me," said Wang Jun.

Zhang Xiang consented, returned to his own ship, and led the squadron. When he reached the walls of Shidou, he called to the defenders to open the gates and allow the Jin army to enter. The gates were opened.

When the Ruler of Wu heard that his enemies had actually entered the capital city, he wished to put an end to his life, but his officers prevented this.

Secretary Hu Zong and Palace Officer Xue Rong said, "Your Majesty, why not imitate the conduct of Liu Shan of Shu, now Duke of Anle?"

So Sun Hao no longer thought of death, but went to offer submission. He bound himself and took a coffin with him. His officers followed him. He was graciously received, and the Jin General Wang Jun himself loosened the bonds, and the coffin was burned. The vanquished Ruler was treated with the ceremony due to a prince.

A poet of the Tang Dynasty wrote a few lines on this surrender:

Adown the stream ride storied warships tall;
With massive chains some seek to stop their way.
But Jiangling's independence fades away,

And soon "We yield" is signaled from the wall.
Full oft I think of bygone days and sigh,
Along the stream, unmoved, the old hills rest,
While I am homeless on the earth's broad breast,
Where grim old forts stand gray beneath the sky.

Therefore Wu was subdued and ceased to exist as a state. Its 4 regions, 43 counties, 313 districts, 5,230,000 families, 62,000 civil officers, 230,000 soldiers and military officers, 23,000,000 inhabitants, its stores of grain and over five thousand large ships, all fell booty to the victorious Jin Dynasty. In the women's quarters of the Palace were found more than five thousand persons.

Proclamations were issued; treasuries and storehouses were sealed. Tao Jun's navy soon melted away without striking a blow. Wang Jun was greatly elated at his success. Sima Zhou, Prince of Langye, and General Wang Rong also arrived and congratulated each other.

When Du Yu, the Commander-in-Chief, arrived, there were great feastings and rewards for the soldiers. The granaries were opened and doles of grain issued to the people, so that they also were glad of peace.

Only one city stood out---Jianping, under Governor Wu Yang. However, he too surrendered when he heard the capital had fallen.

The tidings of all these successes reached Capital Luoyang just at the celebration of the birthday of the Ruler of Jin, and the rejoicings and congratulations were redoubled. At one of the banquets the Ruler of Jin did honor to the memory of the late Yang Hu.

Raising his wine cup, and in a voice broken by emotion, he said, "Today's success is the merit of the Imperial Guardian. I regret that he is not here to share our rejoicings."

In Wu, Sun Xi, General of the Flying Cavalry, went away from the court and wailed, facing the south.

"Alas, ye blue heavens! What manner of man is this Sun Hao to yield thus the heritage of his family, won by the sword of General Sun Jian the Martially Glorious in the brave days that are past?"

Meantime the victors marched homeward, and Sun Hao went to Luoyang to present himself at court. In his capacity of minister, he prostrated himself at the feet of the Emperor of the Jin Dynasty in the Hall of Audience. He was allowed a seat.

"I set that seat for you long since," said the Ruler of Jin.

"Thy servant also set a seat for Your Majesty in the south," retorted Sun Hao.

The Ruler of Jin laughed loudly.

Then Jia Chong turned to Sun Hao and said, "I hear, Sir, that when you were in the south, they gouged out people's eyes and flayed their faces. What crimes were so punished?"

"Murders of princes and malicious speech and disloyal conduct were so punished!"

Jia Chong was silenced, for he was ashamed.

Sun Hao was created Lord of Guiming. His sons and grandsons received minor ranks and other grades were conferred upon his ministers who had followed him in his surrender. The sons and grandsons of the late Prime Minister of Wu, Zhang Ti, who had perished in battle, were given ranks. The victorious leader, Wang Jun, was rewarded with the title General Who Upholds the State. And many other ranks were conferred to the Jin officers.

The three states now became one empire under the rule of Sima Yan of the Jin Dynasty. That is domains under heaven, after a long period of union, tends to divide; after a long period of division, tends to unite.

Liu Shan, the Emperor of Shu-Han, passed away in the seventh year of Great Beginning, in Jin calendar (AD 271). Cao Huang, the Emperor of Wei, passed away in the first year of Magnificent Peace (AD 302). And Sun Hao, the Emperor of Wu, passed away in the fourth year of Prosperous Peace (AD 283). All three died of natural causes.

A poet has summed up the history of these stirring years in a poem:

It was the dawning of a glorious day
When first the Founder of the House of Han
Xianyang's proud Palace entered. Noontide came
When Liu Xiu the imperial rule restored.
Alas, that Liu Xian succeeded in full time
And saw the setting of the sun of power!
He Jin, the feeble, fell beneath the blows
Of Palace minions. Dong Zhuo, vile though bold,
Then ruled the court. The plot Wang Yun
To oust him, failed, recoiled on his own head.
The Li Jue and Guo Si lit up the flame of war
And brigands swarmed like ants through all the land.
Then rose the valiant and deployed their might.
Sun Ce carved out a kingdom in the southeast,
North of Yellow River the Yuans strove to make their own.
Liu Zhang went west and seized on Ba and Shu,
Liu Biao laid hold on Jingzhou and Chu,
Zhang Lu, in turn held Hanzhong by force.
Ma Teng and Han Sui kept Xiliang.
Tao Qian and Gongsun Zan built up quarters,
Zhang Xiu and Lu Bu challenged the bold.
But overtopping all Cao Cao the strong
Became first minister, and to his side,
Drew many able people. He swayed the court,
Without, he held the nobles in his hand;
By force of arms he held the capital
Against all rivals. Of imperial stock
Was born Liu Bei, who with sworn brothers twain
Made oath the dynasty should be restored.
These wandered homeless east and west for years,

A petty force. But Destiny was kind
And led Liu Bei to Nanyang's rustic cot,
Where lay Sleeping Dragon, he who
Already that the empire must be rent.
Twice Liu Bei essayed in vain to see the sage
Once more he went? And then his fortune turned.
Jingzhou fell to him, followed the River Lands,
A fitting base to build an empire on.
Alas! He ruled there only three short years,
Then left his only son to Zhuge Liang's care.
Full nobly Zhuge Liang played protector's part,
Unceasing strove to win first place for Shu;
But Fate forbade; one night for aye his star
Went down behind the rampart of the hills.
Jiang Wei the strong inherited his task
And struggled on for years.
But Zhong Hui and Deng Ai
Attacked the Hans' last stronghold, and it fell.
Five sons of Cao Cao sat on the dragon throne,
And Sima Yan snatched the court from Cao
Huang.
Before him bowed the kings of Shu and Wu,
Content to forfeit kingly power for life.
All down the ages rings the note of change,
For fate so rules it; none escapes its sway.
The three kingdoms have vanished as a dream,
The useless misery is ours to grieve.

THE END

The Immortals by the River-Yang Shen (1488-1559)

滚滚長江東逝水
浪花淘盡英雄
是非成敗轉頭空
青山依舊在
幾度夕陽紅
白髮漁樵江渚上
慣看秋月春風
一壺濁酒喜相逢
古今多少事
都付笑談中

So sung:
O so vast, O so mighty,
The Great River rolls to sea,
Flowers do waves thrash,
Heroes do sands smash,
When all the dreams drain,
Same are lose and gain.
Green mountains remain,
As sunsets ingrain,
Hoary fishers and woodcutters,
And some small rafts and calm waters,
In autumn moon, in spring winds,
By the wine jars, by porcelains,
Discuss talk and tale,
Only laugh and gale.

Maps

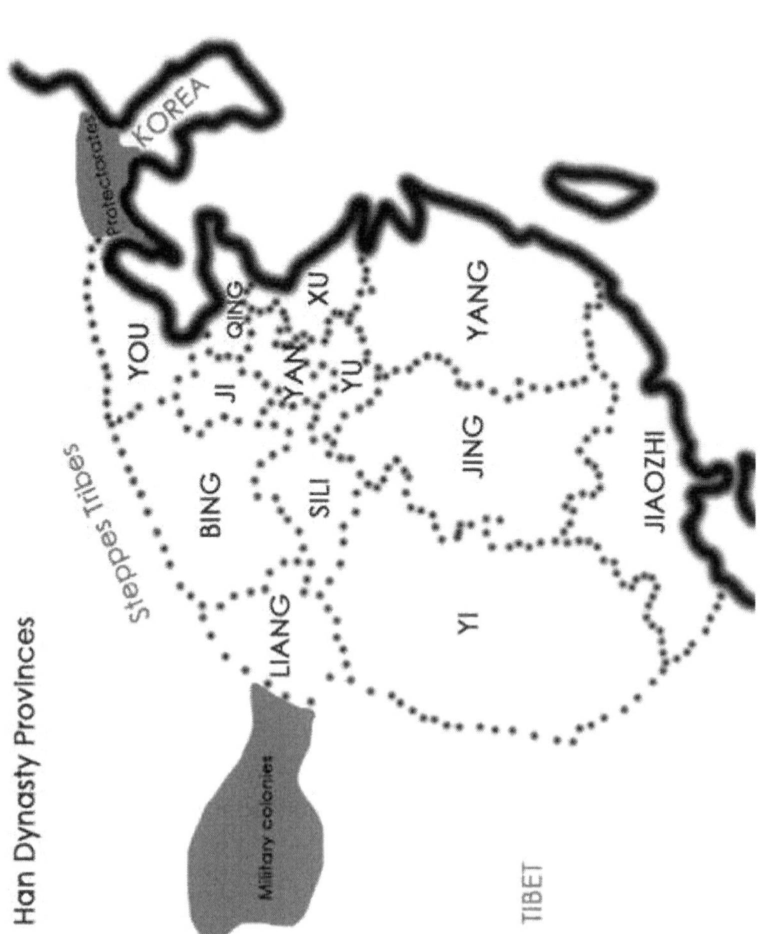
Han Dynasty Provinces
Steppes Tribes
KOREA
Protectorates
YOU
QING
XU
YANG
JI
YAN
YU
BING
SILI
JING
JIAOZHI
LIANG
YI
Military colonies
TIBET

Warlords (190 A.D.)
Steppes Tribes
TIBET
Gongsun Du
Gongsun Zan
Liu Yu
Yuan Shao
Han Fu
Kong Rong
Liu Dai
Zhang Yang
Tao Qian
Kong Zhou
Zhang Chao
Sun Jian
Yuan Shu
Dong Zhuo
Zhang Lu
Ma Teng
Liu Yan

Warlords (208 A.D.)
Steppes Tribes
Gongsun Kang (Cao Cao)
Cao Cao
Sun Quan
Liu Cong
Shi Xie
Zhang Lu
Liu Zhang
Ma Teng (Cao Cao)
TIBET

Warlords (210 A.D.)
Steppes Tribes
Gongsun Kang (Cao Cao)
Cao Cao
Sun Quan
Liu Bei
Shi Xie
Zhang Lu
Liu Zhang
Ma Teng
TIBET

END OF HAN DYNASTY (220 A.D.)
Steppes Tribes
WEI (魏)
Sun Quan
Shi Xie
Liu Bei
TIBET

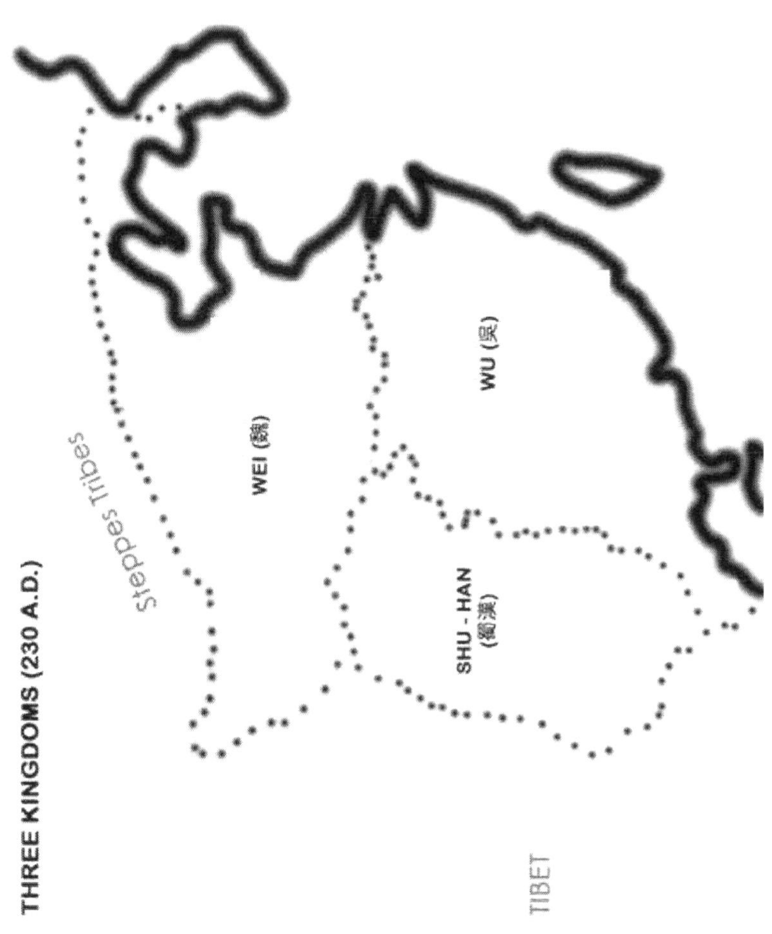
THREE KINGDOMS (230 A.D.)
Steppes Tribes
WEI
WU
SHU - HAN
TIBET

Useful Links

*List of the Three Kingdoms characters:

http://en.wikipedia.org/wiki/List_of_people_of_the_Three_Kingdoms

*List of characters in the novel in order of appareance:

http://www.poisonpie.com/words/others/somewhat/threekingdoms/text/characters.html

*Three Kingdoms Forum:

the-scholars.com

*Rafe de Crespigny Online Publications about Three Kingdoms:

https://digitalcollections.anu.edu.au/html/1885/42048/index.html

*Koei Three Kingdoms simulations:

http://koeiwarriors.co.uk/

*Three Kingdoms browser game:

http://tk.koramgame.com/

---

[i]Five Feudatories: Duke Huan of Qi, Duke Wen of Jin, Duke Xiang of Song, Duke Mu of Qin, and King Chang of Chu.

[ii]King Yu, founder of Xia; King Tang, founder of Shang; King Wen, founder of Zhou.

[iii]Nine Regions symbolized all the lands of the empire. Ancient China was divided into nine regions. But over the time, more regions were created. During the Three Kingdoms period, there were already more than nine regions.

[iv]Lady Zhen, a famous lady in the North of Yellow River (Hebei), wife to Yuan Xi, son of Yuan Shao. When Yuan Shao was defeated by Cao Cao, both Cao Cao's sons Cao Pi and Cao Zhi claimed her, not to mention Cao Cao himself. Cao Pi eventually won her hand, wedded her, and made her an empress. She later became the Goddess of River Luo, according to folktales.

[v]Lian Po commander-in-chief of Zhao in the Warring States period, who made Zhao a powerful state. Liu Xiangru, the Prime Minister of Zhao, was his good friend.

[vi]Ma Yuan (BC 14-AD 49) a general who first served Wang Mang, then join Liu Xiu in restoring Han Dynasty. In his life of career, Ma Yuan contributed much to Liu Xiu's success by putting down rebellions throughout the empire and abroad.

[vii]Guan Zhong was priminister of Duke Huan of Qi. Guan Zhong made Qi a powerful state during the Spring and Autumn period.

[viii]Yue Yi was a great general of Yan. Yue Yi helped Yan overcome Qi, which was a dominant state during the Warring States period.

[ix]Wu Qi, aka Wu Zi, a famous general in the Warring States period. He first served Lu, then went to Wei, his native, and led Wei army against Qin. He made enemies in Wei, so he fled to Chu, where King Dao made him prime minister. Wu Qi made Chu a powerful state; expanded her territory; defended her

against Wei, Zhao, and Han; and attacked Qin. But right after King Dao died, Wu Qi was put to death by his enemies at court. Wu Qi is the author of a military treatise named "Wu Qi's Art of War".

[x]Sun Zi (aka Sun Wu, Sunzi, Suntzu, Sun-tzu, Sun tzu) the author of the famed treatise The Art of War. A general of Wu in the Spring and Autumn period, Sun Zi made her the mightiest state during his lifetime by defeating Chu and conquering Yue. His treatise the Art of War is still avidly read today by many.

[xi]Beginning in the sixty-first year of King Yao's reign, the prosperity of the nation was temporarily disturbed by a thirteen-year flood. It was a terrible disaster, and King Yao was greatly grieved by the sufferings of his people. With some hesitation, the great task of reducing the waters was assigned to Gun, who failed, and for this failure and other crimes, was put to death by Shun, King Yao's son-in-law and co-ruler. Strange as it may seem, Yu, son of Gun, was recommended to the throne by Shun. Later on, Yao would yield the throne to Shun, and Shun to Yu.

[xii]Cheng Dechen was a general of Chu during the Spring and Autumn period. Cheng Dechen fought against Duke Wen of Jin and lost (BC 632).

[xiii]Duke Wen of Jin (reigned 636-628 BC) was ruler of the western state of Jin during the Spring and Autumn period. He and his successors made Jin a dominant state for nearly 200 years.

[xiv]Evan, a reader: "Zhao Yun is my favorite. I don't think that any other character in the novel can quite compare to his nobility and virtue, and few enough could compare with him on any grounds. From Wei, I would say Zhang Liao, and from Wu, Taishi Ci and Lu Meng."

[xv]King Yu was the founder of Xia Dynasty; King Tang, Shang Dynasty; Kings Wen and Wu, Zhou Dynasty.

[xvi]Lu Wang was a master strategist, founding minister of Zhou Dynasty, counselor to King Wen. Before joining King Wen, Lu

Wang had been a fisher, who mediated on the river bank on political events.

[xvii]The mountainous roads to Shu were very difficult. People had to lay planks on the earth to make roads.

[xviii]Sun Bin military strategist, a descendant of Sun Zi. Sun Bin served as military counselor during the Warring States period in Qi. He wrote a treatise named The Art of War of Sun Bin.

[xix]Wu Qi, aka Wu Zi, a famous general in the Warring States period. He first served Lu, then went to Wei, his native, and led Wei army against Qin. He made enemies in Wei, so he fled to Chu, where King Dao made him prime minister. Wu Qi made Chu a powerful state; expanded her territory; defended her against Wei, Zhao, and Han; and attacked Qin. Wu Qi is the author of a military treatise named "Wu Qi's Art of War"

[xx] Bing Ji was a prime minister of Western Han. One day, while riding in his cart with attendants, they came across brawling people by the road. He continued without concern. They then came across a man with an water buffalo panting. He immediately stopped to ask how long they had been traveling. His attendants were puzzled as to why he was more concerned about an ox than injured people. He replied that fighting was a matter for local officials, but an ox panting in early spring (if not traveling for long) suggested unusual heat, which could have disastrous results for all.

[xxi] Chen Ping (BC ?-178) a master strategist of Liu Bang. He first served Xiang Yu but then became a follower in Liu Bang's camp. Served as Liu Bang's prime minister and Empress Lu's left minister. After the death of Empress Lu, Chen Ping played an important role in returning royal authority to the Liu clan.

[xxii]Emperor Wu, aka Liu Che, (reigned BC 141-87) whose reign was longest among the Han emperors. Emperor Wu was perhaps the most influential Han emperor who concerned not only about expanding territory but also about developing trade with other countries (the Silk Road, for example). Emperor paid special attention to longevity, and his court often had elaborate rituals.

[xxiii]Yan state a state in the Warring States period. Located in the northeast, and north of Qi.

[xxiv]Yuan Xi and Yuan Shang were Yuan Shao's sons. Guo Jia was the adviser who planned the scheme for Cao Cao, so that the heads of Yuan Xi and Yuan Shang fell. (chapter 33)

[xxv]Deng Yu was commander-in-chief of Liu Xiu, the founder of Latter Han.

[xxvi]The last king of Shang Dynasty was King Zhou, who was cruel and corrupt. King Zhou had three uncles---Bi Gan, Qi Zi, and Wei Zi---who served as ministers. When these three officials repeatedly failed to persuade King Zhou to repent, Wei Zi resigned his post, while Qi Zi pretended to be insane. Bi Gan stayed and continued persuading the king, who later executed Bi Gan. Later the Duke of Zhou overthrew Shang Dynasty and enobled Wei Zi, Qi Zi, and the wife and the son of Bi Gan. Wei Zi became known as the Duke of Song. Qi Zi left for Korea where he became a ruler.

[xxvii]Yi Yin was was helper and prime minister of King Tang, the founder of Shang Dynasty. After King Tang's death, Yi Yin served his sons and grandson. Soon after Tai Jia, King Tang's grandson, ascended the throne, he committed many faults, and Yi Yin, acting as regent, exiled Tai Jia to Tong Palace---the burial place of King Tang. After three years Yi Yin returned him the throne. Tai Jia eventually became an enlightened emperor. Shang Dynasty lasted for 650 years (BC 1700-1050). It was this act of Yi Yin rather than his services in building up an empire that has made him immortal. Whether he did right in temporarily dethroning the king was open to question, until a final verdict was rendered by Mencius who thought that his ends amply justified his means. This historical event attests the extent of the power exercised by a prime minister in those days.

[xxviii]Duke of Zhou was brother of King Wu, who was the founder of Zhou Dynasty. After King Wu's death, the Duke of Zhou served his young son as regent. The Duke of Zhou completely ended the Shang domination, and he helped establish the Zhou administrative framework, which served as a model for future

Chinese dynasties. Zhou Dynasty lasted for 800 years (BC 1050-221).

[xxix]Huo Guang (BC ?-68) a general and regent of Han. After Emperor Wu died, Huo Guang became regent to three successive emperors, and the second one had been the Prince of Changyi, who was on the throne for only twenty-seven days. Huo Guang had the Prince of Changyi declared unfit to rule and deposed him. Even though Huo Guang contributed much to the empire's stabilization, after he died, he was distanced by the emperor and most of his family were executed for conspiracy charges.

[xxx]Yi Yin was was helper and prime minister of King Tang, the founder of Shang Dynasty. After King Tang's death, Yi Yin served his sons and grandson. Soon after Tai Jia, King Tang's grandson, ascended the throne, he committed many faults, and Yi Yin, acting as regent, exiled Tai Jia to Tong Palace---the burial place of King Tang. After three years Yi Yin returned him the throne. Tai Jia eventually became an enlightened emperor. Shang Dynasty lasted for 650 years (BC 1700-1050). It was this act of Yi Yin rather than his services in building up an empire that has made him immortal. Whether he did right in temporarily dethroning the king was open to question, until a final verdict was rendered by Mencius who thought that his ends amply justified his means. This historical event attests the extent of the power exercised by a prime minister in those days.

[xxxi]Qi was an ancient state on the extreme eastern edge of the North China Plain in what is now Shandong and Hebei provinces. Became prominent under the leadership of Duke Huan and his adviser Guan Zhong during the Spring and Autumn period. It nearly won the empire in the Warring States period.

[xxxii]Chu was one of the most important of states contending for power in both Spring and Autumn and Warring States periods. If other states wanted to be dominant, they had to fight and defeat Chu. Located in the fertile valley of the Great River (Yangtze) in the south, corresponding to the surrounding territory of Jingzhou.

[xxxiii]Zhou Yafu was son of Zhou Bo, the prime minister of Emperor Wen (BC 179-156). After the death of Emperor Wen,

Duke Wu started a rebellion of Seven Kingdoms. Zhou Yafu as a general put down this rebellion.

[xxxiv]Zhang Liang, aka Zhang Zifang, the master strategist for Liu Bang. His family had served the state of Han as chief ministers during the Warring States period. It is said that he received the strategy book of Lu Wang from a mysterious old man. When he was young, Zhang Liang plotted to assasinate the First Emperor, but failed. He later rebeled against Qin. Joined Liu Bang (BC 206) to fight against Qin and then Chu. Recommended Han Xin to Liu Bang. Zhang Liang's insights had earned him the name "The Teacher of Emperor". After Liu Bang won the empire, Zhang Liang was enobled as Lord of Liu, but did not take office, instead he resigned from political life and traveled.

[xxxv]Tian Heng a warrior of Qi at the end of the Warring States period and Qin Dynasty. In his bid to regain the lost kingdom of Qi, Tian Heng rebelled against Qin and fought both Liu Bang and Xiang Yu. Rather than submitting to Liu Bang, Tian Heng committed suicide so that his five hundred soldiers could be pardoned. But on learning of his death, all of his five hundred followers killed themselves.

[xxxvi]King Wen, aka the Scholar King, founder of the Zhou Dynasty, father of King Wu. King Wen did not actually founded the dynasty, but he laid the foundation for Zhou. At the end of Shang Dynasty, the state Zhou of King Wen had already possessed two-thirds of the empire, but King Wen still faithfully served the last emperor of Shang. The final conquest was completed by King Wu and King Wu's brother, the Duke of Zhou.

[xxxvii]Gou Jian was king of Yue during the Spring and Autumn period. Gou Jian had been defeated and humiliated by Wu, but later he was able to fight back and conquer Wu.

[xxxviii]When facing the prospect of a bloody battle, Liu Bang and Xiang Yu agreed to a truce, and they divided the empire into two parts, each part for one of them. The Great Canal was the division line.

[xxxix]Zhang Liang was Liu Bang's master strategist, who helped Liu Bang defeat Xiang Yu and win the empire.

[xl]King Tang founder of the Shang Dynasty.

[xli]King Wu, aka the Martial King, founded the Zhou Dynasty, with the help of the Duke of Zhou, who was his brother.

[xlii]Yi Yin was was helper and prime minister of King Tang, the founder of Shang Dynasty. After King Tang's death, Yi Yin served his sons and grandson. Soon after Tai Jia, King Tang's grandson, ascended the throne, he committed many faults, and Yi Yin, acting as regent, exiled Tai Jia to Tong Palace---the burial place of King Tang. After three years Yi Yin returned him the throne. Tai Jia eventually became an enlightened emperor. Shang Dynasty lasted for 650 years (BC 1700-1050). It was this act of Yi Yin rather than his services in building up an empire that has made him immortal. Whether he did right in temporarily dethroning the king was open to question, until a final verdict was rendered by Mencius who thought that his ends amply justified his means. This historical event attests the extent of the power exercised by a prime minister in those days. Huo Guang (BC ?-68) a general and regent of Han. After Emperor Wu died, Huo Guang became regent to three successive emperors, and the second one had been the Prince of Changyi, who was on the throne for only twenty-seven days. Huo Guang had the Prince of Changyi declared unfit to rule and deposed him. Even though Huo Guang contributed much to the empire's stabilization, after he died, he was distanced by the emperor and most of his family were executed for conspiracy charges.

[xliii]Jiaozhou was a deep-south region, which is now northern Vietnam.

[xliv]Yue Yi was a general of Yan. Yue Yi helped Yan overcome Qi, which was a dominant state during the Warring States period. But he fell victim to court slanderers.

[xlv]Yue Fei (AD 1103-1142) a great general during the Song Dynasty. During his time, northern China was invaded by the Jin (northeast) armies. Yue Fei, as commander of the northern

expedition, was winning victories, when the emperor recalled him because the emperor feared Yue Fei's growing power and that Jin would release his father and brother (both former emperors). Yue Fei was later executed due to false charges.

[xlvi]Jin state occupied the western part of the empire, in the mountainous area north of the Yellow River. During the Spring and Autumn period, under the leadership of Duke Wen and his successors, Jin grew into a very large state, which broke into three states in the Warring States period.

[xlvii]Zhang Rang was one of the Ten Regular Attendants. Zhang Rang won such influence that Emperor Ling called him "Foster Father". Zhang Rang plotted the murder of He Jin, that caused Dong Zhou to seize the capital. (chapter 3)

[xlviii]Zhao Gao a court eunuch serving the First Emperor. Zhao Gao killed the eldest son and supported the second son for the throne after the First Emperor's death (BC 209). In the final days of Qin Dynasty, Zhao Gao killed the Second Emperor and placed the First Emperor's grandson on the throne (BC 206).

[xlix]Two Lius were just founded, armies pass by here. Deng Ai and Zhong Hui compete; both soon die.

[l]Bai Qi a general of Qin. In BC 278, the armies of Qin, led by Bai Qi, conquered Chu and entered her capital Ying, destroying the Palace to the ground.

[li]Han Xin (BC ?-197) was a great general of Liu Bang.

[lii]Han Xin was suspected of rebellion and was arrested by Liu Bang. However, Han Xin said, "When the birds have vanished, the good bows are stored." Liu Bang absolved him due to his merits. But Xiao He and Empress Lu executed him when Liu Bang was absent.

[liii]After Yue conquered Wu, Fan Li gave up politics and traveled. But his collegue Wen Zhong stayed to continue serving King Gou Jian loyally. Wen Zhong later was put to death due to slanders. Meanwhile, it is said that Fan Li, together with the

beauty Xi Shi, had become a wealthy merchant and was doing charity works.

[liv]Emei Mountain one of the most renowned Buddhist and Daoist (Taoist) sanctuaries in China. The mountain is located in the basin of Sichuan Province. The beautiful majesty of this mountain has caused it to be named Emei, "the most beautiful mountain under heaven". Visitors of this mountain are treated to several peaks, bubbling springs, cascading waterfalls, tall ancient trees and abundant flowers along the many mountain paths leading to the many scenic spots and temples that dot the mountain side from the base to the summit.

[lv]Shidou has been a southern capital of China for successive dynasties. A beautiful place, Shidou was considered a treasure by the emperors of Yuan Dynasty (Mongol rule). Located near Shanghai where the Great River meets the East Sea, Shidou's modern name is Nanjing.

Made in the USA
San Bernardino, CA
29 October 2014